The Gap-Toothed Banister

A Tale of Anglo-India

The Gap-Toothed Banister

A Tale of Anglo-India

Juliette Banerjee

NIYOGI BOOKS

Published by
NIYOGI BOOKS
D-78, Okhla Industrial Area, Phase-I
New Delhi-110 020, INDIA
Tel: 91-11-26816301, 49327000
Fax: 91-11-26810483, 26813830
email: niyogibooks@gmail.com
website: www.niyogibooks.com

Editor: Gita Rajan
Design: Shashi Bhushan Prasad

ISBN: 978-93-81523-71-1
Publication: 2012

Printed at: Niyogi Offset Pvt. Ltd., New Delhi, India

For my mother,
Blanche Angela D'Santos
A proud Anglo-Indian,
and a great lady

With love and gratitude

Lines long overdue to you,
who shaped stubborn pride and humour,
my homage is hesitant,
a stumble of words
paltry thanks
for a covenant,
a pact that promised
brighter lights,
broader paths
a shedding of narrow thoughts
and small hopes.

And with these memories
I travel roads you
smoothed, levelled for me

FOREWORD

The Gap-Toothed Banister – a Tale of Anglo-India, is a story of a community with a short genealogy, its people of mixed birth, European and Indian, tracing their origin from the British Raj. Scattered globally, they now form a Diaspora which began with India's Independence in 1947.

The Gap-Toothed Banister, five years in the making, doesn't aim to excuse or explain the community. It speaks of a vibrant people, who acted and reacted to a world which often seemed to misunderstand and sideline them.

Its characters span the latter half of the 20th century, and reflect the abrupt changes in attitudes towards a country fast forgetting to remember old prejudices. The young, like young everywhere, are impatient with the past, the old, resentful of a swiftly changing society. There is love, there is regret. And, however grudgingly, there is reconciliation with the present. It is a love story not in kindergarten hues, but in softer colours of hope and faith.

Part of the wave of immigrants, both from Anglo-Indian and other Indian communities, adjusting to new worlds far removed from their motherland, I have tried objectively to recount the tale of a people trying to live lives, honourable and happy.

The Gap-Toothed Banister is neither eulogy nor epitaph. It is a telling that I trust will be both enjoyable and a reflection of my people's history.

Sydney, December 2012 Juliette Banerjee

"Woo-lloo-moo-loo. Woolloomooloo. Hmmm.

"It's in Sydney, Australia. Funny name eh? Almost sounds like an Indian one." (Laughs disbelievingly). "I have a niece who lives there. Mary Ann. Left Cal some time ago and now is doing very well there. Very well."

"Hello Mary Ann. Hello my girl, hello." (Waves at camera). "This is your Aunty Daisy. These lovely people from Australia are making a TV picture of us AI's. And they are letting me speak to you. Isn't it wonderful? Could you send me an overcoat from Australia my girl? A warm one, please? Foreign things are so nice and all. Not like the rubbishy stuff we get here. I hope you're in the pink in Woolloomooloo. Please write to your old aunt. I'm alone here now, no one left. All dead or emigrated. All gone. Gone. Write to me soon, okay?"

(Excerpt from a TV documentary made in the early 90's on the Anglo-Indian community in India. An aged inmate of an Old People's Home in Calcutta, talks briefly to Australian journalists of life as she sees it in a post-independent India.)

1

Jogging home in a rickshaw under the punishing afternoon sun Grace Renshaw sighed pleasurably at the thought of the Saturday half-holiday. She looked forward to the weekend lunch of sausage curry with potato mash and dal, Abdul their cook served up so well. Then as a dessert, a cool summer mango, and finally, a siesta. Buffered by this promised bliss she was deaf to the noise around her as the rickshaw bumped its way over the potholed street and through the sweaty swath of pedestrians, battling their way through the street, some aggressively, others with a resigned amble, dogs, mangy, sad-eyed, slunk through the legs of the crowd, the odd cow, dewlap gently swaying, nosed through garbage lying haphazardly in the gutter; everywhere was a chaos totally familiar to Grace.

"Aiee, khabadar, khabadar," shouted her rickshaw-puller, as a knot of urchins spilled in front of him. Grinning, the raggedly crew turned and yelled abuse at the rickshaw-man and continued dodging through the turgid afternoon traffic.

"Bloody *chhokras,*" Grace swore to herself. "Wish I could leave all this muck behind."

Her thoughts flashed to the area she had travelled from, an affluent part of the city it contained the nucleus of the business houses. Broad pavements, trees, uniformed doormen in front of several of the glass doors, even the eternal din of the city seemed subdued. Of course there were the clusters of touts shoving tacky goods in front of tourists, beggars crouched on jealously guarded bits of rag singing their dirges to passers-by, pavement stalls where goods from plastic knickknacks and toiletries to recent bestsellers were on sale.

Chaos there too, but somewhat less confronting than this pandemonium she faced on her route home. In a certain light the city hid its illness and looked the gracious city it once was. The silhouettes of buildings noble, imposing, smudged by a murky twilight, but not now, not at glaring noon. Graffiti, posters, the excrescence of a careless citizenry made for a leprous pastiche on walls, pillars. But the city muddled on. It was loved, defended when there was hardly any fuel to defend it against detractors. Alive and vigorous, its sangfroid shrugged off prophecies of doom. A harsh parent it rode roughshod over its children. Love me, it commanded. I am youth. I am age. I wear my deformities defiantly. I am cruel.

The city's devotees bowed down before it and endured.

But even the most besotted of its lovers admitted to oppressive simmering heat, its assault on one's olfactory sense as garbage quickly rotted and corporation trucks, lumbering leviathans from decades past, chuntered by spilling their load without prejudice on anyone in the way. The constant throng of humanity pushing, heaving through streets, the clangour and waves of movement, a harsh tempo with no lull in its rhythm, stunned. Few trees withstood the city's abrasive climate. Quieter by-lanes and richer neighbourhoods boasted jacarandas, tamarinds, frangipani, all of which bloomed briefly during the unbearable summer months. Trees, few and denuded quickly of whatever fruit that might bud, graced some streets, neem trees, hardy and perennial, stood braving neglect, palms, swaying, slender, were often home to the kites, hawks and occasional vulture that made their loftiness, home. Peeling paint on buildings, graffiti created on walls bloodied by the stain of paan juice all combined to mar the beauty of what was a gracious metropolis.

"Ruined, the whole place is ruined." Bob her father often intoned. "Can't maintain any bloody thing, these people. In the old days we'd have water hosed on the streets every morning. Now most gutters and lanes are used as glorified toilets. No pride, no shame. They'll squat anywhere, spit anywhere, muck up any place but their homes. No idea of civic pride, shove them back into huts, that's all they seem fit for. Herd them back to their villages."

Grace had heard this sad sonata most of her life. She recognised some of the truth of it but was frustrated by the passivity that gripped any thought or action to help halt or reverse the decay of a once proud city. A city which boasted a volatile, articulate people whose thought and dedication towards independence formulated the blueprint to a modern India. Now, its vibrancy dribbled away in internecine brawls. The Bengali population, shrill in protests against change, supercilious towards the outsider, dreamed of past glories, inexorably pushed from the seats of power by the merchant, the businessman from western India, juggernauts firmly in the commercial and financial powerhouses.

The rickshaw-puller from the impoverished state of Bihar bobbed before her. A yellowed, tattered singlet clung to his body. Grace stared sightlessly at the serrated back, mahogany skin taut over sharp bones. Her thoughts skittered over the day, work, the grime that seemed to accumulate in streets seeping into her clothes and hopes. She heard her mother's voice tinged with resignation as she spoke of the past. It was a cleaner, brighter, happier place. Of course, it was, Grace always wanted to say, you were young then weren't you? She lacked the courage. A kind person she did not believe in winning arguments and points of order if it meant hurting another.

And she loved her parents.

Twenty-eight years old, Grace was the middle child in a family of three. Bright, gregarious, she had left school with a creditable school-leaving certificate and a scoopful of ambition. Neat features and a dignified manner made up for conventional good looks. Well-groomed, her professional manner commanded respect, if not popularity. Even schoolfriends would joke about her behaviour that was almost patrician; 'la-di-da' they would call it.

"Gosh Gracie, whatcha going to be, next Prime Minister? Mrs Gandhi better watch out then huh?" Much laughter at this comment.

Like the country's most powerful politician, Gracie wore her hair cut severely short and unlike most girls her age did not favour much jewellery or make-up.

With a smooth complexion, glowing, her mother liked to say, and well-defined eyebrows, Grace was confident her appearance presented a professional and even elegant air.

Grace went down the well-trodden path of going to secretarial school, after a year received a diploma testifying to her proficiency in shorthand-typing, bookkeeping and receptionist skills. With a convent education that ensured a level of sophistication, she was soon employed as a stenographer in a multinational firm and easily scaled her way up to being private secretary to one of the executives, a position she had remained at for almost six years. Her colleagues were the usual mix, some younger women, a few older, but men now had begun to infiltrate the citadel of what was hitherto strictly a women's preserve – that of secretary – currently there were four men who sidestepped the feminine 'secretary' tag by re-naming themselves 'personal assistants'. Grace was careful about maintaining a professional attitude towards them but found she was increasingly attracted to a young Punjabi Andy (Arvind) Kaul, and over the last couple of years they began to be seen as an 'item'. At first Grace enjoyed the casual friendship but lately had started to wonder where this relationship was heading. Inter-communal marriages were frowned on, and she grew chill when she thought of the disapproval any mention of marriage this friendship might involve. She thought ruefully of the day she wore a sari and the consternation it caused among her family.

"Why this change in dress," asked her father.

Her brother Carl grinned nervously, he tapped his teeth and wiggling his hips mimed chorus dancers in Hindi-film mode, *"Aiee, aiee, aiee.aieee,"* he sang in a shrill falsetto.

Her mother said nothing but looked unhappy and said the dhobi would probably ask for an increase in his salary with the extra washing saris involved.

"All those yards and yards of material, in this mucky city you'll have to change twice a day, not just once a day," was her mother's dry comment.

Grace was jolted sharply again and stiffened herself to meet the thud as the rickshaw jerked to the ground.

"Memsahib…" the skinny rickshaw-puller, sweat running off wizened, beaten face held his hand out for his fare and smiled gratitude at her generosity.

Grace jumped out lithely and walked up the narrow pathway, a slow climb up the stone staircase that led to her small three-roomed home.

Nimbly she began to climb the gritty red concrete steps. Absentmindedly she smoothed the surface of the worn banister.

She wondered when the rickety rails would be fixed. The wood of the banister gleamed with the polish of years of hands running over it, but rain and damp, twin scourges of wooden furniture in the city, had loosened the balusters, and a series of discordant squeaks accompanied Grace as she ran up the stairs. She idly thought its carved posts always reminded her of pawns in a chess set. Moth-eaten, the relic of childhood, she automatically counted the nineteen steps that led straight up to the upper floor, to the flat at the end of this level.

The line of the old wood, buffed to a velvet sheen, flowed, straight as an arrow, to the newel post, unbroken by flaws in its carved pattern. Missing rails now gave the banister an almost comical look. Grace thought a touch of whimsy could transform the staircase into a jack-o'-lantern, the aged smile in a face where strength had been sapped. A clown's grin masking decay. How old was their mansion, she wondered briefly. Just how many times in her childhood had she slid down the banister. How many games of 'Last Touch' and 'I Spy' had had their pivotal moments on these stairs. A scant and homely feature, the staircase seemed to usher in the sunlight even in shelter of the small portico.

Clutching the shaky newel post Grace's thought flew to the classic Capra film, *It's a Wonderful Life,* when James Stewart's shabby home, shaky rail and all, helps renew and restore his happiness. She gave a rueful smile as she thought of how film–"the pictures"–was powerfully entrenched in their lives. Things invariably reminded her of some film or other. Was this good or not? Did it reveal a narrow frame of mind, or a narrowly lived life? She sighed and hurried up the few remaining steps and wished yet again there was a regular sweeper to keep the surface clean, not the hunchback who made an occasional and lethargic appearance. Poor man, she thought, what a life. His cough was what she recalled about him. A shadow of a man, Grace recalled he moved the broom in a painful rhythm, bent low, scarcely raising his head watching passing feet go by. Dust re-settled when the broom passed over the steps. Why the hell couldn't he swab the steps as well, she thought irritably. Must mention it to that rent collector when he next comes. There was yet another useless idiot. Always with the same smile and the eternal paan chewing, the namaste, a token wish which meant damn all. Took the rent and ran, and so to the next month, with his appearance of studied politeness, the building's stagnation, sealed, set and approved. Ah well, it was better treatment than some other landlords who were monsters to tenants. Grace's reverie ended as she skirted the last step and rapped quickly on the age-darkened front door.

"Gracie, why so late? Come and get out of those clothes and take off those silly high heels," her mother scolded.

Obediently she went to the bathroom and splashed her face with water and ripped off the cotton sari that clung to her with the day's dust and sweat.

"Ouf" she sighed as she pulled on a shabby and comfortable cotton housecoat, "how we have to suffer in this damned heat."

"Mum," she shouted as she combed her hair, "what's for dinner?"

"Cutlets with beef soup and cucumber salad," her mother called back.

Grace grimaced. A heavy meat cutlet was not her favourite meal. Good she thought, the lunch of sausages would make up for that. Abdul seemed to make his cooking almost salt-less. Healthy, she thought, but not palatable.

"Hurry up and come to table, your father's friend, Daryl is coming over for dinner, so I want to tidy the house before he arrives."

"What's he coming for?"

"I don't know, some office stuff I think, you know how your dad loves to talk shop with his colleagues."

Grace had to smile. Her mother, still slim, comfortable, now in her mid-fifties, loved to entertain. Small, her curves gently sliding down to the formless bumps of middle age, Kitty Renshaw brought a balance of practicality to the big imaginings of her husband Bob. Though the family budget was controlled, often strained, it was a rare Saturday spent without someone dropping in to chat and staying on to share a casual meal. Relatives, friends, often a neighbour would visit to talk and the evening would be gone with the lazy contentment of knowing that the next day was a holiday and no one need wake early. They did not have a TV and though a few American films were aired with some world sporting events, none of the family, bar Carl, her young brother, was keen on getting one.

"Better to read the newspapers for the news and talk to each other for entertainment," was her father's sage comment.

So in spite of the invasive power of TV their home held out against the lure of this easy form of `infotainment'.

A knock at the door had Grace hurriedly discard her housecoat and put on a dress and her mother to scamper around the room tidying away the usual scatter of family untidiness, magazines sprawled on the side table, shirts slung on the back of some chairs, the dog's plate left in the middle of the living area of the room, all whisked away from critical eyes.

"Hello, hello, anyone at home," her father's voice boomed through the flat as he stomped in, "come in, and take a pew Daryl."

Grace's heart sank. There would be no chance to have a leisurely lunch this Saturday. She started to eat her lunch rapidly. The mango would have to wait till the next day. One could not slurp into that heavenly fruit with someone looking on. There was little enjoyment in the meal with a guest waiting for her to chat to between each mouthful.

Daryl Jackson was a regular visitor and often Grace felt he had more than a passing interest in her. Older than her by about twelve years her parents liked him, his easy ways and friendly manner. She suspected they were subtly encouraging her to think of him as more than a friend of the family. It was Kay, her elder sister, who appeared to be the flame towards which this drab moth was drawn, or so it seemed. When Kay left for her school teacher's job in the cool of Darjeeling's hills Daryl continued his weekly visits. Accepted as a de-facto family member he was as familiar and as comfortable to have around as Carl's dog Jumbo. Of late though there had been signs that Daryl was slightly giggly when Grace was around. It would have been embarrassing if her parents were not silently approving of the changing situation. Grace steeled herself to smile warmly at the awkward man before her.

"Hi Daryl, how are you?" she said formally as she sat down to chat and thought briefly only her father would use outdated phrases like 'take a pew'. For god's sake, Grace thought, did most people know the origin of it anyway?

"Bloody hot day eh? You look fresh as a daisy, brought the air-conditioning home with you eh?" he whinnied with laughter at this remark.

Grace smiled. What a fool the man sounded, she thought. Imagine having to put up with him for the rest of her life.

She pushed her plate aside and called for the boy to take it away. The cool glass of water, a blessing for a throat parched from summer heat, and from the effect of a rapid swallowing of what might have been a relaxing lunch. She dabbed her mouth fastidiously with the serviette. I hope the pest is happy now he's ruined my lunch, she thought.

"Staying for dinner?"

"Only if you let me," he replied and let off another cackle of high-pitched mirth.

First the heat, then her delayed lunch, now this jackass's self-conscious humour, thought Grace. And now hours of enforced conversation – there went the best part of the weekend.

"Gracie, tell Boy to lay another place for dinner," said her mother.

Happy to leave, Grace quickly went outside their flat to the kitchen, at the end of a communal passageway, and told their cook to prepare for one more at dinner.

She returned to find Carl had returned from school and was talking animatedly with Daryl about a common acquaintance known to have received a Black Belt in karate.

"You should have seen the exhibition he gave, it was wonderful man," enthused Carl. "He could easily act in any Hindi film and earn a lot as a stunt man in some of this action stuff they make."

"I hope you don't waste your money on that bilge," said Daryl quickly, "I know all this singing and dancing around trees is getting noticed in England and America but you can't seriously watch that rubbish can you?"

Carl and Grace laughed at the undisguised irritation in Daryl's tone but neither said anything further. Both knew their parents disapproved of them going to what they called 'Indian' films.

It was even a factor that decided one of their aunts to migrate when her young, school-going sons started singing Hindi film songs that were periodically blared from loudspeakers during festivals or weddings that occurred in the neighbourhood.

"In our days we sang the hits of Frank Sinatra, Nat King Cole, Frankie Laine, remember, 'High Noon' and all that?" her aunt would huff, "not all this nasal stuff. Sounds like their noses are always blocked, no?" Grace couldn't stop giggling at the description of Hindi songs. She still thought of her Aunt Aggie's indignation when she'd hear Hindi songs being played, and yes, years later, the taboo still remained, her parents unhappy when either of their children discussed the Hindi film of the week, or sang snatches of what was the song of the moment.

"It's just a bit of fun, you know," was the usual plea, but their mother would look grim, her silence speaking volumes.

Though neither Grace nor Carl cared for the absurdity of commercial Hindi films, there was not the undercurrent of antipathy towards them evinced by their parents.

"Yes, I think there's a great movie on at the Globe," Daryl was saying, "It's a great drama, has the Redgrave sisters in it," he nodded continually, impressed with his choice, looking at them for confirmation of his taste.

"Hmm, don't really care for all that heavy stuff," Carl muttered, "rather see Sylvester Stallone in *Rambo*."

Daryl pursed his lips and made a sucking noise through his teeth.

"Tch, tch, tch, tch, never mind my boy," he said, "you'll soon see what is quality entertainment when you're older eh?"

Carl rolled his eyes, got up and went into the bedroom calling Jumbo with him. Grace was left to make small talk with Daryl.

An hour and a half later dribbling through fields of question and answer and some forced laughter Grace wondered what it was that put her off this man.

It was not his looks. By standards set he was fairly good looking. Hazel eyes, thick hair, tall, and if a subtle flabby middle was developing, he stood trim and from a certain angle, looked slim. She suddenly realised her indifference had nothing to do with his appearance, it was his air of being correct. He was always used to having the last word and seemed unhappy if someone else finished a subject especially one which did not fit in with his opinion.

"A bore, that's what he is, a bore."

Some hours later, post-twilight time, she smiled at Daryl and quickly rose as the servant came in with the dishes of food to place on the table,

"Come on, dinner's here. It's your favourite dish Daryl, beef soup, and cutlets with cucumber salad."

"Well, thank goodness Bob asked me over tonight then, eh?"

Another laugh and he took his place beside Grace's father and the family sat down to the evening meal.

"What's the matter with Gracie?" Bob Renshaw, large, clumsy, settled himself noisily into bed as he looked at his wife still creaming her face before she joined him.

"Why, what's the matter with her?" Kitty, face greasy with Nivea cream slowly shuffled off her slippers and climbed into bed beside her husband.

"You know damn well the girl's been acting like a fool with that Indian boy at her firm. She'll be in for a rude shock, a bloody mess if she thinks anything will come of it," muttered Bob, "these people only believe in arranged marriages and anyway how could we see our girl marry into a non-Christian family. Goodness knows what they'll expect, you know how they prize fat dowries and fair complexions above anything else. Bloody fools."

He tenderly wiped a smudge of cream from his wife's ear, then leant forward and kissed it. Kitty sighed contentedly. She felt the same sentiments as her husband towards her daughter's association with this young man. Like should stay with like, she thought. Unconsciously she reached out and looped her arm across Bob's ample waist. He grunted and patted her. It was late and they were both tired for any lovemaking.

Fat dowries, what a laugh. She smiled into the night as she considered their month-to-month struggle to make ends meet. Her husband's salary as caretaker for a multi-complex enclave of apartments was adequate, but only just. Carl's tuition fees ate up some of the extra money and with their monthly club bills and an occasional dinner at a Park Street restaurant there was just too much month left over at the end of money, as Bob liked to joke. A fair complexion? With most Indians, the racial emphasis on 'fair' skins, was unspoken but acknowledged. Dark-skinned girls were at a disadvantage and if there was no family background or highly paying professional employment, eligible bachelors were hard to come by. Her darling Gracie was attractive but by no means could she be called fair-skinned, or, as the euphemism went 'wheat-complexioned'. She sighed again and pondered what their lives would have been had they migrated in the late sixties and early seventies along with most of their relatives. Many of her cousins were now well into being part of the granny brigade. Children seemed to have flourished in the new homelands. If there were difficulties faced there was no mention of them. When they came back, usually for Christmas, and roughed it with them in their small flat, she was stricken with embarrassment at how shabby their home and lifestyle must seem to the affluent ex-pats. Her elder daughter Kay, working in a hill school as a games mistress, was impatient with her for what she considered a poor-relative attitude.

"Mum, don't explain or excuse your life to anyone. Yes, yes I know now all our relatives are much better off than us. So what? Haven't we done well on what we have? Dad is respected in his work, Carl is Head Boy at school, Gracie, well she always had to be different, but her job is a good one. Don't put yourself down, you've raised a great family on very little. How many of your cousins can say that?" Kay, rough-voiced, impatient with maintaining the niceties and diplomacies between relatives, protective of their status, grew annoyed when her parents would talk of their missed chances and opportunities to emigrate.

"So we live here, in a smelly lane off a noisy street," Kay would expostulate. "Is it that bad? We have not had to deal with racism as some of our people have had to overseas, oh yes, *yes, yes,* they have been excluded on many levels. Here we live as we want to. We have our club, our church, friends have been around for all our lives, of course there is filth and pollution, and corruption, but that's everywhere in the world today." And Kitty smiled as she thought of that fiery lecture and knew now, whether or not the family liked it, their future lay in India. She yawned soundlessly, moved closer to her husband rumbling now, noisily asleep, and wondered at Kay's naiveté in thinking they lived in a tolerant society. Soon she too was asleep.

Outside the night grew thick with the smoke of the roadside *choolas,* pi dogs scrabbled along the gutters bordering the houses, the honk of traffic gradually lost their power, a stray rickshaw bell tinkled forlornly and monsoon clouds slowly gathered adding to an oppressive heat.

It was the month of May.

In the adjacent flat, a mirror image of the Renshaws', Edward D'Cruze was polishing his shoes for the next day's Sunday church service. He wore a pinched look and as he briskly buffed his patent leather shoes his mouth grew smaller and thinner. Through the thin walls he could hear the Renshaw family as they greeted a guest and later as they started their dinner. He kept no cook. Meals as prepared by his niece Lucy were simple, and generally unvaried. Rice, dal and a meat and potato curry was the staple meal through most days of the week.

On a Sunday he would indulge in a beef roast with a salad and custard pudding, but there was never any mention of alcohol. Let other fools waste money by pouring it away on beer and wine and strong drink, he would stick to water, and on the rare occasion a soft drink of orange or lemonade.

"Lucy," he yelled, "where the hell are you? Hurry and get the hot water ready for my bath." Regular water supply was pumped twice a day to the block of flats, often falling short of giving the dwellers an adequate amount of water. Water was heated in large *handis,* metal vessels, on coal fires in the kitchens. Though it was the middle of a scorching summer Edward 'Eddie' D'Cruze, a bachelor, long retired from a tedious employment in the city's tramways, liked his evening bath water warm. His niece Lucy tended to his needs. She was the only child of his sister killed in a road accident when the girl was just eight. The father too died in the tragedy and there was no option but to rear the little girl himself. Over the past twenty years Lucy's role grew to be maid-of-all-work to her uncle. Her education, pushed along by a desultory attendance at a charity section of a convent school, was minimal. Eddie was not going to spend more than he could on what he felt was an unfair foisting of a responsibility. Tall, soft-spoken, and with a personality attractive in its quiet manner, Lucy for some years now was receptionist at a nearby pharmaceutical outlet, earned a decent salary and had gained a reputation as a diligent, enthusiastic staff member. Eddie was gratified at her success, a success he firmly believed was all due to him.

He put down his shoes and looked round expectantly for Lucy to arrive with a steaming kettle. But there was no sign of the girl.

"Hey, what's the matter, I've been waiting for half an hour. I'll be late for bingo if you don't make it snappy."

Silence.

Eddie, never known for his patience, wheezing and grunting noisily, pulled himself out of the chair and threw the shoe-polish rag down. He twitched aside the curtain drawn between the bedrooms but Lucy was not there. Puzzled he walked to the front room and peered down the common passageway outside the flat, thinking she might be still in the kitchen. But there was no sign of Lucy. The kitchen door was locked and only a stray cat looked up, tail twitching, ready to run lest it be chased away from the overflowing garbage bin. No Lucy.

"Lucy, *Lucy, Lucee,* you downstairs?"

"Lucy's not here Eddie," shouted old Mrs Johnson from the flat beneath him. "But I saw her go out earlier on with that fellow from Raj's garage."

Eddie D'Cruze felt a wave of nausea shoot through him. He tried not to let his mind tell him what he guessed at.

Lucy had left.

She had made good her promise to live with the man he distrusted and disliked. Lucy had walked out on him.

Fury made his voice shake as he thanked his neighbour for letting him know Lucy was out, no point in giving the neighbourhood its share of gossip quite so soon. He quietly shut the door and sat down in the thickening shadows of twilight. In the street outside children shouted playing some raucous game, thumping lorries raced down the street, horns shrieking causing the old overhead fan to shake. It seemed he heard the thud of feet running up and down the shaky staircase and run into his head. He wondered when those flimsy rails would be repaired. Another shabby eyesore. One day that banister would come crashing down. Good, he thought, hope it would hurt someone when it did.

Arrant neglect spread its contempt through that building. Peeling paint. Dog faeces in the passageway. The only notable absence in the overall grime was that of the ubiquitous paan stains. On most walls, on suppurating plaster of tenements, on high aristocratic walls of wealthier areas, on the cardboard box huts of the destitute, the red blood-like stains splashed their signature.

"Thank God there are no Indians here," was the unspoken prayer of thanks for this welcome blankness. "They'd be hawking and spitting every bloody where."

Light bulbs in the passageway were rarely replaced when they blinked out. Noise clashed and clattered its way through the flats from early morning to late night. Unknowingly echoing Grace Renshaw's feelings about the management of their flats, Eddie thought of their landlord, an emaciated tall Bengali. He was seldom seen and rarely met his tenants. Eddie, like Grace, felt an irritation when he recalled the assistant, a laconic clerk who silently appeared on the dot of the second of every month to collect the rent. And then vanished.

Eddie D'Cruze sighed deeply, went back into the bedroom, took his polished shoes and placed them neatly on the shoe rack. There would be no bingo this evening. He thought about a future without a Lucy there to ease the growing inconvenience of ageing. He refused to acknowledge the fact that he had been unfair and unjust in his treatment of her. Even at this moment of bleakness he refused to look into the mirror and recognise the nastiness grown and festered in him. A gecko jerked its way across the wall and he thought of the repulsion Lucy felt towards lizards. He would have to shoosh them away before she would go near the spot.

Lucy.

Eddie D'Cruze eased himself on to his old iron-framed bed, lay down and stared up at the ceiling. He did not light his customary cigarette. He did not turn on the radio for the evening news. Why should things be the same? Everything had changed.

Outside bats swooped, their squeaks and jibbering counterpoint to the raucous melody of the day's end. The nearby muezzin began his melancholy call to prayer. A woman's voice shrilly called to her children, night's ink stained the last streaks of light. Summer heat seeped into the old stained bricks. The air simmered. Eddie closed his eyes and saw his niece Lucy against the red of his eyelids. There would be no dinner set on the table for him. Lucy seemed to nod smugly from the shadows. He sat up abruptly. Sweat made his vest clammy. He got up and went to the bathroom, splashed water on his face. He walked back into his living room, paced up and down the small space left in the crammed room. He would go to the police. He would file a case of theft against her. He would get her back. He would punish her. Punish her.

A rumble of thunder pushed against the thoughts in his head. Automatically he went to the wooden louvered windows to shut them, the room grew stuffy. He waved his hands at a nearby gecko, smelled the stifling wood fire that smoked beneath the window.

"Bloody people. No civic sense whatever. No bloody sense at all. Poison the whole damn world if they could."

He slammed the window shut as the first drops of rain began to spit down. He hated the warm showers that drenched without relieving the heat of summer.

It was the month of May.

On the ground floor of the building, from the corner flat, chanting voices spilled over, individual words forming a high-pitched babel. The Vincents were at evening prayer. This was a month dedicated to special invocations to the Blessed Virgin and every twilight the inhabitants of that hive of a building were compelled to overhear the piety that intruded through the walls to their homes. Crashes, whether of dishes or furniture signalled the end of the evening's activity and slowly the tangle of voices would subside to a murmur and the inhabitants of 16 Lal Chandra Lane would lose interest in the drama played out so vehemently by their neighbours in the tucked away corner flat of the building.

Henry Vincent was a shrivelled retiree, who with his equally shrivelled wife, Fatima, lived a noisy life with a brood of children. Two sons and two daughters crammed into the three rooms. with the eldest daughter married and living with them, the small apartment was crowded, a couple of grandchildren adding to the confusion that seemed an essential part of their existence.

But there was a charm to the Vincents that won them the smiles and friendship of their neighbours. Perhaps it was their complete frankness regarding their familial troubles. No subterfuge was used to explain the daily rows or raised voices. To anyone who cared to ask, both husband and wife would relate the latest mishap and trouble that they faced.

"Yes, my Maria's little boy failed his school exams again. These bloody languages they have to learn, why can't the school keep it wholly English medium, eh?"

At chance meetings, in the stairwell, on an encounter in the street, the Renshaws had unfailingly, after much shaking of heads and nodding in sympathy, learned to leave the Vincents alone without much comment or words of advice, wondering all the while at the vehemence of the couple's day-to-day arguments. Or, on a more dramatic level, Mrs Vincent often slipped in to visit Kitty Renshaw and unburdened the problems her daughter was experiencing in her marriage.

"Calls himself a good husband," the old lady's voice would quiver, "why it's a disgrace the way he never has a job, just lives off her and in our home as well. My two boys and girl have to make space for this loafer." Most of their shared chat with the Renshaws was fuelled by a mutual curiosity, but it wasn't just idle interest, there was help offered when things seemed to get desperate.

Often discreetly a small amount of money was slipped to Mrs Vincent when she would visit. This would cause some annoyance to both Kay and Grace who felt their parents were foolish to believe the sob stories the Vincents spun.

"For goodness sake Mum, can't you see their stories are a load of bullshit," Kay would grumble.

"They're going to use you as a soft touch every time you ask how they are."

Kitty Renshaw would say nothing but wished her girl would be a bit softer in her attitudes towards people. Grace was polite but did not encourage any one of the Vincent family to visit or stay and spend time with her parents.

"What have you in common with them? They're foolish and ignorant," she'd fume, "as you say they're not Anglo-Indian, they're Indian-Christian, aping our ways."

"This from a girl who now wears a sari and has a special friendship with an Indian," her father would murmur.

Grace's face grew sullen and she pressed her lips together tightly, refusing to rise to her father's bait.

"What does it matter what people want to be," her mother said, "if they feel happier being thought to be Anglo-Indian, let them."

"It's dishonest," was all Grace could answer. "Persons who hide and live behind lies are not much as people."

And there's a lot to be said for that, Kitty thought as she waved hello to the Vincents, just back from a family outing, with some of their grandchildren in tow.

To outsiders the ways of life in this microscopic network was surely strange. Christian in religion, and bar the Vincents, Anglo-Indian by community, they were fast dwindling to becoming a footnote of post-colonial India. Grace was inwardly amused at how her parents and relatives clung to their 'foreign-ness'. It was a point of honour to trace back their lineage to a British connection. "Renshaw," her father would say with pride, "a sound English name." His florid face would grow redder, and he'd gaze into the distance, hearing his father's voice saying the same thing to him. Her mother would nod approvingly and almost often would add that unlike other English-speaking and Christian communities, they could trace their family tree back generations with the proof in baptismal records resting in the archives of a small Anglican church down the road.

Grace listened and wondered at what she felt was misplaced loyalty. Even as a young child growing up she puzzled over the lack of feeling towards the country of their birth. She'd often be shushed when she'd ask about how and with whom their English ancestors had intermarried.

"Why this city is truly Anglo-Indian. It was founded by an Anglo-Indian," her father would say.

"Job Charnock, an English trader, married a Hindu widow, saved her from sati. Poor woman, she did not convert to Christianity, but the children were Christians and became the leading pillars of society."

"Big deal," Carl would like to tease, "so how's it that now we are at the bottom of that pillar?"

"No we're not," Kitty Renshaw would retort sharply. "We don't think that only a college education is the way to go. Even without a string of degrees we lead many a profession. Our people are among the best teachers, nurses, office workers – Gracie, take a bow – sportsmen, remember Leslie Claudius, a Calcutta boy, he led the Olympic hockey winners back in the fifties, now where is India on the international sports stage – *nowhere* – we gave the world entertainers, have you forgotten Merle Oberon, Cliff Richard – what are you saying we're at the bottom of the pillar, now *stop* that."

Carl, his lanky frame towering over his petite mother, would end the exchange by smothering her indignation with a rough hug.

"Come on Mum, we're a disappearing mob, the sooner off the scene the better," and Carl would scamper off, dodging a good-humoured cuff from his mother.

"I'll give you something to think about young man, 'disappearing mob' indeed," and only half-jokingly Kitty would close what was a contentious argument about the state of the community. She'd shoot a long-suffering look at her husband and the conversation would come to an end.

Now the Vincents were an anomaly in their tight-knit circle of that shabby little lane.

Their English was halting, but their children had attended good schools, the older son and daughter executives in prestigious commercial concerns.

"The old bribery and corruption at work again," was the unspoken verdict of most. But it was obvious their college degrees had helped further their prospects.

"Still look at the miserable marriages the daughter has made, no dowry I suppose."

"And happy to borrow money from any fool who's fool enough to lend them."

The last remarks a nuanced reminder the Vincents were not really pucca Anglo-Indians. Dowries were a sign of the eastern way of life and thought. Marriage, for the community, was strictly for love. Arranged marriages were considered nothing short of barbaric. They don't think like us, was the general consensus towards this custom. Marriage, as was seen by most Indians, was a business, a merger of families, of opportunities.

"Disgusting," was Kitty Renshaw's verdict. "Gives me the creeps. With the higher education and good job and all that, the girl is now saddled with a drunken clerk, a no-good, who lives off her and is leeching on to her parents. Out and out parasite."

"But Mum, royalty through the ages have had arranged marriages," Grace teased her mother.

"Yes, but the Vincents are not royalty, anyway royalty acts from a sense of duty to country, God and people," her mother countered.

"You do know that the mistresses and lovers are the real marriage partners in these settlements," Grace continued the argument.

"Yes Grace I'm not a complete ignoramus," her mother sarcastically replied, "but I'm still disgusted by marriage for convenience without any softer feelings entering into the partnership. I don't like the cold bargaining that is accepted in most of these Indian communities. There's a heartlessness about it that's dreadful. Awful. It gives me the creeps. Horrible." With a mock shudder to illustrate her feeling on the subject her mother ended the conversation.

Privately Grace thought back to an evening with Andy Kaul, where she had tentatively put forward the whole question of marriage, arranged, as compared with love, a favourite topic with young Indians.

"What will I do with a love marriage," Andy bluntly asked, "sit down and look at it?"

The rhetoric, was final, as it was crude, shocking, and Grace knew instinctively marriage with Andy was out of the question.

He did not love her.

It was a fine friendship, one with laughs and comradeship, but nothing more permanent.

To be fair, and it had to be said, Grace did not love him either. But her pride was hurt. She flinched at the idea of being laughed at by her colleagues and the humiliation of accepting the truth of her family's reading into the relationship.

And here was her mother passing judgement on the marriage of a neighbour's daughter.

"Why does it matter if the Vincentss are not really Anglo-Indians? Isn't it ridiculous in this day and age to store so much by this sort of snobbery? Who gives a stuff whether their grandparents or parents were converted and changed their names to western ones. Why do people have to lie about what they are?" The never-ending debate went on with Gracie contradicting her own feelings about where loyalty should begin and honesty end. The Vincents irritated her, but she ceaselessly puzzled over her parent's attitude towards them.

"Silly fools. All that church going, and that posh schooling, still touching us for the odd tenner eh? ," Bob Renshaw huffed, "old Vincent's father worked as a shop assistant in that liquor store in the New Market, her mother could hardly speak English." The indictment the most deadly against the commandments as set down by her family.

Grace closed her eyes and for a brief darkened second saw how her life might go if she followed these ideas. She would pass on the old war-cry that English was the language of the gods and things outside western norms were third-rate. A notion absurd, but as fixed as their daily rice, dal and curry. Grace grimaced as she thought of the nonsense surrounding her like the all-pervading smoke, smothering, polluting, and essential to their way of thinking. Her thoughts flew to the recent dinner. Daryl Jackson had been irritating with his courtliness. The cutlets were tough, the salad too tart with an overdressing of mayonnaise and the conversation chugged along the well-worn lines of how badly local politicians were managing the state. Rising prices, the changing weather patterns, (even the damned rains now come late, all because the trees were being chopped down) and the coming May Queen Ball Dance their club was preparing were the subjects of the night.

"Wonder who they'll choose for May Queen this year," her mother wondered aloud.

"Hope the girl will be better looking than last year's choice," Bob said, "did have a good complexion, quite fair and all that, her hair was a lovely light brown, but had as much personality as a wet hen."

Everyone laughed.

"Yes, but she was a relative of old Carter, he still pulls strings," this from Daryl.

"*What,* is that old codger still sitting in on the AGMs?"

"What do you think? He'll retire and sit in the shade counting his shekels?" Daryl snickered, "he'll never give up being the boss. Loves hearing his own voice too much for that."

After dinner there was a bit of a singsong, Carl brought out his guitar and strummed it in impressive Presley style. He mugged the wailings of a lovelorn lad and knelt to his mother as he sang in his clear tenor voice,

'Treat me like a fooool,
Treat me mean and crooool,
but lurrve me ,'

and he'd graze the strings, his hand running down the fret-board, ending with an impressive arpeggio. It was good imitation jazz, with a bit of bluegrass and a lot of Anglo-India.

Everyone laughed. They clicked their fingers in time to the well-worn song and sang along with the lyrics. The boy had talent, they all agreed. Few children in other communities could sing like *their* children. Without tuition, without much formal guidance there was always a good voice, a good pianist, a great beat to dance to, to sing along with, to forget that there was a future that did not always align with the colours in their lives. Every day was a party. Music, a bit of shake-a-leg, and the days sped away.

The voices rebounded in Grace's head as she lay hearing the groan of the fan whirring slowly. The heat of May was cruel. Relentless as were some of the traditions that bound families, and as fierce.

Why bother, she thought as she burrowed into her pillow. Let things be as they always were. Perhaps this was the only way to contentment.

But she knew this was as sham a hope as Carl's mock-Presley love song to their mother.

Mrs Edna Johnson, in the flat under Eddie D'Cruze's set her table carefully. The tablecloth was starched from the dhobi's recent wash, her serviettes, all four of them, were folded and placed at neat parallels to the plate. Soup-spoon, table-spoon, fork, knife and dessert spoon formed a correct guard of honour by the side and top of the place-mats. A gleaming glass and silver cruet stand was placed in the middle of the table, salt, pepper in the casters with some vinegar in one of the mini-canisters. Shining glasses held water and on the nearby sideboard in a covered Pyrex dish were rotis kept warm by a thick *jharan,* a bowl of *bhaji* and a bottle of mango pickle–the dinner the family would enjoy that night.

Her son, Fred, was still bathing. The noise of the splashing water could be heard, his wife Hilary was in the bedroom. No doubt reading some of her trashy novels, Mrs Johnson sniffed. Their son, and Mrs Johnson's grandson, Ralph, sat hunched over his schoolbooks. All of sixteen but could be mistaken for just twelve, he was small for his age, his light-coloured hair, eyes and skin a point of great pride. A coloured T-shirt hung on his thin body, a pet pigeon gurgled on the pelmet above him.

"So unhealthy, having that wretched bird near you always," his grandmother, voice husky from a lifetime of cigarettes, slapped Ralph lightly.

"Don't do that," he shrugged away from the reach of her hand sullenly.

"Why do you let that bird roost on your shoulder? Birds carry lice, didn't you know?"

"Better than what some humans carry."

"What do you mean by that, young man…none of your lip…"

Hilary twitched the bedroom curtain aside and stepped into the dining room. She glanced at her son, and sharply said,

"Now let him be Mum. Don't go picking on Ralph, it's his bird, let him do what he wants with it."

Hilary Johnson shot her mother-in-law a sharp look as she gently shooed the bird off and busied herself with the dishes on the sideboard. Tension as thick as the evening dusk gathered. Neither woman cared for each other. It was not just the age-old mother-daughter-in-law standoff where each battled for supremacy in the household, but something deeper, an instinctive difference of character. The husband in Fred most often bowed to the son, and there was a fondness and obvious deference to his mother that caused Hilary's feeling to fester against him.

Hilary knew her body had thickened, her complexion dimmed to a yellowed bleach that matched the patchy distemper of the flat. But she had once been considered a beauty. Had a pick of boyfriends she had, oh yes indeed. So why had she married Fred? Frederick Johnson, polite, quiet, had impressed with his manners, his sober lifestyle. Not for him were the monthly dances held by the church or club that most of her friends attended. No, he would rather go to the free concerts held by the

Calcutta School of Music. He often spoke of his love for classical music and pointed out that many of the popular songs were copied from much older melodies.

Hilary did not want to confess her ignorance, nor her parent's lack of 'culture' or interest in current affairs. The Baker's day-to-day conversation revolved around popular gossip, the recent films showing at one of the few English cinemas and a solemn review of rising prices. She found in Fred a new and novel personality. Of medium height, his skin was scarred by acne, his eyes always seemed to hold a wary expression and when he spoke it was with a slight stammer Hilary found quite endearing. When her father realised she was taken in by the young insurance agent he was not happy.

"Fellow's a dud. Not a spark of life in him. Give him five weeks, *five days,* and he'll have nothing to say to you. Want that to be your life? And look at him, so namby-pamby, bet he's never played a game in his life."

But Hilary, prickled by the criticism sprang to his defence.

"How many men do you know who live with and care for their mothers? Is that less important than kicking a ball around a patch of grass, for heaven's sake!"

Mrs Baker, privately not taken with the solemn young man, had to agree that was a point in his favour.

"Fun and laughter is not everything Jim," she would add, "he seems a nice enough boy."

"Boy…hrumph…he's above thirty-five if he's a day, that's for sure. Bet he's never had a girlfriend in his life before."

"And that's a bad thing?"

But Mr Baker's resistance was worn down by Hilary's obvious preference for the serious Frederick Johnson.

After a short courtship of about six months, they announced their engagement and planned a May wedding.

"It's the month of my middle name – May," Hilary giggled. "isn't that funny?"

Fred smiled. A small twitch of the mouth.

Her mother wasn't pleased.

"You do know May is believed to be an unlucky month for marriages?"

"Oh, go on Mum. Surely you don't believe in all that mumbo-jumbo?"

Mrs Baker sighed dramatically and went about arranging the details of her only daughter's wedding.

Privately she wished Hilary had chosen someone with a bit more spark, a bit more of a personality. She might have been surprised if she read her daughter's thoughts. Hilary was uncertain of her feelings towards her now official fiancée. While she did not want a song-and-dance man, as her father seemed to prefer, she did occasionally wonder if Fred might ever act silly and enjoy the moment. There was also the question of his mother. She did not like the old bag. There was in the old woman's attitude an ill-concealed air of superiority, making it obvious she felt deference was her due. Damned if she was ever going to bend the knee to her, was the private vow of her future daughter-in-law.

Fred, freshly combed hair gleaming with Brylcream entered the room and quickly sat at the table, scraping back the chair noisily.

"*Eeesh...*try to lift the chair when you pull it Fred." To emphasise the point Hilary exaggeratedly lifted the chair away from the table and gently set it down before she sat on it.

"Come on Ralph, leave the homework now, we're waiting to have dinner."

"Wash your hands well, I'm sure you've been petting that bird, you know pigeons are disease carriers. I've told you a thousand times..."

"...leave him be Ma. He knows that. You say the same thing every day like a worn and broken record..."

"Hilary!" Fred scraped his chair back and glared at his wife. Nothing was said. It was all in the swoop of the eyebrows as his face seared into lines clawing his skin into sharp brackets around nose and mouth. After silence had thudded into their evening, he pulled back the chair and nodded to his mother who began serving the rotis carefully, lifting them with the *jharan* before placing them on the side plates. The steaming *bhaji* came next and a small amount of pickle rested on the side of the built-up sautéed vegetables.

"What I wouldn't do for a vindaloo, or a rich beef stew," Hilary thought. It was more a stringency with the monthly budget that kept their table vegetarian than any health consideration. She fought back a smile when she recalled her family's disdain for what they called 'grass' meals.

"Know any Olympic champions who were vegetarians?" her father would ask and roar with laughter at what he considered profound insight.

Long ago. When she was free to decide the food she ate, the friends she could keep in touch with, the opinions she might voice. Long ago. She tore the roti deftly, scooped and spooned the spicy vegetables down. Ralph ate quickly. He took small bites out of the roti instead of tearing it and mixed the pickle with his vegetables.

"You shouldn't bite the roti, Ralphy, use your hands to break it into strips," Edna said, "remember Our Lord broke bread, and blessed it, He didn't bite the bread."

Ralph paused. Nobody spoke. A moment passed, then he took the remaining portion of his roti and began tearing it almost urgently into minute pieces.

"Not so small, not *so* small..."

"Oh for heaven's sake, leave the boy alone Ma." Hilary felt her annoyance bubble again as the old woman interrupted the Saturday dinner.

Fred gripped his roti tightly and sopped the gravy around before taking a large bite of the roll. He made it clear he bit, and did not tear the roti before he ate it. Hilary tried not to let an anger settle. She, as pointedly, tore the last portion of her roti and neatly popped it into her mouth.

The tempo around the table changed.

Fred chewed his food slowly. He didn't look at his family. He seemed to stare steadily at the calendar on the wall.

He'll be late coming to bed tonight, Hilary thought randomly. He'll turn his back and stay that way till I fall asleep. Over the years Fred had forgotten the Morse code between husband and wife. He did not seem to want or care for the warmth of lovemaking. His politeness in public was shiny and people who visited and thought they knew them were impressed by the courtesy he showed his family.

Fine fellow. Good chap. Wonderful husband. Caring father. That was the general consensus, but there was not a great deal of liking for him. The formal etiquette's pointy shards jabbed anyone who took closer steps towards contact with him. Fred's big hands with freckles and age spots were splayed on the table. "He really should not file his nails," Hilary thought. "Men with cared-for hands look funny."

Funny. Funny. Funny. That's what their life had become. How well they acted for everyone. Fred with his careful manners. Ralph, quiet and studious, even her witchy mother-in-law, smiled charmingly, and asked after children, work and health, when people did stop to chat. Smoke, smoke from *choolas,* all of it.

The dinner ended. Their glasses of water were drunk. Fred in abrupt gulps. Edna in sibilant sips. Ralph in a swift swallow. Hilary sucked the water through her teeth, enjoying the cool relief after the spicy food.

No dessert. Fred thought sugary stuff unhealthy. Hilary collected the plates. They did not employ a servant. Fred thought it unnecessary.

After dinner Fred pushed back his chair, rustled the day's newspapers and started to read at the end of the day, the day's news.

Ralph took down the pigeon coop from the alcove above the window and began to clean it out. The pigeon flew down wings beating with a rat-a-tat of an air gun and perched on his shoulder. Edna glared but said nothing.

Daughter and mother-in-law cleared the table. Took the dirty dishes outside to the kitchen and soaked them in the buckets of water there. Tomorrow when the water was pumped through they would wash them. Together locked the kitchen up for the night and walked down the corridor silently back to the flat. Together they slip-slopped in their red rubber Bata slippers into the waiting night.

Later Hilary took out her account books and looked over the day's expenses. The market's expenses had been easy to calculate. Vegetables were cheap. She had paid a higher price for the fresh bamboo, a dish the entire family loved—bamboo salad. She planned a duck roast and prawn and bamboo salad, a 'haas and baas' (duck and bamboo) feast for Ralph's birthday coming up in a few weeks time. It was an occasion to give the vegetarianism a rest. She smiled as she thought of her father, a boisterous man whose biggest joy was being in the centre of whatever his family did. He loved entertaining. Food was a main focus of their celebrations, birthdays, Christmases, Easters, friends visiting, relations travelling back to India from adopted homelands, celebrations were always happening. Her parents never pretended to be anything but ordinary, everyday people. There were rowdy arguments often, nothing lasting, nor deep. Her three brothers brought home friends and almost every weekend was a party, music loud and cheerful, her mother, rarely flustered, pretending to be annoyed at a sudden demand for more people to cater for, and Hilary herself happy to be the only girl, pampered by her parents and looked after by her brothers.

Whoosh.

Gone.

Wiped out by the entrance of a maths tutor, the insurance agent Frederick Richard Johnson, who softly entered their household as tutor, and worked his way to woo and win their only daughter. At first the Bakers were happy a well-placed man was taken with their girl. Hilary was thrilled. At only nineteen she became engaged. She happily relinquished thoughts of career with the future ahead as wife and mother. Fred's mother she had met and though she sensed the reserve at first she thought she understood the feelings a mother might have towards the interloper, the woman who had taken her son's heart and life from her.

What a bleak joke it had turned.

Hilary closed her account books. She ruffled her son's hair as he bent over the books, pigeon still on his shoulder. She wiped the perspiration on her forehead as she went into the bedroom. Undressed for the night and prepared for it with the rituals of brushing her teeth, combing her short thick hair, and like a child, said a prayer when she lay down in bed under her thin cotton bedspread. Mouthing the formula that comforted her through her life Hilary skimmed the years of the quiet erosion of her natural cheeriness, her enthusiasm she brought to her marriage, her initiative, all dwindled before the silence of criticism. Now she was dulled by the constant quiet, her vivacity smothered. Only at night-time honesty before dreams released her, she would briefly relive her life before she became a wife and mother and daughter-in-law.

Chup, chup, she chided herself, go to sleep. Tears make for red eyes. Sleep now, you have to get up early for Ralph's preparations for his coming exams. Mid-term exams needed extra care. Special breakfast to be prepared, sooji halwa, *dalpuris* which Ralph loved, maybe scrambled eggs, a banana, yes that should see him ready for any tough paper. Was it a maths exam tomorrow? Of course not, it was Sunday, then there was a holiday unexpectedly granted by some damned political rubbish. The politicians up to their tricks again – a bandh. How that was supposed to solve the aches and pains of the state was only to be guessed at. What a mess this country was in, holidays for every damn thing, even political convictions. She thought of her son, quickly turning a man, private in his behaviour and thoughts. A good boy, good at maths. Yes, it must be in the genes. She must see he clips his fingernails. Won't do to have ragged nails scratching his paper, making his grip on the pen uncomfortable. Frederick Richard Johnson was good for something, she smiled. He had given her a son who was good at maths. No regrets memsahib, as her father might have said. Now she was hot with the whirr of the overhead fan not helping to whirl away the bullying heat. Sleep, she ordered herself. Sleep.

It was the month of May.

3

"Do you know that Lucy D`Cruze has gone away, left home?"

"What! Really?"

"Was it that man in the garage shop of Raj's?"

"I've seen the girl there many, many times."

"*Chi chi,* what a disgrace. Poor Eddie. Such a good man. Such a shame for this to happen."

"Girls given too much freedom these days eh? All this talk of being equal and all this western nonsense."

"What will Eddie do for his food now?"

"Do you think he will spend money on a cook?"

"Maybe he will board with someone. Old Marie in Number Eleven caters for the old couple down the road. He might think of getting his food from her."

"Oho, oho, such a shame. *Chi, chi.*"

"Did you see her in a sari one day? Given up wearing a dress, going all Indian…"

"Thought too much of herself that girl. Gave herself airs, just because she worked in that chemist shop."

"My Gloria said the manager was very fond of her, not that I'm saying anything, but you know these men and what they are like with our young girls."

"Tch, tch, tch, such a shame."

"Eddie should have kept a stricter eye on her. Poor chap."

"Is that fellow a Christian?"

"Nah, don't think so. What clothes he wears, nothing normal, one of these loose shirt and pyjama things, chappals too and all…And have you noticed the Renshaw girl? Another one with a swollen head."

"Why what's she done?"

"Nothing, yet. But have you seen how she goes around and doesn't talk to any of us?"

"Thinks too much of herself, not like her sister…"

"The teacher in the hill school?"

"Yes, nice girl, always in a lovely dress, or skirt and blouse. Always ready to have a chat. No airs or graces with *her.*"

"Does Bob know?"

"Does Bob know what?"

"That she has an Indian boyfriend?"

"No, no, I mean I don't know if her father knows, but does she really have an Indian boyfriend?"

"Oh yes, and he drops her off after work at the gate and races off on his scooter."

"Oh myee, how badly-behaved. No manners at all."

"Young people these days, no respect for themselves. No respect for their parents."

"A shame, a shame."

"Things changing, not like the old days."

"Tch, tch, tch."

It was the song of the beggar she heard again and again. The keening floated through her mind, elusive, defying a category. Untrained in music theory she knew enough to recognise that the melody was in a minor key. Melancholy, the singer's rusty voice, insistent as a mosquito's whine, beat its circular plaintive cry into her head.

"What are you staring at *yaar?*"

Lucy turned from the small window and smiled at Pradip.

"Nothing, I was thinking how that beggar moves around the locality every day. Do you think people give him much?"

"Don't know. But I do know you are with me, at last." Pradip held Lucy Ridout gently in his arms and rested his face against the nape of her neck. Of medium height he was just slightly taller than her and found it difficult to have her head rest against his chest.

It disappointed him, this unheroic stance when she was in his arms. In his mind he saw the vividly coloured films where the hero towered over the girl and she looked up at him.

He inhaled the slightly spicy smell of her hair. What hair oil did she use, he wondered.

Lucy looked at him and wished she had worn her batik sari. It was light, and less sombre than the plain blue-bordered one she had on.

Almost nun-like, she thought, like the nuns of Mother Teresa, and smiled at the contradiction of their prim garb with this situation.

Pradip ran his hands down her boyish figure. No curves on this one, he thought. Too thin. Hardly any breasts at all.

Never mind, he'd change her diet. Lots of rice, curd, ghee, his mother would say, oil changed everything.

A pity Mother would never know this girl. He could not bring her to his family.

Never mind, never mind all that now. She was here and she was going to be his now. Money? Her job was good wasn't it, and he might be able to get the old man Raj to give him an increase in his salary. Good thing they could live over the garage so there was no rent to be paid. Also Lucy was not a spoilt girl like others of her community. She cooked for her uncle and worked at most of the household needs for him. Pradip sighed. It was so good. It was all he dreamed of – a woman, food prepared for him, and his clothes washed and ironed with all the grease of the garage cleaned away. Sooo lucky, lucky, lucky. Didn't his astrologer say his stars were good? His life would be easy and he would be loved. He never dreamed the past year's smiles and short walks to and from her work would end this way.

It was the mango season that helped change his life. It was always good to breathe the clean air after the rain, eat the fruit, cheap and plentiful, and rub the pulpy seed over his body before his bath. It made his skin smooth. The month of May made him restless. His dreams were full of images he'd feel ashamed of when he woke. He was so hot. He would walk in the rain and hope that his face did not show what thoughts he had of all the women he saw around him. None of the women who came to have their cars repaired looked his way. He'd sneak a look at their breasts and then their faces. The young ones were often too skinny. Flat-chested. He preferred the fuller-figured older women. Saris rarely hid their plump bosoms. Often he'd catch a sly look of compliance from them as he would pretend to busy himself with their cars, keeping near their perfumed presence.

Yes, this one's hair smelt too spicy.

They, the ones who drove up to the garage were rich memsahibs. Often there would be drivers lounging around. Then he'd often have a chat with them. It was stupid to imagine any of those silk-clad women could look his way. Or talk to him. He'd talk to the drivers, quickly spitting out the paan he'd be chewing. One day he might get lucky. He would watch for any woman who'd drive in, he was not that young, he was nearing forty, though everyone swore he looked ten years younger. He smudged the date on his school-leaving certificate so the year of his birth was indistinct. None of his employers ever bothered to check. Age was not important. His skill was, and, as a mechanic he was valued.

He'd whisk a cloth over the car and smile at the women and even if there was no smile in return he continued to rub the windscreen, the windows, the body of the car, smiling fixedly at the women who sat in them, comfortably.

"What witches," he'd curse. "Sitting on their husband's money. Useless bitches, useless."

Then there was Lucy. It was first a smile as she walked by the garage. Every morning on her way to work and back in the evening, she'd smile at him.

Him.

Why, he wondered. She was a memsahib. She spoke English. He spoke it poorly. With a heavy accent. He was educated in a vernacular school, a corporation school the poor were jostled into, hoping once becoming literate they might have a chance to get a job without the usual bribes paid out to grant them an interview with the bosses. School years flew. A poor scholar he now faced an endless round of small backbreaking jobs, some with better employers, some with better prospects, but in the end it was his friend who had an aunt, part-owner of this outlet, that saw him land what he thought at first was a slice of paradise. A steady income beckoned, with free accommodation above the shop.

"*Only* I am asking good behaviour," Sri Raj the proprietor said, a cheek puffed out with a wad of the inevitable paan.

"You have much experience with cars and motor scooters and also other electric goods. No? No? Good, good." Sri Raj squinted at the youngish man in front of him.

It seemed to have happened only yesterday, Pradip thought.

Sri Raj nodded continually. Up and down his head went. Up and down, up and down, bobbobbobbing.

"Wife tells me you are Wiyay's friend? Yes? Wery good, *werywery* good. But look here, friend or no friend, if you cheat me, sleep too much, drink too much tea at the harami *chaiwallahs* there, I will not keep you, okay?"

And he was in.

Ten years ago.

Now here was Lucy looking at him with those eyes that seemed to be laughing at something. Not him he hoped.

"What you thinking?" he asked.

"Nothing. I just like the way you smell of mangoes."

"That's stupid *yaar*."

"All right I was thinking of my uncle Eddie."

"Don't think of that *harami*." He swung her roughly, tighter and bumped his nose against her cheek.

"All right, I won't. But you *do* smell of mangoes."

"I will bathe twice tonight to get rid of that smell."

"No. Don't, I like it."

"Oh."

The cotton sari was wound too tightly around her waist. She wriggled her hand between their bodies and tugged and swathes of cotton dropped to the ground in clumps of colour. Blue, and light blue, almost green. Just like mangoes, Pradip thought. Soft, slippery, it fell away, and Lucy was before him.

The sweeper crouched on the floor, a cross between squatting and kneeling and slowly wiped over the floor with a wet rag. Over and over he pushed the coarse hessian swab, the fan groaned above him, the water spread quickly drying on the red cement. He watched without her knowing he was looking. Looking at the curve of her knees, the soft dips of her ankles, toes stubby, tight buds like those of a child's. He tried to make the work last. Sometimes, in the hour before he fell asleep, when the ache in his body would keep him taut, when he would inhale the *bhang* deeply, his thoughts twisted and curled towards the flat and he felt strong and able to walk up to her and tell her how he needed her. *Bhang* made his crooked body strong.

Arré, arré, he now was Amitabh Bachchan. In hazy visions he'd see her crouch before him, begging him to take her away where he was king and she was queen. She was now crying tears of joy to see the *'bahadur'* bring his horse up to the house. He swung his gun around his back as he pulled her up behind him. Music drowned the sounds of her sobs. Peacocks danced before them as he waved grateful people goodbye. He was their protector. He was the loved leader. Music. It swirled like his thoughts. Lots of pretty girls whirled around and around. He was the hero.

He shook his head and he swabbed the concrete floor lethargically as he heard her voice ask him to hurry with his work. He grinned. If only she knew what he planned. He looked down into the reflection on the floor brought out by the dampened cloth. He rinsed the water from the rough cloth with a deft twist. The bucket screeched along the floor. Now it was just the emptying of the bin into the garbage heap on the street below. Yes, she would give him a cup of tea and slice of bread and he would sink down in front of the main door and dip the bread into the warm tea and have a few more minutes near her. Too soon and his work here was nearly done. He squinted upwards and saw the table at which she sat. Was she looking at him?

Oh no, oh no, but one day, he vowed. One day.

Sunday meant church.

The weather was good, a coolish breeze comforted. Grace got up, threw off her nightdress and after a quick wash, with cold water, a careful choosing of her dress, not a sari, she went downstairs to call Lucy.

It was routine to make the walk to their parish church together. For twenty minutes or less they'd chat about the past week. Lucy, serenely elegant, her slim, tall figure always attracting attention, they'd swiftly dodge men walking close, swinging arms trying to bump into them, aiming at their breasts or legs, or brushing by them aiming at their bottoms. Adept at this unsavoury game of avoid and twist, the two women would step around homeless sleepers, still in a welcome coma after the grinding strain of keeping a living going for yet another day. Past the mad man, who'd smile broadly and ask them if they had seen his dog. Past the spill and smell of an ill-kept road, adroitly manoeuvring over potholes they'd arrive at the church with its stunted spire and dark maroon painted walls.

Sunday Mass, sometimes would be a forty-minute ritual, divided into the before and after of the priest's sermon. A talk rarely evoking comment from either of them. They both looked forward to the celebration of the service when it was taken by the Polish priest who acted assistant to the regular old Goan pastor. "How handsome he is," Lucy would whisper, "so white."

Grace giggling her agreement, solemnly went through the gestures of attending the service without really thinking through the Sunday gospel's message and meaning. The statues were beautiful, rich heritage of the Portuguese tradition. St Joseph, sad-eyed, holding the Christ-child on one arm, a lily in the other, St Teresa, cradling roses, St Anthony also carrying the Christ-child, other plaster figures she could not identify, but all looked sad, no smiles anywhere. The tableau of the crucifixion, the leitmotif of the Christian story, the young man in agony on the wooden planks of torture, His loved ones looking up, that group, Grace privately felt, made a bit too pretty, but essential to the aim of moving any worshipper. Grace loved the colour and drama of the liturgical year. She sank into the unfailing welcome of the purple vestments worn during Lent, the green of the non-happening or ordinary cycle of the church year, the glamorous red of *the* festival, Christmas, and the dazzle of white which signalled the rousing finale of Easter. The raggedly voices that made up the choir were always there, always a soft cushion to rest her random thoughts. She sailed away on those hymns, and with the chant of the service as a backdrop she'd imagine Andy Kaul floating towards her during those Sunday interludes. Here she sat undisturbed. No voices raked through scrabbling to be heard. Their daily demands went on, don't forget this, don't forget that – don't forget those special groceries from the shop near the New Market, the only one stocking smuggled foreign goods – Bovril, which her mother loved, Kraft cheese, Heinz tomato soup, tinned asparagus, luxuries she knew they really could not afford – then there was Carl – his school work waiting for her to look over, of course bills had to be overseen too. It was often tiring. Her father, proud of her accounting, had happily handed over the finances of the home to her. She was tired. The Sunday break was free of the usual necessities of daily living. *Man*, she often marvelled, those in religious orders had it good with no families to look after. It seemed they had no responsibilities the 'world' imposed. She envied the even path of their lives. She was sure Lucy did too.

After church the quick walk home and then after a hasty breakfast, perhaps a rickshaw ride to one of the cinemas for the 10.30 am show. Often the prices were reduced so it wasn't a strain on either Grace's or Lucy's budget.

It was part of the routine of the day. Year after year, they walked in harmony, from their teenage days to now, when both were young women.

She hurried to Lucy's door, next door from her flat and quickly rapped on the front door. Her knock on the door brought Lucy's Uncle Eddie peering out at her, spectacles crookedly on his nose, torn singlet not hiding the thin, bony and strangely hairless chest.

"Lucy's not here." No greeting, no grumpy shout for Lucy to let her know her friend Grace was waiting to go to church.

"Where is she Uncle?"

"How the hell should I know, do you young people bother to tell us anything?"

"...er...will she be back later today?"

"How the *hell* should *I* know? Do you young people bother to tell us any bloody thing?" he repeated through clenched teeth.

Taken aback at the vehemence of his tone Grace stepped back. Lucy's uncle's face was crumpled and sweat was gathering in around his mouth and eyes. He glared at her and pushed the door shut.

She turned slowly and ran down the stairs, the banister creaking loudly as she slid her hand over its silk surface and made her way towards the entrance of their block of flats. She looked at the dust on her palm and quickly brushed it off wishing yet again the cleanliness of the staircase could be better managed. She sighed over one still elegant feature in this block of bricks that she called home. Wondered briefly at the carpenter who fashioned it. Thought of the support its rails gave all of them as they climbed it.

The walk to church was a lonely one. She forgot to keep a sharp eye on the eve-teasers and was bumped into by a couple of lecherous old men.

"Bloody swines," she muttered. She entered the small enclosure that fronted the church. Going in she dipped her hand into the stoup, blessed herself and sat in a quickly filling pew fuming at the odd turn her day had taken. Lucy should have told her what she was doing today. What was the matter? Where was she? Surely she had not run off with that slimy looking mechanic at Raj's? No. No. Never. Not that. *Not that.* Grace was filled with a cold sickness. Surely she could not have risked everything just to be away from that silly uncle. The Mass went on. Responses were given and answered. The sermon was a drone she couldn't remember. She shuffled along the line to receive communion and tried to jerk her thoughts towards the sacredness of the moment.

"Body of Christ", the old Goan priest, Fr D'Mello, intoned as he placed the fragile wafer in her hands.

"Amen," said Grace.

She knelt, feeling nothing, her thoughts confused as she went over the puzzle of Lucy. Had she left her uncle? Had she just left to spend the night with some of her colleagues, Lucy sometimes mentioned a girl at the shop she was friendly with. The choir sang the final hymn. Then it was the final intonation, "Go you are sent forth."

She wished her mother was with her. Her father was Anglican, Church of England, High Church, her father would joke, and though they were baptised Catholics after her mother's faith, Kitty Renshaw was not scrupulous about keeping too strictly to the laws of the church. Grace often laughed at the carte blanche attitude of her mother towards the rules she was supposed to live by.

"I've seen my children grow up as Catholics haven't I? How I live my life is my business. Nothing to do with racing off to church every Sunday." And that was the end of that.

"The Mass has ended, go in peace."

Grace genuflected absentmindedly and walked out into the hot summer morning. She hoped the evening would be cooler and the great May Queen Night would offer some ease after this awful morning.

She retraced her walk back to the lane. It had grown more humid, the glare from the morning sun dazzling. She'd closed her eyes and saw red spots whirling against her eyelids. Where was Lucy? The usual beggars clustered at street corners, the pavement vendors sang their wares' praises. Dogs ran quickly noising out scraps from the gutter, trams clanged and groaned their way along the road. Heat danced in waves above the gritty pavement. Grace suddenly felt nauseous. Her head seemed to have grown as big and as light as a balloon. She forced herself to put one foot in front of the other 'steady, steady' she cautioned. This was all Lucy's fault, she thought angrily. The May morning intrusive, prying, pressed close against her. No comforting cloud was in that sky.

Grace walked on.

The pickle bottles gleamed in the sun. Jewelled, onyx-dark, the marinade glowed. Hilary Johnson reached up and turned them so the jars received an equal amount of heat. She smiled as she tracked the trickle of oil from the lip of the sealed container. A quick wipe with her finger and the bottle was clear. The oil smelled delicious. Mango *kasundi.* Her mouth watered as she lined the half dozen bottles symmetrically. This was something her mother-in-law left to her. Somehow the tedious preparation of cutting the fruit, chopping the spices, then cooking the mixture, was not an enjoyable experience for Edna Johnson.

"Damn smell gets into your skin. Even your hair smells of the stuff."

Good. Very good. Hilary was relieved she did not have the old woman at her elbow, watching every step and finding fault with most of the methods she used. She picked the green and hard mangoes carefully from the fruit vendor, peeled them carefully, sliced them into slender slivers, washed them in a thick mixture of sea-salt. Then she chopped the masalas, the garlic, the ginger, the small red chillies, finally cooking them in a deep *dekchi* of mustard oil. The pickle absorbed plenty of oil and Fred frowned at the price she paid for the premium oil. Doesn't frown when he's scoffing it down with his rotis though, she thought grimly.

Their lunch today was a traditional yellow rice, 'ball' curry and papads. A brief respite from the vegetable menu. There might even be a bottle of beer for Fred and her, a Thums Up cola for Ralph. Edna did not drink and looked faintly annoyed when the chilled beer bottles would be brought to the table.

"Good the hag doesn't drink," Hilary mused. "She's left few enough pleasures for me throughout my life here." And holding that thought she began to set that table for the Sunday midday meal. A knock at the door broke into the morning's drill and Hilary looked up in surprise. They seldom had visitors and with no servants bar the sweeper and weekly visit of the dhobi bringing their washed and ironed clothes she could not think of who might have come calling. Quickly smoothing the creases from her dress and patting her hair she went to the front door and opened it. Standing there was Mr D'Cruze, the grizzled neighbour from upstairs, the least amiable of the block's inhabitants.

"Oh hello Mr D'Cruze, anything wrong?" Normally spruce, quite dapper, he looked unshaven, shirt crumpled, his stare, bloodshot.

"Yes, hellohello... You know my Lucy's left me..." he began hesitantly, he stood there his hands beating a rhythm on his legs, "did Ralph speak to Lucy yesterday?"

"I don't know. Ralph was at school, but stayed late for hockey practice. He came home at about five in the evening." There was pain in his eyes as he looked at Hilary.

"Come in, don't stand outside, come on in."

He shambled inside and looked around vacantly.

"Where's Fred?"

"He's gone out with his mother to buy some grain for the pigeon. We forgot that we had run out of it and the bird is driving us crazy with its rumbling and grumbling," she laughed slightly, "and Ralph is upset as well. Why don't you sit down. Come here, sit nearer the fan. Isn't the heat awful? Can't seem to get cool no matter what you do." Nervously chattering, Hilary watched closely, guessing at the explanation that was to come. She sat down facing him in a wicker chair, and then got up again to bring him a glass of water.

"Why don't you have a drink of water. It's so hot. We need to drink more water than we do."

"My Lucy has left me."

Lucy-in-the-sky-with-diamonds, was the phrase that leapt through Hilary's mind. She liked the girl. Looking at Lucy one found it difficult to believe she was the niece of this sour-looking man. Soft-spoken, she had a manner that withstood the rough, charity-run education her uncle had seen fit to give her. Hilary was silent. Anything she wanted to say sounded silly, false. Of course the people in the mansion knew how poorly Lucy was treated. She was cook, housekeeper, nurse and part-time breadwinner for this shabby, mean man. No one ever recalled Lucy raising her voice in argument, or protest. Older than the Renshaw girls, at least the younger one, and much older than her own son Ralph, she remained a quiet self-contained child.

"Too quiet," her mother-in-law liked to say, "sure sign of slyness."

But Hilary sensed envy simmering there. Lucy was pretty. Her soft complexion, her very calm was an unusual attraction in a young girl.

"Quite the princess," Edna Johnson sniffed. "Should be thankful her uncle gave her a roof over her head. Hate to think what she'd have done without him. Not that young anymore either."

Lucy-in-the-sky-with-diamonds would have probably done well without the rancour her uncle had showered on her.

"I'm sure she's run off with that man in Raj's garage. Run off I tell you." The words came out in a burst of slurred panic.

A mouth that had grown slit-narrow, Lucy's uncle didn't look at Hilary but stared venomously at the pigeon that fluttered down to sit on the back of a dining room chair.

"Why do you keep that bird? Don't you know they carry germs? Breed fevers, even meningitis. Get rid of the thing."

What bloody cheek, Hilary bridled, then reminded herself that the man was under a lot of strain.

"Well it's Ralph's. He's had it since he was little more than a toddler. I can't just get rid of it. And anyway it's always in the house. I don't think there is a chance of it carrying bacteria or anything awful like that."

"Rubbish. These children are so spoilt. Give him a hobby, something like stamp collecting. That'll keep him out of mischief. It doesn't cost a thing and he'll learn from it. Not this sticking his nose close to a ball of smelly feathers."

Hilary, her sympathy dissolving into a growing itch of irritation broke in sharply, "Yes, yes, I suppose you're right. Now that is not why you have come here is it? Why do you say Lucy has left with this fellow from the garage?"

"Why?" Eddie D'Cruze glared, biting his lower lip, tearing off the dried skin there, as he stared at the pigeon, "any bloody fool could see Lucy wanted to leave me. And she would often go alone to that damned shop pretending to get my bicycle seen to when now I know all she wanted was to chat to this, this, this...*bastard.*" He spat out the word, mouth working in untold fury.

"I'm sorry, I'm sorry, so sorry..." she stopped, her voice choked with embarrassment and a sharp slicing of sorrow.

"*Sorry* won't do anything now will it?" He continued to stare at the pigeon. He went on biting his lips, spitting out dried flakes of skin. Hilary tried not to flinch each time he spat. What did he expect her to do or say? The man rarely spoke to anyone, this had to be the first time he had ever entered her home.

"And don't pretend you all didn't know about this, everybody here knows everybody's bloody business. Cursed lot of nosy-parkers."

"I don't think you should abuse like this..."

"So what can I do? Go on as if nothing has happened? Everyone having a good laugh eh?"

"No that's not true at all, anyway if you feel that way why have you come to me?" He looked at her, his eyes filled with pleading and Hilary knew she had to help him.

"Look Mr D'Cruze..."

"Eddie..."

"...Eddie. Don't be hasty about rushing around blaming people for laughing at you or not telling you about how things were going. Believe me, I don't think anyone here guessed at what Lucy intended to do. Why don't you wait and..." Abruptly the old man in front of her put his head in his hands and started to sob, deep heaves. The ragged sound lasted a few seconds and then as suddenly there was a silence. He lifted his face to her.

"No, I'm not going to blame you, I've always known you, kind and quiet. Not like the other bats around here. Not like the old woman you live with. It helps, you know, telling this to someone, it helps. You, you, you're different..."

Hilary looked away. It was confusing, this situation. Her heart went out to Eddie D'Cruze in his moment of anguish, but when she thought of the young woman, forced to blot her life just to get away from him, she felt her breath shortening with anger.

"The only thing I can tell you is to wait and see what happens."

"Yes, you've said that. But what can I *do*. Sit around and twiddle my bloody thumbs? I think the police might be able to do something don't you?"

"No," she almost shouted. "Eddie, do you want your daughter..."

"...niece, *niece*..."

"...niece, to be dragged into a police station and stood before those men. She will be exposed to corrupt men who will enjoy making fun of her in a terrible way. If you want to keep this quiet you must not think of going to the police. You mustn't do that. You know what these people feel about our people. About us and our ways. Please don't do that. It's the worst thing to do."

He stared. Her outburst seemed to sober him.

"So what do I do? Tell me."

She tell *him* what to do? Why did this have to be her decision, how and when did she get involved? A damned nerve this man had, barging in like this and behaving as if she owed him this help. The pigeon fluttered up to the alcove above the window and began its incessant cooing. It was a strange sound, this comforting throaty gurgle in the room. Eddie ignored it and sat there looking at her. There was the sudden sound of a knock and she heard the murmur of Fred and his mother as they stood waiting outside.

Eddie jumped up.

"I'll go now. Don't want to see anyone. Don't want them looking at me with all that slyness. I know how they'll be laughing. I'll go. Quickly." His voice thickened with urgency. He stood up, tugged at his pants, smoothed his hair and stood there. Hilary opened the door and with a slight rise of her eyebrows indicated there was a guest in the house. Fred frowned, his mother stared. This was strange, they had few visitors and Sunday morning was strictly family time "Hello Mr D'Cruze."

"Hello."

Fred and Edna Johnson made their greetings mechanically. Fred smiled. Old Mrs Johnson's look swept over the dishevelled man. The visitor nodded his head, made no answer to the wish. Ralph whistled for his pigeon. He had already opened the bag of grain and held some of it in his hand. The bird swooped down clumsily and began pecking his palm with sharp little jerks of its beak.

"Ralph, do that later. Come now and wash your hands, lunch is about to be served." Edna Johnson's barked message was pointed. A hint to the man there that he was intruding into what was family time. Hilary shut her eyes briefly wondering when, if ever, she might decide the direction of her family.

Eddie D'Cruze walked with stiff steps to the door and formally inclined his head towards Hilary's mother-in-law, her husband and lastly an almost formal bow to her. He slipped through the door and they heard his shoes harshly grating on the steps as he climbed up the stairs to his flat. The shaky rails rattled as he clutched the banister. They heard his door open and close and then there was a silence that seemed to lock them in. Both her husband and mother-in-law seemed to stare at her accusingly. Hilary found herself thinking that rings did not look good on the fat hands of Edna. She found herself not knowing where to start and wondered what they felt about the runaway girl. Or if they'd care much for the pain of the old man she had left behind. Ralph looked at the three adults standing so still and asked, "Are we having a late lunch or what?"

The spell broke.

Flies were everywhere.

They appeared zizzing and whizzing over the food on the table. They hit the closed shutters of the louvered windows. Their light brush on skin carried the grit of the garbage bins that overflowed in the lane outside. He sat on his haunches and thought of the day past. She had been extra quiet today he noticed. Family work had gone by without the usual prodding to polish the corners, or rinse the swab till the water ran clear.

He looked down at his food. It was deep fried corn flour, *suttoo,* with rinds of onion, rolled into a twist. Very tasty. He chewed slowly, sucking his fingers noisily, wondering when he might hear her call to him. When she might cook for him one day. It was not impossible. He had seen many beautiful women start to obey men they once scorned. He slapped at a fly settling on his neck. *Ouf,* he missed. What heat, *hai,* Ram Ram, what heat. Next year an electric fan bought with his savings would keep him cool.

She'd be here and they'd both sit and eat together. The flies gone. The heat gone, gone with the breeze of the fan. He slowed his eating. Hands greasy with the oil from the fried onion he looked into his future with a beautiful wife. He looked into his future without the slop of dirty water, without the smell of garbage, without the voice of women always telling him to hurry, to be quick, to be careful. Bitches. All of them. Except his queen.

Wait and see, wait and watch. All will be clapping. All shouting *jai, jai.* Rose petals will shower them and he will take her to their house. Big. Very big. Lots of rooms. Lots of bathrooms. Toilets. Like the sahibs had, not the holes in the ground. Servants there to hurryscurry, to listen to him and her, obey them. What pleasure. What happiness. What joy.

He slapped at another fly sitting on his knee. Lots of talk. She might read to him. He didn't want to think about the night. That time was special. Even his thoughts shut down before the promise of night. Her skin was so smooth. Like an onion before it browned. *Khubsurat.* Beautiful, beautiful.

He nodded in the afternoon heat, the metal plate slipping from his grasp. A fly settled on scraps of food. His mouth slowly dropped open, he snored raucously, worn out from the day's scrubbing of other people's homes and floors and clearing the garbage their lives had accumulated.

4

Clubland. The rooms, stately, high-ceilinged, kept old stories, prejudice alive.

Grace looked around and saw gathering shadows on this Sunday evening.

The family were at their Club. This was a highpoint in their week. The Club was a nerve-centre for the community. With membership restricted to Anglo-Indians, it was now limping along on funds, sponsorships, the monies received from dances, weddings, functions held in its premises, and the mammoth money-spinner, an annual raffle, a sweepstake of some lacs of rupees. This, of course, *was* open to those of other communities. Once a shining spot, like the lyrics of the Broadway musical, this Camelot managed to exist, but its raddled appearance like the over-powdered face of a once beautiful woman was tragic. Desolate, its terminal condition written in the threadbare carpet, the worn parquetry dance floor, a depleted library, a poor attendance during the working week, symptoms ignored by most members. They gathered, they gossiped, played their cards, bridge and rummy were the popular choices, wrote up credit bills at the bar, discussed the latest films, dismissed the government, 'bloody 420-*wallahs*, the whole jingbang lot', the consensus of opinion, watched their children dance to the music of a four-piece band (piano, double bass, drums, saxophone) of young Goan musicians and finally, flushed, happy, took taxis home to another week of work. A week dealing with inflated prices and a world fast forgetting them, or at best regarding them as curiosities.

Tonight was the night of the May Queen ball.

It was a break with tradition this holding of the dance on a Sunday. But a public holiday stretched the weekend over to the Monday and no one really objected to the change in the day. It was a perfect evening. Fans whirled busily.

"Pray god there won't be a power cut tonight," said Louis Deane, the secretary of the Club. "We do have a generator, but it takes some time to re-start the electricity, and of course everyone will grumble. We should have installed air-conditioning long ago, but the bloody AGM last year decided against it."

"Why, the electric bill won't be that much more than what it is now, will it?" This jokingly remarked by one of the old-timers, suited, looking forward to this red-letter day in the club's calendar.

"Yes man, of course it will be double the money we have to fork out now. Still have to move with the times eh?"

Louis Deane walked away, smile ready to meet the next person who came up to the office. Built like a sumo wrestler, he was employed years ago, partly because of his impressive build. Massive, he had an implacable look that quelled trouble-makers. Arguments were met with a closed stare and words fell away. A retired football coach, his expertise was still in demand by sportspeople and associations like the CC & FC, a wealthy sports club that boasted a celebrity roll-call of members.

Why, he mused, should he answer up to all that went wrong? His salary was not great, he had not been given a raise in years, there were few perks, and recently even the attendance at the dances had fallen off. Funny how the young people now preferred to go to nightclubs, 'discos' and restaurants to have a good time he thought. Why, back in the old days, it was a thrill to be here for a dance, then it was off to Nizams, the famed Muslim outlet for their legendary mouth-watering kathi kebabs, then, if it were really into the small hours of the morning, the Catholics among them, as a final salute to the night's revelry, might attend the early morning Mass at St Thomas' in Middleton Row. Of course it was the 5 o'clock service, the Cook's Mass, as it was known. For only the Indian-Christian servants were up at that hour before going to their jobs.

What fun it had all been. What innocent pleasure. Now it was strobe lighting, noise and thumping electric guitars deafening with their shrill presence. Music? Rubbish, he thought. It was noise. Noise, noise and more bloody noise.

"Hey Louis!" It was the president Mr Coates who hailed him across the hall. "Have you got things under control? Won't want to risk us sweating it out tonight eh?" A hearty laugh and a friendly pat on the back was code for a clear warning to see the night went without mishap. The bonhomie did not match the expressionless eyes behind the thick lens of

John Coates' horn-rimmed glasses. "Yes, of course Mr Coates," he replied, anxiety almost trapping the tone of his voice, "things all A-OK."

"That's the ticket. Everything all right then eh? Yeah, don't want my girl to be disappointed tonight. Mother's very excited, this sort of thing comes only once in a lifetime. Yeah."

Mr Coates's young daughter was one of the contenders for the title of May Queen. Guess who was going to be crowned this year then? Louis Deane grinned ruefully as he nodded and stood besides the president of the club.

God, how long was the man going to hold on to this tenure? President of the club for almost a decade, his hold seemed to get as tenacious as the pollution that blanketed the city. Already it seemed he was a perpetual figure in that hierarchy. Pale, one might say pasty, with a paunch that stretched his waistband, John Coates' voice was the one feature that people remembered. Thin, shrill, it surprised listeners with its feminine quality. The timbre insinuated itself into one's memory. If asked to describe John, it was his voice that flashed into consciousness before his nondescript features did. He looked a successful middleman. One who served well and commanded poorly.

"Well Louis old man, I hope the evening goes without a hitch," he pulled out a handkerchief and mopped his face, "pity we can't organise the weather eh?"

"Well, hope the monsoon breaks soon, Mr Coates."

"Not too soon, not too soon, can't have this evening washed out eh."

"Oh no Mr Coates, that won't do at all, will it?" Louis hoped his slight sarcastic note slipped by unnoticed.

He needn't have worried, for from across the room a voice cut with the accuracy of a well-stropped razor.

"Johnee, there you are. I've been looking everywhere for you. What do you think, Louis has told me one of the judges has phoned to say he is ill and won't be able to make it this evening," Yvonne Coates, top-heavy bouffant hair-do slightly askew, pounced on her husband and fixed him with a reproachful look. At forty-odd years old Yvonne still cut an arresting figure. Trim, of medium height, her complexion was honey and cream, her eyes a light green. The brown hair owed something to her hairdresser's skill but she was considered a beauty by most. Ignore the narrow-eyed gaze, the squashed, foreshortened features, the harsh accent, flattened vowels bouncing along as freely as her ill-concealed breasts and she looked impressive.

Louis's brother when visiting on a short trip from England whistled softly when he saw her, "Hey, *she's* a bit of all right, isn't she?"

He never thought so, but he held his opinion to himself. It would be dangerously impolitic to give an honest opinion of the president's wife.

"Hmm, suppose so." He found Yvonne Coates' raucous voice vulgar, and the overly familiar manner at odds with what he considered the behaviour of a well-bred lady.

"Hello Louis. Looking so handsome and all. Going to set the young girls' hearts fluttering, yeah?" She breathed heavily, and clasped his arm.

Her husband looked annoyed.

"Oh fathers' alive, *why* didn't you let me know Louis? A judge short! God what a catastrophe! Now what do we do?" John Coates took off his glasses and began polishing them vigorously.

"So what are you going to do about the judges eh?" She addressed them both, querulously.

"We all are very excited about this evening, y'know, our Heather is one of the girls going to be judged for the May Queen." She giggled, her constant nodding setting her hair-do swaying in a bizarre motion.

As if he could possibly forget. He gently loosened his arm from her grip and said with a confidence he was far from feeling, "Of course, we'll get someone, don't worry Mrs Coates, leave it to me and I'll get the best judge the club can find," he laughed loudly to show that the problem was a trifling one.

"Okay then. I know Johnee wouldn't want Heather to be disappointed. She's sooo excited, ."

John Coates looked tired and fed-up.

"All right luv," he sighed, "now let's go into the hall and sit with our friends okay?"

"Oh he's so grumpy. Grumpy daddy," she giggled again, "always pretending to be sooo tired."

She took his arm and guided him back to the hall where the band had already started to play its signature tune, a Duke Ellington classic.

"C'mon men, let's hurry and start the ball rolling," she winked at

Louis, who tried to wink back. God, he thought, where am I going to get a judge at this eleventh-hour.

There were to be five judges, four of them outsiders, non-members, only the one among them a member, all on the panel to cast their votes for who would be crowned the night's May Queen.

Two of the judges were English, Jean Alford and Donna Chator, both wives of Anglo-Indian army men, colonels, and he knew everyone applauded this choice. The other two were Anglo-Indians, a local lady doctor, Doris Sims, and Ivan Basil, a head-master of a small primary school, the fifth judge had called in sick. He was the only bona-fide member, popular despite the tag of being 'bookish', an elderly member of the club, he was apologetic for the last minute cancellation and over the phone, sounded wheezy. A revered professor in one of the city's colleges, his quiet erudition was admired by all. *Damn,* why did this have to happen, just as things looked fine. The phone rang breaking into his reverie.

"Hello, Louis Deane here."

"Oh hello Louis, this is Professor Martin. Look I'm sorry for this mess-up, but you know my blood pressure is not what it should be and I've been given strict instructions not to stir. My apologies again," the voice rasped slightly and he went on, "I know there must be quite a fuss going on so if you don't mind I've a lady here who would be happy to step in for me."

Louis let out a sigh of relief. Land in sight, he thought. "Oh I'm sure anyone you recommend is great with us, sir."

"She's Mrs Rupa Jaiswal, the executive head of Henson and Brown, the advertising company, and she says she'll be delighted to be one of the judges for tonight's May Queen Ball."

Louis' heart plummeted. *A Mrs Rupa Jaiswal?* God what were they thinking? Not just an Indian judge, but a *Marwari.* The choice was not the best solution to the evening's dilemma. Disastrous.

"Sure Professor Martin, I'll let Mr Coates know and we'll send the car around to fetch Mrs Jaiswal."

"No don't worry she's got her car and will be there within the half hour. Again, I am sorry for this hitch, but Rupa's lovely, a true sophisticate. Thank you. See you next week when I'm given the all clear my pressure's normal."

The phone clicked off.

Good God, *his* pressure at present was sure as hell not normal. He pictured the faces when he'd break the news of the judge. Bloody hell.

"Sure, sure, a *sophisticate!* Bloody Marwaris," was his own thought. "Woman big shot. They're now getting in everywhere. Chase us out of the city, out of the country, now they're worming their way into the club. Bet she can't dance a step worth knowing. No bloody rhythm to talk of, two left feet with diamonds on the bloody toes and all the bloody fingers too I'll bet. Bloody wog."

He dreaded breaking the news to the Coates. For once he was in agreement with what he knew would be outrage at this choice.

He swore vilely. Bad enough the community was discriminated in most areas, work, sport, the public forums for politics, local affairs, now this unexpected cock-up.

What the hell would a Marwari woman know about Anglo-Indian club life anyway? Indian social dos were the most boring things one could go to. Talking, eating, eating, eating and flashing their jewellery at each other. Weddings were gaudy, ostentatious, what his parents would dismissively call *'khaa, pee, chal'* drills – 'eat, drink and go' without the pleasantries of song, music or dance. "All these people want to do is show off their wealth and their *gulabi* clothes" he'd remember his father saying, "no conversation to speak of." And he'd laugh at the unintentional witticism.

He walked slowly into the hall towards the table where the Coates' party was sitting. Passing the Renshaws at the next table he noticed how attractive their daughter Grace was looking. Wearing a deep green chiffon-like sari her chic short hair had a sparkling pin holding the short fringe away from her face. No other geegaws apart from a single gold armlet contrasting with the brown of her skin.

"Classy," was the immediate thought, "now *that's* sophistication."

John Coates looked up quizzically at him, "what's the matter man, why the long face?"

Louis Deane drew a deep breath and let it out slowly.

He began to tell them.

Outside the night had grown dense. A few pavement dwellers had spread their ragged sheets, bits of plastic and newspapers down for their night's sleep. Pi dogs curled near some of them. Tat, cheap odds and ends, magazines, foreign ones were carefully packed away in glassine folders. Now they relaxed slightly, puffed strongly on the last of their bidis while they chatted and drank a last glass of tea. Smoke from the inevitable wood fires spiralled upwards. Trams still grumbled by. The sounds of the daytime city were growing mellow. Touts hovered at the corners looking for lone men, "Nice fair girl, sahib, fresh from village." Taxis slowed before the awning of the club. A few rickshaws hopefully rang their bells. The city was slowing down. Against this quietening lifescape, a black Mercedes swished to an expert halt besides the pavement. A uniformed chauffeur jumped out and held open the door. There was a ripple of perfume, a rustle of silk, Rupa Jaiswal swiftly adjusted her pallu, smoothed her sari and spoke briefly to the driver before alighting. A quick salute and the man shut the door with a soft thunk, then went around to the driver's seat and got in and slowly drove the car into a nearby side street.

Rupa Jaiswal walked the breadth of the gritty pavement and entered the pillared entrance of the building.

The fifth judge of the May Queen Ball had arrived.

The evening was under way. The noise was deafening. Classic jazz had given way to heavy metal and the young dancers were riveting, mesmeric in their mastery of the new dances. Jumping, whirling, bopping up and down, it was like watching an elite corps perform a military tattoo. Beautiful and savage.

"Can't see the fineness in all this pounding and jumping," John Coates muttered, "looks more a bloody tribal march to me."

He watched his daughter carefully. On the dance floor she looked flustered as she tried to keep in pace with her partner's intricate steps.

"Who is that clown dancing with Heather?"

"Why that's Cedric Smith's son," hissed Yvonne Coates. "Don't look at him like that, you know the family are very well off. He's doing his BCom and is in his final year. See, his mother is looking at us. Smile,

smile," under the shield of the tablecloth his wife dug his knee with her long fingernails. "He's a nice boy."

The rebuke was for the hope that Heather might make a match with this lad.

John Coates wiped the perspiration from his forehead, fixed a smile on his face, and shot a quick look at the surprise of the evening, Rupa Jaiswal.

The lady sat serenely at their table, flicking invisible dust specks off her sari as she watched the scene before her intently.

John felt his embarrassment grow as he recollected his gaffe earlier in the evening. Masking the surprise at her lone entrance and trying to keep his mouth from falling open at her poise, he had fussily scraped a chair forward then asked if she would like a soft drink, a Fanta or a Thums Up perhaps. She had looked at him with a hint of amusement in her brown eyes and in a clear voice said, "Just a straight scotch with no ice please."

It was not a high point in his social graces. He managed to smile and with a tight laugh clicked his fingers for the club bearers, "Of course, of course. Bearer," he called, "one scotch for the memsahib."

His wife was smiling widely at the new guest.

"Myee, I never drink alcohol. Some wine at Christmas, but that's all," she looked for approval around the table but few really were paying her much attention. Mrs Jaiswal, Marwari, executive, and now judge at their May Queen Ball had captured the pivotal place of interest and respect.

The women, Colleen Hindley, Maxine Taylor, and the grande dame of the community, Sophia Lawson, looked eagerly at the newcomer, former misgivings forgotten. Their husbands, and Mrs Lawson's son, Roger were all still standing wearing stiff smiles, as they silently made up a formal frieze around the table.

"Is this your first visit to the club Mrs Jaiswal?"

"Well no, actually I've been here as a schoolgirl when our basketball team won the inter-school sports trophy, and we came here to receive the shield from the president, which was you, Mr Coates. You don't remember me from then do you?" She laughed and looked impishly at the older man.

"I always thought you girls were not encouraged to play sports," Yvonne Coates, smilingly asked.

"No, my family were always sports-minded. My father and brother played a good game of hockey, I've always loved basketball, blame that on the good Loreto nuns. *Us girls,* my sisters and cousins, played quite a bit of sport."

Much laughter at the gentle barb, though Yvonne Coates didn't join in, she just continued to smile.

"Are you still involved with sports?" This from the aristocratic Mrs Lawson, "Does your husband also play hockey?"

The ploy, obvious curiosity into the personal set-up of their guest.

"My ex-husband, I divorced last year, but yes, he plays cricket, at least when I last heard from him he was still fanatical about it."

The casual mention of divorce and the smooth mentioning of her ex-husband evoked a momentary stillness in the group. Divorce was an occurrence that happened rarely. A definite blot on the family, one did not speak of it. Certainly it was not to be referred to quite so easily, even if questioned about one's marital status. A fudge, a white lie was accepted as part of the prevalent social nicety.

Yvonne Coates' smile slid into a smirk. The other women began to drink their Fantas and Thums Up busily, throats working as the fizzy drink helped patch over the solecism.

Roger Lawson sat down by Mrs Jaiswal and courteously asked her if she'd like a cigarette.

"No, thank you," a smile, "I *am* divorced, but I don't smoke."

Roger laughed, a surprised chortle at this sly reference to the ripple her disclosure had caused.

"And, before you ask," she continued, "I'm also a strict non-vegetarian."

This time he laughed loudly, eyes shut, head tilted back, the frail wooden chair rocking slightly in rhythm to the laughter, his collar tight against the riff of mirth till the people in the nearby table looked with open curiosity towards them.

This stylish woman had suddenly made the evening worth attending. He stopped laughing, a bit breathless, and looking at his mother was relieved to see in her steady gaze a slight smiling approval of the exchange. Good. He would not want her to be annoyed by his attention to the outsider.

Indian and Marwari – good god, what an inconvenient combination.

A furtive look at the sari-clad woman and he saw a short, youngish woman, thirty-something at least, a head of glossy black hair swept into a French twist, her figure generous, lending voluptuous curves to the pale cream sari she wore. No glittering jewellery thank heavens, just a broad gold watch, roman figures on its dial, a manly feature on her slightly chubby wrist, and finally, a touch which marked her out among the present company of conventionally dressed women, a tiny nose stud. It was a dark ruby, which complimented the cream of her sari. And the cream of her complexion. Her eyes were classically Indian, large, dark, a bit heavy-lidded when in repose, the look could arouse a man quickly, Roger's thoughts abruptly skidded to a halt. Stop, he ordered himself. This woman is off-limits. She's probably a millionairess having some fun with us poor folk. She probably sees this as a kind of behavioural experiment. He felt unreasonable anger and looked down at her hands, lying still and gently curled near his. No rings. Nails cut short, square, trim with a gloss that became her pale complexion. `Pale hands besides the Shalimar', the line went through his mind as he looked up to see her looking at him.

"What are you going to ask now?" A gentle tease, "my children's ages?"

"Er...um...well no, I mean, hahaha," he stuttered, "I'm not interested..."

"No? How disappointing. I hoped you were."

"Hahaha...yes, I know we're a nosy bunch aren't we? Can't seem to get the yak going without a string of questions."

"Oh I don't mind. It's quite flattering to be the centre of so much attention."

"Really? I think it's awful to come to a social evening and have strangers quiz you about your personal life."

"It's quite magical for me," Rupa Jaiswal looked at him, "no, honestly, I don't go to many social evenings like this, cocktail parties are boring, they're usually tied up with work. Talk, talk, eat, drink and hope that your board meeting the next day is kept happily afloat by the scotch drunk through the previous evening."

Roger was about to answer when he felt a sudden thump on his shoulder. He looked up to see Cedric Smith leaning over him. A wave of whisky breath washed over him as the pudgy man swayed gently and grinned towards the fifth Indian judge.

"Hello, hello, hello. Cedric Smith's the name, and you are..?"

"Rupa Jaiswal, a privileged guest at your club this evening," and she made a formal namaste towards the flabby, heavily sweating man.

"Privileged eh…haha…*man,* you can lay it on can't you?" He ignored her greeting and reached forward and shook her hand keeping hold of it, wagging it up and down vigorously.

"Why don't you join my table for a little while eh? Wife is just dying to meet you."

Her hand still engulfed in his, Rupa looked at Roger, "Why yes, I'd love to. Just let me finish my drink and I'll let Mr Coates know I will be going over to meet your wife."

Yvonne Coates sat stiffly through the exchange looking straight ahead. To a casual observer it appeared as if she were engrossed in the music and dancing before her. The three women alongside were watching the trio as they played out what was sure to be an interesting situation. Cedric Smith, Roger Lawson and Rupa Jaiswal were briefly frozen as each wondered how the other was going to react.

Roger got up suddenly as Rupa withdrew her hand from Cedric's grasp. Cedric Smith rocked back on his heels and took a deep breath as he turned and gave his wife, seated a few tables to the right an okay sign, thumb and forefinger forming a circle.

"See you shortly, all righty then?"

Another thump on Roger's shoulder and Cedric Smith, made a slight bow to the others present there, then walked jauntily back to his place at the other side of the hall.

"My, my, you've certainly made a conquest," Yvonne Coates looked at the young woman, chuckling softly, to show there was no guile intended.

Rupa nodded, but lost her look of ease as she glanced up at Roger who had remained standing.

"Excuse me please," he said, "I have to meet a friend I've seen across the room." With a wave he moved away and Rupa turned towards the people around the table, all facing her with collective anticipation.

There was an intensity in their stares. The silence was broken by John Coates rapping on his glass to summon a passing waiter.

"Here bearer, quick, *jaldi, jaldi"* he turned to Rupa, "what would you like for dinner? Happy with the set menu, or shall I order something special?"

"No, no, I'm quite happy with whatever is on the menu for tonight."

"We have a kitchen here you know. Our chefs are among the best in the city."

Mr Coates glanced at his guests accepting their approval.

"Our Chinese food is prepared and overseen by the owner of Waldorf. The beef kebabs and chicken dishes are supervised by Mario Fernandes, head chef of the Grand Hotel's kitchen. Oh I *am* sorry, I suppose you don't eat beef then?" He looked nervously at her.

Rupa smiled her thanks. "No, I don't, but I will try the chicken. How fortunate you are, I would like to try the Chinese as well but I think tonight I'll decide on Mr Fernandes's menu, minus the beef."

"Wise choice, clever girl," Mr Coates beamed. "I find the Chinese noodles go through me like water. Start feeling peckish after just half an hour. Need to keep up the strength up, can't let that happen now can I?" He burbled on happily. He liked the lady he decided. Doesn't matter if she's a big-wig, he mused. So what if she was a Marwari. All that money and education bound to change them in a generation or less. Evolution. He asked if Rupa would like to go round and introduce herself to the other judges.

"After this drink, I'll straighten my walk and say hello to them."

This caused another chortle from John Coates as he and the other husbands left together towards the bar.

Mrs Lawson, Mrs Hindley and Mrs Taylor rose and excused themselves. They made their way to the ladies' cloakroom.

Yvonne Coates stayed at the table and leaned across to Rupa, "You really have a lovely nose ring, don't mind my saying so but doesn't it hurt when you wash your face or blow your nose?"

"No, it doesn't and I do take it off," Rupa said. She took a long sip of her whisky.

"Gosh, I thought it was fixed. Must be strange having that in your face. Does it feel funny, that red stone gleaming when you look down and all?"

"No. Not really. If you'll excuse me I think I see Mr Smith and I promised I'd go over and meet his wife."

She'd had had enough of the woman staring at her, disapproving and weighing her in the community's scales. Rupa wondered how she fared in her report card? Was it gold stars for a pucca accent? Points taken away for drinking alcohol? She smiled inwardly as she thought of her family and friends and their reaction if they knew how and where she was this evening and among whom.

"Oh Rupa *beta,*" she could hear her aunt Maya's disapproving voice, "all those little clubs and social dances, riff-raffs, riff-raffs. All they talk of is England and the good old days. India and Indians are always bad. They're so ignorant. Neither here nor there, neither here nor there." Rupa smiled to herself as she shook the memory from her mind.

Roger Lawson re-appeared suddenly and walked by her side to the Smith's table.

"Thought I'd give you a bit of moral support. They are nice people but I feel they'd be nicer if I introduced you to them more formally. Hope you don't mind."

She was annoyed. This was uncalled for and as far as she was concerned, as a judge she was supposed to meet and mingle with guests as she wished.

"It's all right, I suppose."

"Look, if you want I'll move off…"

"No, don't make a thing of it. We're nearly there anyway. Come on, do the honours."

Rupa Jaiswal and Roger Lawson fell into step as they made their way to meet some of the members of the club. He took her elbow as he guided her towards them. Unwittingly they presented a picture of a well-suited couple, he tall, commanding, protective towards the petite woman in the cream sari.

"She's a real cunning one," Yvonne spat out the words to her husband. "Look, already Roger is waiting on her hand and foot. And *you* don't have to do the same!"

"What are you talking about? All I did was what any host would do, offer her a drink, ask what she'd like for dinner. Obvious hospitality, Yvonne."

"Yes, I know that. It doesn't mean you had to be grinning at her like a damn fool all the time. Obvious hospitality…huh…rubbish."

"Calm down now…"

"I'm calm, and don't tell me what to do – it's a disgrace. This club not being able to come up with an Anglo-Indian judge for the dance!"

Yvonne scowled at her husband.

"She not so damn young, must be late thirties, talking of you being here when she was a schoolgirl, bloody cheek, not so good-looking, sari so plain, no jewellery, *divorced,* and all, why did old George Martin choose her?"

John Coates felt his head throb with the heat of the night and with his wife's irrefutable logic. He loosened his tie, mopped his forehead. God, he prayed, why wasn't it tomorrow.

"Look," he thought he sounded reasonably hearty, "she's an accomplished young woman, I'm sure she'll do wonderfully as a judge."

"Oh yeah yeah, posh and all that. So fashionable. Nose stud and all. *Divorced,* drinks, wonderful judge, wonderful. Wery posh…oh hello Betty, yes, isn't it a wonderful night. Yes, Heather is so excited. The new judge? *Beautiful*?" She shrugged. "Well, I suppose so. Wery *different* isn't she?"

The president's wife swiftly segued from outraged wife to gracious hostess. She smiled, her high heels rapping a tattoo on the parquetry floor, took her husband's arm as they both re-entered the main hall where the sound of the scat of fifties jazz made talk difficult.

Colleen Hindley leaned across and lightly tapped Rupa's arm.

"My dear, I can't tell you how beautiful that sari is, you look so graceful."

Rupa smiled her thanks. The tumbling together of new names in so short a time made her unsure of how to go about opening conversations. The pecking order was clear, the older couples were to be given preference. Two of the younger couples quietly talking among themselves, after the perfunctory helloes, didn't really make an effort to engage Rupa in casual chat. Roger sat beside her, arm slung behind her chair. The gesture, proprietorial again, annoyed Rupa. She breathed the stuffy air, and one part of her attention was caught by the excellent jazz the quartet was playing. Smoky blues, was it Brubeck or Charlie Parker? She strained over the voices to hear the flowing sound.

"I believe you are going to chat with tonight's contestants," this from an older man probably Linda's husband, was it a Mervyn, she wondered, Hindley.

"Yes, I'll try to, though this short-list is not so short," she joked, as she scanned the brief bio-data of the young women who had made it to this final night.

"Heather Coates is looking sweet isn't she?" This remark thrown in by a severely coiffured middle-aged matron.

"I have not yet had a chance to talk to either the contestants or the other judges, but I'm sure all are talented and all have a good chance of getting that crown."

"Hmm, I wonder if Yvonne would agree with that?"

General laughter at this sally.

Rupa uneasily speculated at the minefield she was about to step through.

"Stop looking so worried, it's a piece of cake," Roger whispered to her, "my mother used to do this thing year after year, it was a breeze."

Your mother, Rupa thought, was the Lady Muck of this place and her word must have been law. I'm an upstart who is not supposed to know this western scene at all.

"What fun you'll have telling your colleagues about tonight," Mr Smith beamed at her.

A good-hearted buffoon, his son, Claude, she learnt the son's name later, curiously attendant to his parents at the table, asking if they needed anything and passing them plates of refreshments. Rupa glanced at the gangly youth who was clutching a serviette to his chest. He continually darted looks her way, and as quickly shifted his gaze away. What was wrong with the boy, she wondered. Shy? Mama's boy?

His mother, Ruth, a pensive-looking woman in a long evening dress sat and fanned herself with a paper napkin.

"Very hot, it's the humidity I can't stand, not just the heat. So very hot, isn't it, *isn't it?*"

Rupa responded by sighing deeply and waving her hand before her face, yes, she nodded, it was stifling. She recalled a college joke that went on those lines, "It's not the heat, it's the humidity." That silly undergrad humour entirely out of place in this setting.

Time was ticking-tocking on. She made her excuses, then, with Roger at her side, went over to the other four judges, all sitting together near the bandstand.

Two of the women were obviously English. *Wah, wah,* she thought, this is what the panel should look like. White and right. The third judge, the doctor, was a pleasant-looking woman who had a walking stick besides her. The only man present was a short, balding, powerfully-built presence, he stood cupping an unlit pipe and stared at her with ill-concealed reproach.

"Hello," she extended her hand, no namastes here, "I'm Rupa Jaiswal and I'm your last-minute stand-in for Prof Martin."

Long and tedious hours later the dance was about to reach the climax of the evening.

In a little while the May Queen for the year was to be announced. Excitement was palpable. Young, middle-aged and the few older guests all discussed the potential winners.

Rupa herself was a bit dazed by the young faces, so hopeful of getting this prize she had been called upon to judge. They were all so innocent, she thought. Not at all the worldly sophisticates she had expected. Their names crowded together in a pastel palette of Shirleys, Sandras, Patsys, Cheryls, Mary Anns, Lorraines, Michelles, Charmaines, Valeries, Anitas, Christines, Christinas, Crystals. All were dressed impeccably. The outfits they wore were, demure, prim, but she marvelled at the quality of material and finish, it could compare with haute couture anywhere in the western world. How talented were the unsung heroes, she thought, the neighbourhood tailors – darzis – who, with little to go on aside from the pictures from the latest fashion magazines sewed and fashioned the stylish clothes for a pittance.

There was no parade of the young contenders, for which she was grateful. No self-conscious walking down ramps, or in a circle, or marching down the hall, the target of well-meaning homespun humour. It was quiet and low-key with a brief chat with each of the girls. Some were teenagers, others a fair bit older, but all were unmarried. The five judges carried notebooks in which they wrote down various details of what impressed them and ticked off criteria already noted there. Poise, general gracefulness, personality, intelligence, social skill, qualities insisted on, all of which had to be remarked on in a positive light. This intensely subjective evaluation was bound to be dangerous. Rupa instantly knew she might prove the deciding vote in what could turn a contentious contest. Thankfully there was only the one winner. No silver or bronze medals were to be handed down to unhappy also-rans. The night demanded a queen, no princesses were allowed.

She spoke to the finalists and soon more or less knew whom she chose. There was to be a consultation of the five judges later and to add to the drama of the moment at exactly midnight the winner would be announced. The band struck up a syrupy dance melody and older members gratefully began to get on the dance floor and start a sedate fox-trot, or at most, a relaxed jive.

Rupa sank down in her chair and eased off the high-heeled slippers. Thank goodness a sari hid these social sins, a total ban on bare feet was the unspoken law here. The men wore Oxford shoes, with dark socks, the women elegant heels. No rubber pumps or sandals at all. Dresses were everywhere. Rupa did note a few salwaar-kameezes among the younger members. There were a couple of saris worn, literally two, a young Goan girl, wife of one of the musicians bashfully pregnant, draped the folds over an obvious midriff, and an older woman, probably her mother.

And there was that chic green chiffon sari worn by one of the contestants. Otherwise the entire picture of merrymaking revellers could have been anywhere in Europe, if you ignored the brown skins and Indian accents. God forbid if you told people here their accents were Indian, *chi-chi,* the put-down description of this community's sing-song cadence. She mulled on the history of India with its continual influx of foreigners. Invaders, outsiders, who breathed the air of a heady indolence, stayed, and were soon absorbed by the vastness of a culture ancient and careless. Stirred into the stew of disparate physiognomies, cultures, religions and accents. Days and years did not seem important, only eras counted.

"Here you are," Mr Coates his hands holding two frosted tumblers of whisky, sat heavily down near her.

Rupa accepted the whisky and moved slightly away from the bulk of the man.

"We are all so excited you know, Yvonne has been preparing Heather for this night for ages."

Oh, no, Rupa winced, here it comes, the big sell.

"So you've met Heather then? Real *pataka* she is too. Never keeps still for a minute, always has something going," he chuckled, fatherly pride softening his voice. "You know she's in her final year BA, enjoys it too. Smart but she wants pulling up sometimes. You know how it is. All fun and games at that age," he took a long sip of his drink, picked at a few potato chips. He continued almost sheepishly, "she is also in the social service group of college. Can't think where she gets the energy to do all she does. Regular livewire. But Mother and I are proud of the little minx, she's a good girl. Doesn't really come to many social functions like this. Rather stick her head in a book. Hahaha. Can't have too much of that now, next thing she'll be wanting to join the feminist nonsense, all those mad women, haha, they talk too much, eh, well, women, it's always their way you know. Aha, here comes Mother."

Yvonne Coates, bouffant straightened, fell into her chair with an exaggerated sigh.

"My gosh, my goodness, these shoes are killing me. *Ouf*, oh man I must get them off. Ah, that's better. How cool you look Mrs Jaiswal, that sari must be warm but you look so comfortable, how do you do it eh?"

"I'm wearing high heel slippers, not shoes, and this sari really keeps one from being too hot. You should try wearing one sometime, you might find you'll prefer it to wearing a dress."

A high-pitched shriek of laughter greeted this as Yvonne, her face puckered, incredulous at the suggestion looked around the table for a back-up chorus.

"No, no, oh me, I really don't see myself in a *sari*. It looks so difficult. And I've never ever worn one, can't see myself getting into one now. It must take you hours to put that on doesn't it?"

Rupa felt the cool air of difference settle around her.

Time gathered its dislikes carefully and was about to lay them at her feet. Suddenly she was the receiver of discontents, of the bad breath of hopes twisted and dreams misplaced.

She breathed deeply and found her mind empty of any kind of response.

Mrs Lawson quietly turned to Rupa, "My dear, I think dresses are so impractical in our weather. Our mothers didn't think of comfort when they opted to wear them."

A silence followed this and Mrs Lawson, ever the imperious matriarch, began talking of the public holiday that followed.

"Isn't it strange having this ball on a Sunday. It won't be the same without the late merrymakers going off to church for the early Mass." She smiled around the table and the slight frost that had built up melted.

A noisy sigh beside her made Rupa aware of her host's relief.

"You don't dance do you Mrs Jaiswal?" He was halfway to his feet.

"Of course I do, I was waiting for when you would ask me to. What took you so long?" And Rupa tucked her *pallu* around her shoulders and holding her hand out to John Coates got up and with a nod to others, walked to the dance floor.

Yvonne Coates turned to Maxine Taylor and began to talk of the dinner.

"Why are they serving so late? Oh of course I'd forgotten that we are having it buffet style. I much prefer being served than lining up to get at the food. So unruly. Really this club is getting so slack. No idea of keeping time. This is damned Indian Standard Time, everything hours later than what it should be," and she shot an irritated look towards her husband, now in the middle of the dance floor, spirited there by a young woman afloat in a cream silk sari and ruby nose stud.

It was stuffy.

The table at which the Renshaws were seated was towards the back of the dance hall near the kitchen. It seemed hotter by the sheer vicinity of this position, the noise of the waiters and bearers scurrying to and fro making the atmosphere clogged, thick.

"Why are they serving the buffet so late?" asked Kitty Renshaw, unconsciously echoing the complaint of the First Lady of the club. She craned over her husband's shoulder to see if the tables were laid and ready for the diners. Yes, she sighed with relief. The two glasses of ginger ale were all she had drunk over the hours they had been here, chips and peanuts totally inadequate to bolster her appetite for the long night ahead.

"Kitty, *Kitty,* there you are, how are you enjoying yourself?" John Coates tried to speak above the din as he whirled by on the dance floor with the glamorous Mrs Jaiswal.

John Coates.

Always John Coates. Like one of those jack-in-the-boxes he seemed to spring up when she thought he was exorcised. And the years melted away.

She nodded several times and smiled in a sprightly way to indicate she was indeed having a great time.

Looking at the VIP of the evening as she danced in step to John Coates, Kitty bowed slightly and marvelled at how the lady could keep her sari so perfectly pleated, as she was swirled around.

These dances were proving quite strenuous now for both Bob and her. She found she was tired the next day, her body aching, her energy zapped. It was time to quietly let the children go by themselves to these affairs and Bob and she would just enjoy it by proxy.

A melancholy settled on the heart of Kitty. Age, which had never bothered her began to loom in a distressingly awkward manner. Her unblemished skin began to slip and develop minute folds which settled over her wrists, neck, her chin; had begun to lose its defined roundness.

"Whatever are you doing Mum?" Grace watched her mother frown, then half-smile, then push a club coaster away.

"Nothing Gracie, nothing. Just being an old fool. Now where is that young man and why isn't he dancing with you?"

"Mum let Carl mingle with his friends. It's bad enough he has to dance with me, *his sister,* through the evening without you wanting him to be at my side. Let him have *some* fun." Grace leaned over and squeezed her mother's hand to take the sting out of the rebuke.

Again Kitty felt the brush of age sweep by her. It was the inevitable move from being the figure of authority to gently stepping aside to the new adults. She looked at her daughter and thought she had rarely seen her look so attractive. Her skin was flawless. The tiny mole near her left eyebrow highlighted their natural sweep upwards. With her short hair haloing a well-shaped head, Grace, her green sari silhouetting her slim figure was what in Kitty's time called a `knock-out'.

"Yes Your Majesty," she joked. "You're right, let your poor brother be off the leash for some time at least until you're crowned May Queen."

"Oh Mum, stop. You know I'm too old. Most of the girls are little more than teenagers. Mrs Jaiswal's long chat with me was nothing more than a common interest in our work, that's all."

"Well, work or not, I can't see many who could hold a candle to you tonight, and don't say it's because I'm your Mum, have you seen the way heads turn when you walk past?"

Grace gave a lop-sided grin. "Wow Mum, what do you want for your birthday? I'll get it whatever the cost."

Kitty looked at Grace and was filled with a buoyancy to think this person belonged to her. She was grateful Grace's job in the city meant she still lived at home. Kay, her eldest, restless and impatient, seemed to have retreated into the hills for most of the year. The three-month vacation at the year's end was too brief and every passing year seemed to take Kay further from the family. The nine-month absence seemed to impede conversation after the initial excitement of her Christmas vacation. She slept long hours and during the evenings she seemed to rather visit friends and go out, than stay and chat with the family. Always an assertive child, Kay had grown strident in manner. Kitty watched with faint disapproval the confidence harden into rigidity. All these thoughts were kept to herself. Never would she divulge them to anyone, not even Bob. Grace looked at her mother and wondered at her sudden silence. A tap on her back woke her up to the moment.

"Hurry up and grab a plate and get to the buffet. All the chilli chicken will have gone and you will have to settle for mutton korma instead," Carl pulled her to her feet and hurried to help his mother up from her chair.

"Where's Dad?" Carl looked bothered. "Why can't you two hurry up, I'm starving. Everyone's grumbling about the food being late and you are happily sitting here. *Hurry up.*"

Kitty deftly swung her evening bag on her arm, hooked Grace's bag on her other arm, then walked with her daughter towards the long, damask-covered tables to where an aromatic dinner was set and waiting.

Outside the month of May simmered and began to softly keen.

The dust in the streets danced in rapid jerks and conjured dervishes that made the pavement sleepers grunt and twitch their tattered sheets closer to their bodies. Rusty leaves rubbed together on skeletal trees. A symphony of sorts was in the making. Rickshaw men tied the hoods of their rickety chariots firmly down.

'Barsaat, barsaat ki raat,' was the warning cry. Cabbies waiting for the night's revellers, sighed happily. If the weather held up here was a chance to drive a hard bargain. Advertising hoardings, their huge cardboard fantasies drooping – Use Lipton's Tea, Buy Better, Buy Bombay Dyeing. Fly Air India – began to flap, their beat against a bass accompaniment to the dry slurry of dust being swept along. A dog yelped, kicked aside by a young urchin rummaging through the garbage. Both needed some sustenance that the day's rubbish might yield. A policeman loomed, his lathi swinging from his belt. The urchin and dog fled. The guardians of the law were generous in their targeting of the poor and homeless. Children often were scapegoats when there were robberies or when complaints were made by local residents about noise or petty nuisances. The policeman walked slowly down the street towards the street's intersection. The traffic island was almost deserted. He was about to stand in for the later part of the night and he was unhappy about the hour and the impending storm. He smacked his lathi against his palm and looked carefully for a child or pi dog to bring it down on. This city was going from bad to worse. He hated beggars, he hated child beggars even more. Thieves, pests, they littered the streets like so much vermin. Heavy boots made his feet hot and heavy. He was tired, he wanted to go home to sleep. He needed his sleep, after this job with its constant irritations he felt his skin and eyes burn. Why did he think it would be an answer to his needs? The pay was meagre. As a street policeman the only bribes that came his way were small ones from the lorries that sped illegally through some of the streets with their overburdened chassis swaying dangerously. They would crash and topple someday. Why should he care? The pimps and touts whined about how bad business was, there were now social workers keeping a close eye on this part of the city. Girls were receiving protection from rescue homes. What did he care? He was nothing in this city. He was a small man, a *chhota lok,* someone of no consequence. He longed to arrest someone

tonight. Someone he could show his power over. Music, western, foreign, came down from the windows of the big building he was standing under. He looked up at the lit windows, the strains of melodies, unfamiliar, at odds with the scene before him, added to his annoyance. There they were, the burra sahibs, enjoying their *sahrab* and music and women, while poor men like him had nothing at all. He swung his lathi and walked on heavily, anger building up steadily.

The wind dropped suddenly. The air was humid, steamy. Yes, he thought, a storm later, definitely. He spat expertly into the gutter and continued his lone vigil on Calcutta's grimy streets.

It was near midnight. In that faux rococo ballroom a strange kinship was forged. The twenty final contestants waited for the witching hour and smiled sympathetically at each other. Oddly, few of them felt the chafing of competition. The girls sat demurely with their parents. A few sat with boyfriends. In between the dances they visited the ladies' room and repaired their make-up and eyed each other for signs of fraying nerves or apparel.

"Watch that petticoat Doreen, it's showing. Knot the shoulder strap and that will keep it from slipping." A swift tug and the offending undergarment was tucked away.

"Fluff your hair from the underneath Ann. It gets better body that way."

"What *fun* this is, isn't it?"

"Myee, I'm so nervous. Wasn't that lady judge sweet?"

"Who? The one in the sari?"

"NO, the one in the *space-suit.* Yeah you dope, of course the one in the sari."

"She's a rich one, big shot in some firm, Dad told me."

"Yeah? Well she's not really the best judge to have for us, is she? I mean, *man,* she isn't even an Anglo and she's with the other old judges, I mean the other English ladies are fine and Dr Sims knows us all, so does old grump-pot Basil but she knows *nothing* about us. Sooo stupid to ask her."

"Hey. Did you see old Mother Coates' face when her old man was dancing with her?"

"*What,* he danced with the new lady judge?"

"Yeah, didn't you notice? He's going to pay like hell for that when he gets home, yeah, hahahaha."

"Yeah, but did you see the buttering-up that was going on? All sweet-talk to get darling Heather crowned queen tonight."

"Shhh...don't yell like that you idiot, someone might hear."

"What do I care? This whole thing is so rigged. I don't know why my mum bothered to have me enter. All this expense, new dress, new shoes, manicure, all for a damned cheap cardboard crown and some applause."

"Hey, don't say you won't be thrilled if you get that cheap crown on your head and won't your Keith be thrilled too..."

"Here, I'll give you one on *your* cheap crown if you pair me off with that Keith McGowen."

"Come on, we know you make eyes at each other. Don't pretend you don't like him."

"...oooh...hi Heather! Or should we say Your Majesty! You really are looking lovely tonight. Your mum must be so proud?"

"Don't be silly. You're all so pretty and your dresses are much more modern than this one. Mum picked it, I wanted the plain peach voile dress, but Mum thought this làme looked better, more sparkle, she said. Well, she knows best. Anyway, what do you think of the new lady judge? Great isn't she?"

"Sure. But, you know, she's well..."

"But what, *what*? Okay she's short and her bottom is too big, but she's very attractive and that sari is beautiful."

"No, that's not what I meant. It's just that she's not one of us is she?"

"Oh what utter *rot.* How can you think like that? That's the sort of stuff our grandparents carried on about. We don't have time for all that nonsense. Come on, this is *now,* not the time of the *raj.'*

"And just what is the time at this moment? Ooh, it's fifteen minutes to twelve..." "Hurry, hurry, *hurry* we've got to be in our places when the winner is announced. C'mon Ann, move it you two, the judges won't wait for you..."

With seminal episodes in life there is often a tremor, a prescience that makes the moment, the day remembered forever.

Though few knew it, the evening's happenings would brand them and bond them.

Smoke made a chiaroscuro of the scene in the big hall. Voices merged into a mellow hum. Faces were beginning to lose the freshness of the evening. Collars were wilted, tables and chairs seemed to lose the polite symmetry of their careful groupings, tension was visible in half-finished sentences, meandering conversations.

Twenty pairs of parents were nervously waiting to see their daughter named May Queen of the Year. Murmurs were already beginning to circulate as to the outcome of the competition. Yvonne Coates fussed with her hair, and nodded animatedly at the babble of talk around. She heard not a word. Her entire being was focused on the night's celebration.

Rupa Jaiswal was sitting with the four other judges. It was decided the only man present, the headmaster Ivan Basil, announce the winner. There had been understandable contention when the five of them had compared their choice. Rupa had been firm about her verdict. Fortunately Dr Sims and one of the English women had agreed with her and the vote for the evening's May Queen was carried three to two.

John Coates caught her eye and waved. His shirt clung wetly to his back. He looked unhappy.

The band was starting to strike up the anticipated rumble of the drums. Some of the young contestants fell about giggling nervously. A few stared solemnly at the stage. Gradually the hubbub of the crowd dulled to a steady buzz. Rupa was filled with an urge to leave. What on earth had she been thinking when she agreed to this? She had had no idea of the consequences of how people might be affected by what to her was just an innocuous evening's entertainment.

The drum-roll was soft and expertly skittered out by the young musician. His eyes dreamily on a middle distance he flicked the drum sticks casually, even carelessly on the skins, the drum's cymbals, the 'high-hat' performing a convulsive, suspenseful crescendo, it rippled loud, insistent, cutting through the night, halting every other activity. The hypnotic thrum finally stopped.

Silence was thick and for a moment Ivan Basil looked as if he did not know what he was there for. He stood up quickly, a stocky figure, squinting into the glare of the spotlight.

"Ladies and gentlemen," he began, rich voice immediately demanding attention.

"I'm pleased to announce the winner for this year's May Queen Ball. After a long and often intense discussion my fellow judges and I did finally come to a conclusion – that this was too difficult a choice to make." Scattered laughter greeted this stock address.

"All these young ladies have been wonderful contestants," he continued. "All were admirable in their intelligence, beauty, poise, and certainly patience, with what has been a long evening and putting up with what might have appeared to be extremely nosy old fogies." More laughter.

"However I will not keep you all in suspense for much longer. But I must thank the parents, for allowing us to pick from among your beautiful daughters the Queen of this Night. And tonight, this year, we are happy to announce that we have chosen – Grace Renshaw."

There was a second's hush before the applause swept over the hall and voices broke through the air like the splintering of glass.

Grace felt her head reel.

It could not be true. She must have heard wrong. She turned to her mother who was clapping frantically. Her father was grinning and Carl was whooping hysterically, his friends yodelling and hooting their joy.

Grace slowly rose from her chair and stood still, stunned by this overwhelming moment in her life.

"What do I do? Mum, what do I do now?"

"Silly. Just smile. Bow. Smile."

Grace looked around at the wave of faces turned towards her. This was never part of her dreams. Something had gone wrong but in the nicest way.

She was Queen of the May. Grace Renshaw.

5

A confetti of congratulations fluttered around Grace. She was hugged, kissed, her hand was shaken in crushing grasps by people she hardly knew. She smiled continuously. The band was blaring the standard *'Congratulations'* score. Sounds built up, words were jumbled, the night turned raucous. She needed a glass of cool water to steady her dazzled mind.

"So surprised," "very happy," "totally unexpected," she repeated to the procession of well-wishers.

Her throat felt strangled. Someone was now leading her to the stage. Where was Carl, where was her father, they should be at her side, not this slick anonymous stranger trotting alongside her.

She was now on the stage. Smiling faces swam up to her. A huge bouquet of pale pink roses was placed in the crook of her arms. The fragrance of the flowers was cloying. Grace hoped the thorns would not catch the delicate chiffon sari. The heat from the dazzling footlights was unbearable, and the strobe lighting from the 'disco ball' began a dizzy pirouette across her eyes. She distinguished her mother and father and Carl still at the rear of the hall, standing proud, defined by the triumph of the moment. She was aware of the chief table at which the club's committee members were seated. The serene Sophia Lawson, cool in spite of the stifling May night, tapping her fan against the table in genteel applause. Her son Roger, leaning back against his chair staring intently past her, towards the judges, Grace wondered who he was looking at. The Hindleys, the Taylors, smiling, clapping. A waiter standing close behind them, balancing a tray overladen with empty crockery distracted by the excitement allowed the slender wine glasses to topple off and crash. Grace was overcome by the urge to laugh. She clenched her jaws in an effort not to giggle. This was not the moment for hysteria. Mrs Taylor glared at the man. Mrs Hindley chose to continue to clap, slowly, politely without much feeling. Roger muttered something to the poor waiter who was frantically mopping up the mess. This was turning into a three-ring circus.

"And here we are, Mr Coates, president of the club will say a few words before last year's winner, Christine Lewis will crown the new queen," Mr Deane, club secretary, mike in hand smiled at Grace, then moved aside for Mr Coates to come forward.

"Aah...yes, thank you, thank you...this is a fine night and what finer way to end it but by giving Calcutta a new reigning monarch," John Coates, stopped, smiled, a brief twitch of good manners, then continued.

"We have seen our judges – thank you judges – give of their time and professional expertise to choose the most fitting girl to wear the crown of May." He turned to a patiently waiting girl bearing a gilt crown on a shiny cushion.

"Ah, here we have not a maid-in-waiting, but a queen, no one could ask for more than that could they? Haha. Come on Christine, we know you're light-headed without that crown on it."

Laughter. Again Grace felt the unreality of the night surge and overwhelm her. She stepped forward and saw Yvonne Coates' unsmiling face staring at her husband as he came forward to guide Grace to the podium. One of the dignitaries, Yvonne Coates sat on stage with the judges, presiding as she had done for years now, over this, the most recent coronation. Grace was aware of the silent disapproval she had incurred by wearing a sari. It was not the done thing to represent the community in a garb not traditionally worn by their girls. The older generation saw it as a change-eroding tradition. Yvonne Coates' background was that of the backbone of Anglo-India – the railways. From a large family, her father, a mail train driver on the South Eastern Railway of India, she was brought up familiar with a sense of struggling survival, always having to make do and pretending to have a level of ease and comfort. It was a pedigree proud of the fact that they had no 'Indian' connection. Anglo-Indians were the life-blood of the British India rail and telegraph network. Quietly, efficiently they had been outstanding in their proficiency and dedication. With a minimal salary and not many thanks for doing a backbreaking job, they carved a reputation that remained sterling even after Independence. In post-British era, detractors grudgingly admitted the country owed much and had returned little in way of an acknowledgement of their service. Bitterness over the offhand treatment the Indian government meted out to them was one of the causes of the huge wave of immigration to the mother-country, England, later to Canada and then Australia. Just a generation removed from those proud workers.

Yvonne Coates resented change. Change, as she saw it, would succumb and yield to a poorly concealed contempt the community was held in. She seethed with rage. She knew how this had all come about – it was, she brooded, the doing of that Marwari judge. O yes, she grimly fumed, it had her thumbprints all over the decision. Discontent engulfed her. She tasted the evening's disappointment, ugly as chipped nail polish and she felt the bite of jealousy claw through her body.

".. a girl so quiet, so dignified, all are taken with her maturity and elegance..."

Yvonne could scarcely keep from rolling her eyes, she for one, had scarcely given the Renshaw girl a thought. So what if she had good posture and a fine bearing, but was she as fair-skinned as Heather, *oh no she wasn't,* her complexion was downright swarthy. Touch of the tar brush there for all to see. Her eyes were dark, not light hazel, or even light brown, her hair was blue-black. Where, she argued to herself, did this girl's attraction lie? Bloody judges were forced into this outcome. Serve Johnee right for agreeing to this damn woman being a judge at their club. *Serve him right.* Let him live with the fact their Heather had lost out due to his slackness. Yvonne Coates did not have a conventionally formal education but she realised her ambitions for her daughter had tumbled about her. Her daughter was her focus, but with her little girl now a young adult there was a certain gap between them, words were not enough, nor the right ones, and Heather seemed to withdraw into a world, a world where she, her mother, appeared awkward, gauche. Yvonne knew the club and its activities filled the emptiness of her life. At this time of her life, fifty years was around the corner, she discovered she wanted to live through the bright and youthful creature of hers who seemed confident of what she wanted the world to offer. Heather was bookish, didn't seem to want to hurry into marriage with any of the young men around, seemed more interested in going off to student camps and living, as she called it, like the *real* people of India. All these ideas were, in her opinion, a lot of rot. Real people indeed – what then were they – phantoms or what? Again the whine of the microphone jerked her thoughts to the present. Static pierced through layers of talk, of people gathered around this camp-fire of security.

Grace now was wearing the crown. Christine Lewis, shorter by some inches, had struggled to place it firmly on Grace. John Coates reached across and with a quick tweak settled the flimsy coronet in place.

Yvonne, conscious of some people watching her, quickly smiled broadly at the winner.

Grace hesitantly, then more confidently began her speech.

"Thank you. That's what I want to say first and last. Thank you for making this night one of the happiest in my life. I never expected that I might be given the honour of wearing this crown. I still find it hard to believe." She turned to the judges and the club's VIPs, "my thanks for voting me May Queen. I hope the coming year will prove you all have made the right choice. Thank-you to the committee members whose dedication and hard work has made this celebration possible."

Then she faced the upturned faces, smiled and blew kisses to her parents still standing at the rear of the ball room, "This for my family, my parents and brother Carl, who deserves a special mention as he had to dance with me tonight to keep me from being a wall-flower," much laughter and another scatter of applause.

"So thank you for making this a wonderful, an unbelievable night... thank you."

The band started up an old Tin Pan Alley favourite and Grace, crown sparkling, walked down into that noisy euphoric haze.

..oh ain't she sweet,
We'll see her walking down the street
I could tell you very confidentially
...ain't she sweet.

Success and triumph intoxicated the young Carl Renshaw. He yelled joyously, sheer disbelief promoting his exuberance. His sister, a beautiful May Queen, she seemed to float down towards his parents and him. His friends had popped open bottles of soda, ginger ale and furtively, a couple of bottles of beer and toasted Grace in the triumph of that moment. After a quick look around, he upped a frothing bottle and drank the icy-cold beer in clumsy gulps. It tasted bitter. How could people enjoy this stuff? He finished the drink quickly and soon found his ears buzzing. Was this then the thrill of drinking alcohol? A ringing of the ears? Maybe if he drank another he would learn to appreciate the brew.

"Hey, Francis," he called to a young friend helping out at the bar.

"What?"

"Any more of that stuff you've got there?"

"You mean you want another beer?"

"Yeah. You got my meaning."

"Take it easy man. You shouldn't put it away like water you know. Beer packs quite a punch."

"Okay *Mum!* Now, before you sound like my dad as well, have you got another bottle or do I have to scrounge around elsewhere to get one."

"Right, right, don't lose your shirt man. It's just that you're still at school, and I really shouldn't be giving you drinks at all."

"Hey, I thought we had straightened that out. It's a special night. I won't do it again okay? My sister's Queen of the Ball man. Give me something to remember it by."

"You want to make it a memory by getting drunk?"

"No, I just want to do something different, something special."

"Getting drunk is different, special?"

"Look, read me a sermon when we're in church. If you don't want to get me a beer, that's all right, I'll ask the other bartender for one and try my luck with him."

"All right, all right, only don't name me if when your parents ask how you got this beer."

With ill-concealed ire a bottle of beer was handed over and Carl wrapped a handkerchief around it as he hurried to where a couple of his friends, Jeff and Jim Sutton, sat waiting for him.

"You took your time, didn't you?"

"Did you manage to get the beers or not?"

"Beers?" He grimaced with disgust. "Bloody hell, I just about squeezed this one from Francis. Why don't you go and get yours yourselves."

The teenagers, bored now that the excitement of the night was over, looked up at Carl sullenly.

"What's the matter with you? Head swollen now that your sis is wearing a crown?"

Carl's smile vanished. A sudden giddiness making him feel oddly daring and reckless.

"Look you creeps, all I'm saying is that if you want beer so much, move off your arses and get it yourselves."

"Oh giving orders now, what next, telling us to shine your shoes and salaam your sister eh? Man, what a hope."

"Whose palms did your Dad grease to get that crown on your sis's head huh?"

Twin voices spat at Carl. He felt tears blur his voice. Shame that he could be reduced to this made him lurch towards the two boys fists swinging.

An outstretched foot neatly caught him in mid-attack and he fell heavily on his knees. Someone's elbow swung towards his face and a burst of pain exploded behind his eye.

Staggering to his feet he balled his fists and said in a muffled tone,

"If you want to take this further come on downstairs. I'll show you whose palm is greased you bastards," he looked round at the corridor, thankful it was empty, no one to witness this.

"Come on then, I'll lick both you shits with hands tied behind my back."

"Sure, sure, *you'll* lick us, c'mon then, quick before you yell to daddy to help you..."

Carl stumbled against the edge of a table and swung his arms towards the screwed up words of malice. With no connection the impetus of his move saw him slam against a half-opened door.

"*Ouf...*goddamit."

His lip split and began to leak a thin line of blood. Tension sprung up suddenly and the three young boys stood in a tight triangle, glaring at each other.

Goodwill evaporated into a contest of wills.

Carl saw the two boys jeering at his happiness. He recalled past remarks that enraged him.

Suddenly in this brittle moment, things became clear. Their sisters were also in the running and had lost out to Grace. A whump whistled by and a well-aimed punch knocked the air from his stomach.

"C'mon downstairs…I'll show you…" Carl gasped.

The three stumbled down the steep narrow staircase and were soon out in the night air. A slight drizzle shocked them into looking at each other, they stepped over sleeping bodies on the pavement and faced each other. Jeff and Jim braced close together and smacked balled fist against the palms of their hands. Carl, former friend and childhood ally, shook his head and tried to gauge the distance between them.

"Right, this is a fair fight, hey…two against one…all right you bastards, let's go…"

A dance of some skill began. Circling, the three shuffled, trying to get a position of advantage. Realising he had backed the two against one of the pillars that supported the covered porch of the club he abruptly, with a shoulder-to-face punch, scored his first hit and heard a satisfying thwack as Jeff's nose blossomed red. Good. A surge of adrenaline and he made a jab at Jim, briefly distracted by his brother's plight, and punched the side of his head sharply against the pillar. Jim's eyes registered shock and he swung but only propelled himself over one of the pavement sleepers and fell prone in a classic pole-axed fashion, stunned. Jeff now pounced on Carl. He leapt on his back and in comical piggy-back style the two clumsily staggered around. Curses, abuse, expletives were muffled as the three sought to hurt and injure one another. By now some of the pavement sleepers had woken and groggily looked on in amazement as three young 'sahibs' wove around, sliding and tripping as they sought to fight.

"*Hai, hai, thamo, thamo,*" quickly they reached out to protect their meagre belongings. Clutching their rags away from this confusion they made way for the brawl to continue in a cleared space.

No one tried to intervene. This did not concern them. It was huge entertainment.

By now the three young men were locked in a tight embrace, straining to push the other to the grimy floor. Arms interwoven, breath coming in gasps, Jeff still hung on to Carl's back. He was trying to sling his arm around Carl's neck and squeeze till he released his hold on Jim. The three swayed through a bizarre dance of violence. The drizzle was now a steady shower, a wind had sprung up and occasional flashes of lightning served as dramatic backdrop to the silhouettes weaving around the broken concrete of the pavement. Dogs yelped as they were kicked away from the melee. Children began to wail as mothers pulled them out of the way of the staggering trio.

The three boys heaved and pushed and staggered on. There was now an audience. Quickly a crowd was magnetised to the spot by the fun of a free show. Grinning, shoving one another for a better view, the population of the homeless dwellers, ignoring the steady rainfall, began to yell for friends to come and see this wrestling match. Abruptly the mood changed with the shouting of an authoritative voice and the thud of a stick falling indiscriminately, effectively parting the mob to lead to the centre of the excitement.

"Bhago, bhago, jaldi, jaldi, police aagaya..."

People scattered. Some fled into the nearby lane. Others melted into deep doorways still watching, caught by the sudden drama. Children howled, a cackle of voices broke the oppressive monsoon night up.

"Aieee...sala, sala..." the policeman's lathi swung down on the three heads seemingly wielded in one mass of thick black hair.

A sharp crack and the struggling, three-pronged tangle of figures fell apart. A body hit the ground. The lathi swung down again. Again there was the sound of a crack. The policeman, tired, angry at this disruption of his round, put all his venom into beating sense into these three boys. His heavy boots stomped on the fallen boy's arm. He'd show these bloody pleasure-seekers who was boss. He'd have them begging for mercy. Fight on his night of duty eh? He'd throw them into the *thana* and give them more of the same.

"Chalo, get up..." he snarled at the prone figure.

He kicked again, taking pleasure in the sound of his boot against this skinny fool, now lying still, inert.

He looked around for the other two boys.

"Aao, come here you. Get your friend up off the ground."

Jeff and Jim Sutton were immobilised. Bleeding, shirts torn, they stared at their friend Carl heaped on the footpath like a pile of dirty linen.

"My god Jim, what's happened."

"This bloody moron has cracked Carl's head open."

"Jeeesus."

"Quick help him. See what's happened. He's bleeding!"

A rough shove and both boys straightened as they looked at the burly policeman preparing now to handcuff them.

"Quick run upstairs and get help. This bloody fool is going to cart us off to the *thana.* Carl needs help."

"Aiee, you...*tum*...pick him up, *pick him up,* get someone to lift him inside."

"You're giving *me* orders, *salas,"* outraged, the lathi rose and was prepared to come down again on Jim. A neat sidestep and a tearful shout to his brother, "*Quick* Jeff. *Don't waste time,* run, RUN, for chrissake, tell someone to come down here and help."

Jeff, crying, tears tracking smudged paths down his face leapt away from the policeman, pushed aside the throng of jabbering onlookers. He dodged through waving arms as they tried to block him. The narrow staircase led on and on. Music deafened. His head hurt, his skin seemed to tingle, scorched, bruised. At last the ballroom opened before him. He looked around for the Renshaws. Where were they? He saw his sister Lisa looking aghast, hand to her mouth, at his stumbling entrance. He tripped, wavered, as his head spun with shock and sudden nausea.

"Where are the Renshaws?' Where's my mum?"

"Omigod, what's happened. *Jeff, Jeff...*"

Faces turned towards him. All expressions save horror, wiped away, all who had become aware of this apparition gaped, silent, stunned. The band playing on, guitars shrilling the legendary Lennon-McCartney ode to the working man.

'...it's been a hard day's night,
And I've been working like a dog
It's been a hard day's night
And I should be sleeping
Like a log...'

Absurdly, it flashed through his mind this single of theirs was the first to have no pronoun in its title, trivia inherited from his parents, avid Beatle's fans, then he was in his mother's arms, collapsing crying, hiccupping with terror, begging them to go down quick and help Carl, help Jim.

Pandemonium smashed through the sedate hall. In a second there was a babel of noise. No words were distinguishable. Kitty and Bob Renshaw were caught in a crush of people. Grace saw her parents looking wildly around as they struggled, racing to the main entrance and stairway. Louis Deane appeared trying to hold some of the people back. Everyone seemed to be shouting.

"Phone the police, hurry..."

"What's happened?"

"Killed? Who?"

"Damned protestors making trouble for tomorrow's holiday..."

"Mob protesting our dance tonight..."

"Who beat Jeff up?"

"...dead...?"

"...dear god, where?"

"The Marwari lady's family have hired thugs to spoil our evening..."

Grace was paralysed. She could not move. She wanted to scream to her parents to wait for her but found she was surrounded by club members, some shouting into her face.

Nothing made sense. Carl. This had to do with Carl. She pushed herself out of the flimsy wooden chair and began shoving people out of her way. The May Queen crown slipped over her forehead, without thinking she wrenched it off and flung it down. The cardboard circlet immediately trampled on by the throng of people.

Suddenly she felt herself being held back. She struggled to free herself then looked up to see Roger Lawson. Holding her in a firm grip he calmly turned her around and began to walk her back into the hall.

"What are you doing, let me go, I have to find out..."

"No Grace, come away. Your parents have gone downstairs. Louis is with them. Come and sit down."

Grace looked blankly at Roger. The lady judge was by his side. She looked distraught, and was murmuring something to Mr Lawson, she could not quite catch what she had said.

"It's Carl? What has happened, I want to know."

Roger looked grimly at her, "Carl, we think, was attacked by a mob downstairs."

"What! Why?"

"From what we know, we think that Jim and Jeff Sutton and Carl went downstairs and were having a quiet drink when a crowd of hoodlums suddenly attacked them."

Grace gasped. This was madness. Why should three young boys be targeted? How badly were Carl and Jim hurt? She leaned forward and caught Roger's arm.

"Mr Lawson, how badly is Carl hurt? Why isn't he here? Where's Jim? I have to go downstairs, I have to be with my parents."

She half-rose, but Rupa held her hand and prevented her from leaving.

"Sit here Miss Renshaw. It won't help your parents if you witness things that will only upset all of you further."

It was the 'Miss Renshaw' that stopped Grace from pulling away.

There was command in her request but coupled with that courtesy Grace found herself automatically obeying this dignified stranger.

Grace saw in the melee her chiffon sari was dishevelled. Her hair seemed to be stringy, wet with sweat. She could smell fear rise off her body, rank and unpleasant.

Without warning she began sobbing, dry, with a series of short breaths she was jerked by hiccoughs of panic, she could not think, she did not want to think.

Mrs Jaiswal held her hands and mutely conveyed a sense of sympathy.

"Gracie, oh Gracie," the strident tone could not be mistaken. Grace swivelled to see Yvonne Coates trotting towards her, high heels making her teeter, she reached the three of them. She stooped and leant down to embrace Grace.

"My dear. We will go back home with you. John and I will see you and your mother safely back. How awful all this is. Poor Carl, poor boy. Poor Jim."

She was engulfed by Mrs Coates' gauzy sleeves. Her nose smothered by the stiffness of a well-upholstered brassiere Grace cautiously fought free of Yvonne Coates's embrace and asked. "What has happened? Will you tell me *exactly* what has happened?"

"Oh my dear, what to say, Carl has been knocked unconscious by some ruffians on the street downstairs. Jim Sutton's also been hurt but not as badly as your brother. The ambulance has been sent for and we are now told the police is helping us round up these goondas."

Her breath still coming in short gasps, Grace looked at Roger Lawson and the lady judge. She wiped the tears from her face, "Will you take me home Mr Lawson?"

She turned to the club's first lady conscious of having breached good manners and clasped her hand. "Don't worry about me Mrs Coates, I know you have so much to see to here. I know you have to look after the Suttons and see to them and their concerns," she paused for breath. "Mr Coates needs you to be with him – so much to do here." She gestured vaguely around the hall. People were milling around, trying not to look towards them.

Yvonne smiled stiffly. She eased her way from the crouching position besides Grace's chair and nodded to Roger Lawson and the lady judge.

"Please yourself Grace. I'll tell your father that you were taken home by Mr Lawson." She pointedly ignored mentioning Rupa.

The girl had manoeuvred her way through a social minefield with diplomatic finesse. Roger Lawson found it difficult to hide his smile. Rupa Jaiswal stared straight ahead aware of the strained feelings, a situation that could have been comic had it come at a less fraught time.

"Well, goodnight then. This has certainly been a May Queen we won't forget will we? The new judge did you proud. The sari, and all, yes, of course, goes well with your skin tone." She nodded in the general direction of the three of them, turned, waved towards Mrs Sutton, standing waiting by the main door of the hall, and walked towards her. A silence followed this and Grace looked disbelievingly at the woman as the implication of her remark sunk in.

Rupa's expression of distaste was swiftly replaced by her concern for the shaken girl.

"Come on young lady. Now let's see you home."

Rupa put her hand out to Grace, I think you might have something to drink before we leave. Try a shot of brandy. It's good to help one calm down in times like these."

"I thought yoga was good," she almost smiled at her feeble attempt at lightening the heaviness of the moment.

"Yes, that can come later. Now we'll have a quick drink and then I'll call my driver and we'll go home with you. Don't worry about your parents, we've seen they are with Carl and we've called my doctor to attend to your brother."

This was miraculous.

In a city known for its philosophy of *'cholche cholbe'* this efficiency was unheard of, unknown.

It was the honey-smooth promise of money that made the wheels turn. Money. It spoke. It got things done. Thank god for Rupa Jaiswal.

Grace reached out for the snifter of brandy that was proffered. She swallowed the golden liquid and winced at the burning graze it left in her throat and mouth.

"Drink up. It's good for you. Strictly medicinal of course." The old joke made her smile faintly. She drank the last of the brandy nosily, careless of the inelegance of her manners. It tasted awful. Why did they talk of alcohol being smooth? It was the harshest thing she tasted since Eno's Fruit Salts.

Both Roger and Rupa looked fondly at the girl as she hurriedly put the glass down, shakily grasped the table as she rose, "Let's go home," she said.

"This has been a hateful evening. I wish I'd never come." Tears were near but she gave a twisted smile, walked between Roger Lawson and the Indian judge, ignoring anxious looks, curious faces.

Grace Renshaw without crown or sceptre wished with all her heart she were far removed from this scene, had never come to this ball, never entered this ridiculous event, never agreed to be a member of what was a fusty remnant of a forgotten time and defunct tradition.

She wanted to be with her brother, her parents. She was screaming inwardly wanting to know how things were going at the hospital. How badly was Carl injured? How had this happened, this was freakish, unheard of. She would get the legal advisor in her firm to help her investigate further into the night's horror.

A sleek car purred to a halt before them. The driver leapt out and opened the doors for them.

Roger helped her in. Rupa got in after her. The driver after closing the doors, went round to his place and starting the ignition drove carefully away from the pillared entrance. The luxurious smell of the leather seats soothed Grace. This was security, she thought. This was the buffer between all that dirt, that squalor. This was where she longed to be for the rest of her life. Cared for by wealth, protected by its power.

The city sped by, she was going home.

6

Bob Renshaw sat on the edge of a rickety chair in the corridor of the private nursing home. He had been waiting, sitting, with short walks up and down that beige-coloured corridor for almost three hours. Kitty had briefly come out of the emergency room an hour or so ago. Somehow she had found a kitchen in that grim environ and rustled up a cup of coffee. Scalding hot, tasteless, it was what he needed. He felt dazed. His mouth dry. Kitty without a word had taken his cup from him and returned to their son. She had not come back, though it was hours since she had given him the coffee. Almost four in the morning, the sky, what he could see from the small window, was black. Rain fell in short temperamental bursts of noise. A quick look at his watch and the hands pointed at three forty-five in the morning. The dark hour of the soul it had sometimes been called.

It seemed a longer time since he had raced in that ramshackle cab after the ambulance, a nightmare ride away from the club.

He tried not to think of how excruciating the journey must be for Carl, if he was aware of it at all.

Kitty sat stoically besides Carl. She held his hand in hers and with a handkerchief that wafted the fragrance of Revlon's Intimate, wiped his forehead. Medicos quickly lifted the stretcher carrying Carl out and to the Emergency Department. Kitty followed.

Bob grimaced at the glimpse he had of his son. Ashen-faced, an intravenous drip fixed to his arm, a makeshift bandage around his head he was hardly recognisable.

What had happened was still a muddle of shrill denials, accusations, a garbled telling which all had but one end, his son being beaten unconscious. The policeman, sweaty, foul-breathed, said he had saved the boy from a rapacious crowd of street-dwellers and related a tale that was at odds with the Sutton boys' account. According to them it was a deliberate attack by the policeman that had resulted in this outcome. He recalled their hysterical repetition of what had happened and sensed an imbalance in their stories.

Jim had spoken of a quiet drink and smoke on the street below. Jeff mentioned a silly disagreement which they were 'sorting out', away from the crowd at the ball. Bob's thoughts slid around the possible happenings. There were untruths here. The stories ran counter to commonsense. The pavement sleepers, emaciated, terrified, denied all involvement, bar witnessing a fight between the young sahibs and then, they said, the policeman who began beating the sahibs up with his lathi. Or so they said.

"Mr Renshaw," Bob looked up to see a young South Indian nurse standing before him.

"Yes?"

"Dr Mitra is waiting to see you. Will you follow me please?"

"Where's my wife?" Bob demanded.

"Your good wife is with the patient."

"Our son Carl. Do you know how he is?" A wide smile, teeth dazzling white against her matte skin, the little nurse, she scarcely came up to his chest, bobbed her head and pointed the way to a swing door to the right of the corridor.

Bob entered and again inhaled the sharp smell of a hospital. He had an impression of a small room, strangely bereft of the usual clutter of a medical man. A plain metal desk with the usual In and Out trays, a phone, a desk calendar, steel cabinets, charts on the walls which he vaguely recognised as diagrams of the human anatomy, framed certificates, all, he hoped, testifying to the doctor's competence. The doctor himself was a middle-aged, greying man. Nicotine stained fingers held a sheaf of papers. Horn-rimmed spectacles balanced on his head and undistinguished features wore a look of irritation, grumpiness. He shot a look at Bob then looked down again at the papers in his hand.

"Good morning Dr Mitra…Bob Renshaw, Carl's father," he began.

"Yes, yes," was the impatient response. "Now, I don't know how this accident or assault happened. You understand this will be reported as a police matter?"

Bob felt a fury bubble within him.

His son's life was at stake and this pompous fool was paper-shuffling with police procedures. Hadn't the man taken an oath to care and preserve life?

"Yes, I know that. How is my son? What injuries has he sustained? I've been sitting out in that corridor for about three hours…"

"Your son has to undergo surgery. We need your signature for that."

" S.s.surgery..." Bob tried to keep his mind clear. "My god, what are his injuries? Will you please tell me how badly he has been injured?"

"There has been trauma to the head, there might be cerebral haemorrhaging. We have to operate to contain the wound. It is essential to operate quickly to prevent further damage to the brain."

Bob felt sick. Saliva flooded his mouth. He swallowed hard.

Would his son recover from this horrendous accident. Where was Kitty? Did she know this? Why had she not come out and been with him to see and hear what had happened to their son.

"Where is my wife Kitty?"

"I really don't know. Now if you would sign this, we will have to hurry to see about procedures for surgery." The doctor pushed papers towards Bob. He looked up at the sudden pause in the exchange.

Bob was looking at him with ill-concealed dislike.

"I want to know some more as to the extent of my son's injuries. I must speak to *my* doctor before I sign papers I don't understand, I must read the fine print..."

"Why are you speaking like this? Am I going to harm you? You know nothing, understand nothing. I am a busy man, you are trying to tell me what to do? I am only doing this, at this hour of the morning, after I received a call from Mrs Jaiswal."

"I don't want any bloody favours here. My son's life is what we're talking about, not about your damned schedule."

Dr Mitra did not reply. He placed the papers on the desk. Deliberately took his spectacles off and began polishing them all the while examining the calendar. Bob had been dismissed.

Suppressing a rage that made him want to strangle the man before him, he turned and walked out and made for his son's room.

"Where are you going sir."

The young south Indian nurse was at his elbow looking worried as he strode toward the restricted area of the nursing home.

"I am going to see my son," he said through gritted teeth.

"No sir, I will go to your wife and let her know but no more than one visitor at a time sir, no more than one..."

He brushed off the entreaties, angrily walked ahead peering at the rooms as he strode by.

The Intensive Care Unit was on the third floor and he began to climb the stairs, the lift, a sign said, was out of order, the nurse had turned away and was speaking to a young orderly.

His breath came in short gasps. He began to sweat profusely. He went over the recent encounter with the doctor and fumed.

"Arrogant swine," he cursed, "these people all the same. A little power and they act like everyone else is dirt. Especially us. *Especially us.*"

"Bob, Bob!"

He stopped and swung around. Kitty was standing at the door of one of the cabins. She held out her hand.

No, he thought, *no.*

He rushed to her and held her hands.

"What's happened, how is he? Why didn't you come down to me?"

"Bob, listen. Mrs Jaiswal just called and will be coming over to see how Carl is. She knows the surgeon here and will try to get them to operate as soon as they can."

"I've just come from that arse of a doctor, who tried his nonsense with me..."

"Why are you talking like this? Are you crazy. This is no time for arguments and dislikes. Our son is lying there badly injured. The sooner he is seen to the better. You cannot afford to let personal feelings come in the way of Carl's life!"

Yes of course. What was he thinking? Distracted he stared at his wife and thought of how clearly she saw through this whole mess.

Sudden fatigue swept through him and he sighed deeply.

"Oh Kitty. Why has this happened to us? Why us. *Why us?*"

"Stop that. Stop that now," gently Kitty reached up and wiped the perspiration off her husband's forehead. "We're all exhausted. The main thing is to see that Carl gets the best treatment available."

"I suppose Mrs Jaiswal will offer her help with that will she?"

"Well if she does, god bless her. I won't say no." Kitty gave Bob's hand a tug and quietly, trying to regulate their very breath, husband and wife entered the room where their son lay.

She stood in the little flat and switched on the lights. Her hands were trembling. It was a good thing neither Roger nor Rupa noticed. She looked around and then down at her sari. The chiffon was crushed. Probably as crushed as the famed May Queen coronet, underfoot and forgotten as it lay somewhere on the floor of the club's ballroom.

Uneasy lies the head that wears that crown, she smiled wryly.

Such a fuss over some foolish feathers. She sat heavily, pushing Carl's Jumbo off the sofa. He gave her a reproachful look and rested his nose on her foot. Mrs Jaiswal sat beside her and looked at her searchingly.

The black of the sky had begun to turn a dirty grey. Dawn. Rain a possibility later, with smudged light on the horizon. No news of Carl. Mrs Jaiswal had promised to send her parents home, when the time came, in her car.

"Don't worry too much Grace. I'll see that your father and mother get home. I'll keep in touch."

If there was such a thing as instant love, it was at that moment. Grace looked at the woman and saw more than efficiency. She saw kindness there. It was not just easy access to money that prompted actions. It was genuine caring. It was compassion. Grace leaned across and hugged her. After an instant's surprise the older woman tentatively returned the embrace and gave Roger an embarrassed smile over Grace's head.

"Now I think you ought to go to bed." Rupa patted Grace a little awkwardly.

"It won't help your sitting here waiting for them to come home. They might be a while. Undress and rest. Need anything to drink, eat? No? All right then, it's a good thing tomorrow's a holiday. I'll come around and see how things are going. If that's all right with you?"

Roger Lawson stepping carefully around an attentive pet dog, smiled down at Grace. He glanced around the flat and saw a comfortable home. Neat, tidy. Family pictures on the walls, one of a daughter smiling and proud with graduation gown and mortar-board, it spoke of middle-class contentment. A conventional three-piece suite, not chintzy, shone with the veneer of carefully polished wood, china knick-knacks, a Wedgewood bowl on a glass shelf and a stack of books, resting with the day's newspaper on a side table. Half the room had a dining table and a set of chairs, a sideboard and a small fridge. A guitar was propped up against an easy chair and a few pages of sheet music lay scattered besides it. He wondered who the musician was, Grace, Carl, the beaming graduate in the snapshot, or one of their parents?

Roger and Rupa stood briefly at the door. They hesitated, with a small wave, left, closing the main door gently with a click as the Godrej bolt slid home.

Grace sat alone in the little flat. She had assured Roger Lawson and Rupa Jaiswal she was fine and there was nothing she needed. Yes, she was collected, yes, she had regained some of the composure she was noted for.

Her thoughts were chaotic. She knew the story, so far as they had been told was a patched-up affair. Both the Sutton boys, one a bit more shell-shocked than the other did not seem to be as forthcoming as expected. Their stories garbled and did not make sense. The policeman, the little she glimpsed of him, all bluster, rank with rain and sweat, was voluble in his explanation. His lathi he swung against his leg. Heavy boots scraped as he shifted from one foot to the other. The Hindustani words made no sense, it was a gabble of high-pitched sounds, without much pausing for breath, she heard it as an angry noise as they inched around the angry knot of people.

"What's he saying," Grace asked Rupa as they bypassed the knot of people surrounding the man.

"Don't bother to stop and ask. Your father is there. Your mother is with Carl."

"Can't I go and see if I can help?"

"No Grace, you'll only complicate matters. You'll help your parents best if you go home and wait for them there."

The advice made sense and the trio stepped around the noise and slipped into the car and sped away from the unhappy scene.

Grace, now sitting in the quiet of the flat, looked out of the window. Already the noise and clamour of the day was beginning to screech and scratch into wakefulness. Women's voice shrill, strident could be heard. They gathered at the communal hand pump, banging down metal buckets, scrubbing and slapping wailing children, filling utensils, everything that required a row and shout was done there and then, in a short while the pump would be started, its whine a signal for their block's households' awakening and day's bustle. It was about five-thirty on a sunny and humid

May morning. Last night's rain washing a sky clear and brilliant.

Her sari she pulled off roughly and threw into the laundry-basket. She suddenly was sick of seeing the past evening's finery. Her armlet she carelessly tossed on to the dressing table. Without brushing her teeth, or washing her face she fell into bed. Staring at the ceiling at the slowly revolving fan she thought of the years she had lain in this room. Small, shared with Carl, it was just big enough to have the two beds a couple of almirahs and a small table they both used as a desk. Pin-ups of Carl's heroes were splashed colourfully around one wall. Bruce Lee looked down at her menacingly, one of the film personas of James Bond was equally grim – she could not tell if it were Timothy Dalton or Roger Moore, another of a sultry, pouting woman – was it Madonna – took up a huge space and then there was a classic black and white print of a brooding Marlon Brando. What was the film *One Eyed Jacks* or *On the Waterfront,* she was never sure. Her parents grumbled at the tacked-up pictures spoiling the white-washed walls. But she knew they enjoyed the lively look of their room.

She thought of times when talk had gone on too long and their parents would thump the connecting wall to silence them. Jumbo's snores would punctuate conversation, Carl, never judgmental, listened to her problems quietly. Almost ten years her junior, she was closer to him than she was to Kay. Kay, though a few years older than her, was quick to decide the rights and wrongs of choices made. Grace was never certain if she was in for a lecture or a pat on the back.

Quickly her thoughts grew liquid. Images of the day floated by, Yvonne Coates started adjusting her crown and then held out a plate of sandwiches, the musicians began to dance towards her, Carl began to play his guitar. She felt herself grow light and knew she was on the edge of sleep. Jumbo snored with a ripple of puffed snorts. When would her parents get home? She wondered what Andy might say when she gave him the news, both, of her winning the crown, and of the upsetting aftermath of the night. Strangely, she then thought of Daryl Jackson. It was odd he had not attended the dance. He was awkward, and though sometimes maddeningly proper, was really quite shy. She really must not be so dismissive of the man.

That was the last conscious thought Grace had as she fell asleep.

7

"What the hell are you doing?"

Hilary Johnson was shocked to see her mother-in-law crouching before the front door, opened an inch or so, with a look of intense concentration.

Whirling around, scowling, Edna straightened and almost tripped. She clicked the door shut and shot the bolt home.

"Why are you yelling?" she asked in a suffocating kind of tone, "Do you want to wake Fred and Ralph?"

"What were you up to?"

"I wasn't *up* to anything. I just was curious as to what the Renshaws were doing racing around at all hours of the night and early morning. Didn't you hear the banging around?"

"No. And I don't really care to know what the banging around was about anyway!"

A look of impatience was shot her way and Edna walked slowly away from the door and made a show of getting the breakfast ready.

It wasn't true. Hilary had been awakened by footsteps running up and down the stairs.

The banister's creak, pronounced in the still hours of a pre-dawn darkness, must have been witness to some disturbance. There had been new, unknown voices. A car's door thumping close, ignition being started several times, tyres squealing, punctuated the time into hour-long intervals. Voices bounced off the walls with urgency. She thought she recognised Kitty and Bob Renshaw's voices. Hours before she had heard the murmur of unfamiliar tones in conversation. Again the purr of a car, not a taxi rattle, had come to a halt before their block's entrance. Three people she guessed, had come up and stayed for a while. She lay quietly listening to the odd playing of some drama in the flat above. Was it Lucy, she wondered? Was Eddie D'Cruze somehow involved in this coming and going? Fred remained still and deeply asleep beside her, arm thrown over his face. Ralph, in the adjoining room was also sound asleep. She could not tell if the Old Bat were up and around, pottering about in the bathroom or just sitting in the dark, nursing some imaginary ache.

God how fed up she was with this set-up. Watching and wondering and waiting for something to break and give. Fred, his long silences and shut-in look seemed far removed from any of them. Ralph, obsessive, spent time hunched over his books or mumbling to his pigeon, blotting out relationships, seemingly friendless. Her mother-in-law, hawk-like, willing more tension, generating a contagious ill-temper.

And where was she among this skein of familial cross-hatching? She just seemed to keep going through the motions of everyday living. Waking, cooking, shopping, keeping the house clean, seeing to the needs and wants of her husband and son. Was this what she had exchanged a life of undemanding ease, and pampered comfort for?

High-heeled shoes tapped on the floor above. Chairs were moved hastily around. Her introspection again tugged back into a wakeful curiosity of what was happening in the flat above.

Then the sound of the tramping of several people walking hurriedly up the path. This followed by a silence save for the scrape of shoes on the ground. A heartfelt swearing as someone must have stepped into unswept rubbish, that littered their pathway. She gave a gurgle of laughter.

"Whazzer matter?" Fred rolled over and with eyes shut, moved around to find himself a comfortable spot in his part of the bed.

"Nothing, nothing. Sorry. Go to sleep."

How could you get a cool spot when the sheets seemed to imbibe and radiate the heat of the day.

She carefully turned on her side, pillow clutched to her stomach and tucked up her nightgown so that her body was free of clothes.

"Whazzer matter with you, can't you lie still?" Irritable, Fred punched pillows and burrowed his head into them.

"Hmm. Yes."

Now if she lifted her head slightly she could see through the thin curtain pulled across the window the perfect black of the sky beginning to scar with the light of another burning hot day. Damn. She hated the summer. Last night's rain bringing no relief it promised, instead an increase of stickiness and humidity. Another thump of footsteps running upstairs. Again the door upstairs banged open and shut. What was going on? She squinted at the wristwatch she kept on the bedside table. It was only four-thirty in the morning. There was still a couple of hours of sleep before the day's grind started. Oh god, please let me get some sleep, Hilary prayed. She did fall into a doze which seemed to last five minutes before the whine of the pump pierced through her head. Her eyes bleary with sleep she jumped up and saw Fred had already woken and was in the bathroom.

Her mother-in-law was probably boiling the water for their tea and baths. Ralph might be poring over his studies, doing some revision for the week's exam. How did she oversleep? Yes, it was because of the cursed disturbance during the night and early morning. What were the Renshaws up to? She pulled her dressing gown hurriedly, not wanting to be seen to be sleeping late on this strange Monday holiday. What was this holiday about she wondered. There was no religious festival, lord knows there were enough of those around, why then this day of rest? She listened to the still of their flat. There was something missing. She could not place what it was.

She jerked the curtain aside and saw her mother-in-law crouched before the front door, hands on knees as she focused on the sounds outside.

Hilary deliberately made her voice sharp and abrupt. Her mother-in-law's shocked response gave her a sense of power.

'Well, what have you heard or seen?"

Edna's silence stretched but an excitement she could not withhold made her blurt the reason for her crouching at the door.

"I think there's been an accident at the Renshaws." she half-whispered. "Something happened at that dance last night. I'm sure of it. I saw some official looking chaps. Sure they were police. They have the *thana* written all over them."

"Why are you whispering? No one can overhear you."

She got a glare and then Edna stomped over to the dining area and began setting the table for breakfast. Fred entered the room smelling fresh, shaved, but still in his pyjamas and singlet. He didn't say a word to anyone but reached over for an old newspaper, no delivery on a bandh, sat down, shook out the pages, folded them into a neat square, already lost in the happenings of yesterday's world as reported by *The Statesman.*

There was a silence, the only sounds the smack of cup against saucer, a clack of spoon again china, toast crunched. The two women covertly watched him, waiting for any sign of communication. Hilary briefly thought back to her home where breakfast was always a noisy time. It was usually interrupted by her father's loud comments and curses at the headlines in the newspaper, her brothers scouring the sports page, and her mother rattling around gossiping about the slightest thing that caught her fancy. The radio would be on, centred to Radio Ceylon, a couple of hours of popular western music, stopping at 9 o'clock, the cook taking orders, cheerfully accepting a half-hearted blame for things gone wrong in the previous night's dinner, pet cats mewing, winding themselves around legs, it was as ever an untidy, slovenly swirl of family life. Here, Hilary saw nothing but order and a sterile precision.

Ralph, yawning loudly, entered the room. He stretched, looked round, staring vacantly past his mother and grandmother.

"Where's Oleg?"

"Never mind that bird," Edna muttered, "sit down and have your breakfast. *Dalpuris* nice and warm. Your mum made them last night."

Hilary glanced up in surprise at the alcove above the door.

That's what was missing, it was the sound of the bird's eternal gurgling. She did not care for the perpetual gargle the cooing sounded to her, but it had become part of the home scene. Going on five years the bird had achieved a notoriety in the flats as it had pecked the landlord on the one occasion he had visited his tenants. Part of her surprise was that her mother-in-law had actually given credit to her for preparing breakfast.

Edna rarely mentioned her, and she wondered what had caused this change in a diehard habit. She smiled into her porridge as she hazarded a guess that Edna wished her to keep the night's drama from Fred. He hated their showing an interest in their neighbours' doings.

"Don't stick your nose into other people's business," was how he put it.

"Where's Oleg?" Ralph repeated. His voice rose. His face was already losing the loose, easy folds of childhood. Lines, faint, but startlingly like his father's, appeared on his forehead, lining his mouth. His eyes darted from his mother to his grandmother.

Fred bobbed his head up from behind the newspaper.

"Where *is* the bird? I miss its rumblings."

Ralph pushed back his chair. He looked angry.

"What's happened to Oleg? Have any of you opened the door and let him fly out?"

Hilary's mind flashed to the door ajar while Edna was crouching trying her best to listen to the happenings in the flat above.

Edna grew pale.

"Ralph, *beta,* I'm sure the bird will fly back."

"What, you let my bird fly out, you let Oleg go into the open, you, you, *you…"* Ralph, his chest rising and falling, his voice thin, accusing, began pounding the table with his fist with each word.

"Ralph, stop it!" Hilary alarmed at the hysteria steeled herself to speak normally.

A look of shock seemed to mummify Fred. He clutched the newspaper and stared at his son, unbelieving.

Edna's face was quivering. Not just her chin, but her entire face was rippling into a downslide of burrows and ridges.

"Son, I tried to stop it. It was so quick. I opened the door just a little bit and Oleg flew past me."

"You *hate* Oleg. You wanted to kill him. He'll *die* out there. The other birds will kill him. I *hate* you, you're a witch. You spoil *everything* …"

"Ralph, that's enough," Hilary stepped round and held her son's arm tightly. "Don't talk foolishly son. Gran didn't mean to let Oleg escape. He'll find his way back.

" He *won't,* he's a house bird, he'll never be able to come back," tears tracked streaks down Ralph's face.

"Don't be stupid," Fred thumped his papers down on the floor. "Any more of this nonsense and I'll give you a good hard backhand."

Edna had gone completely silent. She looked down at her cup of tea. Hilary guessed she did not want to try to drink or eat for fear she might break down and cry. It was astonishing but in this moment of her son's anguish she felt a connection with the woman with whom she had little sympathy or liking.

"Come on Ralph, eat your breakfast. Oleg will find his way home, all pigeons are homing birds, they fly back instinctively."

Ralph stared down at his plate, uneaten *dalpuris,* porridge shoved aside.

Silence.

Slowly the charade of having a meal together started. Edna drank her tea noisily. Fred turned over the pages of his newspaper with a clenched fist. Hilary briefly went over day's chores automatically. First off the dhobi was due with some of their good clothes – the *'tagada'*, then the sweeper was due and she would have to pay the man for the month. After that it was the cooking, the tidying of the house, some laundry, a bit of ironing of Ralph's and Fred's clothes, and if she was lucky in the afternoon a short siesta, in the evening a visit to her parents who lived just ten minutes away. She planned to go alone. Fred and Edna happy to stay away, Ralph with exams looming scarcely expected to come with her. She foresaw the day's happenings, her parent's insistence she stay for dinner, her refusal, a forceful plea that she had her family to take care of. Her father would snort, say nothing, her mother might get moody and fall silent. It was never a satisfying end to her spending time at her home.

Hilary looked at her son's shut solemn face. He had eaten most of his breakfast. With an abrupt push of his chair he stood up and left the table, going into the bedroom. They heard the desk bang shut, a chair moved, Ralph had retreated behind his books. Fred said nothing but the pages of his newspaper were still, as still as his mother who sat twirling a butter knife.

A knock at the door and Hilary, relieved to break the tension, went to open the door to the smiling dhobi, sweating, his raggedly pugree askew with the summer heat, his bundle of starched, sweet-smelling clothes.

"Salaam memsahib."

A rose lay in a chipped plate by the stringed charpoy.

Crows perched on the tin awning over the window and cawed monotonously. It was unusually silent for a Monday and then Lucy remembered that it was a public holiday. Wasn't this holiday really a bandh of sorts? There was a political stand-off between the party in power and the opposition. If she had her facts right someone threatened a 'fast unto death' to promote and publicise the corruption within the ranks of the controlling party. She smiled and thought of her Uncle Eddie's reaction to most of the political shenanigans.

"Bloody idiots the lot of them. *'Fast'*; phooh, it's more a *'farce'*. Gandhian humbug twisted to fit into the pockets of these money-grubs. There's always someone somewhere lying around on his charpoy fasting. Rubbish. Publicity, that's what these beggars want."

Every time. He was like clockwork, pouring scorn at any movement of what politicians sought to do. Chary of change he'd read the newspapers avidly, then tear every proposal, every scheme to shreds with a certain logic garnered from years of being passed over for promotion in his career.

"All the sons and nephews, all the *jaat bhais* of the bosses get in and sit on the velvet *gaddis,*" he'd exclaim. "Degrees by the bushel, but can they write a bloody letter properly? Hah! Have to come and ask me, Mr Poor-Bloody-Sitting-in-the-Corner- Eddie D'Cruze. I've seen enough 'improvements' to know it's a good way to stow another bundle of rupees in someone's pocket. My girl, *we* are fools to stay in this country, should have got out *years* ago."

He'd talk to himself, lips moving, a low mumbling ultimately tapering off with his dressing to go out, either down the road to the church club, or a walk to the nearby open market. Lucy learned to keep quiet when one of these moods of desperation were on him. She recognised the frustration, sensed the hopelessness her uncle saw his life shrinking into.

She looked at her watch saw it was near seven, still fairly early, and wondered where Pradip had gone. There was no work today. The small room was neat, his clothes, the kurta and pyjama he wore hung on the nail tacked behind the front door. A metal tray with their plates and tumblers lay clean and shining, the few toiletries neatly on a small towel in a niche near their bed. How early had he risen, she wondered. After the excitement of yesterday and the awkward fumblings of last night it was odd he was up and away from her.

She sat up, twisted her thick hair into a knot and gathered her crumpled sari to her as she wondered if there was water enough for her to have a shower.

A woman's voice cackling, quarrelsome, drew her to the small window. She peered out and could just about see a queue that stood in front of the hand-pump in the corner of the courtyard. No, she could not have a wash or bathe like the others here. Yes, she had agreed to live with Pradip and share his life but was not going to have a bath in public. Was this a test of love? No, there had to be another way. What happened when it rained, or when either of them fell ill? A bucket in the corner of the room answered her question. A thin curtain, hung by a string looped back from a small space squared off a microscopic portion that was the bathroom. It had a small squatting toilet, a tiny mirror hung on the wall. A bottle of disinfectant was on a wooden shelf, along with a safety razor and a bottle of hair oil. Soap, toothpaste, and a tin of Cuticura talcum powder crowded together in a plastic tray balanced on that little plank of wood.

Well.

Now she knew how to go about all the intimate necessities of the rituals of civilisation.

She wished Pradip had introduced her to the workings of what seemed to be their daily life. Used to a relative spaciousness and privacy, in three rooms shared with just her uncle, she listened to the squawking around the handpump below their nest and wondered if Pradip might be persuaded to move out.

Money? She had enough in her bank to finance a more comfortable lifestyle. Her job was secure. Professionally she had no concerns. Pradip might work in an apprenticeship, she thought, and get a ticket to join the boats in Calcutta's shipping industry. She moved to the charpoy and kicked the plate and the rose off to the side.

Quickly stooping she picked up the plate and held the rose breathing in its fragrance. What a courtly gesture. She rarely thought of Pradip as a romantic. Where and how had he managed to get it? The rose was a lovely touch. She saw it had already curled with the harshness of summer. It petals flecked with brown, looking carefully she recognised it as an Independence. A tall plant with a handsome foliage, it usually had dramatic orange or scarlet demi-double flowers.

Her knowledge of horticulture she inherited from her mother. An amateur botanist, her mother would gently guide the girl among the lines of terra-cotta pots, naming lovingly the various roses nurtured. Lucy trotting after her in cool, damp gardens learnt much and now kept memories alive with the flowers she sometimes would be given to arrange at her place of work. If it were remarkable a child should store knowledge like this, no one gave it much thought. It was the gift and privilege of being an orphan. And a poor one had even greater advantages. Few adults hid their feelings towards her. The world showed her its face with complete honesty. No one was intentionally harsh, but she met with a general apathy, an indifference probably more hurtful.

Uncle Eddie saw in her a duty to be done. She was the only child of his sister and he fulfilled his obligation and responsibility. Perhaps if she had been with him from infancy he might have developed fonder sentiments. But a clever eight-year old was neither here nor there. He accepted the child without great drama. His only insistence that she change her name to his.

"You're no Ridout," she remembered the day, the tone of dismissal, "you're Chloe's girl. You're a D'Cruze. We are an educated family. We believe in an education. We don't depend on family names to get by. No illiterate train drivers in our family. You're now Lucy Therese D'Cruze."

But for all that big talk there was not much of an education given her. She was taken out of the non-denominational school she attended and admitted to a Catholic day school. It was a free-school. A charity affair run by Irish nuns, one which ended at Year Eight. If the pupil was bright and willing to learn they could get transferred to the main school but even there a class barrier was evident. Few completed a secondary education that ended with the Indian School Certificate, the equivalent of the old Senior Cambridge. Most dropped out after finishing with a certificate that ensured a polytechnic training or the inevitable secretarial school diploma. Lucy, quiet and bookish, caught the attention of the headmistress, but opted to leave early, without the recognised ISC. She disappointed her teachers. They were certain she'd secure or win a scholarship from the Anglo-Indian Association. Lucy, a flair for accountancy standing in good stead, quickly mastered bookkeeping and accounts and within a month of completing a course from a small commercial college was offered this job as receptionist with additional duties as accountant. She was ecstatic.

In the cavern of her Uncle Eddie's munificence there was no softness of family warmth. No photographs, save some sepia-tinted ones of him when he served during the Second World War as a medical orderly in the Egyptian war theatre. She used to stare at those snapshots. This then, she thought, was the desert. This was the home of the pharaohs, the magical kingdom of the pyramids, the land where cats were worshipped and legendary woman monarchs ruled. She looked at it and did not see the self-conscious posing of a thin young man, she saw in that arid background a passport to a place freed from habit and routine. One day, she promised herself, one day I will go there.

She never did.

Travel had been a short weekend trip to Kharagpur, a crucial nerve-centre of the South Eastern Indian Railway (holding the distinction of having the longest train platform in the world) where Anglo-Indians held pride of place and commanded respect. The other 'journey', an hour's train travel to Bandel, a small town on the banks of the muddy, treacherous river Hooghly. It was a place of pilgrimage, where the oldest Catholic church in northern India was located. During the cooler months, she and her uncle, with a group from the parish, would go on pilgrimage. It was a picnic, an hour's joyride in the puffing train and then a walk through a tree-lined route to the church, now exulted as a mini basilica. Scenic, its Portuguese structure withstanding neglect and decay, she loved it. She would climb up those steep steps to the terraced shrine where from that vantage point the green of Bengal was spread out. The squalidness and shabbiness of the town hidden by this perspective, was cunningly transformed into something beautiful. That was the sum total of her travels.

She survived.

It was ironic that Pradip had chosen this rose. It flourished in warm weather, the hotter the better.

She could hear her mother's voice clearly.

"See darling, this rose is called Independence. Isn't that wonderful? Remember to be proud you are born in a free country. This rose makes us very very happy."

She smelled in the perfume of the flower deeply. "Now I'm free aren't I?"

Her mother laughed. She swung her hands in hers and tickled her neck with a breathy kiss. Then, face buried in Lucy's curls she recited quickly lovely rhyming lines in her clear voice:

Love, it is the time of roses!
In bright fields and garden closes
How they burgeon and unfold!
How they sweep o'er tombs and towers
In voluptuous crimson showers
And untrammelled tides of gold!

Her mother had laughed again and put a swing into the cadence so that with every closing line she butted her on the top of her head.

"You made it up Mummy?"

"No darling. A great lady did that many years ago. "Someone who knew Shakespeare?"

Her mother gave a shriek of laughter and hugged her.

"You clever, clever girl. No. Other people wrote lovely songs and poetry as well, you know. Now. let's go and meet Daddy. Shall we take him a flower?"

No, she wanted to say. Let this be our rose. Yours and mine. Daddy didn't talk to her like Mummy. He was always hurrying.

"Hurry up Luce. Can't you be quick. Come on, *come on,* we haven't got all day."

Mummy never did that. She saw the tall, lithe figure of her mother. The cotton dress with the pink stripes she liked. Her wavy hair worn neatly bobbed, a couple of hair slides holding her hair back above her ears. The smell of Mummy. A clean soapy freshness, the comfort of her skin, smooth and clear.

They would talk. No question was brushed aside. When Mummy and Daddy walked with her or rode on the scooter there was no easy chat. Everything grew serious. Mummy would shush her then. She would be squeezed between the two on a seat that she was told was a pillion. The rush of the wind when they were riding on it was wonderful. There was a bit of fear, but her cheek against Daddy's shirt and with Mummy's arm around her, the drives would be joyous, the rushing wind stinging her cheeks, making her eyes cry. Often with shopping there might be some bags Mummy asked her to clutch as well. How proud she'd be when between both her parents she was given some of the shopping to clutch and keep safe during the whirlwind drive.

"Hold tight now. See they don't fly away. You won't have anything to eat, no barfi, no sandesh, no hot-gram if they fall out you know," Daddy joked. Her Mummy smiled and hoisted her, small and thin for her age, between them. She loved those trips.

Then came that wet day in May.

Sick with a childhood fever she had stayed at home while both parents went out, Saturday morning, shopping again. It rained that day. An early monsoon storm tossed around the accumulated garbage, dust, it wailed around the closed windows, tried to seep into the cracks between the shutters. She waited for her parents to return in the meanwhile, cough drops near her, she read happily alone in the small flat. Time seemed to go on and she realised that it was much later than the time they were due to return. She was hungry.

Breakfast had been hours ago. Mummy had promised a special lunch when she came home. She was going to have toast with Kraft cheese, tomato soup and mangoes. No curry, no rice, no dal. When you had a fever you did not have rice or curry. She loved the soup and cheese. Her ayah, Tara, was having a nap. She got out of bed and opening the window, leaned from it to watch for her parent's return. Rain swept in, the drops cool and lovely on her hot forehead. The noise of the scooter was always clear, announcing her parent's arrival. But, she thought with the noise of the storm, she couldn't hear the phut-phut of its motor. She brought her head back from the window, wiped the rain from her face and closed the shutters again carefully, battling against the fierce wind. As she was about to wake the ayah she heard lots of voices talking and people all who seemed to be hurrying up to the flat. Puzzled, she was about to go to the front room and open the door, though Mummy had warned her never to do that, when the ayah jumped up and with a gasp, quickly reached from behind her and held her back.

"Nai, nai, mutt jao. Kaun hai, kaun hai?"

Knocks on the heavy wooden door were rapid, impatient.

"Kholo, jaldi, jaldi. Lucy are you there?" It was her Uncle Eddie. "Open the door quick."

She did. Her ayah looked annoyed. Pulling her sari over her head she unbarred the door and looked suspiciously at the visitors. Her uncle and two other strangers stood before them. Uncle Eddie was breathing fast. His hair looked uncombed, his shirt was untucked and he had worn shoes without socks. He looked at her and did something he never had done ever, he took her in his arms and kissed her.

"It's all right Lucy," he said as he kept holding her within his arms. "You'll be coming home with me."

Fear, cold and certain, rippled through her.

She knew.

She was alone now.

Her parents had gone forever. They had been swept away by the winds of that wet morning.

It was the start of her becoming Lucy D'Cruze.

Lucy Ridout faded away.

Long ago, and often it still felt like yesterday. Lucy Ridout had waited in vain for her lunch of tomato soup and Kraft cheese.

"Lucee, Lucee," it was Pradip, he had returned. Lucy quickly folded the bed-clothes, pulled the few pieces of furniture into some kind of order.

"Here, Pradip," she called from the door.

Immediately faces in the courtyard turned to look up at her. Curiosity rampant, she saw the questions tumbling through the minds of the half dozen people out there.

Clutching the vessels used to fill water, they gaped while Pradip walked through them and climbed the stairs up to her.

An embarrassment was evident in the stiffness of his gait. He held some paper parcels awkwardly and on reaching their door, looked down at their neighbours, gave them all a smile, then quickly shoved the door open and almost hopped into the room.

"Bandh *karo,* bandh *karo jaldi,*" he murmured to her.

Lucy grasped the parcels from him and with a deft kick of her foot swung the door shut. He put an arm around her. She looked at him and was pleased to see a longing for her.

They were alone together again.

With retirement approaching John Coates wondered what path his life might follow. He often thought of the open, blank stretch of years ahead waiting to be filled. He had Heather. Heather, busy with commitments, career paths to be considered, a social life revolving around marriage, his pleasure in having this wise and thoughtful young person around the house was, at most, tenuous. He sighed deeply as he reviewed the shambles of the previous night, a night looked forward to with such anticipation.

Yvonne was still asleep. He gave silent thanks for that. The rain of last night had made the day steamy, even more humid. The light bush shirt he'd worn for the morning's work was already rumpled and sweat-stained, he planned to give the car a thorough check-up. There was a wheezy rattle in the engine he was not happy with. After that he intended to go over to the nursing home and see how young Carl Renshaw was progressing. What a mess. What a cock-up. And had it to be Kitty Renshaw's son in the middle of the imbroglio. Kitty, fiftyish now and yet a look from her luminous eyes still able to make him as gawky as any schoolboy. A look from her, the sound of that soft laugh and he zoomed back years when they shared a brief month or so of 'handholding' as it was coyly referred to back then… when he was an idealistic young boy in love with a pretty girl.

Annette 'Kitty' Palmer. She was a year or so younger than him working as a market researcher for his company. His memories fresh as the day's newspapers he could still picture her as she came up to him as he raced into the lift that day,

"Mr Coates I'll be so happy if you'd agree to answer this questionnaire."

He'd been flattered. The attractive young girl had called him 'Mr' Coates. Just twenty-three he was a bright star in the company's firmament. Enthusiasm and a quick mind had caught the attention of the directors and he was quickly absorbed into the ranks of those who were being groomed for future managerial positions.

He loved life. He liked himself.

Then one day a young woman entered his world of well-oiled satisfaction and everything changed. She handed him a three-page questionnaire he had to fill in. By the time he had got to the end of the somewhat pedestrian queries, he was confused and happily bewildered by the vivacious girl who sat looking at him with those large brown eyes. What exactly he spoke of or about was a blur, he knew that he was abruptly elated for no real reason. Here was a girl of his own community who could connect with his sense of humour, his views on immediate concerns, a wry acceptance of the whims of Anglo-Indians, a people they both felt at odds with.

At the end of that morning both had looked slightly abashed at the sudden ease an official meeting turned into.

He had quickly assumed a correct and very formal stance, almost leapt out to escort her to the door of his tiny office and through all the formulae of goodbyes and thank-yous was desperately wondering when he would see her again.

After that he went through days of enforced calm and times when he couldn't understand what had happened to him. A couple of weeks dragged on, he tried to shake off the morass of feeling he was floundering through, work grew grey and slow. His boss asked him once if he needed a holiday. That snapped him out of his foggy mulling. He made every effort to put the peppy young girl out of his mind. He groomed his enthusiasm now. The fervour of work tamped down by a voice and a pair of eyes. How banal. The adolescence, the silliness were laughable. Clichéd. And pretty catastrophic for the balance of his professional acumen. He daydreamed during meetings, he caught himself wishing the day's work was done. It had never happened before. 'Work as life', was once a proud maxim of his, but suddenly work didn't really seem to matter that much.

Where did she go? There was no personal knowledge of the elusive woman, where she lived, where she worked, nothing. He could have asked in the personnel department about her, but he knew that was dangerous, the office grapevine was strong and hardworking. News of his interest would be sure to fan salacious speculation. He went from stern resolve not to think of her to falling into a dullness of spirit. Everything was repetitious.

Then there was his mother urging him to attend the club's dance the following Saturday. He went. His astonishment when he saw her across the dance floor, part of a noisy family group. She saw him and looked embarrassed. A wave, an agonising dilemma of whether or not to go across and say hello. He stood stolidly, smile frozen. What had happened next was all so ridiculous. It was again, as predictable as any trashy romance novella. He was called away by his cousin to meet a young man, an applicant for the position of caretaker of the company's new executive suites. It was a responsible post, an almost round-the-clock surveillance of one of the new high-rise blocks the company had acquired. Situated in Alipore it was still in stages of completion. He walked out to the bar and saw the two men, glasses in hand, laughing, comfortable, relaxed in each other's company.

"John," his cousin Ben, backslapped a good-looking man of about his own age, "say hi to Bob Renshaw."

They had self-consciously shaken hands. The prospective employee was taller by several inches than him, with the loose-limbed grace of an athlete. John envied the man's height, his easy social manner, neither servile nor deferential. Most of all, he envied his voice. He always wished his own voice had been deep and commanding. Something it was not. His voice always annoyed him with its high pitch.

"Hello, it's a nice evening isn't it? Enjoying yourself?" Bob was assured, friendly. It seemed a reversal of roles. Wasn't he the one to take over the social niceties?

"...er...yes...though I don't come to these dos often."

"No, I didn't think you did." That grin flashed again, wide, attractive and a bit silly.

"My work keeps me from a hectic social scene."

"Yeah, I can see that. Regular workhorse aren't you?"

Annoyance surged quickly.

"Well, I'm getting used to the fun and I'm sure I'd get used to the company as well." There was a touch of frost in the reply that the good-looking Mr Renshaw could not ignore.

"Oh I say man, didn't mean to give offence, I know you're a busy chap. I'm usually pretty busy as well, no time to jitterbug my time away." He laughed uneasily.

John immediately grew contrite.

Here was a pleasant young person of his age probably nervous about his meeting with him and he was ready to take offence at inconsequential small talk.

"No offence taken Bob. Why don't we join the others in the dance-hall? It's so bloody hot here. Maybe the cool jazz there will help us forget the heat here."

Bob Renshaw laughed long and loud at the attempt to smooth social clumsiness.

"Yeah man. You said it. I love Miles Davis, don't you? That trumpeter really knows how to deliver the goods doesn't he? He's playing *'So What'*, isn't he? Smooth man, real smooth."

He wouldn't know Miles Davis from Sammy Davis Jr, but John nodded his head like a tugged marionette and said yeah, yeah, *yeah,* this trumpeter could really play it man. They went in together.

Kitty was waiting. He sensed it. This time he didn't just stand and stare and smile. He walked across and asked her to dance with him. It was as if the cheeriness of the attractive Bob Renshaw had given his confidence a boost.

She moved in his arms as effortlessly as a feather. He should have known she'd be a good dancer. Most Anglo-Indians were, and he smiled at his generalisation. He himself was no natural dancer, stiff, and jerky, he moved consciously thinking of the steps in his mind. Not this time though. It was over too quickly and she left him standing there to return to her family. He was determined to continue to dance with her.

He remembered the looks of her family, puzzled at the appearance of this young man, seemingly a longstanding friend of Kitty.

"Kitty never tells us much, do you pet?"

Mrs Palmer, tall, a complexion buffed to appear unnaturally smooth, hair tightly curled in the fashion of the fifties, let her curiosity be felt.

Kitty flushed.

"Oh come on, Mum. Mr Coates is an executive with the company. I interviewed him a couple of weeks ago. I told you about it, you never listen to a word I say."

She flashed an apologetic smile at John and looked quickly at her mother.

He had sat with her family that day and talked easily without constraint or reserve. What he talked of he could not remember. Enough to recall the glow of Kitty's eyes. The reckless lift of happiness that suffused him.

Later, much later, when he was whirling around that dance floor Kitty laughing now, hair falling into her eyes, his cousin had given him a thumbs-up sign which he ignored. It looked vulgar and cheap. Trust Ben to make something nasty out of what was a special time.

"I've never seen you here before Mr Coates. What made you come tonight?"

"First off, stop this *Mr* Coates nonsense. Keep that for work if you must. And to answer your question, yes, this is the first time I've come to one of these shows. No, I don't really care for dancing, real fuddy-duddy, that's me. But now," he looked at her straight and without leaving any doubt in her mind, "nothing will be able to keep me away."

Kitty suddenly shy, looked away.

That August flew in an euphoric daze. After almost thirty-five years, he still remembered exact dates, where they spent them, snatches of their conversation. The weekends were evenings at her home. Nothing was done that was special. It was a relaxed time. During all the time spent in that small flat he was given no privacy at all with Kitty. Occasionally he'd be asked to join in a quick game of rummy with Mr Palmer and some of his neighbours. Kitty would play her favourite records on a small stereo. Musicals. She loved them. *Showboat, Porgy and Bess,* the soupy lyrics and booming orchestration would flood the room. Then dinner was served. Table talk with the Palmers was innocuous. Food, bazaar bargains, rising prices, commentary on the day-to-day politics, nothing really incisive, or provoking.

Mr Palmer was casual in his attitude to most situations and events bar his daughter. His Kitty walked in the light of his love. The elder brother Harvey, as old as he was, came over as serious, somewhat tongue-tied, a bit in awe of John. Quickly he was introduced to the extended family. Aunts, uncles, cousins, first, second and three times removed, made entrances, asked questions. He grew irritable with the parading of what seemed an endless queue of relatives. Kitty's mother, shrewd and quick to pick up nuances, asked if he preferred small or large families. There was a flicker of disapproval in her tone. He mumbled a reply and that evening asked Kitty if her mother approved of his weekend visits. She looked oddly at him and asked if he was not comfortable with her family. Of course he was, he recalled his quick denial. But the truth was that he was feeling overwhelmed by the intense scrutiny he was placed under by them.

On Sundays he took Kitty out. Movies, the 'pictures', as they would call them, one of the few entertainments left in a city drab under a humourless, xenophobic, political regime. He was always too aware of Kitty besides him to concentrate on the screen. He held her hand tightly. Stroking her arm under cover of that darkness. Sometimes they would have a coffee in one of the Park Street restaurants, a walk, slow, punctuated by the silly talk of young lovers they'd go back to her home.

They'd discovered a route through one of the city's small and sparse parks. Under the shadow of its ill-lit paths, in shadowy corners they'd quickly embrace, Kitty stiffly allowing him to kiss her. She'd push him away nervous of the knowing looks of the occasional passers-by. Once when they were whistled at she was furious. She made him promise never to walk that way again. There was a tension in their going out together. Both were wary of being seen by office personnel. As a junior staff member it was impolitic to socialise with whom Kitty laughingly called her 'superiors'.

"Don't be silly." John brushed aside her warning impatiently, "I can be friendly with whomever I like. It's just that while I'm working towards my promotion to this Calcutta management I can't really be thinking of having a girl-friend or anything like that."

"Friendly?" Kitty raised her eyebrows at the schoolboy phrase. She said nothing more. Her silence was eloquent. When they parted, the feeling was strained. John felt nettled. Surely, he reasoned, he had to be cautious about how he behaved while in public. He did have an important position at the office and couldn't go haring around with her like some besotted teenager. The evening was spoilt. Their annoyances hung over them, a miasma of frustration, with unspoken questions, a sense of hurt pride.

Through the week at the office neither saw each other, both were in different departments, both careful not to speak of their relationship to colleagues.

Then came the day when he was called in by the regional manager, Mr Samuel Carter, the only other Anglo-Indian in the firm. It was the beginning of September. There were plans for the coming Pujas, a presentation was to be made for a visiting head of department. He never foresaw how that day was to change his life.

"Look here Coates, you will have to baby-sit the visiting VIP, Mr Sloane's family while he is in town."

"Certainly sir, no problem at all. I'll have to find out what they'd like to do and see. Also, if I may, could I have the company car at my disposal. It's not easy to beat the traffic jam with the company driver, Hussein, coming around to my place at eight o'clock."

Mr Carter chuckled, "Real workhorse aren't you? Yep, I'll see Hussein gets to your place much earlier so you'll be on time to fetch and carry for Mr Sloane's wife around the city. But don't forget you are in charge of the presentation. It's important he like it. You have a month to work on it, so don't waste time."

John struck by the description of him as a workhorse, twice, both by men met recently. He thought with some guilt of Bob Renshaw. He had forgotten his promise to look into the possibility of getting him an interview as prospective caretaker of the company's new apartments. He would look into that immediately.

Mr Carter puffed on a pipe. Very classy. John made a note of trying out a pipe. Has a dignified air to it, he thought. Mr Carter seemed to be toying with another idea as he fiddled with the various items on his desk.

"Look here John, I have a request to make. My niece will be coming over to stay for a couple of weeks. She's a country girl, not used to the big city ways. Or lights," he laughed half-heartedly.

John waited.

"Well the fact is I and the wife are not much company for a young girl, so we'd be grateful if you could take her out a bit while she's with us."

John smiled. "Yes Mr Carter. I'll be glad to show her around."

"It's my sister's girl. Her husband's a railway man, a bit rough and ready, not too relaxed when he's visiting us," a snort and laugh combined, "old story of the in-laws and out-laws eh?"

"When will she be arriving sir?"

"Monday after next. She's a beauty too, giggly, but nice. Don't worry too much about her preferences. She loves Calcutta. Anything here is heaven."

John kept his surprise hidden. He had seen the disdain most of the young 'country' girls had for the city. This was a turnabout.

"What's her name sir?"

"It's Ashton – Yvonne Ashton."

8

Yvonne.

He smiled at the memory.

What a long time ago that was. John met her at Mr Carter's spacious house on Rawdon Street. His mother had been thrilled.

"John, see that your clothes are right. He does live in the south of Park Street you know. None of your grubby bush shirts, and please polish your shoes."

Mrs Coates, widowed for nine years, lavished her attention on her son. She worked as a seamstress in one of the city's fashion designer shops. Refuting the title of tailor, the chief cutter and stylist, a shrewd Nepali businessman, recognised the skill of Mrs Coates and employed her on a generous wage as head 'designer'.

Over the years her flair with the scissors had seen young John attend one of the top schools in the city. It had seen him go on to a tertiary education. There were the luxuries like subscriptions to magazines, an occasional concert, and even short holidays, Puri, or Digha, where they paddled carefully in the wake of strong ocean waves. Diligence and careful cultivation of things fashionable soon saw John getting a job as a minor executive in one of the city's chief commercial concerns. Mother and son were overjoyed. Nothing marred their contentment.

And then Yvonne swam into his life.

She *was* beautiful. And very young. Cream complexion, pale blue eyes, and a figure he forced himself not to gawk at. He wished Mr Carter had prepared him for this blonde stunner. She nodded bashfully when introduced and true to Mr Carter's warning, giggled through most of that first chat.

He had escorted her during those weeks to what was considered the city's attractions. The Victoria Memorial, offering rare soft green lawns in the midst of dull dust encrusted streets. She looked sleepy when he suggested visiting the city's famed museum but came wide-awake when they wandered through Calcutta's pride and joy, the New Market. At the confluence of two of the busiest streets, it was a fascinating parade of the buying and selling, bargaining, a heady mixture of the hawking of goods, sly manipulation of consumer greed, he admired the Sindhi shopkeepers, masters of the soft sell, convince and cajole customers to accept wares from jewellery to swathes of English cotton. Yvonne loved every aspect of this untidy monument to materialism. The target of frenzied appeals to patronise this or that store, Yvonne led him through the maze of stores and stalls, assured in this, her role as discerning shopper. He drifted through that time hardly aware of the urgency of work, of his commitments. He seldom thought of Kitty. Friendship. Kitty and her family had shrunk to an unimportant few weeks of his life.

Mr Carter and his wife were pleased. Yvonne was charming. She hadn't much of an education. As a child of the railways, education was not a priority for the girls in that peripatetic lifestyle. But Yvonne held her own, walking a tightrope during social occasions. She spoke only when she had to, her opinions held in check, her talk was geared to head-nodding agreement with whomever was the most important person in the group. John was mesmerised.

September merged into a cooler and blissful October. The city put on its festive look. People rushed around happily and Yvonne was still in Calcutta. If Mr Carter thought it odd John Coates left work early, and got in late, he never commented on it. In addition he was at Mrs Sloane's beck and call through the working day. He enjoyed the entrance it had given him to the more exclusive city's clubs and Masonic societies. He relished doors being held open, the bowing and scraping that came naturally to most Indians.

At the end of the visit Mrs Sloane had spoken warmly of the young man who had so effortlessly introduced her to the other face of a city that at first confronted the newcomer with its noise and dirt. Then the couple had left for the powerhouse of New York. Mr Carter called John in that Friday afternoon to congratulate him on the babysitting and his presentation. "I have to hand it you John, you seem to have put everyone in a good mood. There's a promotion in this somewhere for you eh?" He breathed heavily, good humour with every breath, puffed on his pipe and with a look at the young manager suddenly said, "You do know that Yvonne will be leaving next weekend?"

"What?"

John abashed at his dismayed response bit his lip and kept quiet.

"Well?"

He fumbled for a reply. Nothing came to mind. Generally quick and easy with words he was shocked into silence.

Mr Carter darted a look at the tongue-tied man before him.

"John, her father's a guard on the mail trains. Her mum, my sister Dawn, is not doing too well. Yvonne is one of five children. If she were married it would help the family enormously. I think you are, er, fond of her. Ah, how old are you – 23, 24 – well it's not *that* young to take the plunge," he puffed long at the pipe, aromatic clouds of smoke haloing his head.

"Do you know how old I was when I got hitched? Just 21. Crazy, no? No. It was the smartest move I made. No more gadding around, wasting time, money. It focused me on what life was all about. Mavis and I have had our share of ups and downs, but it's been a good life. A full one."

He then knew what he had to do, wanted to do. Marry Yvonne. He put the thought of his mother from him. Surely she'd be happy for him. The girl was a step up for them. Mr Carter was her uncle. Suddenly he looked up at Mr Carter and solemnly said, "Is December a good month to marry?"

They both stared at each other then laughed aloud. Mr Carter came around the desk to embrace him, stood back and pointed his pipe at him, "You're counting your chickens before they're hatched aren't you?"

John glanced puzzled at the change in tone and said, "What's that?"

"Have to ask the lady haven't you? She might say no."

And again they both broke into loud gasping shouts of laughter.

The wedding was one of the social highlights of the year. There was a guest list of more than three hundred people. John knew perhaps about twenty of them. He and his mother were shunted along in a maze of etiquette, meeting strangers, being invited to dinners and lunches, greeted now by many who before would not consider smiling at them. The parish priest, an old Frenchman, acerbic, short-tempered, suddenly grew amiable.

It was all quite heady.

The day itself went off quickly without a flaw. The weather was cool, the sun was golden, Yvonne one of the most dazzling brides, the church, one at the fashionable end of Park Street, had seen in a long while. A stranger in a frothy lace confection she was demure, greeting guests, her face out of some Old Masters' painting.

"You look relaxed John." Mr Carter punched his arm lightly.

His mother brushed his hair off his forehead. She did not wave when they left for the honeymoon, nor did she have any words of advice to give. It was a passive mother-in-law who greeted the new Mrs Coates. And after all the noise, the crush of well-wishing strangers they made their escape to Gopalpur-on-Sea. Mr Carter knew the proprietor of one of the holiday homes there.

So off they went, the train, puffing slowly out of Howrah Station, friends peering, waving at them through the tinted windows of the air-conditioned coupe.

Finally they were alone. The wedding night was without much drama. Yvonne was excited. She giggled a lot. Then she cried after the first attempt at lovemaking. She cried after they grew more expert and then giggled non-stop for a good part of that night. He put it down to nerves. Surprisingly for all her golden beauty Yvonne did not have nor excite much sexuality. He felt protective towards her. Certainly she was without any subtlety, her accent with its pronounced lilt, redolent of a careless schooling, grated, but he was taken with her childlike simplicity. She needed a gentle guidance to show her some of the norms expected of an executive's wife.

In the days that followed she'd listen to him but before he could explain his dreams or plans would jump into his lap and tug his hair, pull away the newspapers from him or run down to the beach where she'd scream when surprised with the small sand crabs which scuttled across her path. Conversation was limited to the discussion of their wedding.

"Did you see Mary Anne's dress? Wasn't it a scream? Wearing rose-coloured lace with that dark complexion. How silly of Uncle Tim to get drunk and sing his naughty Rugby songs. Wasn't our cake delicious. Did you like mum's hat? Why wasn't your mum there to wish us at the station?"

He answered with a smile and usually kisses. Yvonne was content with his way of answering her questions.

One of the greatest surprises was when she delighted him by her fluency with the local language, Oriya. As were the servants of the hotel. When the golden-haired lady spoke to them fluently in their language they put their hands to their heads and exclaimed that she was wonderful, wonderful. And so she was, John thought back ruefully.

Five days into their honeymoon and Yvonne was restless. The sand, she complained was everywhere, in her hair, her food, under her nails, she wanted the lights of the city. The food was too spicy. It was unseasonably hot for December in this seaside town. Yvonne pouted, was cool. She wanted to go back and see how the wedding photographs had turned out.

"Why can't we go back now? Surely it's not fixed that we stay here for as long as ten days!"

John, unwilling to think why she was keen to return, unwilling to examine his own eagerness to return to the normalcy of life at the office and the city, was tempted to agree.

"No, it's rude to cut short this holiday which your uncle has given us."

"Oh rubbish. Uncle Sam won't mind. He knows we'd like to be back with the family. Oh *let's* go back home," she softened the demand by giving his ear a quick nibble.

"Well, all right. We'll tell Mr D'Costa we won't be staying till Sunday and leave on Wednesday instead. Remember I have to change our tickets at the station, that'll take doing."

She laughed in relief. "Oh I'm so glad. I'm tired of this quiet. No one to see, no one to talk to, nothing at all happening. Won't it be fun to be back and be called *Mrs Coates.*" She fell on the bed pummelling the pillows in delight.

She stretched out her arms to John. Pushing aside self-doubt and a shadow of unease, John, unbuttoning his shirt, quickly went to her, marvelling at her swift changes of mood.

It was one of his last few days of happiness.

Standing, a rag in his hand, John polished his car. He rubbed the bonnet till the metal reflected his sweating face in a distorted oblong caricature of himself.

He marvelled at how rapidly life had run away from him.

Three decades had vanished into photographs, into the anaesthesia of habit. Life had long since been drained of emotional spark. He lived for the single font of his happiness, his daughter. Born years after their marriage, Heather was a child welcomed with a fervour that bordered on the religious. His in-laws regarded him with scantily clad contempt as the childless years gathered momentum. Their other children had large families, grandchildren seemed to sprout from coughs and sneezes. Yvonne grew obsessed with what she called, biblically dramatic, their 'barrenness'.

John, impatient, lost for words of comfort or companionship, drifted from his beautiful wife. Yvonne grew plump. Her face lost a pliant softness. Her features without the spark of youth developed a bluntness, the large blue eyes taking on the abject look of dissatisfaction.

All the while in the closed and curtained world of John Coates' mind Kitty Palmer stayed and grew stronger with the passing years. He learnt she had also married shortly after he did. With a wry amusement he discovered it was to Bob Renshaw, the applicant he had helped get the caretaker position at the company's executive block of apartments. She had left the organisation months after his marriage and he had resigned himself to living with memories of their short friendship. Then at a function at his uncle-in-law's club she had walked out of the library there and bumped into him.

Both had first stared in shock, quickly covering up the moment with awkward laughter.

"Congratulations. Mrs Renshaw, I believe. How are you?" He shook her hand, then let it fall abruptly.

She had nodded and seemed to be fumbling for the right words.

"You have a lucky husband and a handsome one."

Kitty Palmer smiled without warmth, "Yes," she said, "yes. And you have a beautiful wife."

They both stood smiling, silently looking at each other, after a few seconds he stood aside for her to walk away from him.

There was really nothing to be said. He shook himself mentally and vowed to try be a good husband to the simple and undemanding girl he had married. Childless, they lived without much imagination, but with strict adherence to what people expected of them. Yvonne was active member of committees, church, club, and club sports board. She was kept busy and accepted what their life demanded.

Then, almost fifteen years into their marriage their daughter, Heather was born. It revitalised John. The years of stifled boredom vanished. Yvonne lived her life with her old élan and through their child, was happy, content.

Months, years tumbled by with the comfort of ritual. School years, holidays – they shunned Gopalpur – Heather's childhood illnesses, shopping, minor squabbles, domestic decisions, his growing importance with the company promoting him to chief executive, it rushed along and abruptly John and Yvonne Coates found they were almost old.

Heather now was a young person. She had her own ideas that often seemed estranged from theirs. Life within her circle closed around her and left little space or time for her parents.

So it seemed they had to live with each other again. Tedium swooped. John was desperate and dreaded approaching retirement. He swamped himself with work and now with the club's activities. It was a harsh discipline he forced on himself.

He saw Kitty Renshaw and her family occasionally and felt his heart twist each time. True it was distanced by social differences, but Kitty Renshaw fluttered on the periphery of his life. Kitty was happy. He could sense that. He also sensed she was aware of the chasm between Yvonne and himself. Yvonne had not been burnished by time. Her brassiness was embarrassing. The petulance of youth had hardened to tones of sharp command. She was irritated easily. Now he was too tired to coax her towards any kind of harmony.

Life was routine.

They kept a home for Heather. Most of their doings revolved around her. Happiness was grasped through the satisfaction of being the parents of a bright girl. John was now partner in his company and chairman of the board of directors.

Life was secure.

It was good to be top of the tree. His mother, frail, kept a stern independence and refused to live with her son and daughter-in-law. He kept from thinking of the indifference Yvonne showed towards her. It was a less than savoury side to the competent wife and mother, a factor which had led to his quick disillusion with his wife and his choice of a lifelong companion. He recognised the infatuation and glitter of ambition that had propelled him into marriage. Ashamed of his motivation he forced himself to be accepting of Yvonne's behaviour. That had meant quietly widening and dissolving the closeness between him and his mother. Again he allowed this, and reasoned he paid for his loveless feeling towards his wife by an almost blind acquiescing to her wishes. One of which was that their lives remain distant from that of his mother's. So it went on, and John found himself hardening towards Yvonne. It was, he acknowledged, shaped by his failure as companion and friend to a basically simple girl. He ached with the loneliness of middle-age.

And now he was faced with the prospect of sorting out this muddle with Kitty's son in the eye of the storm.

"Johnee, Johnee, there's a call for you," Yvonne yelled from the bedroom.

Wiping the sweat from his eyes, streaking his face with the grime of the rag, he shouted a reply to his wife and woke up to the present.

Unflagging in their commitment to daily bickerings the Vincents were in the middle of an early morning argument when a grey and white pigeon flew into their house.

"Hey, hey, wha's this, wha's this?" Henry Vincent stopped mid-shout in genuine astonishment as the flutter of the bird cut across the rattle of shrill dissent.

"You must have left the door open Fatima. Get it out. Its shit will be all over the house. Shoo it off, fast, fast. My fathers, *bapre bap,* must you always be so slow," the old man glared at his wife as she stood amazed as the bird settled on a beam near the window.

Fatima Vincent, harried by a couple of hungry grandchildren, both needing to be bathed and dressed, swatted a cloth duster feebly at the intruder.

"Henry, stop, wait, I think – *will you stop"* – this to the grandsons who were climbing on chairs to be nearer to the bird, *"Arre,* I'm sure it's the Johnson boy's pet."

"Chaa – rubbish. How could the bird fly from their flat to ours?"

"Easily. Just open a door or window. Don't need to have a big brain to know that."

Husband and wife stared angrily at each other.

"Oho I'm so stupid eh? You're so smart. Too damn smart. That's why daughter is with us. That's why no-good husband lives with us. That's why damn children…"

"Chup, quiet. Stop shouting. The boys will cry non-stop. *Bahut accha, bahut accha…shsss, shsss…"*

When stressed the Vincents' rapid-fire abuse carried on in a colourful amalgam of English and Hindustani. He thudded a hand on the table.

A cup overturned. Tea spilled over the tablecloth. The two grandchildren began crying. Fatima slammed the breakfast plates together and yelled for their servant to hurry and clear the table.

A young boy, barely in his teens, ambled into the room, and slowly started piling the breakfast crockery together.

He grinned when he saw the pigeon. He pointed up and said to the crying boys, "Look birdie, birdie. Nice. Prettee, prittee. Why you cry? Don't cry. Making too much trouble for Nanee. You want birdie? I'll get for you." He plonked the breakfast things down again on the table and went out to come back with a rickety bamboo ladder.

"Stop, you *ulloo.* Fool, fool, stop," Mr Vincent, spittle flying from rage, grabbed the ladder and pushed the servant boy back away from the centre of the room.

"Let him try to get it, leave him be Henry," Fatima Vincent, hair straggly, escaping from an untidy bun, clutched the grandsons and pulled them off the chairs.

"Let him be," she shouted over the din.

"What are you screaming about? Shut these children up. Can't understand a word you're saying. Damn, blasted bird has already mucked up chair. Get it out. I don't care whose it is. It'll be shitting all over the place."

"No. No. Let bird be. We'll catch it and give it back to the Johnsons later today. Can't you see the boy must be worried, must be looking for it. what's wrong with you?"

"Oh yes, the burra sahibs, those Johnsons, have to run and give them back their bird. They smile at us, oyes, they laugh at us, *laugh,* oyes, but we must be on the right side of the big shots. We have to smile at them. Oyes. Must keep them happy. We are nobodies here. Not good enough for them to say hello to eh? Oyes! *Get that bloody thing out of here."*

The old couple at either end of the small dining table locked in mute anger at each other.

The servant boy dragged the ladder out of the room and singing softly to himself started taking up the breakfast clutter.. He whipped a stained towel across the table spraying crumbs around.

"If you don't take pigeon back I'll let them know bird flew in here and you let it out."

"Oho. You have to be heroine eh? Want to be friends with all the *gora-wallahs.* Don't you see how they laugh at you? Damn fool. Go on. Make an *ulloo* of yourself. I'll have nothing to do with this *tamasha.*" Muttering and dashing about the furniture on his way to the bedroom old Mr Vincent, grabbed the morning papers, and retired from the field of battle. Tacit admission of his defeat. His wife watched, sopping up the spilled tea, making soothing noises to her young grandsons.

The children watching him leave, slowly stopped their bawling. Sniffles now the only sign of distress.

The pigeon looked on.

The sweeper dreamed. It was the same dream. She was laughing and walking towards him a garland held up for him to see. He was striding towards her. Crowds of people muttered around him. He began to beat them away with his broom. She was laughing. The garland was shedding petals over her feet. He had to get to her but the way seemed a long way off. Night was coming on fast. Her family now surrounded him and he was prevented from seeing her. He began to wave his broom around him, it was a weapon, a spear. It was dark and she had gone. At this point he awoke, a deep grief settling on him. He breathed in relief. It had been a dream and she was still his to have. There was no dark blocking his vision. He knew what he had to do and when to do it. He slowly floated back to the day and his life. It had been a disturbed night. He heard footsteps running up, running down, those cursed creaky stairs. Voices too. Loud, strange, not belonging to the block at all. Cars rumbling, their engines huffing out What had happened, he wondered. The dog had not barked. No thieves then.

He rose, uncurling himself from night time wonderings. Shook out his thin cotton sheet, pulled away the *chatai* that was his bed and rolled it in a tight neat swirl, placed it in the corner of his room. Phantoms, *bhoots,* were scared by light. It was what his *didi* had always told him. "Sun chases away bad spirits. Open windows, sweep the floor, roll up the bed quick. Then no *bhoots* will worry you." He always followed that mantra. He forced open the creaky window. Dazzling sun streamed through. Dust motes already thick in the sunbeams. He sneezed and sneezed again.

"Yes, you *salas,* make work for me. All is dust. Everywhere. My work will never clean this dirty world."

He pushed open the door and squinted at the day.

Already the women were at the hand pump with their tin and earthen pots and plastic buckets. "Arrè, why so much *golmal?* Can't you talk quietly? Even the rooster's cry is deadened by your talk."

"Oho, such a big man, a real *lat-sahib,* can't have noise, everything *chupchap.* Go live in a palace then, not here."

"Why don't you get a wife, then you won't be so long-faced, a woman will teach you how to live with noise."

Bitches. He hated the contempt in their voices. He knew they sniggered at his crooked back. How he'd like to see their faces when he'd bring home his *bibi,* real lady, not these slatterns, high-pitched voices always cackling, quarrelling, ignorant, hideous to hear and look at.

He watched covertly. They slapped their children, roughly rubbing the little bodies with soap, rubbing them dry with the rags of towels, all the while keeping up a loud question and answer with each other. How had they ever married, he wondered how did men agree to take them as lifelong partners? A shudder went through him as he considered life with women like them.

Loud, aggressive they shouldered their way through perpetual struggle, the heat, indifferent husbands, gained strength from pre-empting the pain of each day. Many now worked, some as ayahs in neighbouring houses of the memsahibs, there were always children to look after when the young mothers went to their work, some as cooks, others to wash clothes and do light domestic chores, yes, there was work. Now, the luckier ones were even getting work in factories. The money was better. Laws and rules protected them.

He thought about his mother. She was harsh. There was no soft touch that greeted the little boy. He'd run limping after the other children. No one had time for a boy with malformed limbs. Solitary and sickly, he'd stare fixedly while his elder brother played street games.

His father, a Corporation sweeper was usually silent. He'd return from the day's work and smoke in the corner of the compound outside their hut. He'd prepare his chillum and cough regularly, rhythmically. After the first deep drag the smoke smothered the throaty hawkings, and the sweet smell though cloying helped his father sleep through the evening. He'd often lie awake in the night to watch his father hunching over his mother, making a noise like the noise of rustling paper, on and on his father would rock. His mother lying silent, until she'd sense his watching, with a word of abuse she'd hiss at him to close his eyes. "Turn around, go to sleep. I'll beat you if you don't. I'll beat you." Then he'd turn around and the sound of rustling paper continued until it seemed to lull him to sleep.

His father, thin, coughing, eating from the big tin thali, shouting for more, wiping the food from his mouth with a scrap of cloth, his father pulling him by the ear to help him with carrying the rubbish from the garbage heap to the big lorries. How he hated the stinking bundles he had to drag to throw on the unwieldy pile of refuse. Insects crawling on his legs, dogs sniffing at them, rag pickers bickering over scraps of metal, cloth, crows hopping insolently ahead, their cawing and bright eyes mocking his labour. His days in school ended quickly. The family needed money. A job was offered as a road sweeper. He now was old enough to earn a salary. The day began early with sweeping the roads near his house. Then he'd have to see that the local rubbish tips were emptied. Walking up and down those crowded streets the hours seemed endless.

His legs ached and his head swam with the sameness of his tasks.

Sweep, and collect the filth of people.

Sweep, and tidy the mess of the city.

He always feared his father. He knew what might happen if he was late or didn't run fast enough when his father called. He had seen his father bring a stick down on his elder brother and with a single swipe cut his skin open. The blood, the gash of the wound, and his brother's petrified eyes were something he still saw in his nightmares.

His brother had run away from home soon after. There was shouting, his mother weeping, her hair covering her face. Throughout that frenzied time it had taken to accept his brother's loss his father had eaten his meal, noisily sucking his fingers dry of the curried watery meal, he wiped the tin plate dry, belched loudly, never looking up at his wife. Neighbours crowded round their door and asked questions, enjoying the drama of the moment. His brother had vanished. His brother's name not spoken. His mother stopped threatening to beat him. The night time sound of the rustling paper continued.

He did not watch.

One day he realised he was no longer a child. His voice had changed from a thin high treble to a thin high rasp. His face, his body grew strong wiry hair. He had to endure the ribald remarks. He was not thumped away when the men gathered to exchange talk. No longer was he pushed away when the men sat huddled in a pool of lechery. He began to enjoy the new feelings of his body. He started to understand why men were obsessed with women. He listened to the bawdy stories, the smutty remarks, he grinned and slapped his thighs when the married men told of how and when they enjoyed their wives. He was encouraged to shout remarks to girls they passed in the streets, or saw in buses, in rickshaws. He learnt that you could get near them in crowded trams, buses, streets, and touch them. Quickly he slipped into the life of men without women. He heard stories of women who took money to 'do the thing men like to do'. Older men urged him to save his money and visit them. "Watch out for sickness though," he was warned, "these women can give you sicknesses you die from." He was shown packets of rubber balloons that kept you safe.

Everything was galling. He had no money of his own. Every month his meagre earnings were given to his father. His mother washed utensils for the rich folk who lived in the two-storied building in front of their huts. Sari pulled over her head, a jangle of bangles preceding her, she was careful about wearing her sindur in the parting of her hair in the middle of her forehead. "Have to let people know I'm a good woman."

He gathered that unmarried women who worked were bad.

Life for the sweeper was dirty, a grimy business. Every day was like the next. His shoulder ached. His father continued to cough, to spit noisily, to smoke his chllum. His mother was longer at her morning prayers. The tulsi plant in the terracotta pot was sprinkled, the foliage fresh and blooming, in spite of the pall of dust and his mother murmured, lips moving, eyes wide, hands cupped in front of her chest as she stood before it, careless of how the devotion made her late for her work. Then abruptly his life changed. One evening, after preparing his chillum his father's cough grew louder. He did not think it unusual so regular was the habit of the evening smoke. All grew quiet. It was after a while he noticed that the cough and the smoke of the chillum had ceased. Going outside he found his father slumped, head on chest, apparently asleep. The chillum's smoke thinning in the growing dusk. Afraid to touch him he called, "Baba, Baba." But somehow he knew that his father was dead.

He turned slowly and went into the hut to his mother. Relief made him giddy. His father had gone. Gone was the terror, the imprisoning fear. He was free.

His shoulder ached from the jolting bite of the charpoy on which the shrunken body lay, the chant escorting his dead father was a prayer of thanks. Jouncing over the streets his callused feet padding over sharp stones, debris, the last journey of his father, he was filled with thoughts of a future where he could do as he wanted and do as he wished. He lit the pyre with joy and thanked Yama for taking his father.

Freedom meant even more loneliness. His mother he sent back to their village to her younger married sister. In that emptied one room he now reigned as head of what was left of the family. He worked. Day after day his mind empty, his body grew strong with the physical harshness of his work. The perpetual stink of the garbage was the backdrop of his existence. Crows, pi-dogs, flies, companions in his life's journey.

His attention to his work earned him more than money, the supervisors noted his lack of ambition, his dogged regularity with routine and were pleased. No troublemaker, they knew he was a captive of the system for life. Making his way towards a long, dull, middle-age once again his life changed. He was employed as a private cleaner for one of the flats in the locality.

Then he saw her.

And he fell in love.

9

The doorbell pealed loud, the tones sounding the theme of a popular film. He stood there feeling foolish. At forty-five, settled, secure, his life with his widowed mother smooth, free of the burr of domestic concerns, Roger Lawson was nervous about meeting Rupa Jaiswal in the cold, unblinking eye of morning.

The door opened, a cool draft of air-conditioned comfort drifted out, a stocky Nepali servant stood quietly looking at him inquiringly.

"Er...memsahib...?"

"Roger! How good to see you, come on in." Rupa, appearing from behind the silent Jeeves, nodded assurance to the servant, smiled warmly, a dressing gown of handloom yellow cotton transforming her from the glamorous woman of last night's ball into a housewife, busy with the day's work.

"I wondered if you'd care to visit to see how Carl Renshaw is this morning." The excuse was as flimsy as any lovelorn schoolboy's. He wished he had phoned before, or even sent word to her from the nursing home later in the day. How obvious he must look.

"Of course. How kind to take the trouble to ask me to visit with you." She smiled again. There was no sarcasm in the remark. Roger looked at her and detected no underlying irony. He relaxed.

"Have you any further word from the doctor or the medical staff?"

"No, but Dr Mitra lives just a few doors from here. He'll be in later this morning to tell me how the boy is getting on."

"Oh. Yes. I forgot you were a friend of Dr Mitra."

"We were in college together. I dropped out of medical studies to study business management instead. So here I am, marketing manager in an advertising agency that is not doing too well at the moment." She laughed ruefully.

"Would you care for a coffee? I was about to have a quick cup before I left for the nursing home."

"Yes, I'd love that. I'm a tea drinker myself. Too lazy to brew a good cup, that's why. My mother loves a blend of Orange Pekoe and Lapsong, and I've gone along with that. No real preference of my own."

"Well, let me convert you to coffee."

She called out and a young maidservant appeared.

"Two coffees Rani." Rupa looked at Roger. "Would you care for a dosa to go with that?"

"Dosa?'"

"Well nothing goes so well with South Indian coffee as a good dosa, masala of course." She sat before him on a low divan and pulled a side table towards her.

"Hmm...I'll take a pass on that one." Roger unused to this cuisine was again uncomfortable with the culture and etiquette of this assured woman.

"Don't look so apologetic Roger. Not everyone cares for a big breakfast. But you must know that we Marwaris love our stomachs, the reason we have such big ones." She gave another laugh, patting her rounded tummy.

"C'mon, after last night I think you deserve a good breakfast. Let me get you to sample a typical Jaiswal morning meal."

Roger, seated on a higher chair that looked down on the divan looked around for something more on an eye level with Rupa.

"What's the matter? Oh, do you want an easy chair?"

"No, no. I just wanted to sit where I could be level with you."

As he spoke the words, he could have bitten his tongue off. He sounded inept and bumbling.

"Why yes, I think that would be nice. Here, this is just the thing." She pushed a silk-covered hassock-y stool towards him.

"My, it feels I should kneel, not sit on it."

Again as soon as he said the words he felt foolish.

What was the matter with him? Everything he seemed to say sounded gauche.

She raised her eyebrows. The entrance of the maidservant with a tray saved any answer.

A silver tray. Two tall metal glasses, steaming fragrantly, a couple of thalis each with a crisp dosa, two smaller containers, one with dal, the other with a coconut chutney completed the meal. He looked at Rupa. She looked at him.

"Be brave and sample a different breakfast. It won't put on many kilos. This is healthy. Not many carbohydrates, no cholesterol to speak of."

He caught the teasing note and smiled as he shook out a napkin and sliced into the paper-thin dosa.

They both ate in silence. Companionably. He looked surreptitiously around the room. Affluence glowed in every polished surface. He ignored the large heavily ornamented portraits. Her parents or grandparents, he assumed, after a quick glance. Two stern faces looked straight ahead from heavy gilt frames. Books in untidy heaps on a side table, together with the day's newspapers and current magazines made an engaging litter. A series of prints splashed their vibrancy along the walls on either side of a large bay window. No expert on art, he had realised the social imprint of being familiar with schools of painting, this one, a genre he privately thought was a brittle depiction of Hindu mythology. A mid-nineteenth century print, the playful Krishna was seated with Radha in total bliss. Primary colours made their clothes and features leap out at one, the paintings spelt culture and class. His mother would have been puzzled by it. At first glance she would have been put off by the gaudiness and the unconventional features of the subjects. He thought of the framed Mona Lisa that hung in pride of place in his home, the alpha and omega of an interest in, or knowledge of art. This room could not be more different from his home. On the sideboard were a number of silver frames with dramatic black and white photographs of two young boys. Her sons. Confident, grinning, tousled-headed both held cricket bats. Cricket? Of course. The props of wealth. No football or hockey for these children. There were no photographs of Rupa. Neither, strangely, were there any icons of deities. A scatter of Kashmiri carpets divided the room into the living room and dining area. Metal lamps hung from the ceiling and a huge ceramic flowerpot made one corner a flowering bower, philodendrons waved large fronds.

A set of tablas were arranged in a corner and on the wall was a huge tapestry, a scene depicting a village wedding. Gujarati, Roger guessed. Again, he was struck by the joyousness of the work. Was it created by her, by someone in her family? He gazed captivated by its rich colours. He was fascinated by the décor. It was a new experience. Even the smells were different. He failed to identify any of the domestic fragrances–joss sticks, incense? There was a spicy cooking aroma in the room. He breathed it in and felt himself salivate. He was enjoying himself.

Guiltily he thought of the boy in the care of a neurosurgeon, wounded, vulnerable and here he was on this May morning relishing this gift of a woman's company, and delicious food. The young boy's health was ostensibly the reason for his visit. He *was* concerned. But at this moment he owed himself the intense pleasure of breakfasting with a fascinating woman. A woman he wanted to be in his life. He dismissed the silence of his mother when he mentioned this visit, he wanted Rupa to fit into his life.

"I'm not going to say a penny for them, but I'd still like to know what you intend doing after our visit to the nursing home." Rupa looked quizzically at him, a clean thali before her, she called the maid and swiftly their emptied dishes were removed.

"No thought worth mentioning, just savouring this coffee. But haven't yet decided on what we'd do today."

He was thrilled. She had removed the role-play of the dating game by calmly admitting she too was looking forward to a day with him.

"Another coffee?"

"Yes, we've got a bit of time. Visitors are only allowed after 10 am, and I think we qualify as visitors, we're not family."

"You forget that Dr Mitra is a friend, I can go and come whenever I want. Flexible rules huh!"

He laughed. Yes, the old tie network was useful.

A second tray was brought in, burnished metal glasses deliciously cold to the touch were placed before them with some savouries – *murrukus* – she explained, very 'more-ish.'

"Well, what are we going to do for the rest of the day. It *is* a holiday, damned bandh no less. Let's make the most of the traffic-less roads and take a drive to Diamond Harbour. It's quite a different place without the mess of lorries and trucks. And, the company has a small holiday apartment there."

Heaven on a plate, Roger thought. A day with her and in the luxury of a well appointed company flat.

"Let's go."

"Give me a moment. I'll get myself decent, won't keep you waiting long."

Plump, efficient hands brushing back her hair, she pushed herself up from the divan and vanished into the other room.

He sipped the ice-cold coffee, bit into the *murrukus* and thought he had never been so happy.

Carl Renshaw, injured, his life in jeopardy, was forgotten completely. As was the impending visit of Rupa's friend Dr Mitra.

"Hello, hello…is this 454849?"

"Yes, this is the Coates' residence, who is calling?"

"Yvonne? Yvonne…it's Sophia Lawson speaking. How are you?"

"Why *hi* Mrs Lawson. My goodness this is a pleasant surprise, I was sure it was a wrong number, we're having some crank calls and I'm a bit nervous about answering the phone now. I'm well thanks, considering last night's excitement. Thank goodness last night's rain has cooled things down a bit. Did you want to speak to Johnnie? I'm afraid he's out at the moment."

"No, no, my dear. It's you I wanted to have a chat with. Hope I'm not taking up your time?"

"Er…no, of course not. How can I help?"

"Actually it's a silly nothing really, was just wanting to know how well John knew this young woman who judged the competition last night – what was her name again?"

"Rupa Jaiswal."

"That's right."

"Well, Johnee's not here at the moment. He's the one who could answer your questions. I don't know much about her except she's a manager or something or other. And she was picked out by Prof Martin. You know he fell ill at the last minute. Don't know how he knew her. And Mrs Lawson, she's not *that* young y'know."

"Oh."

"She is divorced, with a couple of children."

"Oh."

"Yeah. My goodness, it's strange isn't it?"

"Well no, not really. It's a new world now. Almost everyone seems to have one in the family – a divorcée I mean."

"Oh yeah. Yeah. My auntie's brother's son has just separated from his wife. After twenty years. A shame, a terrible shame. They have a teenaged girl and boy now having to live in a broken home."

"That's so sad."

"But it's nice that Roger seems to have hit it off with Mrs Jaiswal, no? She seems to be very modern and up-to-date. Not at all like the women in most of these communities. Short hair and everything but I wish she'd not wear..."

"Yes. She is good looking and..."

"...a *nose* stud, otherwise she'd be quite attractive. Very funny that thing, it gives me the willies, putting a ring in your nose, like a, hahaha, like a, y'know, cow..."

"Well, it is unusual to see a woman of her class wear one of those, but I suppose you could get used to it. If it's fashionable very soon it will be quite common to see women wearing them."

"What! I don't think I'd ever be easy y'know, looking at someone flashing a stone plonked in the middle of her nostril...hahaha...no, don't think I could ever get used to that sort of ornament."

"I suppose it is odd to see jewels worn in noses, but look at some of the men these days, earrings, and after a while it doesn't look too bad. Quite fetching some of them."

"Oh Mrs Lawson you *are* naughty. What will Roger say! Anyway he certainly seems to like Mrs Jaiswal's looks."

"Hmmm."

"Oh, I do hope I haven't said anything I oughtn't to have?"

"Oh no, no. It's always interesting to talk of other people's lives. I suppose John is over at the nursing home? I was sure he'd go over to see how Kitty Renshaw's son was getting on."

"...mmm...yeah. Sure. He's very concerned over what happened last night. So sad. And that to have happened after their daughter was crowned May Queen."

"Wasn't she lovely. I think she's been the most elegant queen in years. How well she wore that sari."

"Hmm...frankly, well, if you must know, I think we should keep up our tradition of wearing dresses going. Our community is so small that it is important we carry on with our ways. Of course she *is* much older than many of the other girls."

"Really? I think she is only about five or six years older than most of them."

"Well my Heather is twenty – just – she turned twenty in March, a beautiful Pisces, hahahaha, not that I put much in all this astrological rubbish, but our Heather is such a looker, can't think where she gets her looks from…hahaha…the other day one of her professors said she had the rare blend of beauty and brains. But she's not pushy. But then she's so young and all. I think Grace Renshaw is at least twenty-eight, isn't she…steno or something somewhere isn't she?"

"Yes, she's about that. She's been working for some time. One of the top secretaries in the company. Roger tells me that she has the potential to head her own department."

"Really. Myee goodness."

"Yes. She's very bright and has a flair for management."

"Well it must be in the family. I think her mother was doing the same thing years ago."

"Yes. She was doing research for John's company."

"Myee, that was a long time ago. Imagine you remembering that Mrs Lawson, did you know the family well?"

"No, but my husband was Samuel Carter's friend. Samuel was on the board when she was employed, I think he said it was a pity she left the organisation after she married."

"Yeah. Johnnie knew her slightly, I think. We meet at the club sometimes."

"Kitty finds time for so much. She has done wonderfully with her family. Bob Renshaw dotes on her. It's good seeing that in this day and age with couples breaking up all over the place."

"Yeah. I've always told Johnnie they look a really happy bunch."

"They are. Good people. No pretensions."

"Bob is so funny, always ready with a joke. Nice man. No airs and *phutani* with him."

"Look I mustn't take up your time. Thank you for giving me so much of it. Tell John I called. Tell him I'd like to know how that poor boy is going."

"Oh sure. But I think your Roger will be going there and so will Mrs Jaiswal. You'll get all the news first-hand Mrs Lawson."

"That's right. I'm not sure if Roger will be coming home that soon. He said something about meeting friends later."

"Yeah. This bandh gives everyone a chance to have a bit of fun. Roger needs to have time with people of his age I think."

"Oh yes, of course. He's so caught up with business that now I scarcely see him. Flies around the country every other week."

"How exciting. We're going slow now. Johnnie likes the idea of being retired...haha..."

"Why, don't you?"

"Yeah, it's all right, I suppose. But it's hard to keep busy with so much time that we now have."

"Oh Yvonne, you must be one of the only people I know who complains about having too much time."

"Well there are only so many meetings I can go to and now Johnnie doesn't care to go out so often. He's turned a real stick-in-the-mud."

"He'll surely be busy with this investigation of last night's riot, to have to make a formal police inquiry and get that constable to make a statement, and look into this poor boy's accident."

"Yeah. We all will be involved I suppose."

"John has always been a wonderful president and you have been a wonderful first lady of the club. You both do so much, we will miss you if John decides to step down from the board."

"I don't think Johnny is ready to resign or retire from being president Mrs Lawson. Though I've heard people say that he's been there too long."

"Don't listen to what people say, you know that John has given more than just his time to making the club go back to its glory days, when..."

"...when *your* husband was president?"

"Well...yes. Though I realise that was a long time ago and things were different. With so many of our people emigrating it has been hard to keep up many of our traditions and ways."

"That's exactly, *exactly* what I was saying about the Renshaw girl wearing a sari and winning last night's May Queen crown. It's this sort of thing that will pull our ways down. Not that I have anything against wearing saris but c'mon let's show some unity by not bowing to what most of these people want us to do and be. That's why outside judges like this Marwari person should not really have been invited to be a judge."

"No Yvonne, no.. I can't agree with that. It's exactly this that will never get us into the mainstream of life here. We can't be on the sidelines. It's a silly way to go."

"Silly? Well, I don't know about that. It's seems practical and loyal to keep one's ways in spite of being a minority. Why should we change things like dress to please these people who are now in power? I don't see it as *silly* at all."

"Yvonne, I think times change and it's in the nature of things to change along with them."

"No, Mrs Lawson. I'm a railway girl. And I know how you earn respect, you don't just sit down and have it thrown at you. Y'know, if we took to wearing saris and started speaking Hindustani and allowing our servants to see us as being the same as them, it would get us laughed at."

"I don't think so, Yvonne."

"Well you may not *think* so, but I *know* so. My family never mixed with non-Christians or non-Anglo-Indians, or even Indian Christians, and we were one of the most respected families in the cantonment."

"Yvonne, I have to say I think that attitude is not a good one. It's a foolish one. It is not going to get you many friends. No friends at all really. Young people in our community don't think like this..."

"Mrs Lawson, I'm not that old. I know quite a bit about what young people think, my Heather tells me all about her college friends. I may not have finished high school but I'm not a fool. Wearing saris and having any and everyone join our club is a bad thing for our future. Now if you'll excuse me there's someone at the door. Bye."

Both women hung up on their conversations with feelings of utter and complete disgust for each other. Both felt the stupidity of the other. Both were angry. It was a precipitous start to a long, frustrating day.

Kitty Renshaw smiled disarmingly at John Coates.

Her soft face dimpled, the exhaustion of the night evident in the dark circles scoring her eyes.

"Hello John. Thanks for being here."

He caught her hands in his. The unbearable weight of memory swamped him and he quickly released them.

"Kitty. What can I say. I'm so sorry this has happened to Carl, he's such a fine lad. I'm sure Dr Mitra will do everything to see he's one hundred percent recovered."

The door squeaked open. The little South Indian nurse came in followed by Bob Renshaw.

"Hello John. Hell of a hot day out there, rain hasn't helped much." He spoke genially enough but he looked lost, off-balance.

"Bob," John Coates went over to him and embraced him.

Both men stepped back, caught unaware by the intensity of the moment.

The nurse gestured them to move aside and went over to the still figure on the bed hooked up to a wheezing machine. She checked the intravenous tubes, the catheter, his temperature, scribbled on the report sheet that she unhooked from the foot of the bed. Aside from the scratching of her biro there was silence in the small room.

Carl was a small figure hidden by the white sheet, his head crowned with a toque of bandages, tubes running from his mouth and his arm, his chest scarcely seemed to move. Kitty, John and Bob, a trio of hope, watched the young nurse go about the job of keeping Carl alive. She left with a dazzling smile, a small bob of the white-capped head and they were alone, waiting for the arrival of the doctor. After a few seconds the two men cleared their throats simultaneously. They laughed self-consciously, and Kitty watched, a knot of anxiety stifling her breathing.

"Wonder when this Mitra fellow will deign to arrive. Seems to be too busy to care for the one patient," Bob spoke angrily.

"Bob, Bob," Kitty spoke hastily, "remember to keep on his good side. He has Carl's life in his hands. He's under all kinds of pressure. Don't be so quick to judge him."

"Seems to me everything is money, power, and don't forget we are not one of them. No money, no bloody power."

He sounded brittle, bitter. Kitty frowned slightly. She turned towards Carl, her displeasure obvious. Bob touched her elbow and Kitty gently moved closer to him.

John stood immobile, witnessing the private agony of a family. He wondered at their daughter, the May Queen's absence. Exhausted?

Considerate of her parents' agony and wanting to give them privacy?.

Again the silence filled the room.

Voices loud and nearing broke the spell, the door opened and Dr Mitra followed by two young interns came in.

Brusquely nodding at them, he strode over to the bed, and after reading the report and checking Carl's breathing, began to speak in rapid-fire Bengali to his assistants.

After a long ten minutes, the doctor turned toward Kitty.

"We will operate this afternoon, and we need your signature on the agreement forms. Your son has a head trauma and we need to operate quickly to contain any possibility of further damage to the brain."

Kitty nodded. "Certainly, my husband and I will be here throughout. We will sign the papers as soon as you bring them to us."

Dr Mitra shuffled his papers. He looked at them briefly. Again he addressed Kitty. "The operation, should there be no complications, will not be more than three hours. We will need you to be available throughout."

"My wife and I will be here. I think that as parents we know we are needed during this time." Bob stared steadily at the doctor as he spoke. Without emphasis, with authority and a dignity the doctor could not ignore.

"Yes, yes. Then I will delay you no longer – oh *hello* Rupa!"

Outstretched hands and a beaming smile, Dr Mitra enveloped Rupa Jaiswal with a cordiality sharply contrasting with his abrupt demeanour displayed before the visitors.

"What a pleasure to see you here so early. Sorry I couldn't make it to your place this morning. I know I was told you might visit but I didn't think I might catch you at this hour." The tone was obsequious.

Roger Lawson hesitated at the door, not wanting to crowd the little room. He waved across the room to the Renshaws and John Coates.

Rupa moved towards Kitty.

"Mrs Renshaw. Mr Renshaw," she nodded at the couple. Normally articulate it was all she could say. "Hello John. Please. If there is anything I can do don't hesitate to let me know. With the bandh on today there is virtually no transport and my driver will be at your disposal."

Kitty's eyes filled. She cleared her throat. "Mrs Jaiswal, you have already done so much. We owe you forever for this." Her voice broke and she hastily stopped.

"All that matters is that Carl recovers, okay?"

Kitty murmured, "Yes, yes."

Bob Renshaw broke in, he went over to Rupa, and ignoring the doctor beside her, clasped her hand in both of his.

"All Kitty and I can say is thank you. Thank you."

John Coates' mind flew to the night previous, mere hours ago when Kitty and Bob watched their daughter as she stood dazed, in her moment of triumph and used those words in an entirely different mood, in a world away.

Dr Mitra spoke irritably to his two young assistants, he ignored the Renshaws, John Coates and Roger Lawson.

"Only two people in the room at one time, this *is* the ICU you know, not a club," he instructed the nurse, and again with a smile directed at Rupa he left the room.

The room darkened with sudden change of sky, monsoon clouds could be glimpsed, blue-black, threatening. The five looked at each other, Kitty and Bob Renshaw, John Coates united in anger, Roger Lawson and Rupa Jaiswal looking apologetic.

"What a nasty man." Kitty's voice was high and hysterical. "I hope he doesn't treat all patients this way?"

"I'm afraid Anil's manners graduated from kindergarten bully to post-graduate boor," Rupa spoke without heat, as she stated this fact, "I've known him most of my life and he always resisted making friends and influencing people."

"Odious man," Kitty muttered.

The men grunted in agreement. Nothing further was remarked upon, the good doctor's reputation was now set in concrete, healer he might be, Mr Nice Guy he was not. The whiff of discrimination was strong.

The nurse re-entered the room.

She stood there, hands fiddling with a watch pinned to her uniform, and they understood her unspoken request. Like bidden schoolchildren they filed out and made for the foyer where they prepared to do vigil for the rest of the morning.

Outside the rain beat down with a guttural rush. The harsh lashing of water louder than the buzz of the air-conditioning. The air was infected with a dampness that mingled with the sweat and stickiness of the past weeks. Thunder grumbled. Already the walls were growing moist to the touch. For a brief couple of seconds the lights flickered and then came on again, brighter than before. The room sprung into view again, bright, if not cheerful. Everyone gave a laugh of relief.

In spite of the nail-biting tension Kitty felt her mood lift.

Ah, the rain. How she loved it. The worst of summer was over, the year promised only good things from now on, even the humidity between storms was welcomed. Anything rather than the tightening monotony of summer. It was now almost carnival time. The Pujas, birthdays, and the year went faster and faster till it spun out of control towards the happy chaos of Christmas and the New Year. It was a time for falling in love. She had fallen in love for the first time in the month of June. Did John remember, she wondered. What silly young fools they were. How pompous he was and how he broke her heart. Looking at him now, a paunch cutting a clumsy profile, she compared him with her still spruce and handsome Bob. Dear Bob. So faithful, believing, predictable and a little bit dull. She caught John's eye and smiled mischievously.

Surprised, he smiled back raising his eyebrows in unspoken question.

Bob Renshaw glancing at his wife wondered what it was that had made her smile at John Coates.

Rupa breathed deeply, her head resting against the cool concrete of the wall, she admired the quiet strength of Kitty Renshaw. Oddly enough, Rupa marvelled, even though keeping vigil for her son, the impression she gave was one of relaxed acceptance.

The vibration of the rain rapped frenetically against the double-glazed windows.

A crackle of lightning ripped through the clouds, seconds later a satisfying clap of thunder completed the duet.

"Well," Roger said, "I think the monsoons have finally broken."

10

Make him love me Lord.
Let me not give into spite.
Make me make something of this decision.
Don't give up on me.
Make Pradip love me.
Let him learn to look after me.
I'm tired. I want to rest.
I need to have a reward for always doing what I've been told is right.
Don't punish me for stumbling along the way.
Sorry? No, I'm not.
It's a comforting thing I've done.
Maybe the rules say it shouldn't be, but
You know the nonsense laws are..
Keep people kind.
And forgiving.
Give me a chance to be happy
Make me a present of these days.
Wrap my future in safety.
Don't judge me.
Be loving.
I'll be good. I *am* good. You know that.
Try to get others to know that as well.
Look after us. Please.
We need someone to care.
Send us a little more comfort, this leaky roof is hopeless.
Money is welcome, but understanding also helps.
Are You really angry with me?
I won't say give me a sign. That is *so* childish.
I'm not a schoolgirl, I'm not a fool.

I will go on talking to You and hope that one day I'll feel You are talking back to me.

All these years I've been waiting for something. Pradip? Perhaps this is it.

Nothing much. But yes, there has been kindness.

He's not so bad, he's given me the rose Mum showed me when I was a little girl.

There has been satisfaction.

Would it be blasphemy to call you Dad? Well Dad, keep a close watch on things here.

I may have made a huge mistake, blotted my reputation and life.

I hope not.

I'm counting on You to bail me out if things go wrong.

And I know You will. As the servants here are so fond of saying You are my Mother and Father, my Maa-Baap.

So Mum and Dad, keep Your promise to protect and look after me.

I have done a fair share of looking after, it's about time I took it easy.

Give me a bit more from life than what I've been given so far.

So Hear me. Help me.

Glaring in impotent rage at the rain Eddie D'Cruze slammed the windows shut. The wooden shutters had warped and a steady stream trickled indoors, a pool of water spreading on the floor. In the bedroom a leak, a drip of rain positioned immediately above Eddie's bed had spread an irregular patch on the ceiling. He had had to spend the night in the adjacent bedroom, a large metal pan placed on his bed collecting the monsoon's offering. A stray cat sneaked into the flat sheltering from the storm and crouched under the bookshelf. Fur in comical spikes it looked fearfully at the feet of Eddie as he marched around from room to room fastening the little flat against the force of the storm.

"Where are the candles? Sure to be a power cut later on. Where are they?" he muttered.

He rummaged through drawers making accumulated household bits and pieces clatter and clash, the noise subdued by the fury of the monsoon outside. Cockroaches melting into the cracks, a whispering scuttle as he flung open musty cupboards.

"Housekeeper? Look at this, look at this. She never really worked as she ought to have. Dirty. Hiding the muck. Sly. Never spoke much. So what was she doing eh, *what* was she doing? Took after her father's side. No-good, illiterates, boozers, skirt-chasers. Who asked her mother to marry into railway rubbish?"

Eddie's mind jumped back to life as it had been with his sister.

How lovely she had been – Chloe – the brains of the family. The one destined to go on to higher things, no clerical jobs, no typist, no shop-girl drudgery or run-of-the-mill 'womanly' occupations. Not for her was the mediocrity of being someone's dogsbody. She was destined to become a brilliant surgeon, a doctor, a psychiatrist.

Her laugh was infectious, her academic brilliance never diminishing, her personality had an ebullience, a floating goodness of spirit. What hopes their parents had nurtured for this unexpected flowering in their family. Then of course she had met the dashing Ronnie Ridout. It was with the taste of ashes in their mouths that their parents had consented to a marriage a mere five months after their daughter introduced the man to them. How the quick-talking young man had won over their girl they could never fathom. How do these things happen Eddie wondered. It was a travesty of hope, of promise.

It was good his parents' deaths from as innocuous an illness as a bout of flu, spiralling into pneumonia prevented them from the satisfaction of saying an 'I told you so'. And now of course there was the slap in the face that he had suffered from Lucy.

Lucy.

Eddie felt his anger surge when he thought of this most recent betrayal. Her absence was an unhealed hurt. Everything reminded him of her. His life was falling to bits around him. In the span of just two days his routine was shaken. Ashamed, he refused to seek help, refused to talk about this heartbreak in his life. It was a weakness that alarmed him when he found himself near tears. Thinking back on his breakdown in front of Hilary Johnson he ground his teeth in shame. How could he have let his barrier down? What must she think of him? She was the lovely keeper of this block of flats. If anyone had the keys to his respect and admiration it was the still lovely Mrs Johnson. He'd usually mumble a gruff goodmorning, goodevening or a hellohowareyou to her in passing. Almost every day, 'goodmorninggoodeveninghellohowareyou'. A lifetime of being single and self-centred had frozen social affability. His low stock of small talk marooned him. But he yearned to speak, to be at ease in her company. When the pain of Lucy's desertion broke over him it was to her he instinctively fled. And he hated himself for giving in to this weakness. Did she laugh at him?

The years of living with thin, distempered walls separating their lives, were but a painful reminder that they might well live on the other sides of the moon, so far removed were they in everyday contact. The old mother-in-law, wrinkled face set against small acts of courtesy, he avoided, the pinched-faced husband he scarcely saw bar a few Sunday mornings when he'd be out with his son, it was always her he saw, and the air of kindness she exuded. Readily smiling, even when he'd pretend not to see her, a wave, a few words and Hilary Johnson unwittingly set herself as heroine and star of Eddie D'Cruze's heart.

And what had he done in the long dull years without family, without close friends? He had grown into a desk-bound robot, whiling away his life filling forms in triplicate and trying to maintain an ageing and ill-equipped transport system. The once proudly maintained Calcutta Tramways crumbled into a mockery of what it had been. Unable to keep up with the swelling population, trams trundled on, grinding their daily journey through the potholed streets of the city. Raddled, they reminded Eddie of slugs, inching their way, groaning, heaving their way through the clogged veins of the city. Then abruptly it was over. A thin gathering of his colleagues presented him with a HMT watch, a few refreshments served with forced chat, after an hour everyone returned to their work and Eddie went to his work-cabin where he collected his china mug, his footstool, souvenir from Santiniketan, a framed photograph of Lucy and walked out of that tacky building forever.

"Kaun hai?" He shouted at a rattle of the doorknob.

"Hum hai."

It was the bloody sweeper. He opened the door to the crooked man standing there, gruffly answered his namaste, and walked back to his newspaper and sat staring at the day's crossword.

Silently the servant shuffled into the bathroom where the day's noises began, signalling the start of the day.

11

Plucked from dreams, Grace awoke and for seconds, still sleep dazed, looked at the crumpled sari lying on the floor. There was a silence at odds with the time of day. Street sounds were subdued. Even the usual yells of children playing below and the periodic calls from their parents were missing. The rain drummed on the corrugated roof of the huts that fronted the flats on its western side. Then she recalled the bandh. She sat up, propelled by the misery of the night's drama. Guiltily she realised she had slept through her parent's arrival and their departure. Hastily she leapt up and raced into her shower. The water trickled through. The pump had not been switched on, the man in charge had obviously seen the bandh as a day to ease his schedule as well. Managing with mugfuls of water from the vat in the tiny bathroom she finished a quick bath and rapidly dressed and ate the breakfast set before her.

"Abdul!"

Their cook appeared from the kitchen, smiling gently, as he began taking up her breakfast things.

"Haan, missybaba?"

"Saab, memsahib kyaa time chala gyaa?"

"Bahut saverai."

"Saat, sare saat baje gaya?"

"Haan missybaba."

She had slept through while her parents had come back from the nursing home and again left early to be there. They must have had just about a couple of hours rest. A sick feeling crept through her. The deep refreshing sleep seemed a mockery of the agony her family were undergoing. This damned bandh, it transfixed everything. No transport, no shops opened, no easy access to any kind of information. The radio mouthed government prepared statements, there was no clear picture of what was really going on. The dour leader of the party in power insisted that the Opposition were planning the demise of the state. Someone was on a fast unto death. Grace switched the radio off.

Did Kay know of Carl's accident? Had anyone thought of phoning or sending a telegram to her? How had her parents travelled to the nursing home? Rickshaw, or was it through the largesse of the godmother of all that was easy and luxurious – Rupa Jaiswal? How was she to go now and meet them there? The roads surely must be flooded. The phone they used in emergencies was in the local store, and that was closed today. A sudden down-sweep of mood engulfed her. Everything seemed pointless, silly. She thought briefly of her friend Lucy. Whatever had happened to her. She looked around at the flat and saw shabbiness and life rubbed thin. Where was the family going with their safe, forgettable jobs? Was Carl going to make a recovery and how long would that take? She stared unseeingly at Carl's guitar, scuffed along the bridge, its wooden sheen dull, scratched. Jumbo slept soundly, the old pi-dog, Carl's much loved pet, now showing his twelve years in his slower walk and longer naps. A knock at the door aroused her and she flew to see who it was.

"Grace!"

Daryl Jackson stood there, eyes full of compassion.

He stepped into the hall quietly, closed the door. His shirt was wet, hair sleek with the rain. His shoes squelched and damp marks followed him like an old misdemeanour. Her composure faltered, she was alarmed to feel tears gather. He stood looking at her and she knew then that he loved her.

As if it were the most natural thing he put his arms around her and they stood in that small room silent, in harmony.

She started to say something, but he shook his head.

"Come now. If you're ready, we'll go and meet your parents in the nursing home."

"How did you know?" she asked inadequately.

Daryl smiled. "Oh Grace. I know because I have to know. I heard about Carl from Mr Coates who phoned me this morning. He asked me to come over and see how you were. And of course I came as quickly as I could."

This was no filigreed declaration of love. The simple words revealed all Grace wanted to hear.

Why did it have to be this ending, with this hero? Immediately ashamed of her ungrateful thought Grace looked up at Daryl and smiled.

Daryl Jackson was prepared to give her his life. She decided there and then to settle for contentment. She hoped the warmth of her feelings today could grow into love.

Her parent's approval was there, waiting to be given leave to ring out. Their patience rewarded.

Carl liked him. Yes, Carl's recovery had a lot going for it. A potential brother-in-law with a common interest in kung-fu, black belts, ju-jitsu. Never mind the differing taste in film. She now saw lucidly, it was not Daryl Jackson who was the pompous one, it was her. Self-righteous and prim, her distastes were nothing but childish petulance.

Andy Kaul was now fading, a spectre. She looked into the days that would hurry her to a new life. Security lay in this man's avowal. Security and a monotonous tumbling into age, tamping down of the buzz and fizz of her life. She swallowed a sigh.

"Let's hurry then," Grace mumbled, "we have news to get."

"And news to give."

No comfortable domestic sounds punctuated the Johnson's flat. Rain streaked the walls and already telltale signs of mould were discernible behind the thin buff-coloured distemper. The storm which had been blowing and blustering around since dawn seemed to grow becalmed. There was a shivery feel in the air and Hilary sneezed, a soft bubble of sound. The day had gone wrong from the start. No Oleg fluttered around, its gurgle, an annoyance usually, was now sorely absent. Ralph refused to talk to anyone and had chosen to go out with his grandmother and father to see if a few of the neighbouring shops were open. The larder was short of sugar, red dal and butter.

Edna, quiet after the debacle of the morning had told Hilary that if either Fred or Ralph would accompany her she might be able to get these necessities from a shopkeeper she knew. It was about 9.30 am, the sky was gunmetal grey. Their radio reception had been punctured by static, making the news all but incomprehensible. All India Radio's news presenter, speaking with the strangulated accent many thought indicated public school English, announced that the city was peaceful, demonstrators had been controlled, and a member of the opposition had started a fast unto death and could be met at his residence through the day.

"What a joke," thought Hilary. She remembered when she surprised Fred during their brief courtship by asking if he was interested in politics.

"No," was his short reply.

And there was no continuing of that discussion.

Why is it, she wondered, notwithstanding having a charismatic woman leading their nation, most assumed women were uninterested in the happenings of the world. She had been avidly interested in the political doings of the country. Calcutta was riveting with its longstanding Communist party, its leader who kept surprising voters with his longevity and tenacity in staying in office. Even if her interest had been of a somewhat gossipy kind, it fuelled a curiosity that propelled her beyond the ghetto of community and family constraints.

Leaving school before the final year, Hilary had then been thrilled to get a job quickly as a receptionist with an international airline. Her looks undoubtedly had been what leapfrogged her into the workforce. Quick to learn, she had mastered an engaging phone manner and soon learnt how to deal with the public and private demands of a volatile industry. Without a background in any of the fine arts she gleaned a surface sangfroid when talking to the higher-ups of the company.

Again, with English as her mother-tongue it was to Hilary the managers often turned to when dealing with foreign visitors, their culture and manners. The Americans she charmed with a knowledge of their current politics, she recommended restaurants where the best steaks in town were served, and of course, film. She astounded the more naïve with an in-depth familiarity with Hollywood, its beautiful people and the gossip that delighted. Then there were the English. No problem there, Hilary argued to herself, why she herself was almost English.

Strangely enough the English visitors were less inviting, not warming to the slightly cheeky, attractive young girl who manned the front desk. Her forays into conversation were met with a cool formality. There was a slight frost when she attempted a joke or waved a hello.

"Stupid buggers," was her father's response. "Always wanting to look down their noses at anyone they think not pucca enough."

The ghost of racism wavered here but Hilary was not too put off by this slur, and blossomed with the daily honing of her skills by the job's demands.

"The Japanese are lovely, so are the Germans," she once commented.

"Ha ha, took a couple of wars to teach *them* some manners eh?" Neither parent shared her impartial views on the new global powers.

Australians, New Zealanders, Europeans, Africans of Indian origin, Hilary was fascinated by the fact that the world was at her desk. Her enthusiasm was catchy and her bosses realised with a bit of tutoring, Hilary might easily fit into the higher echelons of the company. Her looks didn't do her any harm either. With her dimpled smile and grey eyes, Hilary was a good front person and advertisement for the décor of the organisation.

For more than a year Hilary lived a life that forced her out of her comfortable confines of family and school friends. Accents, she learnt, didn't matter. Appearances were a bonus but in the long run had nothing to do with the worth of a person. She was rapidly growing into a sophisticated woman mixing easily, with a piquant familiarity that seemed to win popularity with staff and clientele.

Then of course Fred Johnson walked into her life and after a flatteringly short period of time asked her to marry him.

Now, a couple of decades later, dulled by domesticity, an innate sparkle gone with middle-age claiming her bubbly personality, Hilary was not resentful, but often fantasised over what might have been. Perhaps she might have commanded a position in the business of travel and hospitality, a field that was rapidly gaining popularity with young women.

Studying her reflection in the small mirror she saw the rounded shoulders, a slight paunch, sagging breasts, and a comfortable band of flesh under her chin, but the grey eyes, the delicate features still commanded a second look. She smiled and thought of the boy who told her she looked like an Anglo-Indian Sandra Dee. Poor old Sandra Dee.

Burnt-out as she was burnt-out?

Most of the scheduled to-do things on life's menu had been fulfilled, marriage, a child, a steady lifestyle. And the daily ache of not being true to whatever the dream was you had when you looked like Sandra Dee. She bared her teeth at the mirror. Pearly white? Hmm, thankfully nothing wrong with them, no fillings yet.

She shook her hair and pulled a fringe over her eyes. She pirouetted before the bedroom mirror. Then laughed softly at how absurdly she was behaving. Behave yourself Hilary Baker. You're not a sixteen anymore. She ran her tongue over her upper lip and again laughed at how this was supposed to be a turn-on for the boys. Well it did things for Fred, no mistake about that.

This bandh was wonderful, a silence gentled the day. She loved the rain. What had happened at the Renshaws last night? A drunken Bob? Surely not. A more proper man she had yet to meet. Did Grace have an encounter with a rowdy boyfriend? No. Grace did not seem the careless young type to indulge in that kind of fun. Strange girl. Not as strange as poor little Lucy upstairs though. How was old Eddie D'Cruze getting on with his heartbreak. Odd that he should come to her to pour out his woes.

She roused herself. A lethargy hung around her. Chores waited. Maybe it was the unsettling midnight storm that had battened her normal bustle. It was time for a mid-morning cuppa. She glanced around and saw a meagre and even mean lifestyle. It had Fred's signature with the cheap furnishings and sparse style. Even the photographs on the wall were framed by a plain wood, plywood, a small black and white memento of their wedding, a picture of Ralph with Oleg on his shoulder, a framed certificate of one of Fred's diplomas, another cut-out of a pretty seaside resort somewhere in the western world – Brazil, Rio, Copacabana – she really didn't know, it was always there with its dazzling sand, blue sea and bluer sky. She found it incredibly silly. A child's kindergarten colouring of what a holiday might look like.

Thank god neither Fred nor his mother insisted on that fixture of kitsch, three ceramic ducks flying up a wall, or a plastic Taj Mahal. If they had, Hilary smiled to herself, she would have probably agreed quietly to tack it up to their stark walls and grow to ignore its banality. She realised that a nail was loose and their wedding picture was hanging more by determination than a sturdy peg. Walking to the tool drawer she rifled through searching for a small hammer or mallet to fasten it when she heard a quiet shuffle outside the door.

Jerked to the present from her mulling she wondered who was standing there, not knocking but waiting for someone to open the door.

"Kaun hai?"

Quiet sounds and the banister creaked with the weight of someone leaning against it.

"Kaun hai'?"

"Kholo memsahib, Kholo. Hum hai, hum hai."

The damned sweeper again.

What did he want this time, she wondered. He had knocked earlier before the family could go out and asked if they needed him to purchase any of the groceries after the official end of the bandh, at 4:00 pm.

Fred had been irritated by the unusual request and curtly told the man they needed nothing.

Edna watched the servant as he wriggled, grinned, and ingratiated himself before Fred.

"He's a one to watch then," she commented, "bet you anything he's planning to pinch a few of the household stores."

"Stop talking nonsense Mum," Fred for once impatient with his mother's usual suspicions, "the man is trying to help us."

"Nahin, nahin, shukria."

Ralph pushed past the little hunchback and looked at his father and grandmother, lips bunched up in a knot of anger. He ignored Hilary, his way of showing his displeasure to her.

How like Fred he looks now, Hilary thought.

The sweeper had stood there, twisting a piece of his flimsy shirt in his hand. He gave Hilary a sweeping greeting.

"Salaam, salaam."

She had smiled and turned away. She wished that they would all leave soon, before the rain started again. The sky looked heavy, no dramatic play of clouds or thunder but a surly foretaste of storms and the subsequent heat that would sizzle through the wet, damp walls and pavements.

With a murmur of words she scarcely heard, the lot of them, family and sweeper, went out of the room and she was alone.

She rifled through the news. Scanned the advertisements, wondered if she ever might have been a copywriter in the advertising industry. A cup of tea retained its warmth, a couple of Britannia biscuits crumbled in its saucer. A crow alighted on the window, its sleek purple black feathers polished, shining. Eggshells and some breadcrumbs from the morning's breakfast were the reason these patrolmen of the city's skies were regular visitors.

"Here, you rascal. Here." The crow jumped down, cocked its head, watched her while pecking harshly at the shards of shell. *Krutkrutkru,* its beak tapping on the wood. *Krutkrutkrut...*

A few more crows circled, flapping noisily. She scraped the dish free of its messy breakfast remains and clicked her tongue at the birds. They cawed back at her. Clever devils. *Krutkrutkrut,* the rapid beat of the beaks a pulse beat in her head.

Krutkrutkrut.

Where was Oleg? The gurgling of the bird so much part of the sounds of the day, the present silence was unsettling.

Blessed relief to be by herself, and not answer to her son, her husband's or her mother-in-law's moods or voices. Different moods, different voices, same demands.

A glance at the clock and she was surprised to see that already it was half an hour since she had waved her family off on their errand.

Now here was her brief respite interrupted by this man yet again knocking at their door.

"*Thero, thero,* I'm opening the door."

With a whine the front door eased open. The rain had already warped its frame, the screech of wood on the concrete floor set her teeth on edge.

He stood there, twisting his raggedly shirt in his hands. Looking into the house he asked if he could finish his work at this hour instead of the usual afternoon time slot.

Hilary was annoyed.

She was anticipating a rare moment of quiet, a cup of tea, a leisurely read of yesterday's newspapers, the bandh had not allowed the morning's papers to be delivered, and here was this unusual burr in the morning's ease.

The hunchback turned sideways he twisted a ragged cloth in his hands. A pang of pity made her change her mind. Let the man do his work at his time. Surely he had a right to take advantage of this damned bandh. . The politicians who were jumping up and down might learn a lesson from the arid life this voter endured.

"Aa jao, come in."

Another screech as the wood jarred on the sill.

She shut the door and it shuddered close.

Oleg perched on the pinewood pelmet in the Vincents' living room. He looked down on the upturned face of Henry Vincent and with a slight bob excreted a splash of milky liquid on Henry's arm.

"Sala, the filthy thing has shat on me again. How long is this going to go on for? I told you this would happen."

"Arré yaar, what's the fuss about, bird's dirt won't kill you. Good luck it brings."

"Bloody rot you talk. Good luck. Rubbish, rubbish." Husband and wife yet again glared at each other. Oleg gurgled loudly.

"Come here you *harami."*

"Don't be stupid. Why are you abusing the poor bird?"

"Chup karo. Let me be. I'll kill the damn thing when I get it."

The old man lunged feebly towards the bird. The bird with a graceful movement skirted the rim of the pelmet and stopped inches out of reach.

"Haramzada."

"No, slowly, *aasté,* it'll fly away if you shout."

"Oh, now I've got to whisper. Anything else I should do?"

"Aasté, aasté."

Henry clambered down slowly from the high stool. He pushed it along the length of the door, under where the bird was now.

He breathed noisily.

"Why are we taking this trouble for some people who don't even care to wish us I don't know. Open the window and let the thing fly out again."

"Get it now. It's closed its eyes. Now, *now."* Fatima ignored her husband's mutterings.

Once again he climbed on the stool. This time he was directly under the bird.

With a lunge he threw a small towel over the bird and it deftly landed on the startled Oleg.

"Aah, at last. Come here, *aaou, aaou,* you bugger."

"*Aasté*, gently, gently."

"Shut up, *chup, chup,* help me down."

With a struggling bird firmly under his arm, Henry hunched down and leaning heavily on his wife, almost slid down to the floor.

"Ooh, ooh, are you hurt?"

Another glare and Henry straightened, shifted the bird and grasped the towel under its feet.

"Now get rid of this damned thing. Open the door."

"All right, all right. I think I heard their front door opened a little while ago. One of the servants I think, that sweeper, cripple fellow."

Fatima shuffled to the heavy door swung it open and looked out. She peered around at the closed door of their neighbour.

"Doesn't seem as if anyone's at home. Door's shut. I don't hear anything now. No sounds of that sweeper, he usually makes such a damned noise."

"The lot of them went out, I'm sure. I heard husband, mother and boy go out. Mrs Johnson must be alone in there."

Henry's thoughts briefly skittered to how that woman could be part of a family that rarely smiled. She was, he searched for the word, sweet.

"Funny we can't hear the servant at work."

Through the thin walls they now heard an odd sound coming from the flat next door. It was of a scraping, teeth-jarring scrapings that was going on bumpily.

Something crashed. They both jumped. Glass? A loose picture, plates?

Henry stared at Fatima. This was peculiar. What was happening next door? They knew the Johnsons kept no servant, but that hunchback. What was this then?

Henry thumped on the adjoining wall.

"Helloo, hellooo…Mrs Johnson, need any help there?"

Silence.

After the thuds, crashings and glass splintering sounds this silence was stranger.

"Helloo, helloo…Mrs Johnson…Mrs Johnson…helloo?"

Fatima looked at Henry impatiently.

"Stop yelling, go and see what's happening…"

"Suppose they think I'm poking my nose in…I'd feel a fool."

"But who's there?"

"You said you heard all of them go out."

A scream interrupted them. Another scream was suddenly cut off.

Their bickering skid to a stop with a thudding down the stairs, and Eddie D'Cruze came panting to their door. He was in pyjamas, a torn singlet and bathroom slippers.

"What was that noise? Why are you shouting for Mrs Johnson? Is she there?"

The Vincent's stared at him, words failing to conjure their concern and curiosity.

"What's wrong, what's wrong? Is it Hilary? Hilary, *Hilary, Hilary,*" Eddie D'Cruze's voice hoarse cracked and unaware of the strange figure he cut, hair tousled, his thin chest heaving, barely covered by the shabby singlet.

"Hey, hey, hey, take it easy, we don't know what's happening. Both Fatima and I heard something falling down, something breaking and crashing, screaming."

"Yes, yes, I heard that too. For Christ's sake we've got to do something, get out of the way, *get out,* move, *move,"* Eddie D'Cruze roared.

Abruptly Eddie broke off and rushed to the closed door and smashed his body against it.

"What's wrong there? Hilary, Hilary, it's Eddie, Eddie D'Cruze from upstairs. What's broken? My god, answer me, say something, just yell, yell to us that you are all right."

Abruptly the door fell open.

The three of them burst through, tripping on each other's slippers, rushed in and stopped, looking at the tableau before them, stupefied.

Lucy watched Pradip as he readied himself for his working day at the garage.

He was wet from his morning bath. Singing tunelessly he scrutinised himself in the tiny shard of a mirror that hung alongside the small barred window. Utterly absorbed in gazing at his reflection, he scraped noisily at his chin, his cheeks, pulling his lips in to wipe the soap off his upper and lower lip. He slapped his face and blew his cheeks out to examine closely if he had neglected a spot. That done he slapped his face lightly.

The sound of the tapping reminded Lucy of her mother and the ritual of bathing and washing which was turned into a game. First her mother would rap lightly on her forehead and sing out, 'Knock at the door,' then she'd gently pull Lucy's eyes and pull them down, 'Peep in,' next she'd tweak her nose and call out 'Open the latch', then, with Lucy giggling delighted, open her mouth 'Walk in', finally the taps on her cheeks with the accompanying 'Take a chair', 'Sit down there,' and as the coup-de-grace, a fist placed under her chin with a rousing 'Good morning Mr Teddy Bear.' And Lucy would roll around laughing and her father would gather her up and toss her till she shrieked and grew red in the face. She remembered. A half-smile still on her face she saw Pradip looking at her.

She read in his eyes a slight embarrassment and a question.

"What are you staring at *yaar*?"

He looks at her as she lounges, queenly, assured on their cotton mattress.

"You look so handsome."

He immediately smiles. Content, he begins combing his hair. Whistling through his teeth he pours oil into the hollow of his hand and begins carefully to knead it through his thick glossy hair. His square workman's fingers threading the oil into his scalp. Over and over again the oil is massaged and Pradip is utterly absorbed. Again he looks up and sees her staring at him.

"What's the matter *yaar?* Why the long looks?"

This time there was a touch of annoyance in his tone.

Lucy shook herself clear of memories.

"Can't I look at you? You are very lookable, you know."

Pradip smiles uncertainly, the English language and its subtleties slipping out of reach.

"Well, why don't you hurry with my breakfast then. This bandh *d*oesn't mean that I can stay in bed. More people will want to come and have their cars, bikes and scooters seen to."

"Well then, it's good then isn't it, business will bring in rupees for Mr Raj and you, won't it?"

"You making a joke?

Pradip frowning, wondering if this girl were mocking him.

Arée, these *firangi* types were never good at respecting men, respecting their husbands. Pradip heard his father warn him against the western-type woman.

"Too much reading and schooling, that's when they start to get different ideas. How can you respect a woman who works in offices with men all day long, who knows what goes on there eh?" And the old man would spit, a red-flecked gob of paan, his contempt for what he felt was a betrayal of the old ways of life.

Pradip saw his mother, sari pulled over her head to skim her eyes, walking with a sideways tilt, carrying glasses of tea, their plates of rice and bottles of water for their main meal, fetching and carrying, fetching and carrying for his father, for his brothers, for him. She'd sit hunched over the wickedly sharp *bonty* shearing the skins of vegetables, the scales of fish, with amazing precision. He'd watch as she would dice and then gather the symmetrical pieces into a palm-leafed tray and place it on the ledge in the corner of their house. There was no conversation. Talk was economical, sparse, and completely practical. Usually it revolved around money. The earning of it, the spending of it, the saving of it and the burning hope of getting more of it.

He recalled bitterly the bidis and paan his father sent him out to buy every evening. But not one laddoo for any of us, Pradip ground his teeth at the memory. He thought of his aunt, his mother's sister. There was a woman he disliked. Slyly urging on his mother to wail about her troubles, looking sorrowfully at him when his mother bemoaned their struggles, all the while enjoying the harshness of a life she was apart from and protected against. Widowed early and childless, she was granted a small pension from her husband's clerical government job. Financially secure she'd help his mother with the occasional food parcel. Their thanks then would be never-ending with her looking at him and smiling grimly as he touched her feet and murmured his gratitude. Yes, he enjoyed the fish, yes he never ate such delicious *gur,* but surely the chutney she brought them was the best in the country, and definitely this aunt was the biggest hypocrite in the world.

"What's the matter Pradip?"

"Nahin, nahin." He threw down the towel and flung the comb carelessly on the small wooden shelf. Roughly he pulled his shirt over his head and

began rustling with unnecessary noise in the cupboard for something. Slamming the doors and kicking shut the warped door he sat down on their sole chair and looked pointedly at the mug and tea kettle still in the bucket waiting to be washed and dried.

Lucy looked away. His tantrum had began to pall. She has lived most of her life with a man who kept his voice and emotions under control. A display of anger or love was unheard of in their circle of two. Was this a childish passion headed towards a quick snuff-out? Raised voices belonged to the class of people they connected with the likes of the Vincents, not polished, not well-mannered. Shouting, screeching at each other, their neighbours privy to their family anger, family quarrels, they were established entertainment in that shabby building.

"Are you ready for breakfast?"

"*Arre yaar,* what am I sitting here for then, to look at myself in the mirror?"

Lucy swiftly rose, and pulled the kerosene stove from under the kitchen table and began the ritual of lighting it, filling the kettle for his tea and readying the flat hotplate for the frying of Pradip's chapattis. Pradip ate quickly, noisily. He scooped the chapattis with the curried potatoes to his mouth, chewed with gusto and talked throughout. He spoke of the dream he had last night, the noise the crows made on their tin roof, the new shirt he needed to wear for a coming visit of Sri Raj's cousins to the garage, Lucy nodding in the right pauses was silent throughout. Finally he looked up at her, he frowned at the abstract look she maintained.

"What will you do today? Are you going to cook some of that *bhaji* you said you'd make this Monday?"

Lucy turned and looked out of their small barred window.

She hardly heard him.

Today was what she felt was genuinely the first day of the rest of her life. So what was she going to do? Nothing much. It was a bandh, the city was resting and she intended to rest as well. Perhaps she might clear and clean this small room to resemble a comfortable home. It lacked a proper mattress, she determined to put one down, even if on the floor, it would be an improvement on the stringed charpoy they both used last night. Ruefully she arched her back and felt her muscles protest. Lovemaking did not do well on sagging rope netting. Besides she was certain the damn thing had bugs in it. The wood and the rough coir matting was an invitation for vermin to burrow in. Yes, she must get rid of it.

Pradip smacked his lips, went over to the small bucket, splashed water on his face and mouth. Obviously content with the breakfast he slipped into a bush shirt, the worn blue-checked one he donned for work.

"Well are you going to see me off or do I have to go without any help from my woman?"

Trying not to wince at the archaic image the words evoked Lucy smiled and went over to him with a small package, chapattis rolled with lime pickle to make his mid-morning meal a tasty one.

She put her arms around him. Pradip stood stiffly, he never seemed comfortable with casual shows of affection.

"What's the matter? Don't you want a little of last night?"

He stepped back.

"Stop that. Last night was dark. We do that when there is no light. Don't be shameless *yaar.* What sort of talk is that? *Chee, chee.*"

Lucy giggled. She tickled his neck and tried to nuzzle him but he pushed away sharply and she stumbled.

"I told you, not now. What's the matter with you? Don't behave like a *rundi, yaar.*"

The words stung.

She stepped back and wiped her hands against the cheap fabric of the sari she was wearing. What a wicked thing to say, was her first thought. What a stupid man Pradip is, was her second. She stared, at a loss for words.

Was this then the cultural difference her uncle spoke of, was this the divide that separated person from person?

Pradip sensing a change in her hastily moved towards her.

"Don't look like that *yaar,* it's just that I'm in a hurry and it's already late, don't know if the bandh will cause trouble with the workers down the street."

Lucy turned away. She swiftly collected the breakfast crockery and dusted the small table free of crumbs.

The door grated sharply as it always did and then as Pradip tried to slam it, an indication of his pique, finally closed. He was gone.

She breathed a sigh of relief. Alone. Alone and free. She stared at the barred window and grimaced.. Overhead the scrabbling of the crows on the roof tapped loud, incessant. The silence was odd, then she remembered the bandh. The silence was disturbed by a far-off row, voices raised in a bees' angry humming. What was unusual about that, there was always a tamasha about something, somewhere.

Without thinking too much of the aftermath of her actions Lucy started gathering her possessions together. Everything appeared tawdry and cheap. The room retained the smell of the pungent curry. Its grimy floor bore stains of previous meals, an altar to hurried living, of quick graceless lives. The calendar with its depiction of a vividly coloured Krishna at play hung crooked on an outsize nail. Time was flying by it seemed to shout at her.

Shoving her feet into her chappals, pinning her hair back, hurriedly tying her sari around her, Lucy, clumsy in her urgency, grasped her small bundle of possessions and wrenched open the warped door.

It screeched open. She pulled the door shut and steeled herself to its ugly sound. She grazed her thumb on the bolt and felt a quick trill of pain jab upwards into her hand. It was not too early, none of her neighbours were stirring. What was the time, she wondered. The bandh had unsettled the natural timings of the day. With the grey overcast sky the light was deceptive. It could be eleven or eight in the morning. No, it must be about ten she decided. What was that row, she wondered. The buzzing grew and she stood on tiptoe on the turn of the stairs trying to see over the wall to the street alongside. There seemed to be a posse of sorts, men in a knot racing towards their little compound. Were they making their way towards this place? What was happening, what had happened? Doors began opening, heads emerged from windows and voices were raised. What was the noise about?

Lucy was riveted to the scene unfolding. The small knot of men spilled into their yard. Shouting, yelling, there was a sense of enjoyment in the wild telling of whatever tale it was they were relating to the eager listeners. In a slow realisation she knew whatever the incident, it had something to do with her. Heads were being jerked spasmodically in her direction. Furtive looks were shot upwards where she stood, still and frozen. In the ongoing gabble of excitement she could not distinguish a single word, not a sentence. Instinct, sharp and unerring told her this hubbub concerned her.

She went down the stairs slowly.

The chatter slowed. Her neighbours looked closely at her, the men stared openly the women less obviously. Some of the children laughed loudly and pointed at her. What the hell was all this about. It was just a day and night she had spent in this dismal hovel, surely not all the rabble there knew the details of how and why she was here. Was this a collective moral outrage or what? She continued to walk towards the entrance of the yard. Without warning one of the men broke away from the group and came towards her. She slowed and stopped, waited for him to open a dialogue.

"Missy, missy…"

"Yes, namaste."

The formality took him aback and he quickly brought his hands together in the traditional greeting.

"Namaste."

"What is the matter? Have you something you want to tell me?" She addressed him in Hindustani.

"Yes, oh yes…*haan, haan.*"

"What is it? Have you been sent here by my uncle, D'Cruze sahib?"

"*Nahin.* No, no no, yes, yes something bad has happened, something very rotten, something I can't tell you, I feel shame, I feel sorrow…"

Lucy felt the bile of nausea flood her mouth.

"*Kyaa ho gyaa?* Tell me."

"Your uncle he needs you now. He is alone and he wants you."

"What! *Why?* This is nonsense. Tell me what's really happened."

"Can't do that missy. Bad thing has happened. You go home now. You will see."

Lucy stumbled towards the gate. She turned her back on the murmur of disapproval as without a word she raced towards the front of that communal patch of land and flew out into the street.

A couple of chickens squawked as they fluttered out of her way.

Lucy D'Cruze was running home.

12

Bob and Kitty Renshaw sat back against the soft leather of the Mercedes and wordlessly stared ahead at the passing city.

It was past noon and the operation was over. Dr Mitra had spoken matter-of-factly of the next few hours as being critical to its subsequent success or failure.

It was always to Kitty he referred when he did speak.

"Mrs Renshaw," he polished his steel rimmed spectacles and addressed the floor, "I have to be honest and tell you that there is a fifty-fifty chance of your son being an invalid with possible brain damage."

Kitty stared silently. Besides her Bob looked steadily at the man before him delivering a potential sentence of lifelong agony.

The doctor replaced his glasses on his nose and this time met their gaze.

"Sorry to be so pessimistic but recovery depends entirely on the patient. Sometimes a complete recovery is possible. Don't lose hope," he flashed a surprisingly attractive smile at them.

With murmured thanks Bob and Kitty turned and walked out of the room and out of the nursing home.

A uniformed Sikh swiftly came towards them and guided them to a waiting car.

Without expressing surprise they got in and in almost complete silence were driven to their home and their waiting daughter.

"*Jesusgod,* what's going on?"

Bob gasped involuntarily as he saw a Black Maria and one of the city's ramshackle ambulances parked in front of their block of flats, policemen striding around trying to keep the throng of people crowding the entrance, lots of shouting, the local youths entering into the confusion by punching the children milling around trying to peer to see whatever there was to see.

Kitty clutched Bob's arm.

"*Slow down,* slow down, it might have nothing to do with us."

"Are you crazy? *Let me be,* there's Grace inside there, Christ only knows *what's* been happening." He shook Kitty's hand off and struggled to open the car door.

The Sikh driver leapt out and opened the door and in English said, "Sahib, some trouble here. I will come with you and see what the matter is."

Bob smiled his thanks.

Kitty looked at the tall driver, her gratitude obvious at this unexpected source of strength.

A policeman came up to them and in Hindi asked them if they lived here.

"Yes, yes, we do, let us pass you idiot. Our daughter is in there. What has happened?"

"Bad thing sahib. A woman attacked in terrible way. Men injured, maybe dying."

"Oh my god." Kitty reeled back into the car, collapsing against the seat, her legs rubbery.

Bob, with the driver, had pushed past the mob outside and raced towards their flat.

Kitty slowly followed, dreading knowing the details of whatever the disaster was that lay ahead.

A rough cordon had been formed with some coir rope, a few policemen were stationed blocking the passageway. They stared at Kitty and let her go without a word.

From the window above Grace leaned out and softly, urgently called to Kitty, "Mum, Mum, I'm all right. I'm fine."

Kitty breathed deep but felt even the breath she took was not enough to contain the relief she felt.

All was not fine in the flat under their own, the Johnson's.

The Johnson's flat was wide open. The door was smashed. The front windows looking onto the passage way had had panes broken. What looked like blood was smeared on their front door. The front room seemed to be full of people. There was no sign of Hilary or Fred, his son or mother. Where were they? What disaster had befallen this quiet family? Who had been hurt? How?

Kitty restrained herself from going into the flat. She could see no one she recognised. Police and she guessed medicos were crowded in there.

Woman attacked? Who was it, the old lady? Surely not Hilary? Pray god they were unharmed. What had happened? It looked a bomb site. Glass littered the floor. Broken china sparkled, paper was strewn around, ominously, torn shreds of cloth lay vein-like threading together the random chaos on the ground.

Kitty stopped herself from thinking. She ran, legs weak, wobbling, up the stairs towards Grace.

"Grace thank god you're all right. What has happened?"

Daryl Jackson emerged from behind and guided both inside. Bob and the driver were downstairs. Voices buzzed. Kitty realised that the door of the Vincents' had also been wide open. There was disorder there too though not as much as what the Johnson's flat had suffered.

"Mum, drink a glass of water. There has been a horrible accident. I'm afraid Mrs Johnson has been seriously hurt."

"Grace, Grace," Kitty caught at her daughter's hand, "tell me she is all right. Poor thing, so frail."

"No Mum, not the old lady, it's Hilary."

"What happened for god's sake, tell me!"

"She was assaulted by that hunchbacked sweeper..."

Kitty screamed softly.

"I don't believe it, I don't believe it," she moaned. Her hands locked together she began to knead them rhythmically.

"Why? Why? Oh god, why?"

Grace put an arm around her mother and a glass of water was offered by a hovering Daryl Jackson.

She took it and gulped noisily.

"How is she? Someone else was hurt, who?"

"Eddie D'Cruze, Lucy's uncle has been badly injured. He's been taken to hospital."

"What has happened to that pariah sweeper?"

"He's dead."

"What!"

"Yes, he cut his own throat when he was caught by Mr D'Cruze and Mr Vincent."

"Oh God oh God!"

"Mum, why don't you lie down now. You're tired. This is awful, ghastly. Ghastly." Grace paused for a minute. She looked at her mother. She softly asked, "How is Carl?"

Shocked at the fact that for a few minutes she had actually forgotten her son's well-being was in the balance, Kitty gaped at Grace and almost giggled hysterically.

"My god Grace. I forgot Carl. *I forgot Carl.*"

Daryl Jackson knelt before the trembling Kitty and took her hands in his.

"Come on Mrs Renshaw. It's been a horrible time. You've had more than your share of worry and strain. Why don't you have a cup of tea and get to bed. Rest."

Hiccoughing, a streak of water dribbling down the side of her mouth, Kitty looked up.

"We all have to pray that Carl will recover, that's all we can do now."

A collective sigh went round and the sudden silence was broken by the sound of footsteps running up the stairs, their front door was pushed open and Bob came in.

His face pinched, his underlip caught in his teeth, Bob walked over to Kitty and knelt before her. He caught her hands in his.

"Oh Kitty, I don't believe this. It's a nightmare. Eddie D'Cruze might die. Hilary has been raped, that cursed man has killed himself."

He sat back on his heels and stared at her.

No one spoke.

There was the sound of a thin wail and Kitty realised it was the sound of herself crying, high, atonal, agonised.

"Mum, Mum," Grace stooped and put her arm around her mother.

"Dad, bring her into the bedroom. Make her lie down. Daryl, get some tea going. "

Kitty allowed herself to be led into the tiny bedroom. Gratefully she let her shoes be taken off, her dress slipped over her head, she slumped on to the pillows, careless of the fact that she was in just her half-slip and bra, she put her arms around Grace and sobbed into her daughter's neck.

"Oh Gracie, Oh Gracie. I can't believe all this is happening. What a hellish day this has been."

Pushing the pillows against the bedstead, Grace gently helped her mother to sit up.

"Where's Lucy? She has to be told of this. Eddie can't be alone during this time."

"I don't know Mum. I don't know where Lucy is living now. But I'm sure she'll be here soon enough."

"How? There's this damned bandh on. Nothing and no one is working, how will she get to know?"

"Mum, news travels. Lucy will get to know, don't you worry."

"Bob. *Bob.* Bob," Kitty's voice rose, she pushed aside Grace.

"Where's your father?"

"I'm here Kitty. I'm here. Why don't you try to rest now? We'll be getting you a hot cuppa and then you try to get some sleep."

"Get Lucy Bob, get Lucy."

"What?"

Bewildered Bob stood besides his wife and for a brief moment wondered if she was suffering from sudden hysteria.

As if reading his thoughts Kitty said, "No I'm quite sane. I do think you ought to go and find Lucy and bring her home. This is no time for Eddie to be alone."

"Kitty, I don't know where the girl is. I think it would be silly of me to go off looking for someone when she is now living with a man we know next to nothing about."

"Oh for god's sake. That is not the point. You have to bring her home. We must see that Eddie knows Lucy is here and near him."

Her voice rising and tears once again filling her eyes, Grace gestured for her father to stop talking.

"Mum here's a cup of tea. Why don't you drink it and for now just try to relax and sleep. You need it."

"Don't treat me like a child. I'll drink the damn tea, which will wake me up, but I want someone to go and find Lucy and bring her here. Don't any of you see that this must be done?"

Daryl Jackson somewhat awkwardly entered the bedroom and carefully averting his eyes from Kitty's state of undress placed the tea on a small table near her.

"Grace," he spoke in an undertone, "your mum's quite right. I think

I'll try and see if I can go and contact Lucy and get her here."

Kitty had slumped against the pillows and was allowing Grace to hold the cup of tea to her.

"Where's that poor boy, where's Fred and where's the old lady? Bring me another cup of tea.

"Look, we don't know much, but we do know that Hilary has been rushed to the emergency ward and the police are not allowing anyone to see her or the members of her family. Yes, I'll get you some more tea."

"How stupid is that. Why can't we see her family?"

"This has turned a police case and I'm afraid they have the last word in procedures."

The fragrance of the tea filled the room. A fresh cup of tea was brought in by Daryl.

Kitty sipped nosily. Grace stood by the bed watching the shock slowly seep from her mother's face.

Daryl and her father stood by looking down at Kitty. Daryl cracking his knuckles repeatedly, looking quite at home in the cramped space.

"Come, I think we should leave Kitty to have a sleep now. I doubt if the tea will keep you awake." Bob took the empty cup from his wife, and ushered both Grace and Daryl out into the living room.

"She'll be okay after a rest. A sleep is the thing she really needs now, come to think of it so do I," Bob yawned widely, stretched his arms and rotated his neck to relieve some of the tension there.

"Grace," he smiled, "Daryl, you two have been wonderful waiting here for us and not rushing around." He looked again sharply at Daryl's smile and suddenly asked, "Is there anything you two would like to tell me?"

Daryl shuffled his feet noisily. Jumbo raised his head and looked reproachfully at this interruption in his nap.

All of them smiled ruefully at the clear message the dog sent them.

"We'll try to keep quiet okay Jumbo? Yeah, it's a dog's life you lead."

All laughed at the old joke and once again Bob looked at Daryl with a question in his raised eyebrows.

With the horror of the past morning still all around Daryl began to tell of their happiness to his old friend.

Outside the sanctuary of the Renshaws' flat there was chaos elsewhere in that contained area.

The Vincent family were milling around the passageway and corridor. Fatima Vincent sat in an old cane chair in the untidy flat, oddly silent. Her children and grandchildren all seemed to be asking questions and recounting the day's events simultaneously.

"Why did you and Baba go into their flat? Couldn't you both have raised some sort of alarm so some *others* might have investigated? You're not young y'know. Baba is not a strong man y'know. It was madness, madness, stupid." This from her son-in-law who, mouth full of the peanuts he munched, kept talking non-stop angrily, occasional sprays of saliva punctuating his fury.

Her daughter Maria had gone along with the police to the hospital where her father lay critically wounded.

"Nanee, Nanee, can we go and see Grandpa, can we, let us go, we want to go."

Three of her grandchildren began pulling at her sari.

Fatima feebly tried to brush them away but ended holding the youngest close against her.

The childish demands held no rancour unlike her son-in-law's outburst.

"Selfish dog," she thought. "No real thought for her or for poor Henry. How he sat there. Dirty singlet stretched over a paunch he seemed to look more unattractive daily.

"Henry will pull through. He's strong. We are not soft people. We are used to hardship and used to helping others." She looked pointedly at her son-in-law who glared back, chewing momentarily slowed at this direct reproach.

"Are you saying I'm soft, or what?"

"No, I'm saying that Henry did right and he'll be all right. I don't think poor Mr D'Cruze will be as lucky."

"Well what made him charge that madman. Didn't he see he had a knife in his hand? Such a bloody hero he was eh?" The sneer was obvious.

Fatima sat quietly the day's stress still oppressive. Her hands trembled and her voice cracked when she tried to speak normally.

"Maybe you could give me a cup of tea. I'm feeling ill."

Why had her children chosen this time to go out and leave her alone with this lump of nothing, she thought.

Her son-in-law squirmed around in his chair and shouted for his young daughter to put a kettle of water on the stove to give Nanee some tea.

"Baba, Ma told me not to go near the stove. I can't do it."

"Ouf, bloody useless child. Get out." Wiping his hands on his singlet the Vincents' son-in-law lurched out of his chair and began the task of preparing a cup of tea for his mother-in-law.

"Will a glass do for you, I can't find the saucers. What's wrong with tea in a glass anyway? All this show of cup and saucers, damn rubbish – *phutani* – "

Fatima sat and watched the show as kettle, cups, glasses were rattled. She thought of Henry who would bring her her tea, steaming and fragrant every morning and afternoon. Henry. Henry, now wounded with a knife wound in his arm and chest. Without warning Fatima began to cry. Tears rolled down her cheeks and her breath came in sudden spasms. She wanted to be near her husband. How she disliked this man, an interloper, who now seemed to have assumed an authority in her home. Why was her daughter so late in returning? What were the police going to demand now? What more was there to say?

They had heard a disturbance in the flat next door and with their neighbour's help had broken into the home and stopped a maniac from killing the beautiful and lovely Hilary Johnson. But he had already done the bad thing. Fatima shuddered. She tried not to block out the nightmare images that jerked across her mind. She saw the hunchback yet again, Hilary's dress in tatters, she saw him vividly, his skinny legs straddling Hilary. She saw Hilary with a small claw hammer in her hand swoop upwards and smash the weapon into the man's body. The howl that pierced the air was animal-like. Standing transfixed by the tableau she glimpsed Eddie D'Cruze hurtle into the crouching man. Then Henry seemed to be part of a tangle of bodies. It was grotesque.

The hunchback, his clothes slipping from his body, Henry, his shirt and sleeve growing a red pattern of scattered stars, and Eddie, head down, grappling with the small man. A knife gleamed within that knot. Hilary lay there, hand clutching the hammer, now stained. She gazed up at them.

Her mouth pulpy, a paan stain of crimson trickling down the side of her mouth, her eyes wide and staring. She had the look of a person deep in thought. It was not, Fatima briefly noticed, stunned or outraged. Hilary Johnson, seemed perplexed. Then there was Eddie, a look of surprise as a rose seemed to bloom on his shirt front. The small servant was at his feet, his neck wearing a smiling red necklace painted by a swift stroke of a knife. She knew she was screaming throughout. A scream steady and high-pitched as her husband staggered towards Hilary and tried to cover her with the tablecloth crumpled on the floor.

"Shhh, shhh, my dear," he murmured, "shhh, don't move." His comforting sounds as foreign to Fatima as the tenderness with which he stroked Hilary's head.

"My girl, my darling"... *"shutupshutup,"* as he turned and hissed to his wife.

Fatima, her screams dwindling to a hiccough, forced herself to look at the crumpled heap of horror at the door.

Eddie D'Cruze was half sitting nearby, a smile on his face. No, it was a fixed grin, his teeth biting into his lip. His eyes towards Henry, "Help, get help you fool. Shout, shout..." already his words were slurring.

Fatima ran to the door and ran outside, she shouted to the faces running towards the flat.

"Police, *call police,* help, they're dying – help, help, *bacchao, bacchao...*"

People streamed by, it seemed the entire locality was racing towards her. No, they passed her and pushed through the open door. There were more yells, shouts. A man raced by gabbling in unintelligible terror. Another dragged a couple of children with him. He was yanking both holding them by their shirt fronts and abusing. "I'll thrash you both you *salas,* this is not a tamasha. Back to your mother. She'll thrash you as well, *badmash...*"

Fatima was pushed aside. She remained standing, looking on as her husband and Eddie D'Cruze were helped by the crowd of people. Hilary was blocked from sight. She became a bundle of clothes. A heap upon the ground. The servant was surrounded by men. Some were kicking the prone body. Others were trying to restrain them.

"Fools, *ulloos,* he can't feel anything now -- pity – leave him to the police."

Much later a turbaned Sikh was in the heart of the muddle. Who was he? How did he come to be here? He directed the knots of people.

Without raising his voice he had organised some kind of order into that hellish scene. Hilary had already been carried away. Into the bedroom she guessed. Henry and Eddie were lying propped by the cushions from the suite in the Johnson's flat. She had been led away by the Sikh and her grandchildren were clutching her clothes. Her son-in-law was yelling something at her.

How long ago did all this happen. An hour, a minute? Her remembrance was confused. It started with that silly pigeon didn't it? Yes, Henry was trying to catch it when both of them heard a crash next door, then the strange noises. The sounds of glass tumbling and smashing. The strange gargling sounds neither of them could identify. What time did that happen exactly? Early morning? She could remember the family grumbling about the bandh. No bread, no newspapers, just a couple of eggs in the ice-box, of course through the night there had been noisy running up and down the staircase. No, no, Fatima fuzzily placed that noise during the early hours of the morning. Up and down, she had heard the thud of feet, up and down and up and down. The Renshaws must have had one of their club nights. Real partygoers those Renshaws. Still it was unusually busy. Their dances finished by two and three in the morning and their coming home was generally a shushed affair, usually Bob's laughter, and the quiet creak of feet as they made their way upstairs to open their front door. Last night it was a careless race of footsteps. Through the thin ceiling Fatima heard the scrape of shoes, the trace of feet as they paced back and forward in the little flat. She had slept though, awakened again to more footsteps, these, she was certain belonged to strangers. She took pride in the fact she could recognise her neighbour's footsteps. Then again there was silence. Was Grace up there alone? No she was sure she had heard a second set of footsteps later. Heavier, a man's tread. It was definitely not Carl's lighter scamper. Nice boy, she thought vaguely. Did the pigeon belong to him? No of course not, it was that sickly looking boy's next doors. Hilary's son. Of course, of course. Yes, yes, her thoughts coming full circle.

Police likely to question all of them now. Yes, her Henry had to be in the midst of all this *golmal*...Foolish man. Why did he have to be in the middle of that mess. Poor, *bechara* Hilary. What was to become of her? How would her family accept this disaster. The old mother-in-law was a nasty one. Never a smile, never a wish or hello. Son a wash-out. How on earth had that beautiful girl married him? Fatima, thoughts randomly bumping into one another, began to feel sleepy. The noise of the day receded. The buzz of her grandchildren lessened. Fatima dozed.

Her son-in-law stared in annoyance. A cup of tea rapidly cooling in his hand. How like this old nuisance he thought, all this trouble to brew the tea and now she falls asleep. He wished his wife would hurry and return to the flat. What was she needed for anyway? Where were his bloody brothers and sister-in-law? Her stupid father should not have poked his nose in what was not his business. How horrible for a servant to attack one of them. Hope the fellow died painfully. See how dangerous it was to allow for any kind of familiarity between servant and master. He would have liked to have put a kick or two into the swine. A good swift kick that would have had the swine coughing blood.

The thought made him smile, his lips pulled back, baring his teeth as he replayed the deadly blow in his mind. The cup of tea clattered and spilled on the floor. "Damn," he stared at his sleeping mother-in-law and placed the cup with a crash on the table hoping it would awaken her. "Get out and do some of your homework, *Jao,*" he shouted to his young son who was lingering near his grandmother. The boy shied away from the irritation in his father's voice and bolted into the bedroom. Fatima Vincent awoke, still wondering at the action of her husband, she now sat and waited with her son-law-law the blustering Joe Gomes, her grandchildren, fearful, her thoughts confused by the ugly muddle next door.

A cool breeze wafted the debris of the street on to the pavement, sent dust dervishes into the clothes and faces of passers-by. The heat of May and the sullen storm had given way to a surprising respite from the sultry humidity.

Rupa Jaiswal and Roger Lawson stood at the gate of the nursing home waiting for her car.

"Wonder why Kabir is so late, it's not like him. I do hope nothing has happened, though it seems to be a time for things to happen." Rupa smiled up at Roger.

"Hmm, probably stopped off for a chat with friends. Or a cuppa at the local *chaiwallah.*"

"No, that's not like him at all. He's a fanatic about time. Would never dream of having time off for a quick cha or *gup.* He's quite a snob, holds himself aloof from casual gossip with other servants."

"You've had him as a driver for a long time?"

"Yeah. About twelve years. I was lucky enough to have a friend recommend Kabir, I needed a big strong man to drive the car and keep the *goondas* at bay. It still seems to offend people to see a woman manage a car on our roads."

She laughed. "Always comes down to having a man around doesn't it?"

Roger smiled.

He had to agree. He recalled his mother talking of the hooting and lewd comments that would sometimes follow her when she'd have to shop alone or walk certain localities where a dress remained a sign of 'foreign' encroachment.

"Hmm. Can't think why you had any problems at all."

"What do you mean?" She looked somewhat sharply at him, her face losing a good-natured softness.

"Hey, what problems would a well-heeled young woman driven around town in her Mercedes by a strong Sikh have?"

"Are you being funny or do you really imagine I have no problems in my life?"

"Well, let's face it Rupa, money smoothens things a lot. I'm sure you have to deal with high finance, stocks, shares and fears of your investments being in the red. But have you ever waited in a crowded hospital corridor for some irritable doctor to attend to you? I'm sure you've never had the frustration of being without cooking oil, or kerosene, or gas, or having the power fail for hours every day. Your friend Dr Mitra runs to your bidding when your children cough or sneeze once too often. Your generator is ready to switch on when the power is off for hours at a time. Have you ever eaten rancid food because you couldn't afford to eat anything else? Ever tucked into chillies, salt and *suttoo* because it's the only thing you can afford? Wealth eases life. It'd be stupid to think otherwise."

He swallowed hard, his throat dry and stared ahead not wanting to see the anger in her eyes. Feeling an unusual rage in him surge he feared the outburst had punctured the sudden friendship.

"I better make a call home to find out why the car is so late."

There was no frostiness in Rupa's voice as she turned to go back into the nursing home, the tone was normal, business-like.

Her bloody forte, Roger thought as he kicked away scraps of paper scuttling near him and waited under the shade of a frangipani tree watching her dumpy figure walk swiftly away from him.

Sparrows chattered in a dusty gutter near him, a *cheel* wheeled lazily high and he heard its high-pitched *'eeeeee'* loop through the air as it rejoiced in the May morning.

13

"My god, can't you let me through. Let me through. I live here. My uncle is here. I have to see him. I have to be with him. What has happened? Tell me, please let me know."

Lucy tugged at a policeman's sleeve as she was barred from entering the passageway of the building.

"Arre, arre, kaun hai, aap thero, thero..."

A burly policeman, sweating and irritable under the scrutiny of a mob of curious locals pushed Lucy with his baton away from the entrance of the building.

The ambulance had long gone. The crowd had lessened but the air of drama was still thick in the air.

Voices were repeating the story in a dozen different ways and interpretations. Children were gabbling and running around, men and women were loudly and simultaneously yelling their version of what had happened.

It was a huge entertainment in their lives.

Lucy began to gasp. She sensed it was her uncle they were excited about. What the hell had happened? Why the police, the ambulances, the electric air of something awful having happened?

She felt her arm being held.

"Come away Lucy, come away."

She looked around to see old Mrs 'Ma' Mills who lived across the road taking her arm and leading her to her house.

"Tell me aunty, what's happened? Where's Uncle Eddie? Why won't they let me into the building? Can't you tell them I live there?"

Lucy spoke in a rush, her voice cracked and indistinct.

"Come in now and rest. I'll tell you what I know, but first calm yourself. It's not going to be easy for you to hear."

Lucy was glad of the sudden relief from the heat and glare of the street. The little house was shadowy, cool.

Mrs Mills looked cagey, her lined face peering anxiously into Lucy's distress.

In the gloom of a crowded living room Lucy heard of her uncle's bravery. Of his heroic tackling of a maddened attacker. She found her throat tight with horror as she visualised the rape of her neighbour, Hilary Johnson. Where were her husband and child now? How were they coping? She jerked her attention to what the old lady in front of her was saying.

"Lucy, come back to your uncle. He needs you. I think all of us here do. You are a clever girl, an example to the younger ones. Our people are so few now. We are kept out of jobs, we are pushed out of our homes here in the central part of the city. Don't think you can't help. You can." All the while Lucy's hands were held in a firm grip, the old lady pausing only when the servant brought in a glass of orange juice for the distraught girl.

Gulping the cool drink she was grateful Pradip was not mentioned nor was he painted a deep shade of black.

She took a deep breath and gently patted Mrs Mills's hands.

"Aunty, I know how I must seem to people here…"

"…your people…" Mrs Mills quickly injected.

"Yes, yes, but I do have a life to live you know."

"What sort of life Lucy? Cramped in a slum tenement with servants as your neighbours? A man who is going to live off you, yes Lucy, he is. Don't be blind, your boyfriend is an uneducated mechanic, a loafer chap, who will bring his family to live off you. Yes, I know it's hard to hear this, but you know it's true. It's true my girl. True."

Lucy's eyes filled with tears and she felt like turning her back on the words of the old woman and going back to the squalid room, going back to Pradip.

The fan groaned above them, then screeched to a slow stop as the daily power cut ended the quota of electricity for the day.

"Oh lord, here we go again. Boy, boy, bring out more punkahs here. Switch off the fridge at the power point. The surge when the current is resumed is bad for the machine you know."

Mrs Mills rose creakily to her feet, sighed deeply, and took the empty glass from Lucy.

"Now sit here. Let's see how we get you to your uncle. Don't worry. I'm sure he'll feel much better when he sees you."

The hubbub of the street grew. People still clustered around the entrance of the building. Lucy clenched her jaw as she remembered the looks she had got from the people gathered around. Some openly curious, others sly with a hint of smirking at her presence.

Damn them, she thought. No one could judge her. Not these fools, not her uncle, not Pradip. Especially not Pradip.

Obviously her fall from grace had been noted, the tom-tom drums carried the lurid tale of her elopement to the locals.

The servant silently entered the room and without looking at Lucy began to roll down the *khus khus* blinds that hung in the narrow veranda that fronted the room. Silently he brought in a plastic bucket and with quick flicks splashed water on the grassy shades. Lucy inhaled the aroma released and was taken back to childhood when she would delight in throwing the water on them herself.

"Not so much Lucy, not so much," her mother would chide her.

The sun would dazzle, the heat sending little simmers of vapour from the curtains. She'd stand as near as she could and smell the heady fragrance of the bound grass and happiness was there and then. Her mother's laughter, the dampness of the grassy blinds, the promise of mangoes later and the blossoming cool that emerged from the grass curtain, it all came back. Cool, so cool.

"Lucy, Lucy," she jerked awake. She was embarrassed to find she must have drifted off into a doze.

"Sorry, I didn't realise I was napping, how silly of me."

"It's the heat that does that, and the shock. Why don't you have a lie-down before we go and see if we can go to the hospital. I have phoned my son Eugene and he will call back and let us know if he can come and pick us up and take us there in the office car."

"You are kind." Lucy was flustered. She knew Mrs Mills's son Eugene was employed in a bank and was considered a huge success in the neighbourhood. "Won't it be putting Eugene to a lot of trouble? It's in the middle of the day and with the bandh making things difficult..." she trailed off looking at Mrs Mills, growing annoyed at her own awkwardness.

"Let Eugene worry about that. Now why don't you come and have a short rest before we go off again. It'll do you good to close your eyes for a while."

Lucy submitted with grace and going into the bedroom, slipped off her shoes and sank on to the bed with relief.

Not a charpoy, she thought with wry amusement, an honest-to-goodness bed, with good linen, a firm support and a solid teak bedstead that could be leaned against.

Yes, she closed her eyes. She was tired. She had hardly slept and that hot stuffy room was not a bower for any kind of lovemaking, her back ached and she blessed Mrs Mills for her kindness.

A door banged. There were footsteps and though she tried to keep her thoughts and mind clear Lucy slept.

Mrs Mills entered the bedroom and looked at the sleeping girl.

She was disturbed as to how to deal with what she had instigated. While she was aware that Lucy had outraged the sentiments of the community, she was sorry for the child. Eddie D'Cruze was a hard, dry stick of a man, she thought. Not the best candidate to bring up a young girl. She remembered Lucy's mother, bright and lovely and headstrong. A hasty marriage with a tragic outcome.

Poor Lucy.

It was turning out to be a typical summer morning. Humid, stuffy, the early morning rain had given way to a heavy nasty sweaty day. John Coates slipped off his singlet and stood in the wafting air-conditioning and felt the sweet blast of cool air slide comfortingly on his skin.

"Johnnie Johnnie, come here a minute will ya."

Yvonne's scratchy voice shredded the comfort of the moment. John sighed and after a pause answered testily.

"What is it Yvonne? I'm here in the bedroom. Why don't you come in here. It's too damn hot outside."

There was a silence and John knew that he had begun a mood that was not going to be good for whatever Yvonne was about to tell him.

He shook out some talcum powder and dusted it lightly on his chest. He looked down at his body and absent-mindedly noted his paunch was ballooning, he could not see his feet. Age, he mused, age.

"Why couldn't you come when I called Johnnie," Yvonne pushed his shed clothes off the bed in an untidy pool at her feet, and looked at him with unconcealed annoyance.

"When did you come back from the nursing home? I didn't know you were home and I had to answer the grande dame Mrs Lawson, who was as nasty as ever."

"Nasty? That dear old lady, why, what did she ask?"

"Oh, you know. Talking about the Renshaw boy's accident. Asking about whether or not her beloved son was here. And boy, did I let her know how stupid it was to get that damn woman to judge our girls. Imagine that girl getting the May Queen crown. Damn fools."

The diatribe was punctuated with much pattings of the bed quilt, dusting of the pillows, smoothing down of the sheets. Never once did Yvonne look at her husband, nor was she still for a minute. Her voice held the resentment, now ingrown, when she spoke to her husband. Her hands moved twitchily, distracting, John who tried to keep his irritation under control.

"Who are the *damn fools?* The judges? The other contestants? All of us who were there? Why are you so angry at the Renshaws? They are decent people. Nothing wrong with them."

"Oh yeah. I suppose you are thinking mostly of the old wife eh?"

"Yvonne. Stop it. You know Kitty and I were briefly friendly when we were scarcely out of our teens."

"…oh friendly were you – I *bet…*"

"We were both young and neither of us seriously considered the friendship was anything but a slight crush we had on each other."

"Oh so you now admit you two had a thing going. *Slight crush* my left bloody eye."

"Stop being petty. Of course we had a short boyfriend/girlfriend period and then I met you."

"Of course now I'm to blame for what might have been eh?"

"Look, what's this all about? Why are we talking all this rubbish and what's this to do with anything now? We're middle-aged, our daughter's life is our focus and we enjoy doing all we can to make her happy. She's not stupid enough to think that not being crowned May Queen is going to upset her life."

"*She's* not stupid eh? I know you think *I'm* stupid, you and Heather, not ashamed of me or anything are you? Still the trashy railway ignoramus aren't I?"

"Yvonne for god's sake stop this ridiculous…"

"Why? You don't talk to me anymore, not that you would before anyway. Our daughter thinks I'm beneath her to talk with and yes, I enjoy working at the club and with the people there. People I like. *Our people.* People who now have to fight for the little they have. Not step into a Mercedes like that fat bitch with the stone in her nose."

"This is cheap. You're sounding vulgar. I can't believe you feel the way you do. What would you like me to do?"

"Do? *Nothing,* nothing of course. Why should I stop? It's the truth. You know it is. Don't pretend that I don't bore you. I know I'm not as clever as either you or Heather. But I'm not an idiot. What I'd like? I'll tell you what I'd like. I'd like sometimes, just *sometimes* to be listened to and heard."

She had begun to cry. Tears were tracking down her cheeks, her nose was running and childlike, she wiped away tears and dribblings with the back of her hand.

John moved quickly and wiped her face with his singlet.

"Don't cry. Don't cry. It's not true what you say. I love you and I admire you. But I'm not happy when you begin to abuse people we know are good and true friends."

Yvonne sobbed against his chest. She wept unrestrainedly, inelegantly without thought of how she looked or sounded. She wondered at his calling them friends. They only saw the Renshaws at the club and had never asked them over to their home. Not too flush with money, she gathered, they rarely entertained in the club and were never seen to invite friends for meals the club's kitchen was noted for. Friends? What was Johnnie thinking of?

In a muffled voice she offered John an olive branch.

"How's the boy anyway? You haven't told me what's been happening to him and how he is."

John smiled. He thought of the Renshaws, distraught, relying on the healing power of a gruff doctor without a claim to comforting bedside manners. Kitty. He shut out the image of her strained face. He turned away from the sight of Bob, still handsome, holding her hands, a world apart from any of the others in that room.

He cleared his throat.

"We won't know for some time. The operation has probably just finished and I don't want to be there. I'd like to give the family time together. Anyway what was the reason you called me, I don't think it was to have this *chat* now was it?"

"Oh Johnnie, the generator is sounding funny. It's making whirring noises and I worried it might stop and we'll have to call the electrician to fix it again."

"Is that it? Funny noises – was that what the fuss was about then? It was too hot to handle for you huh?"

He continued to gently wipe the streaked face and wondered if Bob ever had to calm Kitty Renshaw in these kinds of domestic upsets.

He stared over the slightly greying head and looked at their reflection in the mirror.

A study in domesticity, an ageing man and woman holding each other to comfort and apologise, there was no trace of a revived passion or sensual urge. This is what we walk towards he thought. Compromise, capitulation.

A door banged, the phone rang, Rahman their houseboy called out that the sahib was wanted and what should he say.

John pushed the singlet into Yvonne's hand and quickly pulling a fresh vest over his head went into the living room to answer the phone.

"Mr Coates?"

"Yes, speaking."

"It's Rupa Jaiswal. Yes, hello, yes thanks, I'm fine. I'm sorry to be the bearer of unpleasant news but there has been an incident in the Renshaw's apartment block. No, no, they are all right, but I gather a neighbour of theirs has been molested, the attacker was killed and another two men, both neighbours I believe, are in a critical condition in hospital."

"Holy Christ," John felt his horizon tilt. His stomach heaved with shock. He wiped his forehead and took a deep breath.

"Have you any details as to who was hurt, who died, who are the men in hospital?"

"No. I'm afraid I don't really know much at all. My driver, Kabir, has returned from dropping the Renshaws home and found the place surrounded by police with a heavy guard in front of the flat where the attack took place. I think it would be good if you went over, the Renshaws might like you to go over and just be there."

"Of course, of course."

Kitty's all right, Kitty's all right, Kitty's all right. John's heart pounded. God, why her – what can I do anyway.

"What…oh yes, Rupa, I'll see you there. Thank you so much for calling us."

Hands shaking he replaced the phone and stood a moment to still his mind and his heart.

"Who was that Johnnie?" Brush in hand Yvonne entered the room and looked in some surprise at her husband.

"Rupa, Rupa Jaiswal…"

"What! What'd she want?" The brush was held momentarily tangled in Yvonne's peppered hair.

"Something terrible has happened at the Renshaws' block of flats."

"Huh? What? The Renshaws in trouble again? Damned family's jinxed or what."

"No, didn't you hear what I said – there's trouble at their block of flats, not with them."

"So what's the fuss about then?"

"I'm off to see what's happened."

"For God's sake, why? Why do *you* have to rush over?"

"I *want* to Yvonne, I *want* to…"

There was a pause. Husband and wife looked at each other.

"To make sure Kitty Renshaw's okay then?"

John mutely stood, his face pale, the customary indulgent tone of voice absent.

"Yes."

It was a small word, an admission of the larger truth. Yvonne Coates knew at last and finally faced the fact that her husband did not love her. It was always Kitty Renshaw.

Without the daily make-up, peach lipstick, the faintly brushed eye shadow, subtle powder masking the sheen of perspiration, she looked drab and younger.

"Go then."

She resumed a slow brushing of her hair. Walked out of the room.

Kitty Renshaw looked at her sleeping husband and daughter and marvelled at how alike they looked. Clones. The same facial structure, high cheek bones, slight cleft in the chin, wide mouths, skin smooth and glowing. How handsome Bob was when she met him. He still is, she thought.

Kitty cleared the front room of the scattered disorder. A scarf of Carl's lay across the table. She gently took it and folded it, holding it to her heart. Jumbo opened an eye and ears pricked, followed Kitty's journey across the room.

"Silly dog. Get out of the way. Always tripping us up."

Later she would go down to the Vincents and see how she could help the old lady and those children.

Later.

Now she struggled to keep images of Hilary Johnson out of her mind. Hilary lying prone, bleeding, stunned. Hilary legs splayed, dress ripped away. Hilary, eyes blinded, looking and not looking. Stunned. Mute. She had been told Hilary had been taken to the emergency department of the nearby hospital, the Nilratan Sircar, down the road. A public hospital, it had a dreaded reputation. Go in there and come out feet first, was the black joke. Its dusty corridors crowded with sick, with poor, doctors tired, harried, nurses loud, voice raucous as they scurried about their duties. It was a medieval representation of a health centre. My god…poor, poor Hilary. Where was her son? Was he with his father or grandmother? She really should find out what the situation was now.

Her thoughts flew to the other victims of this horror. Eddie D'Cruze, old Mr Vincent. How were they? Eddie had been injured seriously. She had learnt from the garbled tale poured out by their servant that one of them was critically wounded. Surely Eddie, cautious, cranky old man was the last person who'd rush to confront a knife-wielding maniac. Mr Vincent? If the reality was not stolidly there, Kitty could not imagine that old man in any other manner than that of shaky, demanding husband, incompetent father and grandfather, fading fast into the squalor of his family. Was he hurt? How might an aged man, with little muscle and less strength stand up to the fury of a madman? How were his family coping?

My god. God. God. God. Don't let that happen ever. To my family, to anyone I know. Carl. My Carl. Let Carl get through this. Please. Why did things happen all at the same time? The terror of the past night was evident in the tremor of her head, her hands. Like a victim of Parkinson's. I can't still them. I can't still myself. How proud we were, how happy when our lovely daughter was crowned May Queen. Was it only hours ago? And John had looked at her. She pushed the thought away from her. Not now. Not the same old going over of what might have been. His wife glaring at her, shooting glances at Grace. Kitty literally shook herself. Tea, yet another cup of tea might help this unhealthy introspection. Carl, get well my darling, get well.

She sat down in the little chair by the window and leaned her head against the wall. She thought about getting herself a cup of tea but a sudden fatigue made her close her eyes, her body sprawl and droop in the chair. Carl's scarf slipped from her hands. It made a colourful puddle at her feet. She closed her eyes and gave herself up to the constant daydream. John Coates was telling her he was getting married. John Coates was leaving her for a rich and beautiful girl. He was leaving.

She felt a ripple of terror, felt the hair on her arms stand. Dear God, what was happening. Her Carl, his life caught between health and possible brain damage. Let him live. Let him live. Kitty sank further into the chair and stared out at the corrugated tin roof of the bustee below. Exhaustion and sudden sadness gripped her. She closed her eyes. If only life went on as usual. Bob loving her unconditionally, the children happy in their lives. She suddenly thought of Kay. Lord, she must send off a telegram immediately. She stood up without thinking of what she might do now. Jumbo started at the sudden movement. She remained at the window, thinking, within the unexpected gift of silence. Even the usual vendors who sang out their wares seemed to be absent. Oh yes, it was a bandh. She kept forgetting. No traffic. No nothing. Her throat caught. It hurt with unshed tears. No, this was self-indulgence. It was in no one's interest to give in to her fears.

John. There he was again. Looming always, locked in her memory. Steady, as she knew he was. Slipping back years she saw them both clambering into a rickshaw. It was a rainy monsoon evening and she stumbled back into the circle of his arm. Embarrassed she giggled, he looked down into her face, and lifted her gently into the shabby 'cart'. The rest of the little journey was a silent one, something changed. It was an establishment of sorts. He was there to protect. Or so she stupidly thought at that time. Yet again she felt the old resentment, bitterness at how differently it had turned out. His sudden disappearance from her life. The shaming discovery of his new attachment. The beautiful and well connected girl he had thrown her over for. Even today years and years later she cringed at her humiliation. The pretence of being fine with his leaving her. Deception on an ongoing basis, an apparent acceptance of how things grew or died. Her parents were disgusted. Angry at John. Angrier at her and her apparent nonchalance. She heard clearly her mother saying she had hoped her daughter had more backbone in her to show people that there was indeed rancour and anger.

No. Kitty sighed. She must stop this now. The morning was now afternoon. Bob and Grace were both deeply asleep. Daryl Jackson had long gone. The cook was padding around laying the table and bringing in the dishes of food. A simple dal and rice and an egg curry were what she had ordered. Nothing too elaborate. When would the doctor call?

There was a knock at the door.

Kiitty started.

"Kaun hai?" The classic query for a knock at the door. No immediate opening of a door. Never again. Never.

"Kitty?"

"Kaun hai?"

"Kitty, Kitty, it's John."

Kitty wide awake, terrified that her dream had evolved and more horror awaited her. John was here to tell her about Carl's progress.

Carl had not made it.

That rude doctor had promised them it would be all right. Why was John here? Was she still dreaming?

"Kitty. *Kitty!"*

"Yes, yes, coming, coming. Just a minute."

Bewildered she automatically smoothed her hair, snatched up some of the papers from the untidily strewn centre table. Her mouth was dry.

She might have eaten something to stop stale breath. Carl. She'd will her darling son to come through this agony well and healthy.

The door opened, their servant puzzled looking in at the memsahib dishevelled, greeting this stranger, her hands all fluttery.

"John, what's wrong?"

"Kitty."

They stood facing each other much the same way they had in that hallway of the club so many years ago, both taking stock of what there was to say, of how to behave.

"What has happened here? Rupa – Mrs Jaiswal – called me earlier to tell me of the trouble here. Are you all right?"

"Of course I am John. It's nothing to do with us really. Well, in a way I suppose it is. Our neighbour was molested by a servant. She was rescued by two other neighbours, Eddie D'Cruze and Mr Vincent. The man killed himself, but he also attacked and injured both of them."

"Jesus. It's horrible. How is the poor woman?"

"The boy told me she has been taken to the Nilratan Sircar hospital. Eddie and Mr Vincent are there as well."

"Blast and damn. The lady would have been much better off in a private hospital rather than in that morgue."

"John! This is a police case. It's going to be treated as such. It is standard procedure."

"And you know so much about standard procedure in police cases do you? Do you know how awful it is in that place? Only the destitute go there, or the terminally ill. The staff treat patients like guinea pigs. Once they realise it's an Anglo-Indian admitted they'll delight in neglecting them or being rude to the family."

"What rubbish! Where did you pick up such ideas? What's the matter with you? Have you come here to pick an argument about what went wrong with the manner of dealing with this crime? Which, just by the way, has really nothing to do with either of us, bar the fact that as neighbours we *are* involved."

Anger sparked. John Coates, the lunatic events of the past night and morning forgotten, stared at Kitty, anger drained, remembering his life had been spent trying to blot her from it.

"What is it?" Kitty, temper tamped down, was puzzled by the sudden change in the tenor of the moment.

"Nothing. I guess I shouldn't have presumed to come here."

"John. *John.* Don't go. We're both tired. It was wonderful of you to come with us to the nursing home to see that Carl was given the best."

"It wasn't my doing. We were lucky to have Rupa on the spot. She's the one who pulled strings." He turned, smoothing his expression, trying to look impassive. The dog yelped as he brushed by the sleeping animal.

"Sorry. Didn't see that damned beast. Carl's?"

Kitty smiled. She hadn't forgotten his fear of dogs.

"He's harmless. Yes, he's Carl's." She felt ashamed of the anger that had sprung between them. This was neither the time nor place for argument.

"Come, why don't you sit and have something to eat or drink. Boy!"

Kitty called out to the servant who padded quickly into the room, shooting a quizzical look at the stranger.

"Haan memsahib?"

"Cha."

"Kitty. I really have to go. Say hello to Bob and Grace. She looked lovely last night. Looks so like you."

Kitty smiled at him, the irritation of the minutes past erased.

John. He was here. In her flat. Just another visitor. Just another friend. John was like a ghost whom she tried to push away and suddenly emerged into her life and mind, recalling and reliving moments both painful and ecstatic.

The tea arrived.

John took the dainty cup and balanced it awkwardly on his knee. Steam rose and he stirred the cup, the teaspoon clicking.

He looked questioningly at the drawn curtains which partitioned the room from the bedrooms.

"Bob?"

"And Grace. Both sound asleep. No, I'm not sleepy. It's good to have someone to talk to. If you can call arguments, talk."

"Oh Kitty, Kitty. I'm sorry."

"Why? For what?"

"For everything."

Kitty was silent. She did not know what to say, or how to say it. It was more than thirty years ago that John Coates had broken her heart. Humiliated her in the deepest way love can be betrayed or tossed aside. Here he was sipping a cup of tea and saying he was sorry. How ridiculous this all was. Her Carl was between life and death. Horror had happened next door to her, cataclysmic happenings, and now wedged in was this confession she had dreamed of for long years. This middle-aged, balding and paunchy man was the pivot of her dreams, her foolish self-indulgent secret.

The tea was gulped loudly. John drank the tea without really tasting it at all. Happy for the scalding burn down his throat he looked at the pi dog lying at his feet. Kitty might say something. He might be asked to leave. Anything that melodramatic, or clichéd was still entirely probable. Surprisingly he was calm. Not flustered or embarrassed by this confession. He loved Kitty. And he'd live with his life, ride out the rest of his arid years of his marriage with Yvonne.

"Well, I better…"

"Will you stay…"

They stopped after the joint words and smiled sheepishly.

"John. Let's not talk of the past. It's long gone, our little story. Why can't you accept things as they are."

No, she thought, she was not going to give him the satisfaction of knowing he was centred in her life. In her mind and in her heart. Every day she thought of him in one or other flashback. Even his high husky voice she remembered with a fondness that edged on maudlin. John Coates remained the lover, the loved. Let him squirm. Looking at him she sensed a relief, a loosening of tension, a quiet defiance in the way he looked at her.

"John. Shall we go to the nursing home now, or will Mrs Jaiswal's car come around shortly?"

The abrupt turnabout in conversation startled him.

"I don't know if Rupa and Roger will come over here to pick us up or not, of course, we can phone them but we can go by ourselves if that's what you decide. Aren't Bob and Grace going to come as well?"

"Naturally. We'll have a quick bite, we all had just some toast and tea earlier on, and then I think we'll all go over and find out what the latest prognosis is."

"Kitty."

"What?"

"You *know* what – what is it going to be, another couple of decades of a moratorium on this situation."

"There's no *situation* John. Not on my part. We had a *thing* going long ago. You moved on. So did I. We've both families whom we love. At present my son might recover, he might not, he might have to live with brain damage. My daughter had her moment of happiness smashed. My husband is distraught. And you want me to comment on 'our' situation?"

Liar, she thought, liar. I'm dizzy with happiness at hearing this and I'm going to keep up a pretence of not caring. Like most of my life. A pretence. Damn him, let him suffer. The stuffed shirt, the pompous fool and why for god's sake did Yvonne allow him to wear that garish bush shirt?

"Do you know what it has been like to have to make do? To make do with someone who cannot really talk with you, day after day with work to carry you through to the next week the next month, the next year… oh Kitty." He made a small step towards her, stopped, feeling as foolish as any schoolboy.

"You've done well by that tenet haven't you? The big shot, the beautiful wife, the super life lived in the south of Park Street. Away from the muck of our part of the city? Did you miss it John? Did you really feel so bad about marrying into money? Did you miss our rickshaw rides, our walks in those smelly parks? Have you longed for the sound of the bustee under your window? The *chhokras'* eyes on your daughters as they grew, the dirty remarks, the smell of the slum wearing you away? You missed all this didn't you? That's really a shame. I have a husband too good-natured to ask for a raise in salary, daughters who hear filthy words whispered at them because they wear dresses not saris. Does your lovely Heather have to deal with these problems? Well does she?"

Kitty, out of breath, cheeks pale with rage, stared at the man she loved. Her eyes filled with tears as she realised the exposure of the deep hurt, how powerful still was the influence of this man's rejection of her.

"Mum! What's going on?"

Grace, bleary-eyed, hair tousled, stood in the bedroom doorway. Aghast, she looked at John Coates and her mother facing each other, knew that the last of what she heard her mother say was a post-script of what really lay at the bottom of this scene.

"Grace! Nothing's going on. Mr Coates is here to go with us to see Carl. I was about to wake you and Dad. It's about time we were off to the nursing home. Get inside and change."

Kitty flustered, trying to regain composure turned from John.

Grace slipped into the bedroom away from the direct gaze of Mr Coates. She held the curtain across her body.

"Mum. Any further news of Aunty Hilary and Mr D'Cruze and Mr Vincent?"

"No, no. for god's sake how would I know anyway? Are the police going to tell me personally what's happening? Now why don't you have a bath and get ready to leave with us."

Grace pulled the curtain quickly behind her and shot a small smile at John Coates.

Catching the last part of the whispered diatribe she saw her mother's face, pinched with grief, wearing an expression totally new. She was not aware her mother knew Mr Coates this well. What was it all about? Did it have to do with her win last night? She looked over into the other room and saw her father still deeply asleep. Arm flung over his eyes he looked younger than his age. What had her mother being raging about to Mr Coates? Curiosity buzzing she vowed to ask and find out exactly what the argument was about.

She heard the murmur of talk. There was intimacy in the duet of voices. Her mother's low and rapid, Mr Coates oddly placating. What on earth had her mother said to the man. Surely it was his wife who had some antipathy towards them. Or was it her brother Carl's accident that had sent Mum over the edge? Whatever it was she had rarely seen her mother so worked up, in such lather. Quickly she chose a dress to wear, a light cotton shift, she slipped out of her clothes and standing, shivering slightly in the tiny bathroom, slowly filled the basin with water from the vat. It was a cold bath she would take. It was too late to ask the servant to bring in a *handi* of hot water. She gasped as the cold water sluiced over her sleep-warmed body. This was good. It was what she needed. A refreshing and cold bath. Get rid of nightmares. Get rid of the reality of being Daryl Jackson's 'girl' now.

She winced at the finality of last night's drama. He was a good man and she by all accounts should be giving thanks for having hooked such a catch. A dull catch, her heart thought. You have compromised your freedom for a secure life not a happy one. Never mind. Now she might be able to look Andy in the eye and tell him that she understood that love had nothing to do with marriage. She smiled to herself. No, she would never betray the person she intended to honour and cherish for the rest of her life. The cold water rolled quickly over her skin and the slight summer breeze that flowed into the small room suddenly chilled and made her skin blossom with goose-bumps. Someone walking over my grave, or I have a really poor blood circulation, she wondered. Towelling herself vigorously Grace walked nude into the bedroom.

Her mother entered and without looking at her whisked the bed covers into some kind of order.

"Hurry up. Mrs Jaiswal's car will soon be here to take us to the nursing home."

"Dad's still asleep."

"Yes, I know. He won't take much time to dress or eat. I wanted him to rest after the strain of last night."

"Mum?"

"Hmm?"

"*What* was going on?"

"Going on?"

"Hey, you know – I heard you really giving Mr Coates the works. Nothing to do with last night was it?"

"What do you mean?"

"Oh *Mum*! You know what I mean. Mr Coates was looking as if you had whipped him. Was it something I did or was it something his wife had asked him to do?"

"No, it was nothing whatever to do with you or last night, nor did his wife send him over to make us stand in the corner."

She smiled at her daughter and Grace knew that whatever it was she was not going to be told anything by her mother.

With a sharp tug at the corners of the bed sheets Kitty left the room and Grace heard her softly waking her father.

Intrigued, she couldn't understand why Mr Coates might take the trouble to come to their home to escort them to see Carl. A good man. She had always liked him. How and why on earth he married the ignorant, vulgar Yvonne was a mystery, if not a joke. Most sniggered at the loud, silly woman, who like it or not, was first lady at their club and to some extent faced up as first lady of the community in the broader happenings of the city. Grace caught herself wondering and almost laughed at the irony of her questioning their marriage.

Here she was on the brink of committing herself to a man solely for purposes of social acceptance, her ultimate wearing down, giving in to social pressures. She loved her parents and wanted them to be happy. She hoped she would ultimately find that pot of gold as they had. Daryl Jackson was all right. He would do for her. She switched off the fan. Combed her hair, powdered her face and pulled aside the curtain to greet Mr Coates who was sitting looking at Jumbo. He was still, hands dangling in front of him, his bush shirt rucked up untidily into creases.

"Hello again Mr Coates. Isn't it awful what's happened here?"

"er…yes. Were you close with the poor lady?"

"Of course. We've grown up with her always there. They're a quiet lovely family. She's beautiful. Kind. Funny. Always ready to have a laugh or joke with us."

"I don't think she belonged to the club, did she?"

"No. They're not too outgoing. I think Mr Johnson's busy with his work and Ralph's busy with his schoolwork and the old lady, Mr Johnson's mum, is busy taking care of all of them." She gave a small smile.

"Mrs Johnson's mother-in-law lives with them, does she?"

"Hmm. Yes, I suppose it is a good thing. They seem to get along. No rows. Nothing we hear through these walls anyway." She laughed ruefully.

"Oh. So you can hear everything that goes on because the walls are thin?"

He looked disturbed. He twitched his shirt collar, pulled open the buttoned-up neck, Jumbo opened an eye and looked warily at this stranger sitting in his master's chair.

"No. Not everything. I'm exaggerating. We hear a lot. But only if someone is really shouting or yelling. And we have those quite a bit." She smiled to show the perfidious thin walls were not to be taken too seriously.

"Would you like a glass of water? You seem to be feeling a bit warm."

"Yes. A glass of water."

Grace poured water from a bottle in the fridge.

"Here. Thank goodness the power has not been affected by the bandh."

"Yep. Everything else seems to have been. A bloody mess. All around we have a mess and a stink. Oh Grace, I often wish I had left back in the fifties when it was easier to leave and emigrate *somewhere* – anywhere. I remember the old rhyme we used to sing *'One flew east, one flew west, one stayed in the cobra's nest'*, well we're here all right, nice and close and cosy, stuck with the goddamned cobra aren't we?"

Grace was surprised. The Coates were known for their staunch support to an independent India. They were never heard to pine for the 'good old days' of the Raj, or indicate the strong loyalty to the British Anglo-Indians were notorious for.

"Really? Why? I'd never dream you would feel this way. Why?"

Any reply John Coates might have given was cut off by the appearance of her father.

"Hello John." He put his arm around John Coates in an unusual show of affection.

"Hope the day will be better than the bloody shambles of last night and earlier on here. My *god*, what happened to everyone. The stars really played up, didn't they? Everything's haywire."

His eyes filled and he quickly went to the dining table where he poured himself a cup of tea and took a slice of toast from his side plate.

"I'm sorry. I can't get my head around what's been happening. Look at the horror here. *Fucking* sweeper. Hunchback *bastard.* Worked for years without a hint of trouble. Who'd think the toad would do a thing like this? Good he took his life. He should have let us bloody string him up – bloody *curse.* The pariah should've been left to die in his own shit."

Grace had never heard her father swear like this. It was out of character and in spite of the fitness of the moment, still shocked her.

A short silence passed. Grace shut her eyes and decided not to comment on the outburst, not to say anything.

Bob Renshaw crunched on his toast.

"Dad. Dad. Why don't you get ready?"

"I'm ready. I'm good and ready. Want me to put on last night's glad rags? I'll look good when they tell me my son will never be normal again?" His voice was quiet. But the anger was there ready to spill.

Grace flinched.

Her easygoing father had never ever indulged in this kind of sarcasm. She was not used to dealing with this side of a person she had only known as kind and loving. Always laughing, always making corny jokes. She could not remember his voice ever honed by irritation or impatience. This was new and unnerving.

Bob Renshaw put down his cup of tea and covered his face with his hands.

"I'm sorry my girl. I'm sorry. I can't deal with this. I can't."

John Coates gently reached out to Bob and forced him sit.

"Take it easy, Bob, take it easy. We'll be going soon to see Carl. He's in good hands. Why don't you finish that toast?"

Bob suddenly gave a laugh. He looked up at John Coates, "I never thought I'd see the day when Kitty's old boyfriend would be taking care of me. Really appreciate it old man."

John Coates stiffened. He looked across at Grace and gave her a small sheepish smile.

It was a ticklish moment. Bob nibbled on his toast unaware, or uncaring, of the awkwardness he had caused. Crows perched on the window cawing and Bob threw out some of the crumbs to them. The muezzin began the call to prayer. A fly buzzed and Bob swiped at it.

"Damn sudden sunshine brings out these bloody things." His mood seemed to have lifted. The despair of five minutes ago vanished into a bland acceptance of the day as it was unfolding. John stared at him and gave Grace another odd smile.

"A nice man," Grace thought. "Wonder what happened between Mum and him. If anything."

Kitty suddenly came into the room. She had changed into a skirt and blouse and looked worn.

"What's been happening here? Bob behaving badly, has he?"

"Yep. Up to what I do best. Playing dumb."

Kitty looked quickly at her husband.

"I don't think you do that at all. Hurry up now. It's late and Dr Mitra said we need to be there before six-thirty. Will Mrs Jaiswal be there as well John?"

"Rupa? Don't know. I think Roger Lawson will be there. I think he said he'd be in touch through the day."

"Kind of him." Bob finished his slice of toast, called for the servant to take away the plate. He smiled disarmingly at his wife, daughter and the paunchy man who seemed to have taken over control of his home. He shook his head as if to clear his thoughts. He glanced at his family again. Funny how things worked out in life. Kitty had missed the mark, just as Grace seems to have missed it and perhaps even old stuffed shirt Coates had missed it as well.

It went back decades to that tacky club hall where Bob knew he was the second prize, as he danced away with Kitty Palmer and knew John Coates looked on.

14

It pops into Rupa's head as she waits for Roger Lawson's call and knock on the door that she might be getting too involved with the man and by association with his community. A strange bunch, she thought. Always so eager to trace European ancestry, always rejecting the reality of the times for a dubious white pedigree. A smile flitted as she recalled Yvonne Coates telling her of her Spanish ancestry. "My mum told me that I got my sense of music from her mother, whose grandparents had come over from Spain. And of course there was my grandfather's family who hailed from England."

"Of course. How nice." Wonder what the good lady Coates would say if I asked how that amalgamation took place, she mused. Ridiculous conversation. With no matter or mind in it. Totally vacuous. What on earth was she doing there?

She saw a people with a sense of deprivation, a people who sadly resented the facts of their roots.

Rupa felt a twinge of pity for the woman. Poorly educated, but canny with the alertness of survivors, Yvonne was nursing heartbreak with the bestowing of the May Queen title on another. Clearly she felt Rupa was the prime mover in voting for the Renshaw girl.

Rupa heard the doorbell peal. Roger's here. She seized a brush and began to brush her hair. Was she 'in face' this morning? Did the late night and morning's excitement show in shadowed eyes and dull skin?

The ayah called softly through the door, *"Memsahib,* visitor asking for you."

"Tell him I'll be there. Ask him to sit and tell him I'll take about five minutes."

"Haan memsahib."

She felt a flutter within her and immediately annoyance grew as she chastised herself for behaving like a schoolgirl.

"For heaven's sake. Act your age. He's not for you and never will be." Sharp rebuke.

She scrutinised herself in the long cheval mirror and saw a short, dumpy woman who was fast slipping to definable middle-age.

Rupa, Rupa, stop this, she chided herself. Think of the children.

Tracing a faint lip gloss on her mouth, she tucked her blouse into her jeans and quickly entered the front room.

"Hello Roger. Well here we are again. Her voice was hard-edged, her throat dry.

He looked surprised and nodded a greeting.

"How good you look."

"Rubbish. I'm too wide and short to look anything but a frumpy housewife."

"Accept a compliment graciously, Rupa, it makes everything so much nicer," Roger smiled but there was a wariness in his eyes.

"Like something cool before we leave? No dosas. It's so muggy, we probably have to face more power cuts when we arrive at the nursing home."

"Nope. I'll pass."

"Fine. Think I'll have a nimbu pani, and take an umbrella, it's much too hot out there to go out without some kind of armour."

"Amor?" He twinkled at her and Rupa felt a wave of confusion as she tried to look nonchalant.

"Stop the puns. I hate them."

"I love 'em."

She grimaced and reached for the drink that had arrived, tall and frosted. Wincing at the sharp taste she hoped she looked impassive. Roger Lawson sat patiently and waited for the stylish Mrs Jaiswal to accompany him on that hot and humid afternoon to see how Carl Renshaw's operation had fared.

For the minute that stretches Rupa finds herself turning into her mother.

How will this man treat you? What has he to offer? Has he a good background? Education? Religion? Is he really taken by you or is it your money, your job that attracts? Don't be stupid. Remember the mess of the last relationship.

She suppressed a shudder when she recalled the bitter finale of her marriage. She thought briefly of the months that followed and her involvement with Sunil, a distant cousin whose concern quickly slipped into something more basic.

It had been furtive, both realising the futility of the situation. Related to her on her father's side Sunil was a quiet man, even dull. But his support during the ugly bickering of the divorce had made Rupa depend on his presence. It happened so suddenly, the casual hug that turned into an embrace and then an abrupt clutching and grasping that had them co-conspirators in a proscribed passion.

It lasted a month.

They had been surprised one afternoon by Rupa's maternal aunt. It had been a chilly December and they had both arrived late from the court. A murky morning and a strong dollop of depression made her reckless. Careless of the servants or an unexpected visitation, they sprawled on the divan in the living room. It was sheer pleasure that made the moment last. Clothes strewn about, they lay in each other's arms, the cool of the day banished by their bodies' warmth.

Her children were at her mother's for the weekend and the ayah was asleep in a room down the hall. It was perfect. Horrified to hear a sharp rapping on the front door, they shot off the divan, muddled, untidy.

"Rupa, *Rupa...*"

The knocking grew louder. Then the doorbell was rung. In a moment the ayah would be awoken and run to open the door.

"Get your clothes quick."

Sunil stumbled from the divan, the vase from the side table was knocked over, water spilling on to the carpet.

"Ouf. Hell. Look at what you've done. Hurry, hurry."

Quickly scurrying around Sunil hopped into his clothes and gesturing Rupa to go into the bedroom, squelched over the watered patch now rapidly soaking into the Kashmiri carpet, opened the door.

"Arre beta, what are you doing here?" It was Rani aunty, the scourge of the family. It was her rasping voice Rupa quailed before as a child.

Sunil stood smiling foolishly. The ayah, by this time awoken from an afternoon nap yawned noisily. After a deep namaste she quickly took the parcel from the elderly lady and padded off to the kitchen.

"Where's Rupa? Rupa, *Rupa.* Oi Rupa *beti,* where are you hiding? *Rupa.*"

As sharp as her jars of pickles she constantly prepared, the old lady's eyes gleamed, her mouth downturned with reproach.

"What is this? *Hai, hai.* You two here alone? Such a bad time when Rupa is bearing much sorrow and gossip from everyone? Go home you. You have work to do and Rupa has much to do as well. Off you go. You young ones of today, what is all this nonsense? Too much time at pictures, all is Hollywood, all is falling into arms and kissing and all that *rubbish.* Are the children coming home this weekend? I've brought Devi's plum *kasundi.* See it's kept in the fridge and don't eat too much at one time. It'll give you a cough and put your stomach out. *Arre.* the carpet is wet here." All the while looking stonily at Sunil, she then turned her accusing stare on to Rupa, who emerged from the bedroom, hair combed, a salwar-kameez meticulously fresh and ironed to perfection, with a prepared smile that crinkled her eyes. A charade the old lady saw through easily.

"Rupa?" Roger called softly.

Rupa was jerked to the present with Roger looking at her quizzically.

"Ready to go now?"

Rupa thinking back, laughed at her chagrin and embarrassment. Thereafter the aunt had made it a point to visit regularly, always with her bottle of pickle, mango during the summer months, brinjal and chilli in the cooler seasons, but there was no real need for this overseeing, Rupa sheared away from casual sex. The afternoon meetings with Sunil ended.

With the divorce proceeding over, she found that work in her small agency blotted out much of the messiness of her life. She was focused and relished the day to day wrestling with a lagging business staffed by diffident workers. Steeling herself to be unpleasant she began by dismissing several of the long-time employees. There was resentment and she was abused 'Shitler, Hitler', behind back. There were ugly scenes at meetings with some of the grizzled copywriters and accounts executives. She enjoyed the duelling, she enjoyed the adrenaline rush, and to the surprise of many, the shedding of much deadwood, plus a young, uninhibited staff, the agency began to emerge as dependable, reputable. Her risk-taking paid off and the agency began to make money. The ultimate accolade. She was absolved from former indiscretions and soon her scandalous divorce was a thing of the past. A recognised personality in business circles she earned a reputation for being a fair competitor as well as a formidable creative force. Her firm's ad campaigns carried punch, a quiet naughtiness that turned catchcries. 'Have fun, but first have a Dulex', a campaign for family planning, caused eyebrows to shoot up. It was considered flippant, irresponsible, to actually name condoms. A conservative society was unhappy. There were letters to the editors in leading newspapers, a sure indication of the ad's impact. Grudgingly accepting, the ad world adapted to a pervasive and feminist slant and there was rueful laughter at how Rupa Jaiswal's billboard one-liners did more for women's rights than scholarly debate.

That was years ago. Now with young, aggressive competitors, economic and social changes and dwindling clients, it was a slog to keep the accounts in the black. Rupa was considering selling out. She was tired and resented family time sacrificed to the business. Age was catching up on her, it was a fact and to be forty-three with a couple of teenage children did not present too rosy a future. Rupa sighed.

Roger faced her. Still smiling he watched her sip at her drink.

"Nimbu pani good maharani?"

"Don't be silly today. This boy's accident is so tragic. On top of this there's this horrible incident in the block of flats where the Renshaws live. The stars are going haywire aren't they?"

"Stars? Nah. Don't know much about that stuff. You study the sky, I'll prefer to keep my eye on the ground. God yes, it's unbelievable such a thing should happen. How that man managed to attack that poor woman is a mystery. The flats are tiny, two-bedroomed pokey cubbyholes, everyone can hear everything through those walls. It's unbelievable. Horrible. Well, we better get moving, the streets are still empty because of the bandh, thank heavens. Come on, we should be off now. Your doctor must have some news now. God, I hope things are all right."

Rupa made no comment as they slid into the car. Her silent Kabir, his turban making him majestic, opened and shut the doors for them. The aroma of Rupa's perfume filled the closed car. Roger shut his eyes, enjoying the nearness of this luxury, and the strange quirk that had him enthralled by a possibility of what might be.

"Can't you get them to shut up?"

Lucy stands tired and blinking in the haze of a stifling corridor of this mockery of a hospital and tries to be understanding of the people who crowd everywhere.

"Lucy, this is not a private nursing home. This is where doctors work round the clock with nurses exhausted from having to see to a stream of people, many dying, frightened, most illiterate, all in terror of what the doctor is going to tell them. Where are the Vincents? I don't see them. Surely the daughter should be here. What's her name? Shirley? Maria? She has another name at home – Maya or something like that. Funny customs. Supposed to keep off the evil eye or some such bullshit."

Eugene Mills is irritable. He has not welcomed the thought of escorting Lucy, a stupid trollop in his book, to visit her uncle in this hellhole.

Why the hell couldn't her Indian boyfriend have brought her here. And what was he doing acting escort and help to a damned slutty woman. God, she was living with a bloody car mechanic in a hovel with the rest of that slummy population.

"No, I've not seen any of the Vincent family. Perhaps Mr Vincent is in a different ward."

"Emergency. This is it. Wonder where they are and where the old fellow is?"

A young intern, stethoscope dangling from thin neck, walked towards them.

"Miss D'Cruze?"

"Yes?"

"Come with me. You can see the patient now. Please do not talk much. He is not strong and cannot really be upset by visitors. But you are his daughter I believe? So it's all right."

Lucy lets the mistake pass. She is not about to explain to a harried medico the intricacies of family ties.

"Will he be better soon?"

The young man shoots her a look impatiently.

"You go now and see him. Please make your visit short. He is barely conscious."

Lucy walks down and turns a number of times, a maze, before she enters a tiny cubicle, the hospital smell grows stronger.

Disinfectant and bodies. The mouldy air of disease and illness. She shudders and steps into the cubbyhole.

Her uncle lies immobile. There are several tubes running from him into the hissing machine by his side. His head is shaved

Will she talk to him? More important will he be able to understand and talk to her?

"Uncle?" She whispers. "Uncle?"

Silence. The sibilance of the machine the only sound in the room.

Lucy's eyes fill. Tears stain her face. This was not meant to be. Her future is now melded with the life of this man lying there.

Not guilty. Not guilty. Lucy allows herself the indulgence of clearing her conscience. No, she will not permit this accident to be the cause and effect of her decision to leave Pradip. She sees clearly the life ahead of her in that shrunken space. If her future is to be compromised she rather it be with the certain comfort of language and food familiar to her.

There is a sound behind her and Lucy turns to see the medico waiting. She bends her head and joins her hands in what she hopes is a good 'thank you' gesture. Prepares to leave.

The young man waits for her to come to the door.

"Luce?" A whisper.

She turns back and sees her uncle's eyes open. He is looking at her. Swiftly she walks back to the narrow hospital bed. She holds his hand tentatively in hers. He smiles. The tubes in his nose distort his face.

"*Luce.* Here."

Whether query or statement she did not pause to think.

She bends and cautiously wipes the damp forehead with a tissue.

The medico frowns. She is not supposed to touch the patient.

Lucy ignores the displeasure.

"Of course Uncle Ed. What did you think? Can't get rid of me that easily."

"Tell Chloe you're all right." A whispered plea.

The confusion and mix-up of names pierces her. Her throat seizes. She is moved and stoops again to kiss the seared cheek. Stubble grazes her face and she forces herself to ignore the rancid breath.

A tear travels down from the corner of his eye to the pillow. Are they tears or the effects of the medication?

Stillness settles again. She releases his hand carefully and looks at the medico, smiles self-consciously.

"Come on miss. I doubt if he'll come round again."

Without answering him she allows herself to be shepherded out towards the general area again. The strong odour of bodies, of general congestion and Eugene Mills waiting. He looks edgy. At their approach he quickly comes forward and addressing the medico asks how Mr D'Cruze is. Any progress, he says in a voice that sounds too loud.

"It's too soon. Have to wait to answer that."

The young medico turns abruptly and walks away. He does not give any sign that he is interested nor does he show sympathy.

"Let's go. *Chalo.*"

Eugene Mills, wiping the perspiration from his face ushers Lucy towards the exit, blocked at the moment by a wailing family.

"*God.* All we need now. Bloody city. More chaos. Caterwauling nuisances."

"Well they have lost someone you know."

He looks hard at Lucy and mutters under his breath what sounds like swearing.

Lucy is almost amused. Here is this man who has brought her here, this pitiful place, to visit her injured uncle and he is upset by a grief-stricken family blocking their path.

"Come on, come on. Luckily because of the bandh we can easily walk back home."

Yes, there were no trams grinding their shambolic way through the streets. A hot summer afternoon was brewing an evening storm. Beggars slumped along the street. Some asleep, others keeping a lethargic eye out for an occasional coin flung their way. It was, Lucy felt, a messy picture. If time stood still a framed portrait of the street would be a glob of abstract art. Swirls of chaos, tainted and captivating.

They step carefully around the crying family. Again picking their way over trailing saris Lucy and Eugene make for the entrance.

A child gapes up at them. A woman shields an infant under her sari. She is crying, but breast-feeding her baby.

Devoted wife and mother, Lucy thinks. Discomfort all around, most borne by this emaciated young girl. Everyone in this male-dominated world is put before her. She'll die, if lucky, by forty. This, a country with little respect for women. She remembered her uncle telling her just this, in one of his rare moods of communication.

"These people don't think of women as individuals Luce. Never believe they will give you equal consideration. Or respect. Forget Gandhi. He was the most *un-Indian,* Indian. Most of what he preached is totally unacceptable to most. Do you think most people will acknowledge Harijans are equal to the priests or merchants? Rubbish. Gandhi is a statue, a figure in folklore, he's now another damned god among all the other clay figures, a *'dada'* without teeth. No power in that smile. A dream."

She had not understood what he meant. Recently she had begun to think she knew what her uncle was going on about.

Her steps flag as she is distracted by the group of mourners.

Eugene looks at her, puzzled by the momentary slowing of her stride.

A moment of some unease as he realises Lucy might not return to her uncle's flat.

"I'll need the key to our flat from the Vincents. I think they may have it. I don't have it at present. Tomorrow I'll come here early to visit Uncle and try to let him know I'm there."

Eugene relaxed. He did not know how to broach the touchy subject but he gathered the crisis had been resolved and this idiot girl was returning home.

What a stupid bit of nonsense this woman had caused. The community was disgusted with her. Not just making off with an Indian but a mechanic for god's sake. Living in a slum with squalling families. He repressed a shudder. A quick look at her and he noted the serene features, the dignity in her posture. Well, she was reputedly clever. Not a secretary but quite a businesswoman in the small chemist shop she served at.

"Mr Mills?"

"Hmm?" Eugene started at the formality, few called him anything else but by his name. His mother insisted on the diminutive 'Gene', which he disliked. Now this girl, his own age, was addressing him almost deferentially.

"Yes?"

"Would you mind if I didn't come back to your mum's place? I want to go to the flat and see to things. I'm sure there's plenty to do there."

Should have thought of that before you daft idiot.

"No problem."

Good. It was good she was going as quick as was decent to take up her duty as housekeeper and carer of that poor uncle of hers. Eugene sighed. He looked at her, wondered at the path her life might take from here on. How on earth did an attractive, smart woman stray so wildly from the norm. Boredom? The old imp of perverse?

"Tell me Lucy, are you sure of this decision. I mean," he looked awkward, struggling with words he continued, "honestly, you've been pretty far out in your behaviour. Pretty outrageous. No one's happy. Are you sure you'll stick it out with people talking, probably resenting your being back in your uncle's home?"

He stopped. He took a deep intake of breath and found himself caught by the calm eyes of the woman before him.

"I've never really cared for what the people think or say Mr Mills. I'll be far too busy to wonder or bother much. And frankly I resent your judging my behaviour as 'outrageous' or any other term you care to throw at me."

He flushed. The correctness and the woman's calm defence beating his moral cant completely. He found himself strangely annoyed by her deference. Surely she knew how old he was, not much older that she was. At thirty he could look much younger and was still referred to as a *chhokra* by his family.

"Hey." The tone of his voice conciliatory, "maybe you should start calling me Eugene. I'm not much older than you."

Lucy smiled. Men and their vanity. Her thoughts flew to Pradip and his careful oiling of his hair, the attention to the brushing of the little bristle of hair above his mouth.

"Sure. Eugene."

They had reached their lane. The beggar at the entrance salaamed and rattled a tin at them.

Flies hovered, a tiara around the man's head.

"Maa," the whine so familiar neither Lucy nor Eugene really registered the plea. The smell of urine in the drains was powerful, emphasised as it was by the fragrance of a nearby flowering frangipani. It was the pungent odour that ushered them back on the road home.

As they neared the block of their flats both were relieved to see the entrance was free of the sensation-seekers.

"Gawkers and gapers taking a break for lunch and siesta," Lucy remarked.

"Of course. Can't do without the eating and sleeping, can we?"

"Thank god. I can do without the staring and grinning."

"Amen to that. I'll go up with you."

Surprised she turned to look at him.

"No need. If you give me the spare key I'll be okay. Get the other from the Vincents later. No bogeymen there to frighten me off."

Eugene looked irritated.

"Yes. I know. It's just that the whole of this mess has unnerved us. We'll be looking under our beds tonight. Poor Mrs Johnson. Poor, lady, poor…" he stopped, bit his lip and held out the small key to Lucy.

Lucy was ashamed she had briefly forgotten the tragedy of Hilary Johnson and her family.

"Yes. Of course. Do you think I ought to visit the family and find out how they are?"

"No. I doubt if they are in a frame of mind to be social or shake hands and say it's a fine day."

"I'm not expecting cakes and coffee you know."

God, what an ass this man was, how presumptuous to think she might barge into a tragedy and make small talk.

She closed her hand over the small key and unconsciously tightened it imagining her fist giving a sharp jab to the face before her.

"Thanks."

He stood there irresolute, eyes looking sideways, "Well I'll come up and see how're you going later, will I?"

"It's okay. I'll be fine. The visiting hours won't really matter. I'll go and see Uncle after work tomorrow. I can cook a meal, y'know, to keep me going and good."

He flushed again, the prick of sarcasm finding its mark. It was earned.

"Right. I'll let Mum know that you're home. She'll be around to give you a look-see I'm sure."

He turned and left the flat, ran down the stairs.

What had made him act so protectively? The woman was sensible, even if she had thrown away her good name. He felt ridiculous. As he passed the door of the Johnsons, he resisted the urge to look in. There was a policeman standing outside the door but he heard nothing to indicate any of the family were inside. Where were they, he wondered? Were they at the hospital or at the police station still waiting for the police procedures to be finished. How long before this hullabaloo would end was anyone's guess.

Already the story was growing unrecognisable. Rumours of a grotesque love affair between the molester and Hilary had sprung like weeds, screaming distortions of the truth. One story was that she encouraged the man, another was the man had given her a love potion, another one was that the sweeper's family had wanted her killed over some past slight. Everyone had a gaudy hue to slap on to this horror.

Eugene shook off the morbidity of the moment and quickly walked to his mother's home to let her know Lucy D'Cruze was back in her uncle's flat and to all purposes, fully in control of the messy situation.

Eugene Mills wished she were not so attractive.

Ralph Johnson sat cradling his pigeon in his hands. His father sat in an armchair in the living room. From time to time Ralph saw he drew a deep shuddering breath. His hands hung between his legs, occasionally he picked at his fingernails, looked at them as if considering a manicure. Ralph's grandmother went silently from room to room. She walked briskly, stopping sometimes to retrieve a misplaced cushion, or settle a knick-knack. She even paused to straighten some of the pictures on the wall. Ralph had counted the times she had gone around the three small rooms, it now was going on twenty rounds. Clockwise, anti-clockwise, the old lady marched, eyes bright on the floor picking up specks only she detected. Maybe she'd tire. Ralph was clocking up the twenty-first tramp around when his father looked up and said, "Mum, whatever you are looking for is not here. Sit down, lie down, but *stop* the walking."

Mrs Johnson paused, looked at her son and tiredly asked him if he wanted a cup of tea.

"No. Ralph?"

Ralph shook his head. The pigeon's coo was comforting. He stroked her crop and wished he had a cold glass of Coca Cola to ease the dryness in his throat and mouth. But that was impossible. They had no fridge and his father did not approve of carbonated drinks. A coke was drunk on the quiet, at school or at a friend's house. His mum loved fizzy drinks. He knew that. She had told him almost whispering to him one day. "Ralphie, we're going to have a couple of drinks at Grandpa's. You have your coke and I'll have a beer. Our secret okay? No need to mention this to Dad or Gran."

She had laughed softly and he had too, proud his mother shared this with him. Proud to be part of her world, a world which allowed for jokes, silliness. It was without the grim warnings of his grandmother or the constant seriousness of his father. His eyes filled. God, he prayed, make his mum well. Make her come back to him. How could he live without her, without the brightness that came only with her. His father's eyes, blank now, always scared Ralph. They saw clearly. Without softness, with little humour and plenty of common sense. Ralph never answered his father's questions. He knew his father had the answers. It was no use to try and talk of other things, or a different way of doing things. His father was always right. But not now. Now he sat still and looked tired. Ralph did not feel the slight fear he usually felt when he thought about his father. His father was sick now. He did not speak out his sickness. But he'd fall ill and then there would be no one. Only Grandma.

Ralph brushed his nose against Oleg's smooth head and felt his heart thump against his chest. Why won't this day end! The bandh was over. Sounds that were silenced began again. Traffic beeped and honked and hawked its way through their narrow lane. The dusty May evening, now black with the suddenness of a summer twilight, had come down and had brought the day to its close. He smelt the cooking in other flats. Someone was frying potatoes. There was the usual masala pungency hissing and spitting somewhere. A voice was raised in impatience. And the muezzin began the night's call to prayer. Over. This wicked day was being put to rest.

His grandmother had now gone to the kitchen outside and he heard the clatter of the kettle on the coal fire. In a little while he'd be asked if he wanted a glass of milk. That is, of course, if the milk had not gone 'off' in the heat of the day. No one had thought of buying extra milk for the bandh. The milkman had not come today.

"Ralph. Ralph." His father is calling him. He pretends not to hear.

"Come on. Get up. *Get up.* It's time to help your gran with the dinner now. We will be going to the hospital soon so we have to get ready now."

Ralph looks up and stares at his father expressionless.

"I don't want to go. I'll stay at home."

"What?"

His father is astonished. The boy has remained oddly self-contained through this hideous day. It was his mother, the old lady, who had screamed and raged at the news. The boy, quiet, speaking only when he asked for his pigeon to be fed. At the hospital he had stared impassive at his mother. He had not asked the usual questions Fred Johnson thought he might. Was the boy simple or what? Didn't he know the facts of life? Was he not cut adrift to know his mother had been so vilely abused? Fred stared at his son.

"All right then. Stay home."

"She is going to be all right isn't she?"

At last. Some flicker of caring.

"We have to wait and see."

"Is that man really and truly dead?"

"Yes."

"Good."

The hardened tone chilled Fred. Ralph sat there, a man, the boy had been extinguished. He looked at his father with the pigeon in his arms and said, "Dad, I want to go to a different school. I don't want to go back to face stupid questions. About mum. About us."

"We'll have to see about that Ralph. I can't whisk you out of school and into another that easily. You know it's the middle of the year. It's won't be possible to ask for a transfer and I doubt if you'll get it. But we'll give it a try." Fred was tired. He had not the energy to pretend that he might consider his son's request.

Ralph smiled at Fred.

It was a moment shared.

Maybe things might work out. This nightmare put behind them. They'd move to a new neighbourhood. Couldn't possibly stay on with the whispers and the sly looks of the slum dwellers who surrounded them. He wondered if Hilary's parents might agree to their living with them until they could get new accommodation. His chest tightened. Thrown on people's goodwill. Was there any of it around anymore? He cringed inwardly at the thought of having to ask and depend on kindness and understanding. It never did to depend on kindness – of strangers or worse, of relatives and friends. Fred Johnson felt an icy wave of despair wash over him as he foresaw how life was going to take him through his future.

For now he smiled at his son.

His mother arrived, teapot in hand. Tea was always welcome.

Hilary. He saw her when he closed his eyes. She lay sedated. Immobile. The nurses and doctors brisk, going about the mechanics of getting people up and running, victims of disease, neglect or criminal attack, all of life's handouts. Thankfully no sympathy was offered nor were there covert looks at him. If he had to analyse the reaction it was as if there were not much interest in a matter he knew inflamed curiosity.

He replayed images that refused to leave. Again and again in the flat and clear imaginings he saw the man crouching over his wife. He heard the screams, the grunts, the orgiastic act, his wife, his wife, abused. Smashing the hammer into the monster. Good, good.

Savagely he picked at his nails. He ground his teeth. He glared at the workings of his mind. He knew he was infected with hate. Saliva seeped into his mouth, nauseous, he sipped the tea his mother handed to him. He looked up at her and wondered for the umpteenth time why the entire family had had to go out shopping for a few groceries. Usually his mother would go with Hilary, or he'd pick up something on his way back from work. His cuticles began to bleed. He noted dispassionately the skin around his fingernails were torn. Good. He needed to feel. To feel pain. His hands lost the usual well-tended look they usually had.

Hilary was not particular about the look of her hands. They were naturally fine, slender with smooth contours. The nails pale rose. Oval, she filed them short. "Can't be bothered," she replied when once during their brief courtship he asked why she did not use nail polish. It was the truth. During the years of their marriage she rarely spoke of the fripperies of make-up, or bothered whether there were signs of age around her eyes and mouth. After the birth of Ralph she had seldom spoken of fashion, or displayed much interest in her wardrobe. He noted with faint surprise Hilary did not speak much to him at all, nor did she converse all that much with his mother. Had she been too busy? Was it disinterest? Was it a woman thing? Did women's interest wane as they aged?

His mother still had a lively interest in her dress, her make-up. In fact he was vaguely puzzled by her feminine, somewhat giddy following of fashion and fads. If anyone kept up with the latest in whatever the glossy magazines reported, it was his mother. Strange how Hilary remained untouched by the hysteria over the ageing process or the fact her fashion was usually dictated by practical considerations. What did she enjoy? Who, apart from her regular visits to her family were her confidantes? She seemed happy to be in the house, seeing her family fed and happy. Frederick Johnson went over this catechism and found a result that was puzzling. Was his wife happy or not? Was their marriage a success? Was the whole time together farcical, an obedient bowing down before the altar of convention and approving nods from neighbours? When did they run out of conversation?

He discovered that he did not know much about his wife, her favourite book, film, song, or even food. He clattered the empty cup down on the floor, stood up and walked into the bedroom. Fred Johnson shied away from the word selfish, no, he was not that. Didn't he provide for their security, their well-being, their social status? No, he was not selfish, tired maybe, exhausted after the day's battles, the demanding office politics, the meagre stretching of what was surely a laughable salary, a scrounging for just that bit more to make the bank balance healthier. Paperwork, routine everyday politics, work had distracted him from the meshwork of wife, child, mother. He had not the energy to talk to his family. Even sex, the ultimate connection, he had misplaced. Surely Hilary had not placed importance on its absence? They were far too old for that kind of nonsense. Middle-age, it was the long haul before they could rest easy. Surely that was the way life charted itself?

He thought back to his parents, never really conversing with each other, or indulging in any silliness. He plucked at his torn cuticles. Soon it would be time to return to the hospital. He briefly thought of the two other men also there. Men who had saved his wife from that, that, that – fiend – too late – they had arrived too damn late.

"What is it Mum?"

"Fred, it's too late to go to the hospital. Why don't you stay home and make a phone call?"

"Are you seriously suggesting that these phones work and that there will be someone at that end to give me a clear report of how Hilary is at the moment? Honestly Mum, you put great faith into everything don't you?"

Mother and son stared at each other. Worry sharpening voices, their former deference forgotten, tempers were at flashpoint.

"Can I change my school Dad?"

"What?"

Fred looked at his son, standing still, rhythmically stroking the pigeon's neck.

"Oh for god's sake I think I told you it's not possible at such short notice!"

"But you can ask other teachers about other schools, can't you?"

"Will you *shut up* about the bloody schools? Don't you know what we are going through now? How can you think only of yourself when we are all worried sick about your mother?" Fred whispered the last sentence through clenched teeth. He looked furious and Ralph flinched at the fury in his father's eyes.

"Fred. The boy has a right to think of how he's going to deal with this…"

"Now you keep quiet. It's nothing to do with you."

"Nothing? What am I here, a *shadow*? I have a say in how my grandson copes with this horror. Or don't I?"

"Ma," Fred gripped the back of the chair, "please, I'm asking you. Don't make this day worse than it is. I'm trying to keep myself from going mad. Let's just be quiet. It's not the time to have shouting matches. Neighbours can hear, you know. We are an entertainment for them."

"How can you say such a nasty thing. If it weren't for our neighbours things might have been worse."

"How much worse could they be?"

"A lot. Hilary might have died."

Three people with one thought, caught and held, mortified by the wicked idea of death perhaps being a better way out for mother, wife and daughter-in-law.

"I'm going." Fred turned, picked up an old newspaper, smoothed his hair and walked out of the room.

"Come here Ralph." Surprisingly the boy went over to the old lady and sat down, Oleg, eyes round and incurious continued its gurgling.

"Don't worry your father now. It's a terrible time and we all have to try and deal with how the next days and weeks will be."

Tears ran silently down the boy's face.

Edna Johnson, put her arms around the thin shoulders of her grandson.

"Come now. Cry. You'll feel a lot better. Put that bird away, put it down now, and let me give you a hug. You're my boy, my *chhota* boy. My boy."

Twilight, short and swift, settled on grandmother and grandson, sitting, rocking together in a duet of grief.

15

An unprecedented bonus, that's what this chauffeur-driven luxury was, Kitty breathed deeply enjoying the special smell of the interior of the Mercedes. Its sleek interior, pale lilac-coloured decor, the plush leather seats, smooth silky fixtures enchanted her and almost succeeded in blotting out the mayhem of the past hours.

Her husband and John Coates sat on either side of her. The silence broken by the muffled sound of the wind whooshing by. Kitty ventured a covert look at her husband, relieved to see he was placid, sitting apparently intent on the darkened streets flashing by. John was staring ahead, his eyes looking into some private world. Kitty sighed. Carl. Her prayers, a mother's demands would have to be answered. She quietly reached out and took Bob's hand in hers. Apart from a slight squeeze there was no reciprocal look or change of posture. John, if he noticed, made no sign. Kitty, sick at the thought of what might await them at the hospital thought of Carl.

Her baby. The talented one, the child gifted from birth with a sense of humour. And though she would never openly admit it, her soul mate. Even as a child Carl had immediately clicked with her. She loved him with a fierceness that was illogical. He was the tender one. Offering her his pillow when she complained of a headache, sitting by her when she was about the household accounts and chores, asking questions about her youth and her childhood. Genuinely interested. Laughing at the same silly jokes. A montage of his cheekiness swirled in her mind. Carl and Jumbo, both with old shirts, sitting up and begging for scraps, his mime of the local church choir, then his young, clear, correct voice making the morning shine with the current pop songs. Carl. They were almost there.

Kitty wished she had Grace beside her at this moment. But Grace had opted to visit later with Daryl. Kitty felt an unease when she thought of Grace inadvertently witnessing the row between John and her. Surely John's presence also raised some curiosity. Why hadn't he driven over in his own car?

The car swerved to avoid a bullock cart, Kabir muttering under his breath. Then they drove into the wrought-iron gates and were in the pebbled driveway of the hospital. Bob released her hand. Kabir quickly was at the door opening it for them. Kitty slid out after Bob, John followed and gave a nod to the impassive Kabir. Kitty wished Bob had made some gesture of appreciation to the chauffeur. He always overlooked obvious social graces. He strode on ahead, Kitty and John hurrying to keep up with his long stride. She gave John a look of apology and he swiftly touched her arm, in mute understanding. The automatic doors opened, a blast of cold air greeted them and then it was the smell of the sick that enveloped them.

"Mrs Renshaw."

Kitty turned sharply. It was Rupa Jaiswal, here again, in spite of the early evening heat looking incredibly young and fresh, hurried through the foyer to meet them.

"How kind of you to be here, you really did not have to take the trouble to come here, how did you travel with your driver 'loaned' to us?"

"Don't worry about it. We came in earlier, Kabir is a superb driver. He's quick and efficient." Rupa spoke breathlessly, she smiled with warmth at John and Bob.

"I'm sure it's good news we'll have. Here's Roger."

Roger Lawson, appearing from a door behind a telephone booth, grasped Bob's hand in both of his.

"Mr Renshaw. Mrs Renshaw. Mr Coates. Hello again."

He looked relaxed and after the quick greeting went over to Rupa Jaiswal, and standing near her made up their group, waiting for the verdict of the omniscient Dr Mitra.

Awkward, silent, they all looked at the big clock, cleared their throats, watched the constant stream of staff and visitors going through the room. Minutes crawled by. Every white-coated medical who appeared brought a jerk of apprehension. Dr Mitra was nowhere in sight.

"What time is it?" Kitty looked at Bob.

"If that clock is correct, which I doubt, it's about a quarter past seven."

"Weren't we supposed to be met here by Dr Mitra at 6.30 pm?"

"Come on Kitty, you know all about Indian Standard Time. We'll be lucky if the great doctor comes out at all."

"What?" Kitty's cry caused heads to turn and Rupa went over to her and placed a calming arm around her shoulder.

"Mrs Renshaw, I'm sure Dr Mitra will be here. He is a committed man and will be here if he said he would."

"I'm happy you have that confidence in him Mrs Jaiswal, *okay?* But we're talking about our son here, my son who might not live, might have to live with brain damage and we have been waiting for almost this entire *bloody* day to find out what the great man will have to tell us." Bob, the long outburst almost whispered, looked at the young woman with an accusatory stare.

"Here, here stop this now, please, we are not helping this situation if we start bickering. And Bob, Mrs Jaiswal is not here to answer for Dr Mitra." John Coates returned Bob's aggressive stance with a calmness that quelled the roiling anger in the other man.

The lift door clanged noisily and Dr Mitra stepped out and walked towards them.

"Mr and Mrs Renshaw?"

Bob and Kitty, frozen, stared at the tousled figure of the doctor as he looked at them.

"I'm happy to tell you your son is out of danger." Kitty's 'ooh' was exhaled as a long strangled breath. Bob's hands clenched into fists, he stared, then in a long stride reached Dr Mitra and embraced him, his long arms totally enclosing the shorter, stocky man.

"Oh Mr Renshaw, Mr Renshaw. It's all right. Your son's injury was not as serious as we thought it was. The trauma fortunately did not damage the cerebellum."

The doctor patted Bob awkwardly. "Come on now, man. Your son will be one hundred per cent healthy. Come on, come on. It's all right."

Bob unsteadily came out of the odd embrace and in a half-circle turned to Kitty and grasped her hands.

"Can we go now and see Carl? Or is he still under strict observation?" Kitty still holding her husband's hands asked Dr Mitra, standing smiling awkwardly at the couple.

"He is under strict observation and will be that way for at least another week. But, yes, you and your husband can go and see him."

Rupa Jaiswal, Roger Lawson and John Coates stood mute as the couple before them struggled to cope with their emotions.

John Coates gestured to Rupa and Roger that they should allow the husband and wife some privacy.

"Mrs Renshaw."

"Yes? And please, call me Kitty. You've done so much, I never, never ever will be able to repay you. What is it?"

Kitty, tears tracing swift lines down her face, turned, and like her husband had done before her, clasped Rupa in a clumsy hug.

"Mrs Renshaw, sorry, Kitty, I'm so happy I was there for you all. It was a good thing for all of us I think." Rupa disengaging herself from Kitty quickly came up with a couple of tissues and discreetly placed them in the teary woman's hand.

"Now, mop up and go and see your boy."

Kitty gave a small laugh. She dabbed at her eyes, crumpled the tissue and made another series of wipes across her cheeks.

"Come on Bob. Let's visit our wounded soldier."

Bob slowly took his wife's hand and unsmilingly walked towards the lift. Dr Mitra's dark eyes trained on Rupa turned into a fawning admirer.

"*Aiee* Rupa, looking so young and beautiful and all. One look at you and my patients will regain health eh?"

"Bunty, stop being silly. But thank you, thank you." Rupa laughed apologetically and waved her hands as if brushing the nonsense away. She avoided looking at Roger.

Roger standing slightly behind Rupa, trained his gaze on a middle distance embarrassed by the sycophancy of the man.

John Coates pointedly looked at his watch and tapped Rupa lightly on the arm.

"Rupa, do you think we could leave before the Renshaws? I'm sure they'd like to be alone now. Seeing things are better now, perhaps we're in the way here."

"Mr Coates, I do think the Renshaws will be pleased we all are here. No, I feel they will be grateful we are here with them."

John Coates shrugged, her response surprised him and he realised perhaps it was the presence of young Roger that had placed them into this position.

Love's dream, he thought and yearned abruptly for long-ago days with nothing so demanding as the next day's work and his shy Kitty waiting for him at the bus stop.

"Mr Coates," Roger looking at him quizzically, "I'll call Mrs Coates if you like and let her know we'll be late waiting for the Renshaws."

"No," the word bounced off sharp and anxious. A quick laugh followed.

"It's just that Yvonne might not be there and our servant gets messages wrong over the phone." Again, a laugh, suppressed immediately as Dr Mitra breathing nosily addressed Rupa, "Right. I think I have a call coming through. Will be seeing you soon. Are you going to Vijay and Aruna's dinner tomorrow night?"

"Probably not. The children might be coming down for a few days and I'll be fairly occupied with them, you know."

"Oh yes, of course. Children. *Ouf,* sometimes can be nuisances, eh?"

Rupa made a face, whether agreement or put-down, and quickly said, "Bunty, you are a fantastic doctor. For all you've done over the last night I'll never be able to thank you enough. I'll certainly keep in touch. Call me during the week and we'll meet sometime."

"*Arre, arre,* no need to repay me like this, what are friends for, eh? Just give me a call to let me know how things are with you, and the children of course."

"Of course," Rupa smiled at the doctor's disappearing figure as he made his way towards the lift and was immediately surrounded by a posse of young medical students all talking quickly and urgently.

"It is late. But I'm sure we'll be home within the hour. How wonderful to know Carl will be all right." She did not look at Roger as she spoke.

"Yes. That is wonderful news. Thank god for your doctor."

"He's hardly *my* doctor Roger, but, I know what you mean. At times like this we should thank all our stars for giving us friends like him."

"Again with the stars."

Roger grinned, John Coates smiled and Rupa, guided them almost regally to an anteroom where they continued their wait for the Renshaws.

A fan whirred wheezily and a gecko, immobile, malevolent crept towards the insects around the fluorescent tube.

Hilary Johnson stared beyond her husband sitting mute beside her bed.

He held her unbandaged hand in a grip that verged on painful. Hilary made no response and looked steadily at the lizard as it slithered its way towards its prey.

Her hands were limp. The bruises on her face were marked, gaudy purple crayons slashed jagged lines across the delicate features. A nurse came and went in the stuffy room, not looking at either person as they maintained their still pose.

Frederick Johnson had no words of comfort to give his wife. Inarticulate, he looked at her and realised years of wasted time and moments had bound his tongue as surely as if he'd been struck dumb.

He found it hard to look at her face. The police had finally departed allowing for some privacy.

"You know Oleg has come back." As soon as the words were said he knew how utterly foolish he must sound.

Hilary turned her head. She looked at her husband fully.

"I'm glad. Where is Ralph?" Her voice sounded slurry, the words slow and heavy.

"He's home with Mum."

"Hmm. How, how is he?"

"He's okay. Nothing wrong with him."

"I know. That's not what I meant."

The words were soft, halting. The drugs were making her words garbled and as she gazed at him, Frederick saw the pupils dilated, huge. God, what had they pumped into her?

"Why don't you try to sleep?"

"Oh I will, don't worry."

The springs of the bed creaked as she made an effort to raise her arm.

"What are you doing? Do you want the nurse to come?"

"No, no. My body feels like its cramping. I wish I could turn over on to my side. Help me will you?"

"Hilary, let me call someone to help. I don't know if they'll like you to move at all." He struggled with her, gently placing a pillow behind her head. Her breath came shallow and noisy, after panting with the exertion of trying to turn she lay quietly on bed in much the same way that she had been before.

"Why not? I'm not ill, no bones broken, just another rape victim."

"Oh *Christ.* Why are you talking like this?"

"What do you want me to say?"

"Try to sleep. Sleep. Sleep."

"Poor Fred. So careful about what other people might say."

"No, that's not true."

"Isn't it?" Her eyes closed and a trickle of tears seeped across the purple stains.

"Hilary. You have to rest. Get better. That's all that's important now."

Silence.

The sounds of the hospital grew loud as the silence filled their space.

Fred stared at the covered figure of his wife. The bed linen was not clean. When his mother had remarked on this Fred had looked at her as if she were insane. Did she imagine this was a five-star resort or one of the expensive nursing homes often used as rest and recuperation for wealthy businessmen and their bored children, wives, mistresses.

He was filled with desperation to move away from Lal Chandra Lane. Away from the community in that building. Perhaps her parents might know of a small place they could afford, somewhere quiet and most importantly a place where their anonymity would be assured.

No, that was impossible.

In a small community like theirs this was sensational gossip. He foresaw years of whispered talk, averted looks, and prurient speculations that would inevitably turn part of the city's legends.

"Mister, mister."

He jerked his head up and saw a nurse, frowning as she entered the room, she rattled the enamel bowl she was carrying and strode over to the bed.

"It's time you leave here. She needs rest. Visiting hours long over."

"I know that. I've got special permission to stay the night if I wish."

He was irritated by this young woman who clearly did not feel obliged to show either sympathy or courtesy.

The poor English, the disregard for the unmade bed, the slovenly state of the look of this place underlined what Fred saw as an unattractive professional.

Her hair tightly back, a bit of white starch linen balanced on an oily chignon, she glared at Fred. A rough twitch of a bed sheet and she flicked out a thermometer and shook it with a couple of snaps of her hand.

"Here. Open mouth."

Hilary eyes still closed opened her mouth obediently.

Fred wanted to wrench the instrument from his wife. He clenched his teeth and looked steadily at his wife, trying to ignore the grubbily-clad woman at her side, looking at a stop-watch.

"It is past nine o'clock.' You go now. If you have to stay you speak with matron for place for bed."

Fred ignored her.

Damned if he'd jump to her words. He'd spend the night on this hard metal chair if he had to. Already his back was stiff. The hours ahead promised a sore body as well as a sore mind.

More rustlings. He looked up to see the nurse writing up something on the small board looped over the end of the bed.

The nurse addressed him in Bengali, "She's very tired. Needs quiet. Why don't you go now? We look after her."

Choking down a sharp reply Fred remained sitting. He was not going to give any indication of his understanding or intentions. Let them figure it out. Bastards should have some English if they were to treat people other than Bengalis.

"You go now."

"You shut up."

The words were out of his mouth before he had time to realise how his rudeness might rebound on him.

"*Aiii.* What did you say? I will tell doctor I will tell him I will not attend here. You can't abuse. You speak your English in other places. Not here."

Fred started to answer then kept quiet.

No use at all to fight against the huge force that might be prepared to make life a hell for him and more importantly for Hilary at the mercy of anyone with a grudge against him or his community.

God, why didn't they leave for Australia when her cousins had immigrated? The deep regret cut through his mind. How foolish to think a life might be carved among a people resentful of past privilege and of natural born advantages.

The nurse stomped out of the room. He heard her shrill voice as she repeated the past drama to her colleagues and others in the corridor.

Christ, now he had done it. Hilary might have to bear the brunt of his stupidity. He squirmed on the hard cold steel chair and felt his throat tighten with tears of rage, of frustration. He needed to go to the bathroom. He shuddered at the thought of the lack of hygiene he would face there. The toilets, squat ones, would be a filthy nightmare. Everything was a nightmare.

"Mister Johnson?"

He looked up and saw a young slim doctor, smiling at him.

"Hello?"

"I'm Dr Ghosh. I'm looking after your wife. I hear you have requested to stay the night with her here?"

It might have been the flawless English, it most probably was the normal demeanour and quiet air of the man but Fred felt tears start and blur his vision.

He was embarrassed and quickly wiped them away.

"Yes. I think my wife would like me to be near her. At this time."

"Of course. Why don't you come with me and we can discuss the matter?"

Fred hardly believed the turnaround of events. He was being spoken to with civility and accorded choices he despaired of getting in this place.

Without a word he got up and accompanied the young man out of the room. The noise had abated somewhat with the lateness of the hour. There were still nurses and other staff who were scurrying around. But it was now fairly subdued and an air of some discipline had taken the place of the earlier bedlam that had greeted Fred.

He entered the cell-like room and sat tentatively waiting for the young doctor's words.

"Mr Johnson, first let me say how terribly sorry I am that this has happened," he paused and shuffled with some papers on his desk.

"I know this sounds silly. Nothing I say will make anything different," he looked up, suddenly got up, walked around to Fred and put an arm around him.

"Be brave. This will pass and yes, you'll hear others say the same, but time does heal. You have a wonderful family. Live for tomorrow." He blinked owlishly and then as quickly as he had come around the little desk, took his arm from Fred and walked back to his seat. Fred stared at the grimy wall behind the young doctor. The black electric wires were an ugly loop of ravelling knots. Insects were buzzing around the light above. Shabbiness and ugliness everywhere. No one seemed to care. He concentrated on keeping himself from collapsing into huge, heaving sobs. No one had touched him as much as this stranger. He sat as if petrified.

"Dr Ghosh." The two men looked at each other.

"Yes?"

"Thank you. You have been the only one who has given me hope. You have shown me kindness."

"Mr Johnson, you needn't thank me. Just remember, don't fall into apathy, for that leads to despair."

Fred noted abstractedly the young man's heavily accented English. He thought back to his schooldays when he and his friends mocked their teachers' incorrect pronunciation. How ridiculous all those hidebound feelings. He looked at the man opposite him.

Dr Ghosh smiled slightly. "Would you like a glass of water or something?"

"No, thanks. But I'd very much like you to visit us in our home sometime soon. We'd be honoured."

"There is really no need..."

"Please. I know my wife would want it. We will be moving. So I'll probably try and visit you here to let you know our new address."

"That's a good idea. A new start, eh?"

Fred nodded.

"*Daktar* sahib," an orderly peeped in, and bobbed a greeting to Fred. "*Daktar* sahib, patient in number eleven bed is having some difficulty with pain. Can you come and see him?"

Dr Ghosh rose, with a quick nod to Fred walked out of the dingy room and vanished into the now quiet hospital corridor.

Fred's thoughts leapfrogged into the future. He saw the tedious, tired days he'd face at his work. Quick, furtive looks from his colleagues, sly questions, awkward conversations, everyone clumsily avoiding any mention of the recent tragedy.

Hilary. His centre of being. He saw her pale and still. How still. He must summon up the lost energy to woo her back to health and his love. He must summon up the lost time to woo her back to him. Slowly he arose from the chair and was aware of a nurse behind him waiting for him to leave the room.

"I'm sorry. I didn't know you were waiting for me to leave."

He stumbled quickly towards the door and mumbled a namaste, and walked out of the office. He suddenly realised the nurse had been holding what was to be his bed linen for the rest of the night. She had followed him and had swiftly swerved to come before him.

"This way, this way please."

He walked back to the tiny cabin where Hilary lay, deeply sedated, motionless.

A small camp cot was tucked by her bedside.

"You sleep here tonight okay."

"Thank you."

He reached over and took the bed sheet and thin bedspread from the nurse. He flapped it into place over the taut canvas of the cot and quietly smoothed down the single pillow on it. The nurse had left. He was alone with Hilary. Fred Johnson slipped off his shoes, loosened his collar, unbuttoned his shirt, undid his belt and eased himself on the small bed. He lay there, he made no attempt to curl into a comfortable position to sleep for the rest of the night. He turned to look at his wife. He sobbed quietly. The bitter outpouring was for Hilary, for himself, for his son.

The summer heat coupled with the humidity made the bread mouldy. It caused the food to spoil if left exposed for too long. Power cuts were dreaded.

For those without the luxury of a private generator it often meant hours of stifling heat, sweat and frustration. Candlelit meals were accompanied by insects, children and students peered over homework and everyone cursed a crumbling administration.

Yvonne Coates watched her maidservant set the table, then squinted at the clock and made a moue of annoyance at the lateness of the hour. She could hardly make out the numerals on the clock but refused to wear spectacles.

"It's all right, *thik hai,* hurry and bring the dinner. The sahib will be late tonight."

She had scarcely said the words when the front door opened and John came in. Shaking his head, he threw a parcel on to the hall table and went into the bedroom. She heard the bathroom door shut and heard the gush of water as she knew he was washing his hands. For the umpteenth time she wished the sounds in the flat were not so easily transmitted into the other rooms. In spite of the thick walls and high ceilings, sounds flowed smoothly through the house. Good acoustics, John had once laughingly remarked. She turned her mouth down in a silent sign of annoyance. John made anything into a joke. Even their marriage. She sat down and wondered where Heather was eating out. She had said she was invited out to a friend's marriage. It was the reception, not the religious ceremony and Heather had mentioned the venue, an exclusive club. Lucky Heather to be out, enjoying herself on this sticky, damned May night.

"Hello my dear."

John entered the room, his hair wet from his quick wash. He had changed his shirt and the vest he had worn was torn at the waist.

"Why are you wearing that old thing?"

He looked surprised, "What's wrong with wearing it at home? I'm sure Neeta won't notice."

"Neeta is not paid for us to bother whether she cares what we wear or not. But *I* care."

"Oh Yvonne, you are priceless," John smiled as he reached for the main dish and spooned some potato chops on to his plate.

The sauce dribbled on his plate, the salad looked limp, cucumbers in vinegar and onion rings made up the greens for the evening meal.

"Can't we have a rice and curry meal instead of these side dishes?"

"What's wrong with the chops?'

"Nothing, nothing at all. It's just that on a hot night it's better than having these heavy dishes."

"Curry and rice and dal are not heavy?" Yvonne said this with an exaggerated questioning look.

"For heaven's sake, you know what I mean. A vegetable curry with a good spicy dal is so much easier to eat to digest."

"Your heartburn has nothing to do with what you eat. You're upset. You have not been home for most of the day. Running around after other people's children, meeting and consoling *old friends,* that's the cause of your poor digestion."

John chewed carefully. The tasty chops could have been sawdust. His appetite vanquished with Yvonne's insight.

"Some mustard could kick these chops into some taste."

"Why don't you pick some up from Yasin's next time you go that way. It's on the way to the Renshaws so it will be easy enough to get. Then, oh yes, we'll have plenty of mustard to last a lifetime."

John got up abruptly. The chair scraped on the concrete floor. He wiped his mouth with the napkin, folded it carefully, placed his knife and fork on either side of the plate then as carefully took the plate and smashed it on the floor.

Yvonne gasped. Her hands trembled and she laid down her cutlery and stared at her husband.

Both were stock still, shocked into immobility. The smell of the vinegar was strong in the air.

Neeta came running in and stared in disbelief at the shattered plate with the remnants of the meal, a mess all around it.

"Hai, hai, kya huah?" She looked at the man and woman staring silently at each other and went out of the room to return with a dishpan. Scooping up the food and shards of china she scurried out, wondering what has caused the tamasha between the sahib and memsahib.

"They are both so good. Why for this trouble and anger?" Neeta, cook and general caretaker of the Coates' household for over a decade shook her head in puzzlement over the recent odd behaviour.

"Hai, hai. Getting old. Yes. That's what's happening, both getting old." She emptied the debris of a good dinner into the bin and returned with a mop to swab the smears off the floor.

The sahib was not there. He must have gone back into the bedroom. His glass of water was untouched. The memsahib was sitting and had begun to finish her dinner. Her hair was loose and pinned untidily behind her ears. Without glancing at Neeta she murmured, *"Jaldi, jaldi."*

"Han memsahib."

But there was no real vigour in the age-old command.

Neeta shot her a quick look and realised the memsahib was not really thinking of her nor was she upset by the broken plate or ruined meal.

She dragged the mop slowly over the floor and thought about how the wife and husband were not so easy with each other anymore. They now did not even eat at the same time. Why, the old servant wondered. What had gone wrong?

It happens, she thought. Men and women too long with each other forget to be nice. Forgot to think of each other. It was like a habit. Good or bad, the living together every day, every year, rubbed natures raw sometimes.

The floor gleamed and Neeta backed out of the room glad to be back in the kitchen away from the unhappy scene. What had happened, she wondered again. If only Heather *baba* was here. Then things were smooth. Why did she not marry? She was now almost finished with her college. How much was she going to study? These modern girls, wanting jobs, wanting to be out just like men. All rubbish. Brought nothing but unhappiness. Here her mother and father thought about her and her only and she was hardly at home now. Books. Talk. That's all the *missybaba* seemed to do these days. All rubbish this new way of life for girls. All rubbish.

"Neeta!!"

"Han memsahib."

She quickly snatched a kitchen cloth and prepared to take up the table and lay another place for the daughter who was still not home.

"Almost half-past eight and yet not home. Very bad, very bad. I'm coming memsahib, coming," and fanning herself with the end of her crushed, faded sari she muttered, *"Bapre, baap,* how hot this day. Rain made it worse."

Padding quickly back into the dining room Neeta was surprised to see the memsahib had left the room and was obviously back in the bedroom. She strained her ears to hear the sounds of voices there. Nothing. No *golmal,* no nothing.

The memsahib came out of the room. Neeta saw she was dressed to go out. *Arre,* where was she was going out at this hour?

"Memsahib?"

Yvonne turned a strained face to her. "Neeta, tell the boy to call a taxi. I need to go to my mama's house tonight."

Neeta did not answer, her surprise ill-disguised as she turned to leave to fetch the young *chhokra* who did odd jobs around the house.

John Coates re-entered the dining room.

"Where are you off to Yvonne?"

His wife turned and faced him. "Don't worry too much John. I'm just going to spend a night at Uncle Sammy's. I think the air's too close in this house. Tomorrow I'll be back for some of my clothes. We both need a break. I certainly do. You can tell Heather when she comes that I'll be there should she want to talk to me. I doubt if she will, but it's nice to pretend she might."

"Yvonne don't be silly. Sit down. It's late and your uncle and aunt can both do without this sort of nonsense."

"Nonsense? I wouldn't call this nonsense. It's what I need to do and should have done a long time ago."

"Yvonne. You're blowing this whole thing up unnecessarily."

"No, I don't think so. Maybe I'll get a bit more respect around this house if I went the way I need to go."

"And that's your Uncle Sammy's house?" He smiled.

"Don't laugh. You all always do that. Laugh at me."

"Yvonne. Please. Sit down and think about this, think of your uncle if not about us. He's not too well. He needs his rest and routine. The last thing he needs is for you to come and weep on his shoulder."

"I'm not going to cry on anyone's shoulder. I want a change of scene. That's all."

Yvonne wrapped her arms around herself in what could be read as a gesture of self-protection.

"John." There was no familiar *Johnee.* "We need time out. I'm tired. You are too, I think."

"What are you tired of, you have everything. Beautiful home, servants, people bowing and scraping to the First Lady of the community and club…"

"You think I'm stupid and don't know they laugh at me?"

"No they don't…"

"My accent," she gave a dull laugh.

"You know, I even took a self-help book from the library on how to gain confidence, then there was a book of notes on literary classics, just so I could talk to Heather sometimes without sounding ignorant. I often wished there was a book on how I could talk to my husband."

John stepped towards her, with a twist of her shoulders Yvonne bypassed him and stood, placed herself nearer the front door. She stroked the wood of a sideboard near the door. It was the nicest piece of furniture in the house. Inherited from his grandmother it did not have the sharp lines of the other furnishings, most from the Park Street furniture shops. It had the veneer of age and the dignity of elegance.

"I love this sideboard. So strong. Like you John." She turned once and faced him with a look of frozen politeness on her face.

"Uncle Sammy will be happy to have me for company. I was always his pet. Poor fellow always worked to give me the best. Worked to get me out of the railway ghetto. I did all right with some. But not with you John. Not with you."

Again John made a movement towards her. A strong beep from a waiting taxi interrupted him.

"Taxi aagaya memsaab."

Neeta stood near, the boy hurried in, a wide grin on his face.

"Taxi memsaab."

John watching his wife hurry through the door felt sudden anger replace pity.

He remained quiet, thinking of how accurate the picture was Yvonne painted of their marriage. He had been bored most of the years of their time together. There were no high points of any drama. It was a bland flow of years most spent in his working at his career, recognition as a lucky couple within the community. His mother's death, a sudden succumbing to what had first been a simple bout of flu, had made him privately morose but it was the birth of their daughter that helped pull him through a flat succession of years. Yes, there was that. Heather. His beautiful, thoughtful girl. She quietly put up with her mother's brassiness. Father and daughter, they quickly, unknowingly, cruelly, established a partnership which excluded Yvonne. Jokes they laughed over, which Yvonne thought silly, later similar tastes in film, books, even, despite the ballyhooed difference in age, music. Yvonne, practical and happiest when casually gossiping or planning the next social outing made it clear she had no patience with the discussions John and Heather enjoyed.

"All these stories, they're just stories. You see a picture, read a book, sometimes it's nice, sometimes rubbish. Why go on about it? It's nothing personal. The way you two go on!"

John quietly gave up on trying to pull Yvonne out of her supreme self-absorption. Life seemed to be less noisy when he nodded throughout the long and aimless chats. Though dishonest, it eased their relationship, it achieved a veneer of compatibility.

The din of everyday life receded and John and Heather were happy in this cocoon, a flimsy comfort, on the edge of a quickly vanishing lifestyle in a confused, confusing community.

And then there was this May Queen debacle and Kitty Renshaw's tragedy. Kitty who seemed to have walked into his life with an abruptness that equalled her vanishing all those years ago. He had behaved badly then, and now he was behaving badly again.

John sighed. A man pushing sixty should be thinking of grandchildren, serenity, not this maundering fallback on mistakes past.

"Sahib?"

Neeta stood holding a paper bag. She eyed him warily.

"Kyaa?"

"Missybaba kyaa time phir ayega?"

"Nahin janta."

He looked at the paper bag. Neeta held it out and he saw it held some knitting wool Yvonne had bought to start a shawl for some charitable fund. She was excited over a planned autumn fete. Already she had a knitting 'bee' going. John was aware of an untidy profusion of tea-cosies, babies' booties, scarves, socks and other woollies in the house. Yvonne had unravelled several old cardigans and was re-using them, knitting with more gusto than skill.

When he once remarked that a shawl looked more dust mop than wrap she was hurt and went around with a frozen face. Stupid. What a waste of years their life had accumulated. All that genteel behaviour, just masking indifference. Just play-acting. Even their sex life was routine. Yvonne, excited more by family rows, neighbours' lives, club functions, he had gone along with the charade but now he was fed-up. He wanted a breath of honesty. And seeing the home of Kitty Renshaw, the ease between husband and wife had sharpened his longing for what might have been.

Inside the living room the phone began to ring.

What now, he thought. At this hour, who the hell was this?

"Sahib. Phone."

"*Aacha, aacha,*" Impatiently he stomped into the living room and took up the receiver.

"Hello?"

"Dad?"

"Heather!"

"Dad. I'll be spending the night here with Urmila. Is that okay? Her mum will drive me home tomorrow morning."

John immediately felt irritated by this new hitch in the expected routine.

"Why? Is something on that you can't come back tonight?"

"Oh Dad. It's nothing. Just fun having a girly night with 'Lila. We'll soon be back in college with little time for anything but slog then. Don't be mean. C'mon smile now."

Against his will John smiled.

"There, that's better. How's the Renshaw boy? Mum told me the awful news. Anything further? How's mum?"

"First things first. I'm smiling now, but you really ought to have been back tonight. Carl Renshaw seems to have pulled through. More serious than a headache but there'll be no lasting damage. Your mum? She's off to Uncle Sammy's for a few days. Feels she needs a break from the household chores."

He heard the silence as Heather's surprise hummed over the phone.

"What happened?"

"Happened? Nothing."

"Come on Dad. Mum wouldn't up and leave for Uncle Sammy's just like that."

"Oh well if you must know she was annoyed I went off to visit the Renshaw family." He foundered slightly not knowing what else to say. It sounded absurd even to his ears and he wondered if his daughter had ever had an inkling as to his connection with Kitty. Had Yvonne mentioned it to her in a rare moment of confiding in her daughter?

In a quieter tone of voice Heather asked, "Dad, could it be that Mum is really upset that I did not get that wretched May Queen crown?"

He laughed, relieved.

"No pet, no. Mum must have been really angry with me. Nothing to do with the May Queen Ball. Thank god."

"Oh."

He sensed her bewilderment. Her mother never really angry. Least of all with her father.

"Do you want me to come home then?"

"Don't be silly. This is a storm in a teacup. Your mum will be fine. She needs a break. Let her have a few days off from the round of keeping us fed and watered huh? She'll be fine." And so will I, he wanted to add.

"Okay. But it's strange, Mum going off like this." After a second or two she quickly added, "Oh Dad, she's not ill or anything?"

"No. I'd have told you if she were. Now please, enjoy your girls' night out and give my best to Urmila and her parents."

"Well," dubiously, "all right then. But I'll be home early. If Urmila's mum can't drop me off I'll make my way home by tram. Things are fine now, the bandh*s* over."

"Yes. Now off you go and have fun. Be careful."

"Bye Dad."

He dropped the phone back and breathed deeply. It was difficult pretending things were all right to his child. Intuitively she guessed that her mother's behaviour indicated something was seriously wrong.

John put the paper bag with the wool on the side table. He smiled when he saw the neat rolls of coloured wool. How like Yvonne. So enthused by an almost childish aim, which, he knew from experience, would be felled by the small jealousies that seemed to spring from these sorts of plannings. How many times before had he seen her amazed and hurt by what she thought were slights and meanness of her peers.

He walked to the bedroom and realised he had not really eaten all evening. The dinner had been somewhat melodramatically ended with his smashing a plate.

Hungry, he called for Neeta. She came wiping her hands on her sari.

"*Haan* sahib?"

"Omelette." He smiled at the woman.

"*Ji haan, sahib.*"

He knew she had a soft spot for him. A master who never questioned kitchen accounts, and rarely interfered with upsets in the daily happenings among the pots and pans.

He picked up yesterday's newspaper. Headlines shrieked about the latest political nonsense. Well the bandh was over, that was a blessing. Now perhaps these damned fools might let them get on with the business of business.

He kept an ear cocked for the phone call from his uncle-in-law. The old boy still had plenty of clout in the business and he hoped this row with his niece would not upset the tenure of life.

"Sahib."

Neeta stood with a steaming plate piled high with omelette the way he liked it, and a generous portion of fried potatoes, tomatoes and onions on the side. He smiled at her, nodded a thank you.

Putting the newspaper down he pulled in the chair, sat down and picking up his knife and fork sliced through the fragrant dish before him.

16

Old Mr Vincent stared in disbelief when he saw his daughter sitting besides his hospital bed.

"What's happened? Why are you here? Where's Ma?"

"Baba, you're awake."

He snorted. "What does it look like?"

A smile greeted this barb and his daughter, she who had married so badly, had been given such a fine education, came over and laid a hand on his forehead.

"Oh Baba. Don't you remember? You were injured while trying to help Mrs Johnson."

He looked up at her, this goodlooking woman who had so disappointed them both, his Fatima and himself.

"I remember. How is that poor woman?"

"She is still confined and the police have yet to make a formal inquiry."

"Inquiry? Why? That *harami* attacked her and Mr D'Cruze and I beat the hell out of him. He's dead? *Sabash!* Good, good. *Bahut aacha.*"

"Baba, Baba, don't upset yourself. Try and stay calm. You need to think of yourself now. Mrs Johnson has her husband with her and she will be all right with time."

"All right? *All right?* Are you mad? No one is right, after something like that happens to them." He glared at his daughter.

"Yes. I know. What I'm trying to say is try and get better so you can come home to Ma. She needs you."

Silence.

"What is your Joe doing? Can't he help around the house while I'm not there?"

"Baba. We are talking about Ma here. She needs you. Joe is there and yes, he looks after the children and sees that the house is running okay." She sighed. Unspoken criticism of her husband was thick in the air and she had long since given up trying to defend her husband.

"Please Baba. Don't fight with me now. Joe is the way he is. I can't change him. He is a loving father and he cares for me in his way." Even as she spoke Maria steeled herself to believe the lie. Her love for her husband had long dwindled. Her husband's charm and good looks were things of the past. Unemployment had dulled him. The quick wit was overtaken by a repetitious resentment of all his failures. Everyone else was to blame. He disliked his father and mother-in-law but was passive in his living with them, avoiding the responsibilities of a householder. Maria busy with the demands of her work had less time to pander to his rants. Physically he was growing into an old man. Sporting a paunch, a face lined with furrows that serrated once fine features, Joe Gomes now looked years older than he was, he brought no contentment to his marriage or his life.

Maria sighed and wished things were different.

"What are you sighing about? *I'm* the one who should sigh."

Maria smiled. Her father, even from a hospital bed had lost none of his snappiness.

"I know Baba, I know."

He twitched at his bed cover. Reached a hand up to his bruised head and grunted softly at the pain.

"Why can't I go home today?"

"No. You need to be under observation. We don't know if you are completely healed or not."

"What do you mean *healed*?"

"Baba, you suffered a concussion. At your age, it's not a good thing. Complications could set in later you know."

"Complications, what complications? My age is the complication. Will die of it, *bas, khatum, hogaya,* sooner with this knock on my head."

Maria stroked her father's hand.

He looked up at her and sudden tears welled in his eyes.

"Please *beta.* Take me home. I want to go home."

"Baba, Baba." The child, now mother to the old man lying there, bent down and wiped her father's tears away.

"Of course you'll go home. We all want to have you back soon, but now have a rest here. Worry these nurses, some of them quite pretty..." she laughed shakily.

Her father did not answer. He lay with his eyes shut. Without warning he said,

"Maria, tell Joe to go. Give that *ulloo* his walking ticket."

"What?"

"Tell Joe to leave the home. You need to be without that lump of nothing. *Beti, beti.* I know how unhappy you are. Live with us. Be happy with your children. This man is no good for you, no good for the children and he doesn't bring your ma and myself any happiness either."

Anger unexpected and sickening in its intensity swept through her.

"How unfair you are, Baba. You know Joe has been unlucky. He is wonderful with the children and he does help you and Ma so much. Why are you saying these things?"

"Beti, I don't want to upset you. You are my darling. But admit the truth about this man. He is a leech. He has a soft life because of you. Surely there is not much love left in you for him? How long are you going to support him? No one can respect a man without a job. Leave him…" he stopped and gasped. Breath short and energy spent, her father looked at her and both knew the truth of his words.

"Baba, I can't do that. I can't. I have not the strength to tell him to leave me. It is wrong, unkind. My children must grow with a father, even one who is jobless."

Maria stared at her father. How fortunate her parent's marriage. To live with someone you love, that was sheer luck. To be with someone you really love. How often does that happen, she wondered.

The grasp on her hand slackened and Maria realised he had fallen asleep.

She quietly loosened her hands and stepped back from the bedside. Soon she would leave and go back to the noisy house where her mother was fretting about her father and her husband surly as the dinner might be late.

He can buy something from the Chinese restaurant nearby. Cheap food, tasty, and a treat for the family to eat out. Tiredly she looked at her watch and saw with a shock it was past eight.

A long, long day.

There was nothing to look forward to but the shoutings of her children and the sullen silence of a man she was quickly growing to loathe.

That and her own lies. Depression grew and clamped down fast on her chest. She breathed in shallow intakes and started when a nurse entered the room.

In chaste Bengali she greeted the neatly dressed woman.

"I am going now. Look after my father. He gives you trouble I know. But he is a kind person. Think of him as your own father."

The nurse nodded, her features indifferent, she then took the chart at the bottom of the bed, read it and replaced it, all without a word.

Maria gathered her bag and a large paper container which had her father's clothes. She shuffled the contents into a neat pile and left her father asleep, dreaming no doubt of a happier time.

Brave Baba.

Rupa and Roger sat in a little restaurant off Park Street. It was dark, smelt of stale food, and the waiters who stood apathetically seemed to be more intent on watching rather than serving them. The air-conditioner rattled and the prawn cocktail they were picking their way through was limp with watery mayonnaise and a mild chilli sauce.

"Is it that bad?" Roger grinned at Rupa's obvious distaste.

"I've tasted worse." Rupa smiled and privately thought she had never had so much fun before. The city outside muffled by plate-glass windows was its usual rambunctious self even at this late hour. Everyone was yelling. Motorists sat on their klaxons, streams of hired labourers carried goods precariously balanced on their heads and made a quick and skilful way through the throngs of pedestrians. Goods were being touted their quality shrieked out by war cries. A few tourists who looked shell-shocked tried to walk and take in the sights of this 'huzlefuzlebad' of a city as Mark Twain had christened it. Feet scuffed up mini clouds of dust and grit, a swirl of murky water pooled in a gutter and Rupa wondered for the umpteenth time why she had not uprooted her business after her divorce and taken her family to the civil south. Bangalore. Now the burgeoning centre for foreign investment. Even some of the hill stations – Ooty, Conoor, names that spelt a cool relief from incessant discomfort.

Calcutta. She had been born here and though a boarder at the prestigious Loreto convent in Darjeeling, she had considered Calcutta her refuge. Every year during the three glorious months of the Christmas vacation she was indulged by her parents. In spite of her grandmother's frowns she cycled around their apartment block down the early morning streets to the Maidan. There, with a couple of neighbourhood friends they'd buy some of the steaming hot 'trash' food of wayside sellers. Delicious, the fiery hot channa and potato 'chaat' was washed down by the spicy tamarind juice. Then back again, trying to beat the office crowd it was a race back home. How quickly that time had gone. Cheeks reddened by the sudden change in climate from hill station in winter to the mild winter of the plains, they were noted, often enviously, as 'apple cheeks' the rich kids from the hills. Shaken from her reverie she grew aware Roger was staring at her bemusedly.

"Stop, don't say a penny for them, for I'm only looking at the mess we live in and wondering why and how we do it."

"Do you mean this fantastic, fierce city of ours?"

"Hmm. How is it your family decided to stay Roger?"

"Not all Anglo-Indians were in love with the thought of life under some other sky."

"A white man's sky surely."

"Yes," the smile slipped at her flippancy. A slight frown of irritation crossed his face. "True, but there were other reasons for staying."

"Like?"

"Well. Most of our family members were here. Just a couple of them migrated. And anyway my mother loved being a memsahib. Servants, leisure, the club, her committees, she lives and has lived a life of privilege and ease. I can't imagine her queuing at a supermarket or carrying groceries home – or vacuuming, hanging out washing or any of the stuff you have to do if you live in any of the western countries."

Rupa laughed aloud.

"Roger. Of all the reasons I've thought of for not emigrating these seem the silliest."

"Really?"

"Yes. Really. Surely you know how easy it is to maintain a lifestyle with all the mod-cons available. No more reliance on servants. The dignity of doing things for yourself."

"So, Miss Self-Reliant, why are you still here? Or is life with no driver nor bearer too bleak to contemplate."

"Now. Don't be angry. I didn't mean to laugh. It's just that your community seem to focus on the little things of life."

"Excuse me Mrs Jaiswal. Try living without them before you call them 'little'."

"Uh oh. I sense a quarrel." She covered his hand with hers and smiled at him.

"Roger. Face it. The reasons, or the chief one that your people are here is that they still have some stake in the country. In another country they would vanish. No aptitude for communal work. Not much of a sense of history. No interest at all in academics. And the greatest indignity of all, not accepting an India of and for Indians."

"How harsh you are."

"No. I don't think so. Be honest. Isn't it true?"

"Rupa. I've been born into what has been a fairly well-off comfortable family. I've never heard my parents or grandparents denigrate India or Indians. We consider ourselves Indians who belong to a westernised community. And an English-speaking one." Roger paused for breath. He looked at Rupa but she was silent. They both sensed a moment had arrived which might define which way their future could go.

"We're loyal to India. My uncle is a Colonel in the Indian Army. They fought with honour in the wars with China and Pakistan. My cousin is a professor in a college in Madras. My grandfather was a lecturer in biology in Jadavpur University. My sister is a music teacher in the Calcutta School of Music and a public relation manager in one of the leading commercial businesses in the city."

He leant back in the imitation velvet chair, "Now. Are my credentials to your satisfaction?"

"Roger. Silly. Of course I don't mean *you*. But you are not your community. Surely you can't deny most of your *'jaat bhais'* do not care to admit to their Indian connection. The girls I was with at school got into a tizzy if asked what their Indian connection was. The colour of their skin was a badge of honour and lord help us if their eyes were coloured or hair not quite dark brown. It was supposed to prove without doubt they did not really have any 'blood ties' to India." She smiled as she made the speech but the tone was serious.

Roger twisted his mouth in reluctant acceptance of her summation.

"Oh Rupa. Of course the community has been frivolous, in their aims, their decisions. Their loyalty. But can you deny they have had to fight against a wave of prejudice after Independence?"

"Sure. And haven't they deserved it?"

Roger fell silent. He thought of the constant reference to 'these people'. It was a phrase, he had grown up with. A favourite aunt had in an undertone confessed that though she "rode in their cars, and chatted and was seemingly friendly, she never was comfortable with *them*," It had shocked him at the time and disappointed him to think that this intelligent woman was so blinkered. It had caused him to re-think many of the truisms of his life. He seemed to have been caught in the cross-hair of vague suspicion on one side and an active bewilderment on the other.

Anglo-Indian girls seemed puzzled by his stance. In a simplistic answer to every problem they said they felt and knew things were better in foreign countries. This country was fast slipping down after the British left. It was a line and thought easy to fall back on when times were tough. As times were tough right now. Visiting girls, and taking them out, dating, an American concept seen on screen, not really in their lifestyle, was fraught with hazards.

His parents, acknowledged leaders of the community, were held in regard. However John Coates and his wife were only tolerated. Most laughed unkindly at the loud and gaudy presence of the parvenu wife Yvonne.

The Lawsons, Roger knew, were still the unquestioned leaders of the community. As such, girls were nervous when asked out by him. But in honesty he found he never really cared for any of the young women deemed suitable for him. Then his father died and he was abruptly the head of the family. In his thirties he was no longer the young son, he was the man of the house. His mother grew more reclusive and gratefully relinquished the running of the household to him. They slipped into a comfortable routine. His mother looking after the immediate concerns of home, the financial aspects his responsibility. Without really noticing it the quest for a wife receded and mother and son accepted their life together, a life rich with security and the esteem of their small circle.

Until now. Rupa. She had presented an entirely different set of values, a different lifescape and set a horizon that was lavish in its difference.

"Roger."

"Um…"

"Why so far away? Are you angry?"

"No, no of course not," he laughed, a muffled sound that had worry somewhere in its bumps of sounds.

They left the restaurant, prawn cocktail half-eaten, waiters duly tipped, and decided to go back to her flat.

"Kabir, *ghar chalo.*"

In the privacy of her flat, they stood facing each other duellists, tentative, uncertain. "Oh, come on now. Let's not argue. It's been an exhausting weekend and we should be celebrating the recovery of that young boy."

"Yes." He smiled, the one-word answer receiving a puzzled look from Rupa.

"It's the trouble with the Renshaws' neighbours now, isn't it? Has anything come of the inquiry into that tragedy?"

"It's the policeman who assaulted the boy. No doubt about it."

"No no, I meant the molestation of the poor woman."

"Yes. I just didn't want to talk about it."

Rupa looked at Roger amazed.

"Why not?"

"It's death, Rupa. It's poverty. It's exploitation. It's all those things. I can't help but think of that wretched man. He killed himself you know. Awful. Two other men have been injured. That family has been marked forever."

Rupa stared at her hands. She had nothing to say. She kept from the balm of banality.

Roger cleared his throat. "Look I'm not articulate. I put things terribly. But this has a ripple effect. The community will be affected in ways it has not even realised. I don't think I'm going to make good company Rupa. It's better that we stop seeing each other. You know what I mean."

"No, I don't really. Why has this anything to do with our friendship? We are not a couple or anything like that for godsake."

"Aren't we?" Roger smiled slightly. "Don't be naïve Rupa. You know how the grapevine works. Even now I'm sure your friends, relations, colleagues, have come to know that you are in the company of an 'Anglo'."

"Who's going to spread the word? My servants?"

"Yes. And the good Dr Mitra."

She laughed, surprised at his acumen. Their two-day encounters quite possibly solidified into gossip fodder.

"Well then. There's not much to be said, is there. You seem clear about how we bow to convention. But hey, neither of us are babies you know." Her logic was artless. Irrefutable. No commitments were made and at this absurdly early moment in their relationship, it was presumptuous of him to think she might even consider him in light of something more than a friend.

He began to feel foolish. A hot blush of embarrassment spread over his face. How stupid, how gauche he was. Why should a wealthy woman bother to take the few meetings and some compatible moments as the beginning of something serious.

"Darling Roger. I'm sorry if I gave you mixed messages. Of course I want your friendship. But anything else is pretty impossible. From all points of view. Think of what your friends at the club will say. I'm a Marwari. Whoops number one. A divorcee. Whoops number two. And that nose ring, whoops number three, four and five."

Roger didn't match her wide grin. He felt angry at being treated like a not too bright schoolboy.

"Fine, I'll just let myself out. We'll know about the Renshaw boy and no doubt you know someone high up in the judiciary who can rap that policeman's knuckles for him. Can you pull strings for a broken woman and her family. No? How strange. I thought you might fish out something from that box of contacts of yours."

Rupa listened to the diatribe impassively, then walked slowly over to the man in front of her. She placed her hands on his shoulders and lifted her face to his. Instinctively he bent and received the kiss she offered. He felt a rush of emotion, a shock and thrill as she slipped her tongue into his mouth. It felt fishlike, this exploration of his mouth, then she moved away, took his hand and led him to her bedroom.

"C'mon my darling Anglo. We're not babies. Let us celebrate the end of the bandh. And we won't be disturbed, the servants have a day off."

He followed dazed and speechless, fumbling with buttons, praying his breath was not stale. Life had thrown him a lifeline.

This was bounty, joy.

Joe Gomes looked blearily at his wife as she scurried around the room.

"When is the old man to be discharged?"

"I told you that we have to be there by 10:00 am, to sign the papers of release and see we have a taxi to bring both, Baba and Mr D'Cruze home." Maria looked at her husband still in pyjamas, unshaven at this hour of the morning. She had had to take a day off from her work to arrange this. Wiping her hands on the *jharan* she went to the door to give Lucy a call. Thank god for Lucy. Calm, unflurried in spite of the drama surrounding her, over the past week the young girl had visited her uncle and realising Maria found it difficult to juggle her work schedule, her children's school hours and housework, quietly brought back news of her father, old Mr Vincent. Fortunately both men, amazingly resilient, made recoveries that confounded the Jobs among them.

"I'm ready to go Maria. The taxi will be here shortly, I hope. Just remember to take another carry bag for we might need more than what we've got; to pack all the medicines separately."

"Oh. I'd forgotten that. Oh no, what'll we do. Will a plastic bag do?"

Joe inside the flat grinned and helped himself to another *dalpuri*. Better them than me, he thought, then sobered as he saw the day ahead with his mother-in-law to be seen and tended to.

Unlike her husband Mrs Vincent seemed to have retreated into a quiet place in her mind where neither her family nor home concerns impinged any more. She cooked the meals, half-heartedly checked her noisy brood of grandchildren but showed little interest in her husband's recovery or the affairs of the neighbourhood. If anything she was averse to hearing or talking of the progress of the past week.

Maria noticed when any mention was made of the recent tragedy her mother grew still, or walked away into another room. It was a reversal of the person Maria had grown up with, Ma – once always keenly interested in the world around her. Not for her was the political nonsense fudging its way through life. Or gossip of glamorous celebrities. Her interest which once piqued at the diet of her neighbours, what they wore, who they married, the children they had, the rumblings of discontent of the couples around them, now seemed quenched. She sat listlessly, rosary in her hands, beads slipping through her fingers, as she gazed at some private vision of her own. Even her habitual twitch of annoyance of having her son-in-law around the house faded into a passive acceptance. Occasionally her daughter lost patience and might sometimes ask her to speak up, not mumble, but Fatima Vincent was secure in her own world, not so much aloof, but far away from daily noise and loud voices.

Maria shut the front door and glanced at her husband still at the breakfast table. He was hunched over the newspaper. Her mother sat before the window, the radio was on and the announcer's voice was a soft mumble, nothing distinguishable. The children were at school. The early morning's hurry was slowing to the mid-morning lull when nothing save the bustee's habitual noise was heard.

"Joe."

"Yeah? What's it?"

"See that the bedroom is ready for Baba. Have the bed shifted more to the window so the light will be better for him there. Okay?"

"Yeah. Sure."

"Did you get that new prescription made up?"

"Yeah. For god's sake you've asked me that a dozen times this morning. I went to Thomas' last evening and had the medicine made up. Your parents owe us about Rs150 for the stuff I've had to get over the week."

Maria looked at Joe with a stare that could have meant anything. She shooed away flies hovering around the butter dish. Her thoughts regretful, not bitter. She often marvelled at how she ever thought him attractive. Neither his personality nor mind had improved with age. Joe Gomes, once a keen football player, games coach and friend, had deteriorated into an encumbrance, sloppy and dull. Their children were disinterested in their father. He was there. He had neither puckish wit of their grandparents, nor the enthusiasm of their mother. The respect showed him was automatic. Obedience, a habit.

"Joe."

"Yeah." He glanced up still immersed in the newspaper.

"Will you do me a favour and see that Ma has her cocoa and tablets with them. By 10.30 sharp."

"Okay, okay. God, do I ever forget it?"

"Yes. You did. Yesterday."

"Well, it was so bloody hot and the power cut was not making it any better. And anyway the old lady was having a shut-eye. Probably did her more good than any pills could."

"Joe. Please. No excuses. Try and give Ma her medicine at the correct time. Please."

"All right. All right. What am I? Some sort of servant here. An ayah to your mother? Bloody hell, all I do around here is pick up after someone, the old lady, the children. Next you'll want your food cooked I suppose?"

A knock at the door cut short the rant.

"Maria. Lucy here. Ready? The taxi is here. Don't worry I've got an extra bag for their stuff."

Opening the door with a jerk, Maria ignored her husband.

"Hi Lucy. Thanks so much. Yes, I'm ready. Joe will keep an eye on the house for us. Have you an extra key for your door? It's a good idea to have one cut. Always helps if it should be misplaced or forgotten."

Lucy sensing the tension in the room, smiled at Joe.

"Let's go then."

The two women walked away from the stuffy room. Outside things were normal. The bustee children yelled their lessons collectively in the nearby mosque, the heat of the day had not reached its peak, dogs shambled about in the overflowing rubbish bin, their taxi driver looked impatient and pointedly tapped the running meter.

They scrambled into the cab and with a jerk the creaking vehicle swerved through the lane into the road beyond.

Lucy and Maria looked ahead watching the crowded street rush by. It was a short journey and within minutes the hospital loomed besides the messy roadside squalor.

"Here." Lucy handed the surly driver his fare and without help from him wrestled the bags out of the cab.

"We will be at the same spot in half an hour's time – *aacha*? Here, in front of this entrance? Don't be late."

"*Haan, haan.*"

The cab reversed and drove away at breakneck speed from the hospital.

Picking their way through the sprawl of people sitting in the forecourt of the hospital, the two women ignored the smells, the obvious misery of the waiting patients, and entered the room where their father and uncle were waiting to be released back into the world.

"Smile," Lucy jokingly said.

"Will do," she grinned and Lucy thought that if she laughed more often Maria Gomes was an attractive woman. "Baba is always cranky this time in the morning."

"Gosh Maria, Uncle Eddie is a ray of sunshine the day through."

Both laughed. It was meagre humour, but the women felt the stress of the day lift slightly.

"Good luck then. Will meet you in front of the office window in about ten minutes. Don't leave without me."

Again sharing a rueful laugh Maria Gomes and Lucy D'Cruze squared their shoulders and walked towards meeting their men.

Men who shaped their world, men who were now entirely dependent on them.

"I'm here Uncle. Don't worry, I'm here."

Eddie D'Cruze, heavily bandaged, stood in the centre of the small room. A little less upright, his tone of voice lacking some of its former stridency, Lucy's father in all that mattered, held out a hand to his niece.

"Lucy."

Grace Renshaw stared in surprise at her sister.

"Kay."

"Oh don't tell me it's such a surprise. I'm not that bloody heartless to keep away from my brother's bedside. How are Mum and Dad?" Kay, pink-cheeked, breathless with the effort of climbing the stairs with two heavy suitcases, thumped her young sister heartily and stooped down to quell the hysterical welcome of Jumbo.

"Get down you stupid beast. God, you smell. Why don't you give this dog a good bath, Gracie? Smells like the damned streets outside."

Trying not to wince at the rebuke, Grace grappled with the leaping dog and yelled at the boy to come and help with the luggage.

"*Jaldi, jaldi.* And see the lunch is made for Kay *missybaba.*"

The servant grinning at Kay, a favourite with the servants, took the suitcases and lifted them lithely into the bedroom.

"*Salaam, salaam.*"

"Abdul. *kaise hai?*"

"*Bahut aacha, missybaba, bahut aacha.*"

Kay smiled and quietly slipped some notes into their cook's hand.

"It's good to be back Gracie. I think I've been away too long. Mum and Dad now need us."

Grace looked blankly at her sister.

"What do you mean?"

"I mean I've given up my job at the school."

"What! No."

A huge grin spread over Kay's face.

"Yes. Yes, I have. Relax. It's a transfer. The school is setting up an extension here on the plains and I've been promoted to headmistress. How's that for efficiency?"

"Ouf. God in heaven, you sent my blood pressure up just now."

"Why? Nothing going wrong at work is there?"

"No, no. It's just that with Carl's condition, both Mum and Dad are finding it less easy to make ends meet."

"Nonsense. Dad has his part time work still going at the complex and Mum does a bit of free-lance accountancy which brings in something. What about that annuity Dad put away last year. Won't that mature soon? Get down Jumbo."

"Yes. True. But Carl needs special care. Physiotherapy, extra lessons for his school work, probably a nurse coming in a few days a week, medical bills, all are going to be an ongoing expense. We have to tighten belts Kay."

"Sure. It's not dire. Gracie. Don't be a baby. We'll manage. We always have. And now I'm here it'll be less of a strain to juggle budgets."

Kay lying prone on her small iron bedstead kicked off her shoes and sighed.

"I tell you Grace it's so good to be away from the constant sound of children." She laughed. "Not quite the thing for a future headmistress to say huh? No, it's good to be in charge, and I'm going to get things going, lots of changes planned for the old establishment. Just see me go."

Grace smiled. It was so like Kay. Impetuous, a doer. Not content to watch or sit on the sidelines Kay brought a sense of well-being and commonsense into the home.

"And I believe congratulations are in order. Got that fuddy-duddy at last did you? More than I could do."

Grace flushed.

She had forgotten Kay was once thought to have been sweet on Daryl Jackson.

"Hmm. Yes. It's still a bit up in the air. We haven't planned anything as yet. Want time to get going with all that sort of thing."

"All that sort of thing? My gracious girl, are you in love or what? I think you might have the date somewhat fixed. God knows the old dolt has been waiting long enough."

"All right, all right. We've had not even a week to really think about the fixed day. Kay, what's the matter with you? Don't you realise what we've been through?"

"Yes, sure. But I think I can see love when it's before me and somehow my darling sister, you don't come over as being lost in love."

For the second time in a matter of minutes Grace felt a flush spread over her face.

"Kay. Not everyone goes into a tailspin when they plan to marry."

"`No? Well pardon me for thinking a bride-to-be should show a bit more excitement than you seem to be doing."

Grace didn't answer. Kay's honesty forced her to look at the life she was about to enter. Safe, secure, but Grace could not bluff herself that there was much passion or tenderness in that future.

"So What do you suggest I do? Give the man his marching orders? See Mum and Dad horribly embarrassed?"

"Gracie, Gracie. I can't believe I'm hearing this. This is your life we're talking of, not some social outing you know. You will have to live with him your life through. A pretence wears down. It's not fair on Daryl. It's not fair on Mum and Dad and it's certainly not fair on you. Wake up. It's not too late. People are tough. I can see Daryl coming over for dinner *for years* even without you as his missus. Jumbo, Jumbo, get off the bed now. *Smelly dog, smelly dog.*" Kay pushed the still excited dog off the bed, reached out and yanked her blouse over her head, unhooked her brassiere.

"God it's humid. I'd forgotten I'd come down from the sweetness of the hills to this mucky furnace."

Grace started as there was a knock at the door.

"'Who could that be? Mum and Dad will be in only after two."

She walked to the front room and opened the door to see young Ralph Johnson standing there.

"Hello Ralph. What's the matter? Need anything?"

Ralph looked at her. Unsmiling he swallowed briefly. "Hi Grace."

They both looked at each other. For the umpteenth time Grace thought the teenager looked small for his age, how old was he she wondered, fifteen, more likely sixteen? After the horror experienced the Johnsons were rarely seen outside their flat. It was as if sound had been quenched. Rumour had it they were preparing to leave the mansion. No one had seen or glimpsed Hilary. The old lady was quick in her visits to the kitchen outside and avoided neighbours. The odd stand-off was difficult, no one knowing how to bridge the awkwardness, the trauma. Fred Johnson strode out to his work in the morning, returned in the evening without a glimmer of anything unusual in his face or manner. He returned wishes formally but the stiff greetings signalled no overtures to conversation were welcome. The boy was seen lingering around the door, busy with his pigeon, but he too did not talk nor continue any dialogue apart from the routine good morning or good afternoon.

"Grace."

"Yes. Come on in Ralph. My sister Kay is here. Remember her? She is a teacher in Darjeeling."

Kay had come into the room, fresh blouse over the skirt, and watched the young boy as he stood in the room, bending down to pat Jumbo.

"Sit down Ralph."

"Er, no, I just wanted to ask you a favour."

"Sure. What is it?"

He fidgeted, looked at Kay, glanced at Grace and quickly averted his eyes.

"Grace, I want you to take Oleg."

Taken aback, knowing how dear the bird was to him Grace bent down to look into the boy's face.

"Oh Ralph why?"

"Surely you must know Grace, you *must.* Don't ask, please. Just say you'll take him. He's no trouble. Jumbo won't mind him being around. He's easy to keep. No fuss with food, a bit of grain, bread crumbs, fresh water, no walks or anything. Just take him – please. He's quite old too. Don't think he has many years to go."

Grace felt her throat tighten. It was obvious why the boy was distancing himself from all things familiar, loved.

"Why if you really want that Ralph all right, I'll take him. Carl will love him. You know how he loves anything that crawls, slides, hops or slithers."

"Yeah. That's why I chose you to take Oleg." Ralph's eyes misted. He rose abruptly.

"I'll bring him over this afternoon, if that's all right with you. And thanks again. And I better say 'bye now. We'll be leaving here in a little while and I don't think I'll get the time to wish everyone."

He stuck out his hand, the gesture precocious for a teenager. Kay came up from behind Grace and solemnly shook his hand. Grace then held his small and dry hand and with a quick movement put her arms around the boy. She felt his instinctive stiffening. There was a brief hug as he pressed his head against hers.

"Goodbye Ralph. Don't forget us. Oleg will be safe and loved here."

"Oh I know that. It's just that I don't want him anymore."

He smiled thinly, lips pinched together, waved with a funny raising of his elbow. Then he skipped off to the stairs where they heard the banister creak under his hand as he swooped down to his home. Ralph's footsteps were clear all the way to his front door. It opened.

And closed.

17

Yvonne did not realise that she was pouting.

The past week had been dull. Her uncle and aunt asked no questions of her, the few childhood friends who were still around found it awkward to pick up a relationship that had lapsed over the years. She behaved with extreme correctness. Laughing often at nothing much. But there was an edge to her gaiety, a hint of the determined and anxious to please. Time crawled by, the days punctuated by a daily call from John. He made proper conversation with no hint of any trouble between them. She asked about Heather, the servants, the daily meals and the state of his health. She did not go to the club. There was no news from John about the Renshaws' trouble, nor news of how the police inquiry over their son's assault was progressing. The calls ended with the perfunctory 'keep wells', and 'love yous'. None lasted more than a couple of minutes.

She briefly wondered about the other trouble which she had scanty details of, the molestation of one of the Renshaws' neighbours. When she asked her uncle he looked upset and said that she had better ask John about it. And that, she decided, she would never do. Everything seemed to revolve around those damned Renshaws. What was it that Kitty Renshaw had she didn't? She saw Kitty, an ordinary middle-aged woman. All right, granted she still had a slim figure and a mop of black hair, but she was not too fair, quite dark actually, had no other accomplishments bar her free-lance work with some accountancy stuff she did, and of course what she did have was a rather well-preserved handsome husband.

Well all right he was not too smooth an operator, but good-natured, ready to have a laugh and a joke. Not like her unsmiling John. Always so damned serious. Always scurrying off to some urgent work, or to head some committee or other. Where was the fun she longed for? No parties, not real fun. John hated it when she insisted he dance and jive at some of the club's socials. Oh yes, Yvonne's face furrowed in annoyance, but he managed to dance all right with that Marwari fatso. All charm then.

No complaints when the nose-studded snob twirled around in her sari. Looked thrilled he did.

Yvonne felt anger surge. Why did John always shoot down her tastes? Her style of dressing, her topics of conversation, even the choice of the pictures they'd go to, rarely was met with John's approval. A damned wet-blanket. Yes, her life through she had given in to his judgement. No more. She might just go back to the small town Jubblepore she had grown up in. Her cousins were still there. Retired now, their children married and happily settled in Canada. Surely there might be a welcome for her there.

She toyed with the fruit salad on her plate. The air conditioning was too cold and the plates were icy to touch.

"Boy!"

The cook came in flicking a dirty *jharan* at some of the flies that had come in with him through the opened door.

"Ho gaya. Le lo," She pushed away the plate, drank long from the glass of water before her and pulling away the white serviette from her lap, tossed it aside, crumpled and now imprinted with her lipstick.

"Ji haan."

Without another word the old servant skilfully removed the half-eaten meal and piled the plates together before straightening the damask table cloth. He left, carrying with him a kitchen odour of onions, garlic and the smoke of a coal fire.

"Ouf. Can't Uncle tell Karim to bathe," Yvonne muttered as she pushed back the chair and wondered what she was to do with the rest of the muggy afternoon.

She slowly wandered through the large darkened hall, shutters carefully pulled against the summer simmer. Magazines and books were stacked neatly on a centre table. She ignored them. Never a reader Yvonne was glad of the lightning bolts of TV news to keep in touch with whatever was the accepted hot topic of the day.

What exactly had that damned bandh done? The Opposition – who were they anyway – ugly old men, most of them, were happy "some of their demands had been met". What demands? Yvonne wondered. They should do something about the damned electric supply. When, if ever, was the power going to resume a normal routine. She'd meet politicians at an occasional cocktail party at John's office and was wise enough to smile prettily and paste on a demure look while talk revolved around the various political issues and agendas. Privately she wished some of the men would not wear their dhotis and slippers to the functions. The buttoned-up Nehru coat was so much more elegant. Nice lines without the folds and billows of that floppy pantaloon thing. She smiled as she thought of John's horror when she suggested that he put down a dress code for office functions.

"Are you crazy?" John was aghast. "We'll be regarded as good as traitors if I dared suggest such a thing." It was one of the few times she saw him angry. "It's part of our national dress, if you like, our heritage. Don't you realise how we'd harm our community if we dared do such a thing? Bad enough we are still looked on with dislike, we'll hammer another nail into our coffin with this. You *are* bloody unthinking aren't you?" It was the most severe reprimand he dealt her. After she had screamed back that he didn't understand her at all nor did he care to, he had looked at her with exasperation and quietly walked out of the room.

Yvonne quickly learnt not to voice opinions about his friends or colleagues, their ways or their habits. Over time at social dos she honed the art of diplomacy. She ate daintily with her hands at weddings, though she refused the offering of paan graciously, 'an allergy', she lied, prevented her from enjoying the so-called delicacy. Privately she shuddered at the thought of the garish red staining her mouth, its sharp taste coating her tongue as one chewed and chewed and chewed on what was basically a narcotic. May as well wear one's gums out on a wad of chewing gum. She gained a reputation for being an affable hostess, one who didn't really converse too much and was generous with her hospitality; food and drink at the Coates' table was plentiful.

"Yvonne." Her aunt came through the veranda to the living room. Grey hair framing a kind face, her aunt still looked imposing, even with a shabby dress whose hemline dipped, the thin cotton fabric clinging to her thin figure with the perspiration of a noon-day heat.

"What's the matter Aunty?"

"Nothing pet. But Karim tells me you did not enjoy your lunch today."

"Rubbish. I couldn't finish the fruit. I was too full," she patted her stomach and smiled disarmingly at the elderly lady.

"Well, he's a bit upset and thinks you don't care for his cooking."

"No, no. I just don't have too much of an appetite that's all. I'll tell Karim I love his chicken tikka. No one can serve it like he can."

Her aunt smiled.

"Be a good girl and tell him will you? He's old, like me, and welcomes compliments especially from the lovely *missybaba.*"

"Go on. Surely he knows better. He's a real butterer-up, old Karim. Says that to everyone who comes here doesn't he?"

"In a manner of speaking, yes." Her aunt smiled. Yvonne. She was fond of the girl. Pity the marriage had not worked out as hoped. Yvonne refused to shed her small-town mindset and though middle-age had broadened her body it had not done the same for her mind. Yvonne at fifty-something still the 'silly filly' of seventeen.

"Why doesn't that husband of hers try to talk to her sometimes," Sam Carter would growl. A daughter in all but name the old man never pointed a finger at his niece's stubborn adherence to ways and fashions of a time long gone.

"That daughter's as bad. Too big for her boots with that uppity college and those college friends filling her head with a lot of nonsense. Looks down her nose at her mother. And her father aids and abets with her."

"Sammy, you're being unfair. John's a wonderful husband. He's never said a word to Yvonne. He's been a good partner and caring parent. I know you don't think much of him, but hasn't he done whatever you suggested? He has proved himself, you said so yourself. The company's profits owe much to his guidance."

"All right, all right. My god, Mavis, what are you, this man's PR or what?"

"No. I just don't care for you to lay blame where it shouldn't be laid. Be honest Sammy. Whatever went wrong was hardly John's fault. I know he doesn't appeal to you for whatever reason, but that's not why the marriage has gone wrong. Yvonne is, and always has been, spoilt rotten. And John has done his fair share of pandering to her every whim. She loves being spoilt."

"Spoilt? How can you think that? Do you know how her family had to scrimp to get from day to day? The Indian railway is not known to be generous with its employees. After Independence our people were shunted out with nothing much to retire on. Christians in the senior positions were Indians, South Indian Christians mostly, some with even more of a prejudice against Anglo-Indians. Rotten buggers, riddled with jealousy against AIs. Mean as snakes and as dangerous. Don't you remember that Mangalorean, what was his name, Lobo, Ferris, or something, who publicly announced he would not consider employing Anglo-Indians? The one who refused to talk to my brother, socially or at work. Bloody upstart."

"Yes. I know, I know. But Yvonne had loving parents. It's all a child really needs. Yvonne was the precious one. The fair golden-haired princess, nothing was too good for her. And she turned good for nothing much."

The sentence sounded harsh. She regretted saying it as soon as the words sounded.

After a telling couple of seconds Sammy snorted loudly. He retired from the argument with ill-grace and his wife knew that nothing could alter his views on his beautiful niece.

"Well Aunty," Yvonne's voice cut through Mavis's train of thought, "do I go in now to compliment Karim, or will I send him an invitation for this evening?" Yvonne looked quizzically at her aunt. "What are you looking so serious about? He's only a cook, it doesn't matter if I say I like his food or not?"

"Of course it matters, Yvonne. Karim is more than a cook, sweetheart, he's not just a servant. He's family. He's been with us forever. Surely you know that. He's worth his weight in gold. Go on now. Just thank him and say how you enjoy his cooking."

Yvonne grimaced. Unconsciously reverting to petulance that marred, she bit her lip with annoyance and slowly walked out of the room and towards the kitchen.

Mavis Carter heard her fluting voice, shrill, as she spoke to Karim.

Unthinking. That was Yvonne. Her cocoon of comfort had to shatter. It would surely come as a shock long overdue. John Coates needed to deliver a few home truths to his wife. The sooner he did that the better. Then and only then would that family survive. At present they were drifting away from each other. Then only might the three of them find a balance of honesty and comfort in each other.

Yvonne returned beaming.

"Well how did you go with Karim?"

"Oh wonderful. I told him his dinner last night was great."

"That's nice…"

"But I did say that his soup was too peppery."

Mavis sighed.

Nothing outside the immediate periphery of Yvonne's world meant much to her. Karim was a cook and as such didn't really figure as important enough to establish a rapport. Mavis briefly wondered how this implacable woman kept her marriage from fraying much earlier than it had.

Yvonne looked at her aunt expecting words of praise. The moment passed.

"Come on Yvonne. Why don't we go to the New Market and look for some new material. I hear the Sindhi shops have a new stock of lovely English cotton."

"Oh Aunty, lovely. Just the thing to get my mind off all this rubbish. You do know what makes me tick don't you?" She turned luminous eyes towards the older woman, looking at her with an appeal of apprehension and concern.

Mavis smiled. Yes, she thought, she did.

From the odour of stale cigarette smoke Fred Johnson knew his mother had been puffing on her favourite brand of 'coffin nails.'

"Mum?"

"Do you mind opening the windows wide after you've finished with those Charminars?"

"Sorry Fred."

"It's all right Mum. Just see that the smoke doesn't linger in the rooms."

"Does it worry Hilary?"

"No. But I don't care for the room to reek like it does after you've smoked."

"Sorry, I think I'll have to stop smoking, it's too expensive and my cough seems to be turning worse." As if on cue a sudden fit of coughing racked the old woman's body. She coughed long and loudly. Fred went silently to the table and quickly poured a glass of water.

"Here. Drink up. Now hurry and finish your packing. I want us to leave here by the weekend. I've asked some of the workers in the firm to give me a hand with the furniture. Luckily our office peon has a nephew who is bringing his lorry over so we can do all the moving at one go. So please see your stuff is ready and we don't have to come back and make another trip."

Edna Johnson, her face red from coughing, looked at Fred and nodded.

"Don't worry. I don't really have much to pack. My old sewing machine, some clothes, that almirah, my bed, the tin box with the photos and albums, that's about it really."

"Do we have to take all that junk, can't you get rid of some of the old papers."

She looked at her son and for once Fred remained silent knowing that what he asked for was unreasonable and unkind.

"It's not junk Fred. It's our history. I'm not ashamed of where I came from or what I am. If you are it's a shame and a pity. You will have little to tell your son when he asks questions of you. No one cares to have a blank page when they want to know about their families. Remember that."

Fred quelled before the dignity and truth of his mother's advice and began to take down some of the pictures from the walls and wrap them in newspapers. Edna turned away. She felt tired and reluctant to go into the bedroom to see to her daughter-in-law. There was no talk to be had there. Edna was at a loss as to how to engage the convalescing woman. Most conversation veered off into areas that were taboo. She had to be careful to avoid mention of the neighbours. No mention of servants. Even the normal asking of how she was feeling or whether her injuries were healing were dangerous areas.

Hilary for most of the day lay silent. She spoke to Ralph. She answered questions with a minimum of words. Her expression was bland, blank. The bruises were gone now. Her skin seemed fairer than before, the sallow hue now pale, pasty, Edna privately thought. Within a week she seemed to have grown plumper. Unusual, after the horror of her assault she might have lost, not gained weight. Her eyes were underlined with dark half-moons, hair looped over her ears, brushed untidily and held back with a couple of hair slides. She ate listlessly and only showed signs of enthusiasm when that damned pigeon strutted into the bedroom. The bird seemed to have grown fond of her and now flew often onto the bedstead, cooing its constant gargling call. When Edna went to shoo it away Hilary had sharply asked her to let it stay there.

"Leave Oleg. He's a good sound to hear."

Edna stopped immediately and later asked Ralph to see the bird's grain was also placed in his parent's bedroom.

He looked surprised but brought out another saucer for the bird seed and seemed pleased and happy to have Oleg given another site in the house. Fred did not mind, or if he did made no mention of the change in the bird's routine.

She looked around the bare room.

It had never been a cheerful home and now it looked stark, stripped even of the scanty claim to a personality it once had.

The buff-coloured walls looked sadder with blank rectangles, pale, where pictures had been removed. The floor grimy. No, Edna thought, no hiring of another sweeper, not for a long while yet. The furniture, shrouded in coarse hessian, made for islands of lumpy objects, dead and even sinister when the evening light painted shadows. Everything had changed. Her pretty daughter-in-law a semi-invalid, listless, scarred by memories. Her stodgy son refusing to admit to the catastrophe, going on with his life as if nothing had happened. Thank god for Hilary's parents. The stop-gap of their home which they offered before Fred found a new flat. They had to move out of here. She flinched before the silence that greeted their every appearance. Ralph seemed to fare normally in his school. He attended his classes, worked longer at the required homework.

"A distraction, that's what his school is now, a distraction," Edna mumbled to herself. She sat down in the darkening room and fumbled in her skirt pocket for a cigarette, but remembering her promise to her son, slowly crushed the packet ruthlessly.

"No. I'll throw them out. I'm too old for this sort of comfort. Besides they're too bloody expensive now." She sat back on the covered sofa. The hessian prickly and rough, against her skin, she leaned back and stared at the ceiling. She was tired. What were they now going to do? Live each day as if nothing had happened? Nurse her daughter-in-law back to health? Her grandson back to some heart? How was that to be done? New neighbourhood? How might a job help with Hilary's recuperation? Surely the stress of working again might push the past back a bit. Edna felt her assurance sinking. The customary gung-ho spirit had been doused. She was tired. With luck, she smiled, she might die before this horrible year was over. The sound of shuffling from the bedroom and Hilary stood before her.

"Hilary. Do you need anything? I'll get it for you. Ralph just went upstairs, I think he went to wish Grace Renshaw goodbye."

"No. I don't need anything. Just thought I'd sit here for a while. Want to move out of that room. Makes me feel useless, sick. This is nice." She looked around the stripped room and lingered on the bulky blocks of covered furniture.

"Nice?"

"It's quite a move isn't it? I feel like we're playing a game of house-house. You know, shifting, getting new household appliances, new curtains, different views." She stopped, and looked at her mother-in-law.

"Oh Edna. You don't have to walk on eggshells around me. I'll mend. So will Fred and Ralph. The only person who won't have to worry about mending is you. Always the strong one. You've always known that haven't you?"

Edna smiled in surprise, her eyes wary. Not given to soul-searching she had rarely thought of herself in the third person and hearing Hilary talk of her 'strength' was almost unnerving.

"Rubbish. We're all rubber balls. Plenty of bounce in us you know."

Hilary looked with sudden affection at the older woman.

"What a lovely way of putting it. And only you could have put it like that." She walked over to Edna and sat on the edge of one of the hessian-covered chairs.

Absently stroking the rough material she stared into the afternoon. Fred promised to return early and Ralph mentioned that he wanted to gift the Renshaws' with Oleg. Funny. She was going to miss that bird's perpetual warbling more than she imagined.

And again she heard the door rattle, saw the face looking down at her, sweat running down on her face, foul breath smothering her.

"Hilary."

She flinched. She unclenched her hands, leant against the arm of the chair and looked at her mother-in-law, wordless, wan.

"Stop." Edna, suddenly the matriarch, every inch of her commanding authority, willing Hilary to heal. "Stop now. Hand me some newspaper and we'll pack the crockery away. No, not now, after we've had our lunch. It'll be good if we get it out of the way," Edna's prosaic words sheathed the gentle admonition.

The door rattled and Ralph pushed open the heavy doors as he came into the room, flushed, bright-eyed.

"Grace will take him Mum."

Hilary forced herself to move away from the memory of the pungent smell of sweat, garlic, onions, the filthy rag smothering breath, stopping thought, hard arm rammed against her throat.

"Good. If she's happy it's all right isn't it? I'm sure Carl will love him. Oleg now has a lovely family to himself."

"Why are you leaving Oleg *here?*" Edna glared at mother and son. "We don't need to give gifts to *anyone* here."

"No. It's what Ralph wants. Let Oleg stay. Birds like their familiar settings. He won't be happy with our shifting, and Mum's flat is noisy. It's on the main road and my brothers won't care for his droppings all over the house or his constant warbling."

Edna sniffed loudly.

"We don't have to have any memories left behind here. I like that bird."

Ralph laughed. It was unusual. The boy's eyes crinkled, he looked at his grandmother with genuine affection. The adults stared surprised.

"Why Gran, you won't have to worry now about lice or fevers. We'll all be healthy without Oleg's dirty habits."

"Heartless boy," Edna waved her spoon at him in mock-anger. "Don't you want him to come with us? Won't you miss him?"

"Leave it Mum. Let's eat." Slowly, favouring her left arm, Hilary began setting out plates and cutlery for their makeshift lunch.

The fan groaned above them with its asthmatic wheeze. The heat of May was showing off its strength. After monsoon downpours the humidity was merciless. The dust motes slid down the ray of sunshine. Wasn't that how some Greek god entered a beautiful maiden's room and 'had his way with her'? Always men had to have their way. Human or gods, it came down to the one thing – brute strength, bullying, overpowering. A sickening fact of life.

Hilary wiped the perspiration from her neck. "God it's so hot. Pray the power doesn't go off in the afternoon."

The three Johnsons sat down and after a look from Edna, Hilary took up the heavy *dekchi* and carefully began ladling out the dal.

Flies buzzed, in that sweltering summer morning that family around the table swatted at them absently.

Life went on.

Carefully, so as not to disturb her sleeping uncle Lucy set the dishes on the sideboard. She folded the table-sheet and seeing she still had time before she caught the bus to work, set about quietly arranging the array of medicines besides her uncle's bed.

"Luce."

Damn. She had hoped to leave before he awoke.

"Yes Uncle?"

"Are you leaving for work?"

Lucy grimaced to herself.

"Well, yes. It's almost 8.00 am, the later bus is so crowded, I have to get this one."

A short silence was broken by the phlegmy coughing of the invalid.

"Are you sure you'll be okay during the day?"

"What do you think I am, some sort of loony? I can answer the door and feed myself. And go to the bloody toilet myself, thank god, I can still think young lady, and don't you forget it."

Lucy smiled wanly. Her uncle was better.

Again a short silence followed.

"I'm sorry."

"It's okay. Just rest. Read. Try and sleep. Your medicines are beside you and Kay Renshaw will call in during the afternoon to see that things are all right."

"Kay will be here again?"

"Yes, Uncle I told you she offered to come and look in on you during the days I'm at work."

"Why isn't *she* at work?"

"Come on Uncle you know she's down from the hills to see Carl. He's still at that nursing home. Count yourself lucky to have neighbours like the Renshaws to lend a hand when we need it."

"Sure, sure. But I really don't care for that thumping woman to come around asking her questions and treating me like one of her pupils. Bloody nosy-parker that's what she is."

Eddie D'Cruze ignored the pulse of grief that seized him. Hilary, my Hilary. Hilary. Hilary. Hilary. The first thought when he awoke. The last thought he had before he lapsed into sleep. Her face. Her eyes staring past him. He pushed away thoughts of the beautiful woman who vanished from his world.

"Kay doesn't mean to annoy, it's just her way. She's a good sort. Just lie quietly and she won't bother you. Everyone is concerned about you, Uncle. You know that." She studiously ignored the tears that welled in her uncle's eyes. If only he knew how she longed to talk him out of his sorrow. That she knew he yearned for a lost love. Hilary Johnson never was his and never would be. I understand, she wanted to say, I've loved too. I've lost as well. Shaking herself from the slide of self-pity, she pushed around the mess of medication on the table besides him. Pradip. The strongest memory was of his hair oil, its overwhelming smell that still hung around some of her clothes. How quickly his mother had arrived. From the bits and pieces of news that trickled to her there was now talk of a marriage being arranged. Quick smart, Lucy thought, before there was a chance of the wicked memsahib returning.

Her uncle looked at her. He continued his rambling.

"Well I wish she'd stop her gob when she tries to gossip about how we're going or when you are going to leave me again, bloody hag, hasn't she a life of her own. She seems to suck blood from everyone around her." He laughed wheezily, made a vulgar sound and looked quickly at Lucy to gauge her reaction.

Pradip vanished. Lucy felt the trickle of anger starting.

"Who? Who is this blood-sucker?"

"Kay Renshaw of course, who did you think I was talking about? Were you listening at all? What's wrong with you? Can't you really pay attention or is it too much to ask?"

She had a vision of herself taking her handbag and smashing it over her uncle's head. When were people going to leave her alone? She knew the curiosity was at fever pitch over her aborted affair with Pradip. If people only knew how free her life had become. Pradip had tried to visit, tried to talk her into coming back to his life. But the efforts were half-hearted. Both knew the equation had changed, neither considered a change of lifestyles.

She no longer found his presence exciting. The odour of his hair oil, cloying. She was ashamed to discover that, yes, she was embarrassed by him. His lack of a formal education, his complete floundering in her world, the sad attempts at copying a style of speech or accent floundered. It was not love at all. It was a holiday from the sterility of life with Uncle. Lucy paused in her bustle around the room. How relieved she was to return to the comforting security of routine. How distressingly short the time taken to learn the lesson.

"What about Kay? What has she done to annoy you?" Lucy hastily asked as her ongoing silence puzzled the old man.

"Ha. Thought you'd wake up to that one. Well, you know her sister Grace seems to have hooked that old stick who hangs around, what's his name, Jackson?"

"Yes?" Lucy thinking briefly 'hooked' was not the word to describe the relationship. The man had hoped for years to marry into the Renshaw family.

"Well I think that dear Kay seems to have put the kybosh onto that."

"What! Why do you say that?"

"Hahaa," a wheezy laugh, "not so sick that my mind has gone, eh?"

"No, no one ever said that. Really, tell me why you say that, or has Kay said something to you?"

"Nah. But every time she comes over to look me up, that silly fool always appears as if by magic. Doesn't he have to work?"

"Daryl Jackson comes here in the morning?"

"Are you deaf, or didn't you hear what I just said. Yes, the fool hangs around and Kay is all flustered and leaves quickly after doing her duty by me – hah!"

"But Daryl Jackson has his work at that hour in the morning. How could he come over at that hour?"

"I don't know. I don't know. I'm telling you what happens. I have a brain and it doesn't need much to put two and two together.

Grace is soon going to get a shock when older sis tells her she's been thrown over."

Lucy frowned. She hated the gleeful way her uncle related the incident. She was fond of Grace and if this were true then it was a nasty thing to happen.

Kay, she hardly knew. But she found Kay's loud voice an irritant. As a young girl she and Grace had deferred to Kay automatically. When Kay graduated with honours it seemed her family relinquished a good measure of their authority to her. Kay left soon after to teach in a prestigious hill school in Darjeeling and Lucy watched her go with a sense of relief. Her friendship with Grace was a quiet one, and she sensed Grace was not unhappy to have the uncluttered time and space left by Kay.

"Well. It's not our business but I think it a pity when families have these kinds of problems divide them." Lucy clattered a few bottles to indicate she was about to leave and was not interested in their neighbours' lives.

"Bosh." Her uncle snorted. "It's good to know what the other fellow is up to, in this case the 'fellee'. Kay is a clever one, we all knew that didn't we? God, her college was thrust down our throats. Everyone from here to Howrah Bridge knew Kay Renshaw was going to college. I remember old Jackson looking moony-eyed at the Great Brain when she graduated. You must have been too young to remember that party when all he did was hold her plate for her when she went around being congratulated. I think she thought she was too big for such an ordinary fellow, does something in Bob Renshaw's work, eh, assistant caretaker of that apartment block or something – but nothing much has happened over all these years has it? No queue asking for her hand in marriage. Time is going on. She's on her way to being left on the shelf." The old man paused, overtaken by a bout of deep coughing. "Take it from me," he continued, "if she lands this chap she'll be very clever indeed."

"Oh Uncle, stop talking like this." Lucy actually shook her shoulders to rid herself of the small spitefulness her uncle was pouring into the room.

"Horrible. I feel sorry for Grace. She's been a wonderful girl, a good girl. Why must she have to deal with this sort of betrayal?"

"Oh for heaven's sake. Don't be dramatic. Your own nonsense has made you see everything on a screen. I don't think Grace will mind at all."

"You're so sure of that?" Lucy spoke angrily. Her uncle, sick or not, seemed to have morphed into a gossip.

"I'm not *sure.* Who the hell is sure of *anything*? Was I sure you'd return here? Eh? Was I sure you'd leave? Am I sure you won't run away again?"

Lucy fell silent.

The accusation was fair enough. She was not going to continue this conversation. It was an ugly revelation, one that did not enhance the character of Eddie D'Cruze. He glanced up at his niece, peering into Lucy's face, his eyes wrinkled, sly.

Silence in the room stretched.

Lucy put the finishing touches to the small room, looked at her reflection in the bathroom mirror. The blue-bordered sari was the one she had worn when she first moved into Pradip's room. The sari she had worn when she and Pradip first had sex. It wasn't making love. That idea belonged with flowers and softness and a well-ordered room. Nothing could be further from all those foolish ideas. She still flinched from the recollection of that lumpy cot and the dingy room. One surefire way to fall out of love. Throw in some poverty. She recalled the cheeky thought that the sari resembled the saris the nuns of the Missionaries of Charity wore. Who knows, Lucy thought, even that random thought might have worked to bringing her back into the fold. Mother Teresa wielded power in high places. The memory of that awkward bumping and twisting on the narrow cot was not the expected glorious initiation to sex and certainly not love. She smiled and with obsessive neatness pinned her hair back behind her ears. Expertly her fingers flew as she speedily folded the sari pleats into the petticoat waistband, straightened her choli, slung her handbag over her shoulder, and with a smile and a fleeting thought tossed towards the shaky romance of Grace and the Jackson man, raced out of the flat.

18

Sounds easily travelled from the thin ceiling above to the Vincents flat below. Mrs Vincent, sitting quietly at the dining table stared at her husband as he slept through the morning chaos of the children preparing to go to school.

"Sheila, Michael, stop that. Have you both got your tiffin ready?" Maria harassed, spoke automatically as she tried to tidy the messy room.

"Yes Ma," both children, smart in their starched white uniforms clutched satchels, with one hand, still taking sly punches at each other.

"What's the matter with you both? Can't you be still for a moment? Your dadu is not well. Be quiet."

Joe Gomes stumbled into the brightness of the room. He was still half-asleep, unshaven and groggy.

"Tell these brats to pipe down, can't you? You should let your grandfather sleep?"

The children snickered.

"What's that? You don't be too smart or you'll get the back of my hand."

Maria ignored the outburst and hurriedly bundled the girl and boy out of the room.

There were no farewells to Joe or their grandmother. The door slammed shut. Footsteps raced towards the front of the passageway, then were soon lost amidst the jumble of noise that was the song of the morning. The flat emptied, felt hollow. Joe glanced at Fatima sitting silently and noisily pulled the teapot towards him as he prepared to pour himself a cup of tea.

"Why hasn't my place been laid? Where's the toast? Hasn't Maria made my hardboiled egg? I'm now expected to make my own breakfast?"

Fatima closed her eyes and shut the complaining man out of her mind.

Soon. She would tell him soon. He could not live here indefinitely, jobless, while her daughter struggled to keep everyone happy. After whispered talks over the past nights, Maria had agreed Joe move back to his parents until such time he get a job and hopefully also get a flat. With Henry's now shaky health and her own not much better, it was time her daughter pushed her husband to try and carve some kind of independent life away from here.

Joe glanced at his mother-in-law. She continued to sit, eyes closed, hands loosely holding the day's paper.

"Old bat. Bet she's up to something."

Joe, scratched his stomach thoroughly, yawned and went back into the bedroom where Fatima heard the sound of the bathroom door slam and the sounds of running water which meant Joe was filling the basin for his bath.

"…'time, 'time," it was a weak cry from Henry. The brief respite over Fatima, a tired sixty-eight year old, realised she wanted to sit by her husband. It was time they looked at each other without the noise of family. They would relax and chat to each other in their mother tongue. Speaking in English had put a strain on their comfort with each other. She now longed to put away the spoons and forks and cutlery Maria had insisted they use when she went to college. No, it was time to stop the play-acting. She wanted to return to her youth and a freedom of life. Henry always ate with his hands when he was sure the rest of the family was eating out. Then husband and wife were comfortable and dispensed with some of the etiquette enforced by their daughter.

Fatima was tired. She could not now be bothered by appearances. No, she needed to ease back into her way of life. Surely they deserved it. After decades of trying hard to shoe-horn their way into a community amused by their efforts to integrate, the pretence had to be scrapped.

Lumbering up from the old easy chair Fatima grunted as she prepared to see to her husband. No, she thought, I'm not young anymore. I need a rest. I want to sit here forever. With my Henry. I don't want grandchildren around me. Just Henry.

"I'm here Henry. Wait a bit. I'm here."

Roger Lawson walked home in a slight drizzle. He still found it difficult to believe the events of the past afternoon.

Rupa. He could taste her perfume. He lowered his head towards his shirt and inhaled deeply. Yes, there was the faint musky fragrance she wore. When he asked the name of the perfume she shook her head.

"Well it's not Pears soap. Hey, let me keep it a secret. A little mystique is good. Why don't you call it Rupa then."

She pulled his head down and buried him in her warmth.

He smiled sheepishly at the thought as he stumbled into a sleeping beggar.

"Sahib, sahib," a crumpled figure unfolded and held out a supplicant hand to him.

Without a thought Roger pulled out a note and dropped it into the astonished man's palm.

"Aiee." Murmured blessings, a huge salaam, a glimpse of a shocked and wizened face. Eyes big, rheumy. Indian-poor. Roger hurried away. He did not want to attract the attention of more of the destitute huddled asleep, all along the pavement.

It was ridiculous, this euphoria. He grinned. Unexpected and dizzying, Rupa's calm offer and acceptance of a relationship with no mention of marriage seemed to be paradise on a plate. How this worked out was something that might yet hold the threat of a bitter-sweet finale. But it was the here and now he was indulging in. Let the morrow take care of itself. Rupa was his. For now. At present he was walking home and trying to prepare some credible tale for his sharp-eyed mother. He didn't really care to look at what might happen.

A few drops of rain splattered down and he quickened his steps. He disliked the aftermath of a monsoon drenching. His skin itched and his sinus flared up in the heat that followed a typical summer shower. The garbage heaps were pulped to a sodden mass. Humidity was thick enough to cut through, mould sprouted on walls, shoes, books, the piano went out of tune, the wires slack in the damp and heat, monsoon relief carried a heavy penalty. Roger still felt the slick sweat between their bodies. He wished their lovemaking had happened in the city's winter. He loved the season of cool, of holidays and of the sheer childlike pleasure of festivities.

He wanted to show off to his new love the happy chaos that heralded Christmas. In spite of the cynicism that surrounded that time he enjoyed the vitality of the season.

He bounded along the road. Perspiration trickled between his shoulder blades. Roger Lawson, in his early middle age had been deflowered. By a wealthy, dumpy Marwari. A divorcee with two children. Modern, she headed her own business. Most of all Rupa was a woman who did not want nor consider marriage. Who could ask for anything more? He had kept from telling her he was a virgin. That bit of show-and-tell might come later. For the moment he grinned, he had acquitted himself well. The lady didn't have complaints did she?

He slowed his walk and remembered he had not arranged when they meet next. Stupid. How foolish was that. Excited by the thought of the next time both had forgotten the simple plan and routine of their now changed and charged lives. The traffic had started up in earnest and the squalid mess of road skill-or-kill was in full blast. He had re-entered the real city. It was a few streets away from the placid oasis of Rupa's street. Already the division of wealth and need had taken place. The gutters clogged with rubbish had turned slushy. A car honked excessively. God, couldn't these fools keep the noise down. Why was there the need to blare those things? He stepped quickly on to the pavement and grimaced when he saw his pants had been marked with the dirt of the puddles. Inevitable.

"Roger!"

He stopped and looked around.

It was John Coates. His car was wedged between a bullock cart and a couple of rickshaws.

"Hey Mr. Coates."

The door was opened and he hopped quickly into the plush car.

"What are you doing here?"

"I could ask you the same question."

Both men smiled.

"Make it a 'John' now Roger, you're old enough."

Roger smiled and nodded. He inwardly squirmed. John Coates was a figure he had grown up regarding with if not awe then respect. Samuel Carter, his uncle-in-law, before him, had been the pillar of the club and the community. School functions, social, church occasions, and the annual family picnic seemed to be held in place by the presence of the Carters and later the baton passed on to the Coates.

"So what are you doing here in the middle of the night? Or were you returning from visiting Carl Renshaw?"

"No. I was at Rupa's."

"Umm."

A silence followed. The car wound its way through a series of potholes and jaywalking pedestrians. Remarkably John Coates did not honk. He patiently slowed for streams of people without losing temper or swearing at the nonchalance of the public, insolently diving and ducking their way across the street.

"Oh Calcutta." He shot Roger a sideways look and laughed. "This city muddles on doesn't it?"

Roger nodded. He rarely ceased to marvel at how the citizenry managed to get any kind of work done. In his own circle of work he did not allow a too easy an attitude to work.

The small printing business he was in charge of was quickly gaining a reputation for reliability and good prices. The printers were content and he seldom had to contend with union issues. A fair wage for a fair day's work was a promise he adhered to, this and a fluency in Bengali helped avoid contentious issues. He had done well in spite of the general xenophobia the country was heir to, anti-English language factions going after differences of opinion, dress, religion with lethal *lathes.* If there were murmurs about the fact that English still held sway in a free India, they were quelled in the face of his basic common sense. The business was well-run, honest, put money in pockets and food on the table. It allowed for peace of mind. His employees knew he was a just man, jingoistic nonsense faded away. That was Roger Lawson's gift, he was accessible to everyone. He talked easily, without condescension, to the humble compositor or the wealthy businessman, with equal ease. But now he was not comfortable. John Coates was not the man he wanted to meet. There was now the involvement stemming from the horrendous mess of the May Queen Ball.

"Roger, it's none of my business, but watch your step with the fair Rupa."

"How's that?"

He smiled, but he was angry. What business was it of anyone to give him advice as to his personal life and to make a bad pun, his affairs.

"Roger. Don't take it amiss but these people are very different from us. Rupa's a lovely girl, but being together with her will open a can of worms."

"Mr Coates, John, I'd never think of turning my back on your advice, but surely this is a matter between Rupa and me and no one else."

"Yes. I'd say it was. But this is hardly the usual involvement with the girl-next-door. Rupa is rich, no, she's wealthy. I need hardly say she is from a community known for their clannish ways. There will be, to put it mildly, hell to pay, if this relationship is made public."

The car had come to a halt at traffic lights.

Roger felt incoherent with rage. How dare his life be open to this kind of scrutiny! So what if he was in love, yes, there was that too, this was not just a sex romp, why should he be answerable to the elder statesmen of his community.

Did every alliance have to start with a scramble for money! In this time, day and age, did communities have to view any outsiders with suspicion! He thought of his lover and felt prickles of desire sweep up his body.

John glanced across at him. The car started again. He drove smoothly and now the roads seem to have emptied, the journey was less jerky, even the potholes seemed to have lessened.

"Apart from the money Rupa has, why else do you think it's such a bad idea to for us to have this 'thing' going?"

"Roger. I don't have to spell it out but Rupa is an experienced woman. She has children. She is known in circles for a pretty free-and-easy lifestyle."

Again Roger felt a cold sickness start, he could taste the saliva as it surged in his mouth.

"What are you saying?"

"I'm saying it's not a good idea to throw in your lot with someone who has such different ways from yours Roger."

"Why don't you say clearly what you obviously want to John."

"Right. Then I will."

The car had come to the Lawson's house. Roger could see the servants as they relaxed in the small compound outside the house, the day's work coming to an end. It was too hot to be doing anything else. John Coates' breathing rasped unpleasantly in the confined space of the car. It was growing hot as only a post-monsoon heat can escalate. Sweat trickled from John's spectacles onto his cheeks. It could be mistaken for tears, Roger thought.

"Rupa Jaiswal has had many suitors Roger. Many. She is known in her circles as a free-living socialite. A swinger, I think the term is. Her divorce was not amicable. All kinds of dirty linen were aired. Her husband agreed to her having custody of the children only on consideration of her not marrying again."

"How the *fuck* do you know all this?"

John winced at the expletive.

"Take it easy, take it easy. I made it my business to know about her after all that happened at the May Queen Ball. She suddenly seemed to be everywhere. Of course I'm grateful to her for what she did for Kitty's boy, but we can't go accepting that kind of help."

"Why not? Didn't do Carl harm did it?"

"Sure. Sure. But look here Roger, are you prepared to live the kind of lifestyle she lives?"

"What sort of lifestyle is that?"

John shot an apprehensive look at the angry man besides him, he took a shaky breath and plunged to what he hoped might be the death-blow to this ugly situation.

"Roger, you know she's had several affairs and is at present the mistress of the great Dr Mitra? How can you, in all good faith, continue a friendship with Rupa? Have you thought of your mother? Have you given a thought to what the gossip will be like in and out of the community? How it could rebound on your business? Theirs is a way of life so different from ours it really cannot be compared in any way."

"I can't believe this." Roger sat numb, immobile. He stared at the windscreen wipers as they squeaked away droplets of rain.

"My boy, we've known your family all our lives. Don't be flattered by charm. Or wealth. It's not easy this decision of yours but surely you see the pitfall of where this situation might lead? Surely not happiness."

"Like the one you made by throwing over Kitty Renshaw."

"*What?* What's that?"

"Oh please. Everyone knows you fell into a tub of butter when you married old Carter's niece. People know. People talk. And yes, an involvement with a struggling girl was not as lucrative as marriage to the well-heeled Carter family."

"Shut up. *Shut up.* You know nothing. How dare you assume to judge me when all you've heard is tittle-tattle from those filthy gossiping bitches in the club." John spoke quietly, hands clenched on the steering wheel. He did not look at Roger. Both men stared straight ahead.

One of the servants had come to the entrance of the passageway and was looking curiously at the two men sitting in the car.

"Sahib. Salaam." He made as if to open the car door.

Roger waved him off and turned to John Coates.

"Much as I appreciate the advice John, I think I'm of an age when I can make decisions, for better or worse. Don't ever think of talking to me about what or how I choose to live my life. I don't take to condescension. Even from a pillar of our community. Go to hell." He made a mock salute to John Coates and turned quickly and almost ran to the front door of the house.

Once inside he stopped, breathless and called for the cook to make him some tea. He switched on the fan, then realised it was the time for the daily power cut and he had not yet seen to the repairing of their erratic generator. Automatically he took out his handkerchief and wiped his face of the sweat of the day. Must have a bath, he thought.

The encounter had left him speechless. In his mind he replayed the past conversations and found several things he might have said which would have put him as the victor in both morality and wit. Bloody hypocrites. Who gave them the right to arbitrate in anyone's life? He started as his mother suddenly emerged from the bedroom.

"Roger. Roger. Where have you been?"

Hair disarrayed after her nap, Sophia Lawson, unseasonably clad in a heavily embroidered dressing gown, absurdly overdressed, looked at him quizzically.

"What's wrong?"

"Nothing. Why should there be?"

"It's just that I didn't know where you were and you are looking upset."

"Oh Mum, you always are so dramatic. I'm just hot."

"Where were you?"

"At Rupa's. Surely you know I was having lunch with her today."

"No."

The monosyllable had a hint of frost in it and Roger wondered at his intuitive mother, she always seemed to know the tempo and pulse of his life.

"Mum. I'm a big boy and yes, I'm serious about Rupa. It's the first time I've felt anything about a woman and I think Rupa feels the same way about me."

"Roger! You can't know or imagine how your life would be taken over by this woman."

"Mum. Don't say things like that and her name is Rupa. I thought you liked her."

"I do. But not when she's plans to thwart my son's life."

"Thwart – what a word. Oh for chrissake's sake stop the drama. How can she possibly ruin my life?"

"Roger. Don't shout. I know life slightly better than you. This is a wealthy woman we're talking of. She is not little stenographer Shirley down the lane, flattered by you taking her out. This is an executive and someone from a community we don't have a lot in common with, nothing in common with at all. She's a Hindu. She's a divorcee. She's a single mother. A couple of children I'm told. What on earth can you be thinking. A life with someone whose life is settled. A life that will be open to gossip and ill-feeling. Do you think her people are going to accept a middle-class Anglo-Indian man with no connections and no serious money?"

"No. I don't see it that way. She's a tough woman. She's been through a hard time and I think she's – fond – of me."

Roger hesitated over the sentence. He shied away from the juvenile sounding 'love'. Did in fact Rupa love him? He felt ill when he considered John Coates' revelations.

'Mistress', had a medieval ring to it, 'girlfriend' sounded childish, silly. Unbidden the word 'whore' leapt to his mind and he immediately shut it down. Was it true? Should he ask Rupa outright about her life and the squalid whispers, rumours he was desperately hoping were rumours, about her bohemian way of life.

The phone rang.

Mother and son looked at each other over the shrill sound.

"Take it."

Roger walked to the small hallway where the phone was and spoke into it.

"Yes. The Lawson's residence."

"Roger?"

Breathy, even whispery. He knew the voice well. He had joked that she sounded like the iconic Jacqueline Kennedy.

"Rupa?"

"Just called to let you know our plan to go to the sitar recital is off. Can't make it I'm afraid. I've news an old friend has just flown in from America and I've to act hostess for a couple of days." She laughed ruefully. He could imagine her flicking her hair behind her ear as she spoke, a gesture he remembered with a spasm of desire.

"Who's this friend, do I know him?"

"Roger. How like a schoolmaster you sound. No, I don't think you know her. She's a cousin of Dr Mitra's. We've been schoolfriends and go back years. What's the matter?"

"Nothing. Nothing at all."

"Hmm. You sound strange. Tell me. I sense something's happened?"

Roger sighed. Words fled. He floundered between explaining all to her and the easier and slippery task of pretending nothing had broken his world. Nothing had smashed his perception of how love was, how love is.

"Roger."

"No. Rupa. I think I'll have to take a rain-check for my going over to your place for the time being. A problem at home. Well not a problem as such, but like you, I'm supposed to play host to some of Mum's relatives who are arriving from Canada. It'll be a blast. And that's a euphemism." He laughed.

"Well. This is sudden. I suppose the family and the elders have to be appeased. God knows I have to do it all the time. Right. I'll wait for your call when your familial duties have been done. Next time tell me when you expect any overseas guests okay? Bye for now."

"Bye."

He put the phone down and realised he was still with a fixed smile on his face. A line from a poem learned in school came to him 'smiling the boy fell dead.'

Roger turned to find his mother fussing around with a cup of tea.

"Mum. You don't have to pretend you don't know what's happening."

"Roger. I'm sorry for you. But if you have decided to stop seeing

Rupa I'm far from being sorry. It's a pity you seem to have fallen in love with her but I think it's for the best."

The platitude fell between mother and son as they looked at each other, sensing the skinny comfort it offered.

"I'll have that tea now please."

The matriarch moved away. She had won. The slut was ousted for the moment. Her son retained his dignity and everything was as it should be. With a groan the overhead fan slowly began its futile dance against the heat.

"Thank god the power has come back," his mother fanned herself exaggeratedly.

"Yes. Now I'll think I'll have that shower. It's been an exhausting day."

"I'm sorry son."

Roger smiled.

"It's all right Mum. Dinner can be late tonight." He hated the sound of his voice, strained and high-pitched. "It's all right," he reiterated.

Nothing was further from what his feelings were. Everything was wrong. He recalled the bluster of John Coates. He looked at his mother unseeingly. He continued smiling.

Sophia Lawson breathed long and deep. Her son was once again the reasonable man he was; he never intended to have anything to do with that woman. Things were back to normal. She smiled with exquisite insincerity and turned back to her bedroom, determined to right her fractured world. Grey hair poked out of the twisted knob of hair.

Roger looked at his mother's back, ramrod straight. The body language was telling. No, she was not the queen and reigning monarch of the community. She was an old lady. A stiff, unbending, inflexible matriarch.

He thought of Rupa. She had not behaved like a hysterical fool, as if she ever would. No, she would laugh, toss their interlude aside and perhaps make plans for the next day's office schedule.

Roger Lawson knew he was lost forever. Come next week and Rupa would be there. He set the teacup down carefully and went back into the hallway to make the call to Rupa. To tell her he was hers. To tell her he was ready to settle for whatever she offered. He didn't care.

He blinked at the light that seeped in from under the pulled blinds. His head felt heavy and he couldn't turn without risking sharp edges of pain running down to his neck.

"Carl."

His mother was looking down at him.

"Hello. Feeling better today?"

"Yeah. A lot."

"Good. You've been sleeping a lot y'know. Days and days. Lazy rascal, that's what you are. Hurry up and get well and come home. We're missing that damn music of yours and Jumbo is off his feed." Bob looked at his youngest child and fought hard to keep his voice from wobbling. No good if the boy sensed his emotion.

"Com'n home quick." Bob boomed too heartily for the little room, "Fireworks to celebrate. Kay is here as well, you know that. She'll visit you tomorrow. We are not allowed to crowd you out you know."

Carl clenched his jaw. The thought of his elder sister with her carrying voice did not help his pain.

"Sure. Nice to think of a full house again."

"Carl. Rest. You don't have to speak. Just blink your eyes if you want answers."

"I can talk now," he croaked.

"Shush. We know you can. But it's better if you just rested. We're happy to tell you all the news from the mansion."

Carefully news was filtered to the patient. The Vincents' lapse into unusual quiet come evenings, no prayers, no quarrels, the D'Cruze's new servant and his fragrant curries that wafted through to all the flats. Another threatened strike by the corporation workers, which meant the garbage would overflow yet again, power cuts getting more frequent. Daryl Jackson's gift of baskets of mangoes that no one really had an appetite for, Carl smiled, poor Daryl. He little knew what a handful he had got when he decided to marry into this family. Grace rolled her eyes. Carl grinned. Their telepathy conveyed their constant silent amusement over yet another Darylism. The man was a natural fall guy. How on earth was Grace preparing to endure a lifetime of sobriety with him? No mention was made of the Johnsons' tragedy or of the debacle at the May Queen Ball. Not a word as to the arrest of the policeman, or the subsequent coolness that had sprung up between the families involved. The Sutton boys seemed to have been blotted from collective memory. Carl turned his head and watched his sister. Grace. He'd welcome the time he'd spend with her during his convalescence. Kay. He groaned. He'd forgotten she'd be there too. Oh well. Can't have everything. Jumbo. He was drowsy. He felt the faces swimming away.

Kitty laid a hand on his forehead. He opened his eyes and gave her a crooked smile.

"Mrs Jaiswal?"

Yes, yes, of course the Marwari lady was fervently blessed. One way or other if it had not been for her he would have been a goner. None of this might have happened. Little justice, and less than adequate medical expertise. God bless the glitch that had her acting judge that awful night.

Carl's breathing, shallow, held them in its rasp and rhythm.

Kitty continued to stroke her son's forehead.

News, more of it, could keep till Carl got home. Difficult to tell him Jumbo had a rival in Oleg now. The pigeon was firmly entrenched in Kitty's affections. Early evening light shone on the family as they played their fragile games willing their son and brother to health. Willing themselves to keep from touching wounds, opening hurts.

That could wait.

19

Kay Renshaw stared at Daryl across the small and crowded room.

She felt guilty. She felt unbearably happy. At last the silly man had plucked up enough nerve to tell her he loved her. And it was another fine mess he had got her into, as Oliver Hardy famously said.

An hour ago, after bathing Jumbo Abdul had announced that, "Daryl sahib was at the door."

Flustered, she raced to change her damp housecoat and wear something flattering.

Daryl.

Daryl, whom she had asked to forget her all those years ago. Here he was now the fiancé of her young sister.

"Hi. What do you want? I'm trying to prepare Jumbo for his master's return." Her tone abrupt, her face wrinkled in an effort to look normal. Foolish. Her reaction as silly as some of her teenage pupils.

"Kay." The space between them huge.

"Hmm."

"Come on Kay, you're not making this easy for me."

"I don't know what you're talking about."

"Don't be schoolmarmish with me Kay. You know damn well what I and you know; that we have to settle this now."

"Daryl Jackson, you have a nerve, you have. Five years is a long time to fall back on. And neither of us made promises."

"You insisted I didn't write. You admitted you were wanting to move away from the family. I was left dangling, waiting and hoping your dad would continue inviting the good family friend over in spite of a fall from grace."

Both startled, and smiled half-guiltily at the pun.

"So what happens to Gracie then?"

"What happens to Grace depends on you now doesn't it?"

"For shame. You've asked her to marry you and you so easily break an engagement on the strength of my being here? What kind of rubbery conscience do you have?"

"Don't talk of conscience. I know Grace is not in love with me. Her acceptance was not that flattering. We both knew it was compromise. I was just there in the wake of Carl's accident. She knew it and so did I."

"Great. If I hadn't arrived when I did you both would have married without a qualm, without a shred of feeling. And then how would life have gone on for both you clever people?"

"Kay. That never did happen. And somehow I think it never would have.'

"Really?"

"Really. Truly."

"Well, I hope Mum and Dad were aware of this arrangement."

"Please. Don't make me feel worse than I'm feeling."

"Daryl."

"What?"

"I should send you on your way." Kay whispered, her eyes filling.

"But you won't will you?"

Daryl stepped around the damp dog, for once without the hesitance in his demeanour. He reached and clasped Kay's hands.

"Kay. So much time's lost. We're not that young. Let's put the past away. Why don't we marry? Quietly. Without a big fuss. We can't forget Carl."

"Or Gracie." Kay looked at him steadily.

Daryl pulled Kay to him. "Don't make things hard. I know Grace will be all right."

He bent his head to Kay's. She looked up at him, glad he was taller than she was. Daryl Jackson seemed to have lost the foolish air, he looked confident and they smiled at each other, content.

There was a scraping on the front door and the cook entered the room, a covered dish in his hands.

Embarrassed Abdul looked at the floor and shuffled into the room. He ignored the couple and with a deliberate clattering of plates began to fiddle with the crockery.

Kay and Daryl moved apart. Jumbo began a noisy scratching, leg thumping as he made a thorough job of routing out fleas.

"Missybaba. Khana."

"Haan Abdul."

He left the room without looking at either of them. Daryl and Kay began to laugh.

"How typical. The first one to know about us should be old Abdul."

"I'm not thrilled when the news gets to your parents."

"And Gracie?"

"Kay. I've told you Grace is not the one who will be disappointed."

"Oh. My parents will be then?"

"Well. I think I'll be seen in a poor light, letting down the younger daughter and all that."

"I'll be seen as a Jezebel or what?"

"Stop being melodramatic. Bob and Kitty are sensible people who will understand…"

"Gracie is their daughter y'know. It will be seen as a jilting of sorts."

"Kay. Why are you so sure of how your family is going to see this…"

"Because *I* feel guilty."

Daryl fell silent. Kay sat down and began to stroke Jumbo's head.

Steps were heard coming up. The banister began its song. A creaking of those shaky rails, the grit of the unswept steps amplifying sounds. Three pairs of feet made their way to the flat. Kay felt her stomach knot. This was not what she had envisioned. This was not why she had returned home.

"Oh hello. Daryl. Kay. What are you two up to here eh?" Bob glanced at them, then with a sudden sharper look walked to the dining table where he picked and began shuffling through the newspapers.

Kitty and Grace had gone into the bedroom.

Kay and Daryl stood awkwardly, like two schoolchildren caught playing truant.

"Do you two want to tell me something?" Bob looked over his spectacles.

"Um…yes Dad. I'd, we both have something to say, but I think it'll wait till Mum and Grace come out."

"What are you waiting for Kay?"

Kitty and Grace re-entered the room and both looked faintly puzzled at the charged atmosphere.

"Grace."

Kay walked over to her young sister and put out her hands to her.

"What..." Grace held Kay's hands, momentarily confused. She shot a look at Daryl and she knew. It was in Daryl Jackson's sheepish hangdog look.

Her father looked truculent. Her mother, lips compressed, did not look happy.

Grace felt a huge relief. Thank god. It was a massive weight off her chest. No more Daryl. No more wrestling with the ethical problem of a marriage based on mutual respect without love. The freedom. The dizzy prospect of being free again. Grace chuckled.

"Kay. I'm happy. I really am. You and Daryl should have done this a long while ago. You will both be so happy. I don't mind, I know this is shocking but I don't care. I think Daryl understands what I mean. Mum, Dad, don't be angry. This is the right thing. This makes sense."

Bob glared at Grace.

"I've never understood you Grace. And I'm disappointed in you Daryl. Can't you make up your mind? Do you want us to be the laughing stock of everybody? Particularly Grace?"

"Nonsense Dad," Grace sat down and pulled her father down besides her on the small rattan sofa.

"Mum, listen. No don't frown, listen. Daryl and I are good friends but nothing more. Yes, we might have married. But luckily Kay came home and I think we realised the mistake we'd have made. Don't you see how happy they are, they've always been in love. Our 'involvement' happened because of the shock of Carl, and then all that horror of poor Hilary Johnson's. Nothing more. I was lonely, so was Daryl. We both like each other better now. Don't we?" Grace paused, a little breathless.

Kitty stared at her daughter and her clear logic. She bowed her head, a tiny affirmative nod. She didn't trust herself to speak.

So be it.

"Daryl, you'll be staying for dinner then?"

"Cutlets and beef soup? Of course." Lugubrious, arms swinging, he ambled over to the table and with a shaky laugh nodded. Of course he'd be staying.

Grace took charge of the domestic world in a couple of fluid sentences.

Her parents, her sister and her future brother-in-law moved around the table and Grace called to the boy to serve dinner, it was late and all of them were hungry.

The two young women looked at each other over the bed where the invalid lay sleeping.

"Oh Grace, what happened?"

"Lucy, Lucy. I've been set free."

"What? What are you talking about? Calm down. I can't understand anything. What *are* you babbling about?"

Grace swung Lucy around in a girlish whirl.

"Hey. Watch it. This room hasn't the space for your crazy ways. Tell me what's happened."

"No more Daryl. He's gone. He's history. I can make plans. I can go places. I can tell him he's a crashing bore now. He's going to be my brother-in-law after all."

Both stared at each other. They giggled. Suddenly the absurdity of the situation hit them and they began to laugh out loud. Unrestrained. In the way the young laugh when life is simple. They staggered around clutching at furniture, doubling up at the absurdity of the moment. Clutching stomachs they wheezed with laughter. Hiccoughing, faces scrunched, eyes bleary with this abrupt hysteria.

"Don't, don't. My tummy hurts. Stop it."

"Oh Grace," Lucy wiping tears from her eyes, gasped and hiccoughed again.

"Lucy. Lucy. What a pair we are huh?"

"So what now? Plans? Changes of plans? Your parents must be upset. I mean they must be happy for Kay but it's a funny sort of way for things to work out, I'm sure they think your heart is broken."

"No Lucy. I think they guessed I'm relieved to be on my own again. There's life waiting. Think I'll think about moving away – Canada, England – no it's difficult now to get there, maybe Australia."

Lucy felt laughter swell as Grace punched her arm.

"The great thing is that we both told our men to beat it!"

"We told the men to beat it, and we're off and running." Grace whooped with another gurgle of laughter.

"Tell the men to beat it, to beat it, to beat it, to beat it, tell the men to beat it and indeed we have…" after Prof Higgins' self-congratulatory song in *My Fair Lady,* Grace and Lucy clapped hands in a catchy rhythm.

The invalid stirred, disturbed by the fracas.

Eddie D'Cruze glared up at Grace.

"What're you doing here?" His voice, even from a sick bed had lost none of its truculence. "Shouldn't your sister be here bossing me around now?"

"No Uncle. I've just come over to have a chat with Lucy."

"Hrummph. You're making noise enough to wake the dead. What's up?"

"Nothing much Uncle. Grace has been telling me about her work that's all."

"What does she work as, a circus clown? So much *hahahehe* at her office?"

The girls started off again, breathless puffs of giggles they both tried to suppress.

"Get out both of you. I'm tired and need to rest."

Eddie D'Cruze, envious of the young women's gaiety, turned away. He closed his eyes and looked into the darkness.

The rectangular hall of the club lay dark and silent.

A few bearers padded its length carrying trays for the few members who were in the smaller rooms either playing cards, or chatting, relaxed, at ease.

August is a quiet month. There were no festivities to celebrate. True the fifteenth was Independence Day but it was not in the culture of the country to have western style dances to remember what had become a solemn pause in the nation's workings. There were march-pasts, speeches, some commercial firms had a holiday, schools had elaborate assemblies and young people listened to the old people's talk. Much was said about the historic past, a shining future. but not much breath was spent on the immediate present. A benevolent chaos was one way of describing the muddle in the country's direction.

"Year's flying isn't it?" Cedric Smith mumbled into his rum and Coca-Cola.

"You can say that again." Louis Deane, sitting in the glow of a dim lamp, enjoyed the lull in the club's activities. "Don't know where time goes."

"Think this year's Christmas gala will be as good as last year's Louis?" Cedric Smith spoke, not really intending to follow up the thought.

"Who knows? There's going to be a new look that's for sure." Louis Deane smiled to himself.

"Yep. Never thought I'd see the day that the Coates' would not be presiding at the big table."

"Shame about the spilt-up. What a bloody shock that was."

"Yeah. I felt sorry for the missus. She was all right. A bit loud, but heart of gold and very generous." Cedric sipped his frosty drink, delighting in its burning cold.

"Wonder how Mr Coates is faring in Canada. Bloody shock that was. Bloody shock."

"Still, it's all for the best. Club needed new blood. About time we had fresh faces and different voices. I think most were happy to have the Sutton's step in and take over as First Family."

"Hmm. Don't care for how all that trouble was hushed up though. The boys seem sneaky. And you know, the Renshaws now don't come in at all."

"Give them time. They'll be back. I hear one of their girls married, no not the looker, the other one, the school teacher."

"Where did the gorgeous May Queen go?"

Louis Deane saw again the green chiffon sari, a golden armlet and a shining cap of blue-black hair.

"Didn't you hear? She's off to Australia."

"Good heavens. That was quick and sudden. Why? She held a good job. Was well-liked. What on earth made her do that?"

"Who knows? Boy-friend trouble, boredom, wanting to cut the apron strings, distant places hold enchantment you know…"

Cedric Smith in that dim lit room felt a gnawing grief. The young were leaving in droves. The communities' most precious commodity, youth, vanishing into a vacuum. He prayed daily his son might marry and decide to throw in his lot with those who had decided to stay in India. Why did a first-class girl like the Renshaw girl have to leave? Surely there were excellent prospects for a girl with her talents and ability? Another one gone. Giving to a foreign country all India had given them.

"Mr Smith?"

"Oh I'm here all right. Not asleep. Just putting off heaving myself out of this chair and going back into that muggy night. No chance of a taxi now I suppose."

"I'll try and get one of the durwans to get one for you. Special security now after that horrible mess. A new policeman and a special doorman. No risk of any more muggings. The Suttons are hyper-careful about this, and with good reason."

Cedric Smith, lumbered to his feet. Tilted the glass to drain it of the last few drops of rum and walked heavily to the steps, and down to the vaulted porte-cochere to wait for the taxi Louis Deane promised he would call for him.

August. He did not care for the month at all.

20

Five years is not a great deal of time in the grand scheme of things.

Grace Renshaw, standing in the crowded suburban train, wondered at where time had gone. Here she was, far away from what once was her life. In a land bright, bland, comfortable. Still, after this length of time, with a secure job, a home she owned, and a couple of cats who were beloved companions, her waking thoughts reverted to her homeland. It was festival time there now.

The Puja pandals would be going up. Children going berserk in a fury of impatience for the big days. Five, or were there more days, when dressed in their best, most of Calcutta throbbed to the Goddess who promised deliverance from the heavy woes and lighter irritations that irked her devotees. Not a Hindu, Grace grew up with the sound of conch shells heralding a cooler season, a more relaxed time of year. The train juddered to a halt. It was still a good fifteen minutes before her station. She dreamed of faraway places as tidy houses, doll's houses, sped by. No chaos here. How different from the landscape she was used to. From point of view when perched high in a rickshaw, seeing the city's streets, and on the rare holiday out of the city from those wondrous trains. Paddy fields, cows, palm trees, emaciated village folk always ready to wave as the train roared by. The children grinning as some ran alongside the train.

No comparison to this, stretches of shops, ribbons of cars weaving their eternal journey towards distant horizons, billboards, shopfronts, car yards, the emergence of high rise blocks obscuring a wide sky, how different. Miles of mass-produced conformity, mind-boggling.

"Stand clear, doors closing." The tinny recorded message warned.

Another station to go and she would be home.

The young Asian man besides her shifted his briefcase and smiled apologetically as he bumped into her.

"It's all right."

She noticed a couple of men shooting covert looks at her.

She was still a head-turner right? She recalled her mother's proud description of her and felt a pang for that far-off time.

Shaking herself mentally she counted the assets gained by this decision of hers to leave all the familiar and beloved behind her – a prestigious position in a leading publishing house, an apartment or 'unit' of her own, a bank balance that was so healthy at times she wondered what she was supposed to do with all that security – she was busy over holidays and weekends with pleasant colleagues who welcomed her *chic*, which considering her origins, puzzled them. Still it was a mini-triumph not to be regarded as exotic any more.

The train slowly stopped.

Grace Renshaw, a beautiful woman in her thirties stepped off and walked to her car parked in the nearby side-street.

It was jacaranda time. The purple blooms lay scattered on the pavements. It was a brief beauty they bestowed on the sprawl of suburbia. A couple of weeks at most and then the royal swirl of colour disappeared.

The little Mazda she'd leave in the station car park through the day, purred her to her block of units, the uphill drive a quick one, without the city's asthmatic clog of traffic to contend with. A passing pedestrian, bowling along in the spring breeze glanced at her before crossing the road, her rapid walk reminding Grace of Kay. She wondered if Kay was happy being wife to Daryl Jackson. She was pretty sure she was. They were made for each other. Confident, slightly impatient of most around them. Daryl and Kay were supremely secure in their choice of life as assistant caretaker and assistant principal in a prestigious English-medium school in the city. Happy pair.

How fortunate she was to have shaken the illusion of having a life with Daryl. She had had a lucky escape.

She used her remote control to open the garage door, edged the car in as it quickly closed behind her, walked up to her second-floor flat. The frosted glass of the front door gleamed and the carpeted corridor smelled strongly of a chemical flower fragrance.

Entering her home she briefly went through the menu for her dinner. A couple of sausages left over from the dinner last night, some canned soup, a few celery sticks and some tinned rosogollas she bought from the Indian corner shop, and it was a feast fit for the gods. She smiled thinking of poor Abdul and how she'd complain about his concern for her demands for salt in his cooking.

She was tired. She wanted to have a long bath and relax for an hour or so of completely mindless TV. Junk food for the mind. As public relation person she was glad to shed the smooth persona of her public face. Scotch and Soda leapt on the sofa to greet her. Their meows more accusatory than welcoming.

"All right, I'm hurrying with your food. How's my favourite couple been today huh?"

Twin pairs of green eyes stared, the basilisk look perfected in these sleek creatures. Bowls of chicken wings duly presented, Grace dropped her shoes carelessly in the front room, stripped off her cotton blouse and stepped out of her designer pants and clad in just bra and panty, stood briefly before the wide glass bay window looking onto the smooth lawn and thick border of trees that fronted the block. What a very civilised scene she thought. Quickly drawing the blinds she grinned thinking of how her mother might react to her casual disrobing in front of the window. What the hell, it was a different country where the motto seemed to be 'let it all hang out'. Good and healthy. Removed from the regime of a smothered and smothering lifestyle.

Aaah, it was good to wear what you liked, how you liked, without incurring the wrath of the watchers and gapers.

Bless Daryl and Kay for causing her to make this move.

Her mind switched back years to when the family had walked in on her sister and then fiancé sitting close, murmuring, looking startled and yes, guilty, as they moved apart.

She remembered how upset her mother had been. How her father had stayed to hear out Kay and Daryl's predicament. How she had insisted to her mother she was relieved her sister Kay had realised how foolish she'd been to refuse Daryl's offer of marriage years before. It was comic now even farcical to think back on that painful interlude. Again she fell into a little reverie.

She once more heard herself all those years ago, say coolly, "It's good you two seem to have realised finally you were made for each other."

Daryl had turned red, his good-natured face confused and upset. Biting his lips and looking a prize idiot. The hangdog expression pronounced in his downcast face.

Kay fussed about the room, for once her voice mumbling and indistinct, avoided looking at her younger sister.

Grace replayed the scene over in her head. She saw Jumbo sprawled between them, the dog panting in that stifling heat, an inevitable power cut stilling the relief from the old overhead fan.

"For heaven's sake. Stop this drama! Daryl I'm not going to sue you for breach of promise. It's a relief to know you and Kay seem to know now what you should have done years ago. No, Daryl, I'm not heartbroken. Hey, don't look like that, you're a friend. Really. I know Mum and Dad and Carl are happy and pleased that things have turned out this way. Yes, pleased and happy."

God, how priggish she must have sounded. A sudden re-construction, her swift re-writing of the mythology of romance as acted out by the Renshaw girls.

Her father, never quick with his choice of words, looked unhappy. He held out a hand stiffly to Daryl.

Her mother had emerged, pale, eyes wary, as she bobbed an acknowledgment to Daryl and moved to give Kay a hug.

The couple stood awkward, fidgety, everyone tense, the silence suddenly broken by Jumbo's sudden bark as Abdul balancing a stack of clean dishes entering the room almost stepped on the sprawling animal. Laughter broke the tension and the rhythm of the evening picked up its dropped chord.

The wedding that followed, a scarce two months later, was quiet, small, and, in the opinion of all who mattered, a triumph of diplomacy.

Grace smiled. The scene vanishing as the cats wound around her legs. Thoughts long ago and as fresh as the sea breeze that sometimes blew through her suburb. Perfectly preserved relics of the past that were always there at her heels.

Before turning the stove on she switched on the ghetto blaster and chose an evening raga CD to soothe her night away.

It helped with her sleep. It refreshed her. Again she remembered how scornfully her family had regarded any music not western. Here she was, hankering after the sounds of that time and place. How pure this sound. Uncomplicated. She yawned and yawned again, widely without inhibition, sounding a loud, breathy 'aaah', of content. She dropped inelegantly onto the leather couch.

Slipping further down on the sofa she decided to have a late dinner. A nap was what she needed now.

Half-asleep, images of Jumbo, crazy mongrel dog, bounced towards her. Carl came up then, laughing and happy.

Was this Andy? Andy Kaul? Yes, there he was avoiding her, walking distantly into darkness.

That creak. The banister. Always there. Its presence steadying against a careless fall. A fresco of children's faces, Lucy, Ralph, Carl, pressed through its gaping spaces. Here she was, a child again, sailing down its silken beam. Aaaah, the final stomach-churning gasp while she leapt off on to the ground. It defined her childhood. Yes, the flats would float away if not pinned down by that sturdy wooden frame. Again the image turned misty. Her parents locking up the flat as they prepared to leave for an evening out. Abdul shooing the stray cats away from the bin near the top of the stairs. The dark there. The walls suffused with the daily coal fire's smoke. And the light never quite as harsh as the light outside. The heat not as feral. Subdued, the stairwell offered shelter from every weather. Rain, summer heat, or winter's bite. A portal. The banister, a sentinel watching, calmly knowing all that had happened before and perhaps all that would happen again. Then as dreams go the image fades. And vanishes.

Now it was her boss, Mr Jameson. The flat accent asking for his 11:00 am shot of caffeine and a blueberry muffin. It was the bright today of her world now.

Grace roused herself and gazed into a slow twilight. Amazing how it was still light at nine at night. She was looking forward to an early night with a good book. She thought back to dinners at home. The adults talking and laughing. For hours and hours it seemed to her as a child. Time was elastic. Servants were there to take a plate away or bring one a glass of water.

Here the days were chopped into identical bites. A working week that started 7.30 am to 7:00 pm. Mondays, Tuesdays, Wednesday – also known as Hump Day – then Thursday, late night shopping preceding the resuscitating Friday and the meltdown on the Saturday and Sunday, maybe a film, a walk in the nearby national park, a visit to a new bistro, chatting with a few friends, when come eight o'clock on Sunday night it was ready to start all over again.

Oh well, there was something about routine. There was something to be said about a treadmill. It did prevent a running down. Those squirrels never seemed bored. Just desperate. Australia had no squirrels.

Lucy, she said in her mind, Lucy my friend, I have no regrets. Really. No regrets at all. But I wish you were here.

Grace turned her thoughts ruefully to the immediate task at hand. Yes, she must find something to read. TV was rubbish. The couple of channels with worthwhile programmes aired them late into the night and she invariably fell asleep before they ended.

A book. Always the answer. Books to hide behind. Books to keep the world from intruding too sharply into uncomfortable corners of her life. A book to put her to sleep. Hmm, a good future to look to. A good future.

Sleep and dreams. Lovely.

Slowly she began to lay a place for her solitary dinner. Contentment welled as one of the cats rubbed against her legs. She had found her place. The view was satisfying, the prospect soothing. Not like some of her straying thoughts or indisciplined longings. Yes, it was almost festival time back home, but she was far from all that noise, the joyous yelling. She was here. Far from that time. Far from that place.

Grace, staring unseeingly at her elegant dining setting, realised with a faint chill she would always dream of India.